The Writing Desk

"Rachel Hauck enchants us again! Tenley and Birdie are bound together by the understanding that creativity is a guiding force and that their stories must be told. A tale both bittersweet and redemptive, *The Writing Desk* is your must-read."

—PATTI CALLAHAN HENRY, *NEW YORK TIMES* BESTSELLING AUTHOR

The Wedding Shop

"I adored *The Wedding Shop*! Rachel Hauck has created a tender, nostalgic story, weaving together two pairs of star-crossed lovers from the present and the past with the magical space that connects them. So full of heart and heartache and redemption, this book is one you'll read long into the night, until the characters become your friends, and Heart's Bend, Tennessee, your second hometown."

—BEATRIZ WILLIAMS, *NEW YORK TIMES* BESTSELLING AUTHOR

"*The Wedding Shop* is the kind of book I love, complete with flawed yet realistic characters, dual timelines that intersect unexpectedly, a touch of magic, and a large dose of faith. Two breathtaking romances are the perfect bookends for this novel about love, forgiveness, and following your dreams. And a stunning, antique wedding dress with a secret of its own. This is more than just a good read—it's a book to savor."

—KAREN WHITE, *NEW YORK TIMES* BESTSELLING AUTHOR

"In *The Wedding Shop*, the storyline alternates between past and present, engrossing the reader in both timelines. There are certain elements that are more obvious to the reader than to the characters, and it can get slightly frustrating waiting for the characters to get a clue. However, this is short lived, and the ways that God's provision is shown is heartwarming and can even increase the reader's faith. The weaving in of characters and plot points from The Wedding Dress and The Wedding Chapel adds depth and meaning to the gorgeously rendered tale."

—*RT BOOK REVIEWS*, 4 STARS

The Wedding Chapel

"Hauck's engaging novel about love, forgiveness, and new beginnings adeptly ties together multiple oscillating storylines of several generations of families. Interesting plot interweaves romance, real life issues, and a dash of mystery . . . Recommend for mature fans of well-done historical fiction. "

—CBA RETAILERS AND RESOURCES

"Hauck tells another gorgeously rendered story. The raw, hidden emotions of Taylor and Jack are incredibly realistic and will resonate with readers. The way the entire tale comes together with the image of the chapel as holding the heartbeat of God is breathtaking and complements the romance of the story."

—RT BOOK REVIEWS, 4½ STARS AND A TOP PICK!

The Wedding Dress

"Hauck seamlessly switches back and forth in this redeeming tale of a shop with healing powers for the soul. As Cora and Haley search for solace and love, they find peace in the community of the charming shop. Hauck succeeds at blending similar themes across the time periods, grounding the plot twists in the main characters' search for redemption and a reinvigoration of their wavering faith. In the third of her winsome wedding-themed standalone novels, Hauck focuses on the power of community to heal a broken heart. "

—PUBLISHERS WEEKLY

"*The Wedding Dress* is a thought-provoking read and one of the best books I have read. Look forward to more . . ."

—MICHELLE JOHNMAN, GOLD COAST, AUSTRALIA

"I thank God for your talent and that you wrote *The Wedding Dress*. I will definitely come back to this book and read it again. And now I cannot wait to read *Once Upon a Prince*."

—AGATA FROM POLAND

The Royal Wedding Series

"Perfect for Valentine's Day, Hauck's latest inspirational romance offers an uplifting and emotionally rewarding tale that will delight her growing fan base."

—*Library Journal*, starred review

"Hauck writes a feel-good novel that explores the trauma and love of the human heart . . . an example of patience and sacrifice that readers will adore."

—*Romantic Times*, 4 stars

"A stirring modern-day fairy tale about the power of true love."

—Cindy Kirk, author of *Love at Mistletoe Inn*

"*How to Catch a Prince* is an enchanting story told with bold flavor and tender insight. Engaging characters come alive as romance blooms between a prince and his one true love. Hauck's own brand of royal-style romance shines in this third installment of the Royal Wedding series."

—Denise Hunter, bestselling author of *The Wishing Season*

"*How to Catch a Prince* contains all the elements I've come to love in Rachel Hauck's Royal Wedding series: an 'it don't come easy' happily ever after, a contemporary romance woven through with royal history, and a strong spiritual thread with an unexpected touch of the divine. Hauck's smooth writing—and the way she wove life truths throughout the novel—made for a couldn't-put-it-down read."

—Beth K. Vogt, author of *Somebody Like You*, one of *Publishers Weekly*'s Best Books of 2014

"Rachel Hauck's inspiring Royal Wedding series is one for which you should reserve space on your keeper shelf!"

—*USA Today*

"Hauck spins a surprisingly believable royal-meets-commoner love story. This is a modern and engaging tale with well-developed secondary characters that are entertaining and add a quirky touch. Hauck fans will find a gem of a tale."

—Publishers Weekly starred review of Once Upon a Prince

THE WRITING DESK

ALSO BY RACHEL HAUCK

The Wedding Shop
The Wedding Chapel
The Wedding Dress

Novellas found in *A Year of Weddings*
A March Bride (e-book only)
A Brush with Love: A January Wedding Story (e-book only)

THE ROYAL WEDDING SERIES

Once Upon a Prince
Princess Ever After
How to Catch a Prince
A Royal Christmas Wedding (novella)

LOWCOUNTRY ROMANCE NOVELS

Sweet Caroline
Love Starts with Elle
Dining with Joy

NASHVILLE NOVELS

Nashville Sweetheart (e-book only)
Nashville Dreams (e-book only)

WITH SARA EVANS

Sweet By and By
Softly and Tenderly
Love Lifted Me

The WRITING DESK

RACHEL HAUCK

ZONDERVAN

The Writing Desk

Copyright © 2017 by Rachel Hauck

This title is also available as a Zondervan e-book. Visit www.zondervan.com.

Requests for information should be addressed to:
Zondervan, *Grand Rapids, Michigan 49546*

ISBN: 978-0-310-35127-6 (HC)
ISBN: 978-0-310-34159-8 (TP)

Interior design: Mallory Collins

Printed in the United States of America
17 18 19 20 21 / LSC / 5 4 3 2 1

Dedicated to: My aunt, Carol Hayes.
We dreamed of this, didn't we?

ONE

TENLEY

This should be her night of triumph. To be the queen of her world. An acclaimed, bestselling, award-winning author with the literati bowing at her feet.

But tears snuck along the rims of her eyes, blurring the Manhattan scene slowly passing beyond the limousine's window. Though her Fifth Avenue apartment was only a few blocks from the award venue, her publisher had insisted on sending a luxury ride.

"You're quiet." Holt, her boyfriend of eleven months and eleven days—yes, she counted—leaned to see her face.

"Nervous I guess." She offered a conciliatory smile, holding her clutch against her middle. If her mother texted, she'd want to see it. Not that she expected to hear from Blanche Albright. But tonight was a big night. "I think they'll find out, you know . . . the truth."

"What truth? That you're a great writer?"

"That I'm a hack."

Holt moved against her, pressing her against the limo door. "You're the Gordon Phipps Roth Award winner for Outstanding Debut Novelist. Enjoy it, Tenley." His hard kiss came with a mocking laugh. "Sheesh, you're the envy of every novelist in New York.

A Roth Award?" He fell back to his side of the wide seat, smoothed his tie, and checked his morphed appearance in the tinted window. "You can write your ticket. Literally. Just like all the others."

"But I'm not like the others, am I?"

She was legacy. Words like *nepotism* and *payoff* had rumbled through the publishing world when the Gordon Phipps Roth Foundation announced Tenley Roth, the great-great-granddaughter of America's beloved storyteller Gordon Phipps Roth, and daughter of the frequent *New York Times* bestseller Conrad Roth, as this year's winner.

"Is this how the night's going to go? You being surly over winning an award founded in your family's name?"

"I think they gave it to me because of Dad." She'd said it to Holt a hundred times since they announced her name. Over dinner. While getting ready for bed. Walking down Fifth Avenue after an evening out with friends.

"The foundation uses a select team of judges. They decide. If I were you—"

"Which you're not."

"—I'd drink this in until I was loopy with adoration. You're a descendant of literary geniuses. Me? I hail from greedy bankers, Wall Streeters, and slum lords who robbed the poor to pay the rich."

The limo slowed for a traffic light.

Yeah, she didn't have a lot of compassion for Holt. A struggling screenwriter to be sure, he hailed from old New York Knickerbockers. The Van Cliffs. Their fortune was legendary, rivaling the Vanderbilts' during the Gilded Age.

He pretended to hate money as a way to relate to the starving artists in their circle, but his clothes closet and shoe rack said otherwise.

"Do you think he'd be proud?" Tenley said.

Her father had penned beloved thrillers and mysteries until his untimely death two years ago rocked the publishing world. And destroyed Tenley's.

Black ice. On his way home from a book signing upstate. Tenley had been writing in a coffee shop when she got the call. Holt, only a friend then, sat a few tables away.

"Yes, Tenley, he'd be proud. So would Gordon."

She'd sold over a million copies of *Someone to Love*. Embarked on a national book tour and appeared on talks shows. Even did a quick spot on *The Tonight Show* with Jimmy Fallon.

From her beaded clutch, her phone pinged.

Holt eyed her. "Want to turn off your phone? You're a celebrity tonight. Try to act like it. Give the people what they want."

"It might be Blanche."

"Blanche? Are you serious?" He sighed. "I don't know why you even care what she thinks."

But it wasn't Blanche, it was Alicia. Her best friend from college.

Wish I was there. Go get 'em. Addison May is feeling
better. But all my clothes smell like baby puke. Yay me!
Hugs.

The limo glided to a stop, finding a rare vacancy along the curb, the driver announcing through a set of speakers, "Loft and Garden."

This was it. The Manhattan rooftop venue was her introduction to New York's elite literati club. Here, for a few hours, all of New York City would be at her feet.

She'd hobnob with the aristocrats of the publishing world, mingle with the glitterati, the wealthy and famous, smile for photos and selfies.

But tomorrow? Back to reality. To a deadline she knew in her bones she could not meet.

The doorman opened Tenley's door. Before she could step out, Holt leaned across her, handing the man a folded bill.

"Give us a few, please."

"Yes, sir." And the door clapped closed.

Tenley made a face. "Holt, what are you doing?"

"Well, we've been together for a while now." Sweat dotted his high, smooth brow as he fidgeted, slipping his hand in and out of his tuxedo pocket. "I believe we've taken this relationship as far as we can."

Tenley's phone pinged again. She snapped open the clutch, reaching for her phone. Despite her doubts, the Gordon Phipps Roth Award was quite an achievement and Tenley wondered if her estranged mother just might wish her well.

But before she could read the screen, Holt snatched her bag away.

"Turn off your phone, Tenley."

"Just let me see . . ."

"It's not Blanche." He slid across the seat, his brown eyes wide behind his dark, struggling-writer glasses, the slightest hint of a beard on his aristocratic cheeks. "I'm trying to talk to you about us."

"You never want to talk about us." Her phone rang this time, chiming over and over. Couldn't be Blanche then. She only communicated through long, single text messages. "Holt, let me check this." She retrieved her bag. "It might be Wendall or Brené or someone from the foundation."

Wendall Barclay and Brené Queen were her publisher and editor at Barclay Publishing, a small but ancient and esteemed New York house.

They had launched her great-great-grandfather's career, her father's, and now, quiet possibly, hers. If she didn't succumb to—

"Answer your phone." Holt's sigh ended with a growl.

Tenley caught her breath as she peered at her phone. It was actually her mother. Blanche.

"Who is it?"

"Blanche. She called." She never called. She texted. Once or twice a year.

"She can wait. Call her after the evening."

"What if she wants to congratulate me?"

Holt laughed. "I don't know why you care so much about her opinion. She didn't care about yours when she walked out on you."

"She's still my mother." But Tenley felt the sting of truth in Holt's assertion.

Nevertheless, Barclay Publishing had invited Blanche Hastings Roth Williams Albright to Tenley's award ceremony. She was hopeful. Maybe, for once, Blanche would go out of her way to be there for her. Fly up from Florida for the occasion.

But when Barclay's assistant called to confirm Tenley's personal invitations, Blanche was not one of them.

She stuffed her phone back into her bag and turned to him. "You have my attention. What is it you want to say about *us*?"

Holt leaned in, flirting, adjusting his nerdy but sexy glasses, a mass of his dark hair curling over his forehead, an object cupped in his right hand.

"We're both twenty-nine, in the prime of our lives, know what we want, working in our chosen careers."

Where was he going with this? "Do you want to write together? Because I'm barely a novelist, let alone a screenwriter."

"Tenley, for crying out loud, will you marry me?" He held up the blue ring box, slowly raising the lid, revealing a blinding diamond. "I bought it new for you. Not from the family jewels. Tiffany's."

"Y-you want to marry me? Holt, we've never even talked about it."

Her phone rang again and someone hammered on the limo window.

"Tenley? You in there?" Wendall, her publisher. "We've been waiting on you."

She glanced over to see Wendall squinting through the dark window, his voice bouncing off the glass.

"What do you say?" Holt took her hand. "You and me." The cold ring slid down her finger. "Is that a yes?"

"Tenley!" The door opened and Wendall peeked in. "Let's go. You two kids can make out later." The gregarious publisher took her hand. "Your public awaits."

"Tenley?" Holt followed her out of the limo.

"Holt, I, I, wow . . ." She pressed her hands against his face, kissing him. "Can we talk about it later?" She laughed low. "My brain's a bit muddled right now."

"Absolutely. The night is yours."

Outside the limo, a small crowd cheered, applauding. In the lobby, she was greeted by late-arriving guests as well as members of the media, along with the Oscar-winning actress Nicolette Carson.

"I'm a big fan," Nicolette said, stepping into the elevator as the doors slid open. "Ezra Elliot might be my favorite hero of all time." She eyed Tenley's red gown up and down with an approving nod and then, with a gasp, snatched up her hand. "What's this? Oh my stars . . ." Nicolette mimed being blinded by Tenley's diamond. "I think it is *literally* one of the stars. This is amazing."

"We're engaged." Holt leaned between them from the back of the elevator, beaming.

"Engaged?" Wendall's voice could be very loud.

"Tenley, are you engaged?" The reporter from Channel 7

pressed against her. "Can we have details? How did he propose? When are the nuptials?"

Tenley laughed, waving them off with her right hand, tucking her left close to her side. "You'll just have to wait and see. Tonight is about the great Gordon Phipps Roth and the world of literature."

She could crown Holt for this. Just bonk him on the head. Twice. And for a moment, Tenley believed they rode the slowest elevator on the planet.

Nicolette offered her hand to Holt. He all but drooled. "Holt Armstrong, if I'm not mistaken."

"Which you are not." He laughed a bit loudly.

"I recently read a screenplay by you," Nicolette said. "It was hilarious. I loved it. We should talk. Tenley, do tell. He had to be the inspiration for your hero in *Someone to Love*?"

Tenley smiled, the elevator quarters growing tighter, the weight of the diamond on her finger along with the mantle of expectation inspiring a cool sweat down her spine.

"I suppose." She squinted at her boyfriend of eleven months and eleven days, trying to see him through the starlet's eyes. She'd forgotten his appeal, the cut of his jaw, the intellectual glint in his eye behind those dark-rimmed spectacles, and the full plump of his lips.

If he wanted to believe he was Ezra, she'd not disappoint him. But her father was her inspiration. The book poured out of her in the months after his death. The writing, the process, the emotional mining of words proved to be her therapy, her way of commanding grief.

She never imagined that showing the manuscript to her father's literary agent, Charlie McGuire, would lead to a multi-book deal with Barclay Publishing.

But now that grief and pain were in her rearview mirror, Tenley found writing a chore. A strain. Void of creativity and inspiration.

For her July deadline, she'd written approximately zero words. Zero. The very notion washed over her with a suffocating panic.

She inhaled, pushing out when the elevator doors opened, grateful for the pure April breeze rising up from the street.

The Loft and Garden venue, aglow with romantic light, stood as an island among a river of city. Overhead, the stars sat as twinkling members of the audience.

Fans, colleagues, fellow authors, and friends surrounded her, congratulating her.

"So proud of you, Tenley."

"This is your night, girl."

"How do you feel about winning an award set up in your great-great-grandfather's honor?"

Finally the head of the Gordon Phipps Roth Foundation, a distant cousin, Elijah Phipps, rescued her. "We have a seat on the dais for you. Tenley, I can't tell you how proud we are that the board selected you as this year's winner. I know they regret never giving it to your father. We can't wait for your next book. My wife raves about *Someone to Love*."

Tenley took her seat on the dais, her gaze drifting over the guests, esteemed and otherwise, and wondered how she got here.

In her grief she'd stumbled upon this path, writing, as a way to figure out her life. So why, in this auspicious moment, did she feel so unbearably lost?

TWO

BIRDIE

DECEMBER 30, 1902

She wished to escape. So much so her legs twitched of their own volition. Each time, Mama glared at her in warning.

Nevertheless, Birdie maintained decorum, perched on the edge of the red sitting room divan, sipping her tea and listening to Mrs. Opal Smith drone on about the season.

". . . they say she's never recovered from her husband's death. I daresay I believe them."

"I'm quite sure I'd faint dead away should anything happen to my Geoffrey." Mama sipped her tea. She must. It would be the only way to hide her exaggeration.

Birdie suspected Mama would never expire or wilt away should Papa pass on to the other side. Though she should weep and wail over losing a man as kind and loving as Papa.

"But she's holding her annual ball." Mrs. Smith peeked at Birdie. "I suppose you'll be at the Astors'. Shouldn't a girl of your advanced age be betrothed by now?"

Mama's teacup rattled against the saucer. "Mrs. Smith, is that what everyone is saying?"

She shrugged. "I've no idea. I ask of my own inquisitiveness." She raised her tea cup, as she'd most likely done in every society drawing room across the city, musing over the same curiosities.

"Mr. Shehorn and I agreed Birdie's education superseded marriage. Rather opposite of common practice for young women, but she is a bright girl. We did not want to frustrate her. She is forever reading books and scribbling stories, talking of mathematics and sciences." Mama spoke as if an expert on the matter, but Birdie's intellectual interests frustrated her. It was Papa who had insisted their daughter spend four years at Wellesley.

Mama had pitched a fit. Hidden away in her room for nearly a week, having her meals brought to her upon her "sickbed."

She wanted Birdie in a marriage match. One that would advance her up the social ladder. Seeing Mrs. Astor fade with ill health and heartbreak left an opening for another woman to lead New York, and thus American, society.

Mama aimed to be that woman. The new queen of the elite. Then pass the crown to her daughter.

"How did you find Wellesley, Birdie?" Mrs. Smith said. "Haven't you just graduated?"

"I found Wellesley a splendid place of knowledge, friendship, and spiritual challenge. I'd not trade my years there for all of Mr. Vanderbilt's gold."

Mrs. Smith gaped at her. Mama gasped. Then the two chortled together.

"She is so droll, Mrs. Shehorn. How do you manage?"

Mama eyed Birdie with a dark glint. "We find a way."

"Now that you're home, surely you mean to find a husband. You're twenty-two unless I miss my guess. My Aimee and Ruthann married at seventeen and eighteen respectively." Mrs. Smith leaned toward Mama and Birdie with a proud smile. "A duke and an earl."

"Yes, I recall their weddings," Mama said. "I do hope they are faring well in their positions."

"Yes, quite well. Though I'm anxious for grandchildren. So, Birdie, do you have your eye on a young heir? A duke of your own perhaps."

Birdie lowered her gaze, hiding the blush on her cheeks. Must Mrs. Smith remain so determined to ascertain her marital aspirations?

"No, I do not. I don't see marriage as a necessary requirement to live a fulfilling life."

"Birdie!" Mama's rebuke was clear.

Mrs. Smith laughed. "Then what on earth do you plan to do with yourself? Do you not want children? Don't tell me you'll be like the godless progressives, having affairs without marriage, spawning unwanted illegitimates."

"Mrs. Smith, I'll have you curb your coarseness in my drawing room!"

"I beg your pardon, but what am I to make of *your* daughter's assertion?"

"Not that she'll live in sin, certainly." Mama shuffled in her chair, clattering her cup against the saucer, a slight mist glittering across her forehead. "We have Christian values in this family."

"Well, of course you do." Mrs. Smith offered a conciliatory smile. Upsetting Mrs. Shehorn would not serve her reputation. "I didn't mean—"

"Of course I want to marry," Birdie said, smoothing the discourse. "I've just no one in mind as of yet. Didn't Edith Minturn Stokes not marry until twenty-eight? See how happy she and Isaac are now? Don't you think love is a factor?"

"Yes, but not as grand a factor as the young people make of it today," Mama said, dabbing her forehead with her handkerchief.

"Yes, I quite agree. Love must win the day but it is not a requirement for marriage. Position and advantage must determine the suitable mate." Mrs. Smith spoke with the utmost authority.

Birdie burned at her words. Such an arrangement might have suited Mama, Mrs. Smith, and their mothers, but it would not suit Birdie, a woman coming of age in the twentieth century.

From the hallway, the grandfather clock chimed the hour. Three o'clock. Birdie set her tea aside and brushed her hands over her gown. Surely Mrs. Smith would take her leave. She'd been visiting for more than thirty minutes.

Birdie must make her way to Barclay Publishing's Broadway office within an hour. She needed time to slip upstairs, retrieve her hat and coat, run up to her writing room under the attic eaves to gather her new manuscript from her desk, and then sneak away, hoping the private brougham she asked Percival to order waited for her on the corner of Fifth and Fifty-Seventh.

". . . surely as an heiress, you've a selection of suitable mates."

"We are discussing now—"

"What?" Birdie didn't care about her interruption. "I've been in no such discussions."

"Birdie. Don't make Mrs. Smith uncomfortable. Tell me, what are your New Year's plans? We're heading to the Berkshires. The Van Cliffs built a cottage there and we are looking forward to seeing it."

"The Van Cliffs. How wonderful. We are planning our annual grand ball here . . ."

Birdie faded from the conversation. What was Mama up to now? With whom was she talking about marriage? Oh, why must she constantly control, dictate, and demand her way? Even while at Wellesley, Birdie felt her taut reins.

From the fireplace, the flames crackled. Beyond the frosty window, the day faded from sun to the promise of snow.

Birdie's leg twitched. She must be away or she'd miss Mr. Barclay. She'd tried to set an appointment with him but he refused to see her, so she was going to impose the element of surprise. Either way, she *must* retrieve her first manuscript and present him with another.

Because the idea of *A View from Her Carriage* being read by thousands . . . well, it made her blood run cold.

Percival stepped through the drawing-room door. "Mrs. Astor has come to call."

Mrs. Smith jumped up, smoothing her hand over her hair. "Caroline Astor? Here?"

"Do escort her in, Percival." Mama beamed, rising to her feet.

Birdie exchanged a glance with the Shehorns' trusted butler. *Do not let my brougham go. Please.*

"This is quite an honor, Mrs. Shehorn." Mrs. Smith nodded her respect. "Mrs. Astor has not been making personal calls as of late."

"Indeed not."

After her husband's death and her own failing health, *the* Mrs. Astor did not call in person. She sent her card and nothing more. This rare visit all but crowned Mama the new head of society.

Yet, as Mama sought her lot in life, Birdie must seek hers.

"Mama, if you'll excuse—"

"Shhh, I do not excuse you. Stay put."

"Yes, Mama." Birdie felt instantly a child again, ruled by a demanding if not harsh mama whose approval she desperately sought.

The grand dame of New York society graced the doorway. Mama moved to welcome her.

"Mrs. Astor, do come in. To what do I owe this honor?"

And so Birdie sat with her elders, listening to the idle conversation, a sound so dull in her ears she imagined she could hear the coming snowflakes forming.

The grandfather clock struck the half hour. She must be away. Glancing from Mama to Mrs. Smith to Mrs. Astor, she did the only polite thing she could do.

She rolled her eyes back in her head, exhaled a loud gasp, and swooned out of her chair.

TENLEY

She stood in her loft workspace, staring at the bronze and gold Gordon Phipps Roth Award sitting on the edge of her desk.

Inspire me!

But instead the scene, the setting, and everything about the space intimidated her.

The desk was a family heirloom passed down from her great-great-grandfather. He wrote his first novel, *When Hearts Are in Love*, at that desk. And his third, the one that defined and launched his career, *The Girl in the Carriage*.

Dad wrote his first novel at the desk. Blanche had recently abandoned them, and Grandpa moved the desk and accompanying chair from his apartment to theirs.

"Your heart's broken, Conrad. Time to write that novel you've been promising to write," he said.

The Roth family writing gene had skipped Tenley's great-grandpa and grandpa. Great-Grandpa became an accountant, working in a downtown Manhattan office for forty-five years. Grandpa became a reverend and stood in a midtown pulpit for thirty-two years.

Yeah, Tenley didn't see her path in either of their lives. She'd followed Dad happily down the author trail until she realized, lost in the woods of sudden success, she had no idea what she was doing.

He was supposed to have lived another twenty-five years, mentoring her, teaching her, perhaps walking her down the aisle and bouncing her children on his knee.

After which she'd write her great American novel. Instead, he died at sixty-two, and Tenley wrote a simple romance.

The light falling through the high dormer windows shifted, draping a stream of gold across the desk, picking up the shine of her trophy.

Oh, how she longed to *feel* the acceptance, love, and honor exemplified by the sculpture of a hand holding a book.

Instead, she trembled at her own failings. She'd only be as good as her last book. Her only book.

Pacing over to the desk, Tenley knotted her hair into a loose bun, inhaled long and deep, and sat down.

Opening her laptop, she stared at the blank screen, shifting around, slouching, then sitting tall. She resituated her chair, pulling it close, then shoving it back.

Nothing felt comfortable. The chair and desk didn't work for her. But she couldn't see herself chucking them away after Great-Great-Grandpa and Dad had written so many great novels right here.

She'd written *Someone to Love* at Starbucks in the midnight hours because sleeping alone in the apartment without Dad haunted her.

"Okay, wisdom of Great-Great-Grandpa Gordon and of my father, I'm on deadline. You've been there, done that. Help me!" She rubbed her hands together with expectation, then propped them on her keyboard. "Ready? Go!"

Nothing.

Large sticky pages stuck around the attic wall held her ideas and outlines, character-journey notes, and possible epiphanies.

But nothing struck a chord. The moment she sat down to write, she went blank. As if she was, well, not meant to do this anymore.

Slumping down in her chair, she pressed her hands to her face. "I don't want to be a one-hit wonder!"

Growing up with Dad in Murray Hill, she had watched her father hover over his typewriter night after night, muttering to himself, often yanking a fully typed page from the roller and wadding it up for the trash.

It was one of her chores to pick up his pile of discarded pages and toss them in the trash can. Oh, if she had half of those pages now she'd be well on her way to a story.

One of Dad's stories, but a story nonetheless.

Staring at the ceiling, she counted the exposed beams down the length of the room. Hmm, fifteen.

After Dad's death, she needed change. She rented out their apartment and bought a renovated space on Fifth Avenue. By then she was dating Holt, and somehow, without any discussion, their two dwellings became one.

Tenley raised her left hand, staring at her bare ring finger. Since his proposal two nights ago, she'd tucked the ring in its esteemed box and left it there. You know, for safekeeping. It was almost too beautiful to wear. To dunk in dishwater or get clogged with cold hamburger meat.

Back to work. Tenley sat forward, facing her computer.

Give me a story.

She'd heard that plea boosted from Dad's gut many, many times. "*God! Give me a story.*"

God must have answered, because Dad produced book after

book, but Tenley was not privy to his faith formula. He kept his faith quiet and simple, not shoving it at Tenley like he felt Grandpa had done to him.

Tenley admired Dad's faith. Felt it at times. Heard his prayers. Listened to his testimonies of small miracles. It was just that Dad never told her how to get some of that wonder-working power for herself.

How do I believe?

"Tenley?"

She snapped around at Holt's call, posing her fingers on her laptop keyboard, the front door clapping shut behind him. "I'm up here."

Waiting for his footsteps in the attic stairwell, Tenley left her blank story page to check e-mail. Nothing important other than fan e-mails she'd read later.

While hearing from fans was the pinnacle of being a writer, their gushing praise over *Someone to Love* would only feed her desire to write an even better book while reminding her she had no idea what she was doing.

Below, she heard Holt moving about the apartment. It was his ritual to leave for a coffee shop every morning at ten, write until three, and return home.

When his footsteps faded into their bedroom, Tenley stood. She might as well call it a day too. Staring at a blank screen and playing umpteen hands of online euchre counted as a workday, right?

As she reached for her phone, a new text from Blanche pinged onto the screen.

Are you busy?

Tenley slowly sat. She'd meant to call her back the other night but never got around to it. After the ceremony, Wendall gathered a large crowd for drinks, including Nicolette Carson and Oscar-winning director Jeremiah Gonda. Swept up into the pageantry of the evening and the assurance of Jeremiah that he was pursuing the film rights to her story, Tenley forgot all about Blanche.

Sorta. What's up?
Can I call you?

Hmm . . . Blanche typically only reached out on Tenley's birthday and at Christmas. Not on a random week in spring.

Sure.

Her phone rang the moment she hit Send.

"Tell me, how's the weather?" Blanche always led off with a weather report. "I always loved spring in Manhattan."

"Warm, sunny, gorgeous. H-how's the weather in Florida?" Not that Tenley really wanted to know, but she should keep up her side of the conversation.

Afternoon light filled the loft's dormer windows, and the scent of warm lumber perfumed the air.

"There's no place like Florida in the spring. It's wonderful, simply wonderful. Have you ever been down here in the spring?"

"Not that I recall." Blanche left when Tenley was nine and the Roth house became one of survival. Not of luxury trips to Florida in the spring.

"Not even for college spring break?"

"I went skiing." Once. When her best friend, Alicia, made her.

"Then you must come down. Really. Do you remember Grove Manor? You were here as a girl. Isn't that wild? Anyway, the place is lovely. Inspiring. The backyard slopes down to the seagrass and right out to the beach."

"Did you really call to talk about the spring weather and the beauty of Grove Manor?"

Their cellular connection went silent.

"Blanche?"

"I recently had a bit of surgery. For cancer."

"Cancer?"

"A small lump in my breast. We caught it in time but the doctor wants me to do a round of chemo. There's a new treatment he wants to try. It's intense but should zap any lingering nasty cells."

"You have cancer?"

"Had. Let's speak in the positive."

"When did you have surgery?"

"A few weeks ago. My sister came to be with me. Your aunt Reese."

Aunt Reese. The name evoked a distant memory. Tenley never saw Blanche's family after she left. Her world consisted of Dad and Grandpa. "Extended family" was a bit of an anomaly to her.

"So what do you say?" Blanche said.

"About your cancer?" What was she wanting? Needing? "Pretty rough business, cancer. I'm sorry to hear—"

"No, no, I mean about coming down. I need someone with me during chemo."

"Me? Why not Aunt Reese?"

"She had to go home. Her youngest is graduating from high school. Besides, we were about to kill each other. Three weeks is long enough for us to be under one roof."

"Blanche, I can't come. I've got a deadline."

"You can write down here. There's a library on the second floor. A beautiful, huge space with lots of light. You'll love it."

"No. My life is here. And my fiancé."

"You're engaged?"

"Just."

"Oh, well, congratulations."

"Thank you." Tenley tucked her bare ring finger under her leg. "I'm sure you can find someone else to help you. I really do wish you well." In moments like this, she wanted to whisper, "I'll pray for you," but it seemed so foreign and hypocritical. She rarely prayed. And if she did, it was for herself. "How long is the chemo?"

"Once a week for four weeks, then every other week for four more treatments. I'm hoping it won't knock me out, but chemo hits everyone different. The doc says I should have someone with me. Especially since this is a new treatment. The pamphlet informs me I'll feel worse the longer it goes on. Fun times. So, will you come down?"

"You want me to be your caregiver?" Bold. Even for Blanche. *I abandoned you, but now I need your help.*

"In a word, yes. Say, bring your fiancé. The house is plenty big. You two can have the whole upstairs. There are lots of windows overlooking the Atlantic. A spectacular view. Except for chemo days and those following, I'll be on my own." A forlorn echo tinged her upbeat, chipper request.

But Tenley recognized the vibe. It lived in her chest. "Blanche, I can't."

"Tenley, I won't beg but please give it some thought. I wouldn't ask if I had another option."

A flash of anger gave way to quiet tears. This wasn't fair, putting the burden of her care on Tenley. She had a life. A fiancé. (Sort of.) Plans! Hills to climb. Mountains to conquer.

Blanche had her season, her carefree days of chasing whatever rainbow caught her fancy. And now she wanted Tenley to drop everything to tend to her?

"It's only for twelve weeks. Until the end of July."

"Which is exactly my deadline."

"I see . . ." A standoff of silence weighted the call. Blanche broke first. "So, can you come? The doctor wants to start treatment next week."

"I-I don't know, Blanche." An out-and-out no seemed heartless. She'd talk to Holt and he'd remind her of everything Blanche *wasn't* to Tenley growing up, and she'd settle the matter in her heart.

"Can you think about it?"

"I'll have to talk to Holt."

"When?"

"T-tonight, I guess. Blanche, if I can't come, what's your backup plan?" When it came down to it, didn't a rumble with cancer trump a heart-choking deadline?

"I don't have one. I'll have to go it alone."

Tenley made a face. "There's no one else to help you? You have money. Hire someone."

"It's you or nothing, Tenley."

She sighed. "Okay, well, I'll let you know—"

"Oh, forgive me, but congratulations on the Gordon Phipps Roth Award. How very proud you must be. I know I am." Blanche's voice stumbled, weary and rough. "You know your dad is looking down from heaven, cheering you on."

"Thank you." Tenley brushed the wash of emotion from under her eyes. This . . . this was what tripped her up. Why did it matter what Blanche thought? Why, in the core of her being, did Tenley crave her approval?

"How do you like the writing life? Conrad seemed to take to it like a duck to water. Of course, that was after I left. When I was married to him, he was a janitor."

"He wanted the everyman life experience."

"Yeah, well, you don't have to be a janitor to experience life." Dad had quit his editing job at the *New York Post* to get "out of the four walls to see how the world lives." A move Blanche never accepted. "So, are you a natural? Sure you are. It's in your blood."

"I don't know . . ." A natural? Nothing about writing seemed natural at the moment. It was hard work. Hard, hard, hard, a million times hard work. "That being said, Blanche, I think you should find someone better qualified to be with you." More tears. More craving in her soul to please this woman. "I live on Diet Coke and coffee. I barely cook for myself, let alone for anyone else."

"I need someone to be here when I'm sick. Can you make soup from a can? Run to the grocery store? Take me to appointments? That's all I need. Maybe some light housekeeping. Throw in a load of laundry. Tenley . . ." Blanche's voice sobered. "I'm scared. There, I said it."

"I-I'd be scared too."

Blanche's long, deep breath vibrated over the phone and through Tenley, melting her resolve.

"Then you'll call me? Let me know . . ."

"Sure, I'll call you." She felt sick, angry. Yet a swirl of regret painted her emotions, her thoughts, her soul.

However late, Blanche was offering Tenley something she'd dreamed of her whole life. More than literary achievements or a handsome fiancé. A chance to know her mother.

"Chemo starts next week, kiddo. *Please*, come down. Please say yes."

Breathing back a sting of tears, Tenley promised to think about it.

"I'll call. I promise."

She'd just hung up when Holt bounded into the attic, a wild

glint lighting his august face. "Pack your bags, babe." He pulled her from her chair, spun her around.

"Why?" Tenley laughed, releasing a piece of her burden. "What's going on?"

"Paris, babe. We're going to Paris."

THREE

BIRDIE

She walked through the Barclay Publishing office doors as the clock in the box-shaped reception chimed four. Gathering her breath after sprinting up four flights of stairs, Birdie approached Mr. Barclay's secretary, Mrs. Petersheim.

"Miss Elizabeth Candler Shehorn to see Mr. Barclay." She glanced toward his door, which remained closed. Daniel Barclay, Founder, Publisher, Editor-in-Chief was etched in the clouded glass.

Should she go on? Daughter of a wealthy shipping magnate with the blood of old New York in her veins. A Knickerbocker. An heiress. An authoress-in-waiting.

"Miss Shehorn, was he expecting you? Mr. Barclay is a very busy man, and it's near the close of business."

"I only need a moment of his time." She'd not be dismissed by this man. Not like before, when she'd made an appointment only to be left waiting in reception as he escaped out a back door with Mrs. Petersheim as his accomplice.

Well, not today.

After pretending to faint in the drawing room—which created

quite a ruckus—Birdie retired to her room, where Percival—bless him—had set out her coat and hat for a quick escape. She had no time to retrieve the new manuscript from the attic. Never mind, today's meeting was about her former submission to Barclay. The one she must retrieve.

Birdie snuck down the back stairs and through the empty kitchen and raced toward Ol' Mo's shed, where he waited to escort her to the brougham. What would she do without Percival and Ol' Mo? Her allies. The rest of the staff was too intimidated by Mama to aid Birdie.

At last! Barclay's office door swung open and the man himself appeared, his voice low, emanating a reassuring tone to the lean, wild-haired man he escorted from his office.

"Everything will be just fine, Gordon, I assure you—"

Birdie froze, boring her fingers into the thick brocade of her reticule. Gordon Phipps Roth? The man, the author himself? She might swoon. She adored his work. Had read his books at least a dozen times. Her governess, with Mama's blessing, had finally banned her from them for a whole year.

"Surely there are other fine authors with which to engage your-self."

While Papa had declared, "How can a man know so much about romance? He'll fill your head with fairy tales, Birdie."

"I don't know, Papa," Birdie spryly answered. "Why don't you inquire of romance from Shakespeare, Hawthorne, or Longfellow? Perhaps Robert Browning."

"Miss Shehorn." Mr. Barclay drew up short, his expression sober. "Hello. Was I expecting you?"

"Since you escaped on me previously, I thought I'd surprise you this time." Birdie clutched her reticule, affixed her smile, and tried to appear confident. Mr. Barclay was intimidating enough, but add the presence of Mr. Phipps Roth and, well, she was nearly weak.

Mr. Phipps Roth addressed her with a vivid gaze. "Not *the* Miss Shehorn? The one I read of in the papers so often?"

"One and the same," Mr. Barclay said. "May I introduce Mr. Gordon—"

"Phipps Roth. I've spent many a happy evening in front of a fire lost in your stories."

"Well now, what an honor. I never tire of hearing from a fan, but from one so beautiful and accomplished . . . Is it true what they say? You speak three languages and are the most sought-after partner for the season?"

"I don't know how *they* compose their stories but yes, I speak three languages, and no, I am no more sought after than all the fair ladies of the season when the dance is gay and the music lively."

Truth was, she was well past her debut. At twenty-two, she was practically an old maid. Thus Mama's hint to Mrs. Smith today raised her suspicions. Her cautions.

But that was neither here nor there in this moment.

"A modest girl," Mr. Phipps Roth said with a glance at Mr. Barclay. "Refreshing. Miss Shehorn, how did you know I was here?"

"Actually, I'm here to engage Mr. Barclay." She twisted the handles of her bag around her gloved hand. "Again."

"Again?" Mr. Phipps Roth frowned. "Daniel, are you putting off this young beauty? What is your business with Barclay, Miss Shehorn? A job? A typist or secretary?" He laughed. "Surely a woman of your means—"

"A novel," she blurted with vigor. "I submitted a novel to Mr. Barclay for his consideration." And she was desperate to retrieve it.

"Have you now? Isn't that splendid?" Mr. Phipps Roth seemed most amused. "Daniel, what's the delay? Give her the kindness of your time." Then to Birdie, "Take heed. You must have alligator skin to endure the trials of publishing."

"I've nothing but the toughest skin." This shared moment with Mr. Phipps Roth caused her heart to soar. Authors must stick together! "However, Mr. Barclay seems to think I'm more of a bother than any kind of talent."

Mr. Phipps Roth popped the publisher on the back. "You must see her, Daniel. Give her a chance. Put it on my tab."

"Perhaps I will," Barclay said, squaring his shoulders. "She keeps showing up like a hungry pup."

"Because you've given me no answer regarding my manuscript." Birdie raised her chin, grateful for the iconic author's camaraderie and subtle endorsement.

"Give the woman an answer, Daniel." Mr. Phipps Roth reached for her hand, bringing it to his lips. "Until we meet again, Miss Shehorn. A true princess of New York. I look forward to reading your work one day very soon."

He was younger than his craggy appearance portrayed. At first glance, he appeared to be a desperate old man, but Birdie knew him to be near his thirty-second year. He'd been first published at twenty-five, producing four exceptional novels.

"Then we are in agreement, Mr. Phipps Roth." She smiled, cutting a coy glance toward Mr. Barclay, who watched the exchange with dubiety. "I look forward to your next book as well."

"As do I. Remember, Miss Shehorn, never let anyone steal your dreams. You must guard them with all your heart."

His gaze locked with hers as he bent to kiss her hand. "I'll remember, Mr. Phipps Roth. I'll remember."

Once Mr. Phipps Roth exited, Mr. Barclay steered Birdie into his office wearing a scowl. Holding a chair for her to sit, he maneuvered behind his desk yet remained on his feet.

"I've five daughters, Miss Shehorn," he said. "I've witnessed every pitiful, angry, manipulative, begging, pleading expression a girl can muster for her father. I'm immune to them all." Jerking up his pants legs, he sat with a harrumph.

"My manuscript, sir—"

"Miss Shehorn, are you not from one of New York's oldest and wealthiest families?" The handsome publisher with graying temples shuffled the rubber-banded manuscripts to the edge of his desk. "Why do you seek publication? A girl of your stature must have more than one proposal of marriage. My wife and daughters read your family's name in the papers weekly during the season."

"Do you always believe what you read in the papers?"

His stern demeanor broke into a smile. "I suppose I do not." Clasping his hands behind his head, he peered out the window, the visage of Manhattan rooftops rising and falling beyond the pane. "But if I can believe the papers on this count, didn't your family recently return from yet another grand tour? Egypt and the Far East?"

"The editors rather lack news if they report on another Shehorn grand tour."

"I trust you all fared well. I've always longed to see Egypt. Is it as exotic as they say?"

"It's quite remarkable, but I daresay the pyramids are easier to scale than your publishing house, Mr. Barclay."

He laughed and made a show of checking his pocket watch. "What can I do for you? My family is preparing for dinner. I'd like to be home on time."

Birdie sat up a bit straighter.

On a dare put forth by her former Wellesley roommate, Birdie had submitted her first novel to Mr. Barclay the summer after graduation.

"It's so romantic, Birdie. You must try to publish it. Did you really have such a summer with a handsome earl in York, England?"

She submitted *A View from Her Carriage* to Barclay Publishing in June with anticipation and excitement. Could she become a published authoress? Sleep eluded her for the first week. Then Papa's grand tour became a lovely distraction.

The summer passed into fall and when Birdie returned home, her hands trembled as she sorted through her letters and packages. There was nothing from Barclay. The silence awakened her fears.

What if Mr. Barclay spoke to Papa? Or worse, Mama. They passed one another in church every week even though the Shehorns never spoke to the Barclays.

"Begging your pardon, Mr. Shehorn. What of this tome your daughter penned about falling in love with an English earl?"

Oh, she must retrieve it. What had she been thinking, submitting such an intimate story? What if Barclay published it and Eli read it? While the story and characters were fictional, the underlying truth would be evident to one in the know. That one being Eli.

Clearly, her head had been clouded with fancy publishing dreams.

Her second story was better suited for publication. Less intimate. Less personal.

"Actually, sir, I just want the story returned to me."

"We return all manuscripts. Did you leave a return post?"

"I did."

"And you've not received it?"

"No, sir."

He regarded her for a moment, then reached for the side door, disappearing into the offices and the working sounds of telephones and typewriters.

The hands of the clock behind Mr. Barclay's desk were poised at four thirty. Mama would knock on her door at five. She must be away soon.

She sighed with relief when Mr. Barclay returned not a moment later. "My editor tells me your manuscript was returned, Miss Shehorn. In August."

"Returned? But it couldn't . . ." She launched herself toward the door, peering into a long room lined with desks. "I've not seen it." Which one was the confident editor?

"Might I suggest you check with your servants? You were away in August. Perhaps they set it aside and forgot." Mr. Barclay pulled her into his office, gently shutting the door. "It's beginning to snow. We should both be off."

"May I speak with your editor? To be sure?"

Mr. Barclay slipped on his coat, his weighted sigh stealing a piece of her courage. At the side door he called, "Hamlisch, can you come in, please?"

A portly man with a grand mustache and pencils stuck behind his ears entered, his gray eyes bloodshot and bleary.

"This is Miss Shehorn. She has a question for you." Mr. Barclay popped his hat upon his head and folded his arms.

"You're quite sure you returned my manuscript, *A View from Her Carriage*?"

"We return all by courier. I'm quite sure."

"D-did you read it?" She gripped her hands into fists, waiting for his critique.

"The one of the young lady fallen for an earl?"

"Yes, yes, that's the one." She perked up, smiling.

"It was quite good. But not for our needs right now."

"Should I seek publication elsewhere?" She glanced between Hamlisch and Mr. Barclay. Time had healed her heart's yearning for Eli. She'd written a more fictionalized heroine the second time, not an image of herself longing for the man Birdie had left four thousand miles away. The man of whom her parents would never approve.

This time the hero was nothing like Eli. She'd modeled him after her dear departed brother, William.

"That I cannot tell you. But do keep writing, Miss Shehorn. You'll have your name on a book one day."

"I have written another—"

"There, are you satisfied? I am." Mr. Barclay urged her toward the exit. "See the snow? I don't want to tread through it home. Come."

The publisher paused to speak to Mrs. Petersheim while Birdie took the stairs to the lobby. She must drill Percival to find the location of her returned manuscript. Had it been given to Mama? Or Papa? Or burned in the incinerator?

She didn't want the world to read her raw, real emotions for Eli. She'd like to keep the book for herself.

"Good night, miss." The doorman held the door as Birdie stepped into the brisk afternoon, snowflakes swirling in the fading gray light.

"Good night." Tears swelled as she stood on the side of Broadway tugging on her gloves. "Might you hail me a cab, please?"

The doorman waved down a passing hansom, aiding her inside, then shouting to the driver to carry on.

In the rock and rhythm of the cobble streets, Birdie headed home. She'd gained nothing of her intended mission. But the words of Mr. Phipps Roth clung to her soul.

Guard your dreams. She pledged in the moment to do just that. Without exception.

ELIJAH

This would be the last of it. His freedom. Once January came upon him, his obligation and duty would rule the day.

But for this merry New Year's weekend at the Van Cliff estate in the Berkshires, he would be the man he wanted to be. Not the one he must become.

Leaning on his cane, he rang the bell, his valet gathering his things on the steps. "What do you think of this cottage?"

Benedict tipped his head to see the highest spiral peak. "Astounding."

"Lovely country, what, this Berkshires." Elijah motioned to the surrounding woodlands. "Puts me in mind of York and my beloved Hapsworth."

"Nothing will ever be as grand as Hapsworth, your lordship."

Elijah laughed. "It's back to 'your lordship'?" Benedict had been his batman in South Africa. They'd been through hell and back. Shared untold horrors of the Boer War. He was more of a brother than a manservant.

But the dictates of war differed from the dictates of society. Arranging for Benedict to be his valet meant they both must return to the ways and customs he held before Her Majesty called him into service for queen and country.

"You think you'll go through with it?" Benedict had a way of cutting through formality. Which Elijah allowed.

"I've given my word. So yes."

"For gentry and title?" Benedict's laugh lit his eyes.

"For hearth and home. A new battle we wage." Elijah leaned toward him. "To keep things as they've been for four hundred years."

At once, the ornate grand door eased open, slow and heavy.

"Your lordship, welcome." The Van Cliff butler, Sheldon, stood aside for Elijah to enter, commanding a footman to aid Benedict with his bags. "Begging your pardon, but a cane?"

Eli tapped his knee. "The war had its way with me."

"Then we are grateful for your safe and sound return."

"As am I." He removed his gloves, handing them to Benedict, whose tall, broad build dwarfed the young footman beside him. He too bore the marks of war. A bayonet cut ran from his left ear down his cheek and around his jaw to his chin. "This is my man, Benedict."

"Very good. Your rooms are ready. Alfonse is in the library, your lordship. He said I was to send you in upon your arrival."

"Then off I go. Benedict, make yourself useful to the house. Hosting a large party is sure to strain the staff." Benedict needed to be busy. It was his way of fighting off shell shock.

"Of course, your lordship."

Eli followed Sheldon through the expansive main hall with the grand staircase to his right and a large fireplace with a sitting area to his left.

Though a set of tall and wide doors, he entered the library.

"Lord Montague, sir," Sheldon said with a bow, closing the doors behind him.

Alfonse, an American mate from Cambridge, folded his newspaper, a spry grin on his handsome mug.

"My good man." Alfonse embraced him. "Welcome to our humble abode. How'd you find the ocean journey?"

"Cold and windy. I'm glad to be on land." The friends sat in adjacent chairs, the fire crackling in the marble fireplace.

"Are you looking forward to the season? Mrs. Astor's ball is after the first opera of the year. Are you on her list?"

"I've been informed I am." Eli stretched his hands toward the fire. There were moments when a chill ran through him no heat could reach. A remnant fear of his enlisted duty.

Alfonse passed Eli a glass of port. "You never said in your letter, but I assume a young lady is the main reason for your journey."

Eli leaned his cane against his chair and sipped the dark drink. "I've been given new orders. Apparently while I risked life and limb for my queen, my mama and Aunt Sylva arranged for my future. What are matters of the heart once the women have taken the reins?"

Alfonse did not laugh. "For men like us, marriage is about joining powerful families, adding wealth to the coffers, making alliances that cannot be broken."

"Yes, and all the royal marriages across the continent have prevented us from war."

"There's the cynical chap I remember." Alfonse smiled, sitting back, motioning to Eli's knee. "You won't be drawn into many quadrilles with that knee."

"Proof my luck hasn't completely run ashore."

"So, who is she?"

Eli hesitated. "Do I have your confidence?"

"Most assuredly."

"A Miss Rose Gottlieb."

"Rose Gottlieb?" Alfonse's expression conveyed his approval. "Beautiful girl, if not a bit young. Just came out last year. She's rich as the dickens. Her father is the newest of the Wall Street tycoons making waves."

"Seems he's most agreeable to send her to England with a large dowry in exchange for a title. A countess and future marchioness."

"And you're skeptical because?"

"How can a marriage be founded on one partner's need for capital to rescue his family's poorly managed estate and on the other's desire for social recognition and esteem? A title if you will. Doesn't it leave you rather cold?"

"Not at all. I'm looking at a bride myself. Brokered not because we're moony-eyed in love but because our families are a match. Because we bring power, fortune, and I daresay good looks to the union. We are the future of our nations, Eli. Don't begrudge your duty. Embrace it."

"I'm an Englishman. Of course I embrace it."

"Have you seen her? Rose?"

"In a photograph." He carried it in his pocket during the voyage over, wondering if theirs was a love matched in heaven. "She is quite lovely."

"I think she'll win your heart."

Eli saluted his friend with his port. "I'd like nothing more." He'd given his heart to a lady once. But they'd lost touch during the war. How? A question to which he had no answers.

"If all else fails, marry for money, then seek the one you love. Take her as your mistress."

Eli gulped his drink. "Is that your plan, my man? Do you aim to say so to the lass as you're proposing? Otherwise, you defraud her."

"What? Have you gone moral on me? What happened to 'as many lasses as possible'? Our escapades in London—"

"War has a way of purifying one's heart. In the darkest of nights there is only one thing on your mind—Should I be required to stand before the Almighty, will I find myself in His favor?"

"So the Earl of Montague, the future Marquess of Ainsworth, has found religion." Alfonse shook his head. "I never imagined I would see the day."

"Not religion, my good chap. But faith. It comforts me at the deepest level." Especially when he was to marry a woman he did not know or love.

"You're a better man than I." Alfonse refilled their port glasses. "Now, give me the truth. How was it? The war?"

"Beyond the pale."

"As I feared. I did, and it may surprise you, offer prayers on your behalf. I'm most glad you're home safe and sound." His cheeky grin sprang up. "Bum knee aside, you're still the handsomest chap I ever knew."

Eli laughed. "Don't start. We're not university men anymore. That was another time. Another life. A different Elijah Percy." He raised his cane to the library shelves. "The library is impressive."

"Mother had the house commissioned by Rotch and Tilden. I'm sure it seems small to you, being an English lord living in a castle, but it's quite spectacular for us Yanks."

"I was impressed at first sighting." Elijah pushed out of his chair and wandered the lengthy, well-stocked library, a portrait of Mrs. Van Cliff adorning the high wall between two bookcases. "Your collection rivals Hapsworth's. And you have modern conveniences. Plumbing and electricity."

"Father insisted. Cost him twice the price, but we're fixed for the future." Alfonse lit a cigar, sitting back, relaxing, looking like Eli's father rather than his friend.

"Who's the lass you're pursuing?" Eli reached for a Gordon Phipps Roth novel. He'd read one on the way to Africa. Enjoyed it immensely. The romance of the story reminded him of Birdie Shehorn and how she made him feel alive.

"I'm not at liberty to speak yet. Discussions are not concluded, but as soon as I've the final word, you will be the first to know. It's a good match. She's from an old family, educated, beautiful. Has a mind of her own, I'll tell you."

"She'll have to have her own mind to be your wife."

Alfonse laughed. "Let's hope Rose is the same. You'll need a strong woman to make the transition from American heiress to British peer."

Sheldon entered, carrying a silver tray. "Coffee and cake. I thought you'd want refreshment from your journey, your lordship."

Alfonse anchored his cigar in his teeth, rising to inspect the refreshment, thanking Sheldon as he exited. "When you visit, Sheldon is on his best behavior. I think he misses jolly ol' England."

"He's better off here." Elijah poured a cup of coffee, sweetening it with cream and sugar. "Many estates are failing. The mines are depleted. American agriculture competes with ours, thus the value of our crops is a quarter of what they were. Meanwhile, our wage bills increase. Not that we have as many workers as before. Service workers are migrating to the cities for positions in factories or the shops."

"Thus your financial quandary." Alfonse took up his coffee and a slice of cake, returning to his chair.

"Yes, thus." Elijah joined him, his stomach rumbling, the idea of cake and coffee stirring his appetite. "We have to change our ways. Many estates have been destroyed."

He thought of longtime family friends, the Tarboroughs, who lost everything at auction, then had to stand by while dynamite tumbled their precious Blanton Castle.

"Eli!" Gertrude, Alfonse's young sister, burst into the library, her smile like the sun. "You're here. At last, the party can begin."

"Alfonse? Who is this vision of loveliness?" He greeted Gertrude with a kiss. "Surely not your younger sister, Trudy?"

"Stop, you're only feeding her already lofty opinion of herself."

"He's jealous because I inherited the good looks in the family." Gertrude made a playful face at her brother. "Did you tell him?"

"Tell me what?"

"Tomorrow night the party is in your honor. Mother is bursting with pride that you're here. Is it true? You won the Victoria Cross?"

"Word travels fast across a vast ocean."

"As good news should. We've told all our guests."

"So just who is coming to the celebration weekend?" He glanced at Alfonse. "You never told me."

"Just a few families. The Shehorns, Vandergriffs, and Martins."

"The Shehorns?" He fought to suppress his grin. "How pleasant. We know them. From their '98 grand tour. They stayed at Hapsworth for a month."

A treasured memory. He first met Birdie at the Cranston's. He had walked into their ballroom expecting the usual peers when he spied a vision of beauty.

Miss Birdie Shehorn. She captured him completely. To his dismay, she had the same effect on half of his London peers. From ballroom to ballroom, night after night, Eli was met with the question, "Have you been introduced to Birdie Shehorn, the American? She's a delight."

Seeing an opportunity to marry Eli to American money, Mama invited the Shehorns to Hapsworth Manor for a month's stay. Eli thought he'd touched a bit of heaven when they agreed.

But Mr. Shehorn had no interest in investing the Shehorns' well-earned fortune into the failing system of British landed gentry.

When Birdie left, peering at him through the carriage window, he feared he'd never see her again.

"Eli's to marry Rose Gottlieb, Trudy," Alfonse said. "What do you think of that?"

"I think Rose is a lucky girl, but we're coming upon 1903. It's high time you men learn women are not merely your commodity to be traded for favors and money." Gertrude huffed as she sat on the couch with a large slice of cake.

Alfonse pointed to his sister. "She's training as a suffragette."

"Good for you, Trudy." Eli moved to the dessert tray to pour a cup of coffee. "I agree, women are not the commodity of men. Even in marriage."

"So the future Marquess of Ainsworth is a modernist?" Trudy eyed him, looking beyond his thin veil. "Might I make a prediction?"

"Oh no, not this. Tell her now, Eli. You don't know what crazy fortune she'll tell."

"I'm not telling fortunes, Alfonse. You need to talk less and listen more." Trudy faced Eli. "You will marry for love. No matter who it is. Mark my words, it will be for love."

"Love is a very expensive commodity," he said. But her expression, her tone, the vibrating intensity in her blue eyes captured him.

"Mark my words."

"So I will. And I hope, my dear Trudy, you are correct."

FOUR

TENLEY

She rode the train to Larchmont. To her best friend, who lived in a white cottage with red shutters and a picket fence.

"What are you doing here?" Alicia made a face as Tenley barged through the door into a cozy country kitchen. "At five in the afternoon?"

Alicia lowered her one-year-old, Addison May, into the high chair and poured a mountain of Cheerios onto the tray.

"Holt wants to go to Paris."

"The rat fink. The nerve . . ." Alicia retrieved two Diet Cokes from the fridge, then yanked a chair out from under the table, stomping the legs against the tile. "Paris! What's he thinking? Taking you to the redneckville of Europe." She passed Tenley a cold Diet Coke. "I tell you, he's trouble."

"Very funny." Tenley popped the top of her drink as a gulp of sunlight fell through the windows. "You know I love Paris." Seeing the City of Lights had been her college graduation present from Dad.

"Then why are you here, not home packing, calling me from your phone, shouting, 'I'm going to Paris'? Is there a better place in the world to write? In the shadows of Hemingway and Fitzgerald . . ."

the Eiffel Tower. Think of the lights, the music, the French bread. Never mind the romance." Alicia swigged her pop as if parched and drained. "What's the problem?"

Tenley averted her gaze. "Blanche called. She's going through chemo and asked if I'd come to Florida. Help her out."

"Blanche?" Alicia sat forward. "The woman who abandoned you wants you to help her? Oh, the irony." Alicia pulled a face. "Is she intent on ruining your life?"

"She's going through chemo, Alicia. And I don't think she's intent on ruining my life."

"You defend her?" Alicia shook her head. "Look, I'm sorry she's battling something as heinous as cancer. I wish her well. But how does that put you on the hook to help her? She abandoned *you* twenty years ago. You've seen her—what? A dozen times since then? Each time she waltzes into your life on her terms and exits the same, leaving you with emotional whiplash, wanting nothing but her love and approval. Neither of which she has ever given you in any great measure. I say go to Paris and I'm sorry if that sounds selfish. No. No, I'm not. I blame your dad for this. He taught you to forgive her."

"He loved her, Al. Always did. Besides, his religious roots wouldn't allow him *not* to forgive her."

Even in his most broken state, Dad never uttered a disparaging word about Blanche. Nor would he tolerate one from Tenley.

"She's your mother and you will respect her."

"What does Holt say?" Alicia tossed back a swig of her drink with a glance at Addi, whose face was covered with Cheerio bits.

"Paris, of course."

"For once I agree with him. So how did this Paris gig come up?"

"Nicolette Carson—"

"There's a name I didn't expect. Where did he run into her?"

"She was at the Phipps Roth Award. She invited Holt to a

screenwriting and film symposium she's hosting. By invitation only. So it's an elite crowd."

Alicia wagged her finger at baby Addi. "Look what you made me miss, young lady."

Tenley smiled, running her thumb over her bare ring finger. Alicia's shallow scolding meant nothing. She'd walk across cut glass for her daughter, for her family, and not think twice.

Married right out of NYU, she and Drake bought a house one block away from her parents, who still lived in the house where she grew up.

Tenley envied Alicia. She had family. Close and tight, sharing every birthday and holiday, watching each other's houses when one or the other went on vacation. They circled the wagons when sickness or hardship hit.

Tenley had Dad. And Grandpa until he died. They did their best. But when tragedy struck, there were no family wagons circling.

If not for Alicia's family, Tenley would've stood alone at Dad's funeral.

Alone was the loneliest place on earth.

"Where are you on your book?" Alicia said.

"Same place I was last time you asked."

Wide-eyed, Alicia filled Addi's tray with more Cheerios. "Isn't your deadline coming up?"

"Yep."

"But you got nothing?"

"Zip, zero, nada."

"Then you have to go to Paris. Find some inspiration. Oh—" She reached for Tenley's left hand. "Let me see your ring. I saw a picture in the paper but . . ." She made a face with a quizzical glance at Tenley. "It looked much bigger in the photo. And sparkly. Where's your ring, Tenley?"

"In its home." She pulled her hand free, hiding it under the table. "The Tiffany box."

"Why—"

"I don't want to gunk it up with soap and stuff . . . you know . . . hamburger meat or whatever."

Alicia spewed her mouthful of Diet Coke. "Hamburger meat? When did you ever make a hamburger?"

"Look, this isn't about the ring or when I ever made a hamburger, which, for your information, was my senior year of college."

"Right, when you almost caught our kitchen on fire."

"And you dated one of the firefighters for six months. You're welcome. Back to my problem."

"Easy. Go to Paris, then go help Blanche. How long is the symposium?"

"A week, but Holt booked an apartment for three months. He wants to write there."

"When does Blanche need you?"

"By Monday." Tenley rose from the table, the caffeine from the pop energizing her anxiety. "Blanche assures me Cocoa Beach is an inspiring place to write. Her house has a huge library I can use. She said she should only need me on treatment days and maybe a few days after if she's sick."

"Who will cook? Clean? Run errands?"

"Me, I guess."

"Then you're both doomed. You can't write if you're so distracted. Look at how far you've gotten with all the time in the world."

"You don't need to remind me. And I haven't had all the time in the world. I've done a second book tour, interviews for radio, TV, and print. I've attended book fairs. It's exhausting being a success."

More exhausting to realize it was all a facade.

"Then you need Paris. A sort of beautiful isolation. You can't go on a promotional junket or call in to a radio show if you're in Paris. I swear, Barclay has kept you running with promotions, book clubs, special appearances, this thing or that."

"People miss my father."

"It's not just about your dad. You wrote a great book. Don't cut yourself short."

Tenley drained her Diet Coke and dumped the can in the recycle bin. "Tell me what to do, Al."

"What do you think I've been doing?" she said. "Apparently your heart is telling you something different. You know, if you go to Paris, you could get married there. Wouldn't that be amazing?"

"Married in Paris?" But she'd never really said yes, had she? "Al, I don't wear the ring because I never really said yes. He asked me in the limo on the way to the event. Then Wendall knocked on my window and opened the door, telling us we were late. Holt slipped the ring on and I—"

"Went with it."

Going with it was Tenley's superpower. Only child of a single dad, she'd learned to roll with almost any situation. The upside was very little ruffled her. The downside was very little ruffled her.

Except failing when everyone—*everyone*—anticipated success.

Otherwise, she lived with a man she wasn't sure she loved. She accepted a book deal she wasn't sure she'd earned.

"Go to Paris, Tenley. Blanche is the past. Holt is the future. Book writing is your calling. Figure out if your answer to his proposal is yes or no. Spend sunny afternoons writing. Take weekends in the country. Dream. Drink good wine, eat fabulous cheese and great bread. Make the kind of love that destroys the bed."

Tenley's eyes watered. "You should be the writer." She peeked at her best friend. "You know it won't be like that, Alicia. We'll work

44

until midnight, when one of us will look up, realize the dinner hour has passed, and all we have in the fridge is leftover Chinese."

Alicia laughed. "Even in Paris, leftover Chinese is romantic."

"There will be no romance. That went out the door the first time we . . . well, you know."

"So use this opportunity to find the spark again."

"I'm not sure there ever was a spark."

"Never?"

"A small one. I was in so much pain after Dad died. I'd see Holt at the coffee shop and he became a sort of solace, a friend in the night."

"Go to Paris, Tenley. Write. Find your passion. Get married in a country chapel if you're so inclined. Gain five pounds. Do it. Just don't debate it ad nauseam. Indecision makes people unstable."

"Exactly. I feel like I'm free-falling." Tenley slapped her hand against the faux-wood tabletop. "Paris. I'm going to Paris, and I'm going to love it. And Holt. Find our spark. Commit. Write an amazing book."

With each confession, her words swirled and inspired, raised her soul to confidence.

"I can't believe I let Blanche mess me up. Again. You're right, she's been doing it since she left twenty years ago."

"Although . . . " Alicia said, low and slow.

"Alicia." Tenley covered her face with her hands. "Don't! You always do this. I make up my mind, then you present a different view."

"I'm sorry, it's how my brain works. Paris is great, but helping your mom could really change your relationship with her. Give you what you've always wanted."

"I'm twenty-nine years old. I don't need her approval. Or her affection. It's enough we text and e-mail a few times a year." Lies. Fat ones. Dripping from her lips.

"Yet here you sit in my Larchmont kitchen, wondering if you should go to Florida or Paris."

A sheen of tears exposed Tenley's true emotions. "I guess I do wonder if going to Florida would change things between us. Is this my chance to have a relationship with her? What if the cancer defeats her? Would I always wonder . . . ?"

"If saying yes to her would've been a turning point?"

Tenley pressed her forehead to the table. "Yes. Maybe that's why she's *asking*."

Alicia's warm arms came around her shoulders. "Go to Florida, Tenley. It's what your dad would want. I think it's what you want, or you wouldn't be here. This is a time for Holt to support you. Be there for you. Trust his love, Ten."

Tenley raised her head, peering into her friend's beautiful eyes. "How did I ever deserve you?"

Alicia laughed. "You stalked me all the way to my dorm room."

"Excuse me, but as I recall, you broke into *my* dorm room pretending it was yours."

But it was fate, or God, who brought them together as roommates their freshman year at NYU.

"So, Florida it is."

"Al, do you think I'm with Holt because I'm afraid to be alone? Is fear why I have writer's block?"

"Tenley, those are questions only you can answer."

From her chair, Addison fussed, demanding attention and sending Cheerio crumbs over the side of her tray with a quick swish of her chubby hand.

When Drake came home, Tenley headed out, turning down an invitation to dinner. She yearned for the train ride home to think. To be.

As she walked to the train station, a low, familiar hum began in her chest—the melody of the song she'd known since she was a child. She didn't know its origins. Dad and Grandpa claimed they'd never heard it before.

Nevertheless, it was Tenley's song. One that comforted her in her darkest hours. An omnipotent voice singing, "Do not be dismayed, do not be dismayed, you don't have to worry or be afraid."

FIVE

BIRDIE

Percival greeted her at the front door, helping her out of her coat. "Is the coast clear?" Birdie asked.

"Yes, if you move quickly. How did it go?"

"Not as well as I'd have liked." She'd pondered her meeting with Mr. Barclay the entire ride home, mystified by the disappearance of her manuscript. "Though I did meet Gordon Phipps Roth."

"How splendid. I know how you adore his books. But"—Percival leaned near, whispering—"nothing of your own work?"

Percival was the only one in the house who knew the height of Birdie's writing ambitions. He protected her attic space from the prying eyes of nosy maids and lazy footmen. Even demanding Mama.

"He claims the manuscript was returned to me." Birdie checked her appearance in the hallway mirror. Her hair was in place, but her cheeks were pink from the cold. Much too vibrant for an ill woman who'd spent several hours *napping*. "Which brings me to you, Percival. Did a package arrive for me in August? Perhaps a footman stored it away while we were gone? Maybe mistakenly gave it to

Mama? Read *Miss* Shehorn as *Mrs.* Shehorn?" If Mama discovered Birdie had written a book, let alone submitted it for publication, she'd dismantle the house to discover how such a travesty could go on without her knowledge.

Then she'd rail until Birdie's spine vibrated. When that ended, she'd enter a season of silence, not speaking to her daughter until she determined Birdie had been properly punished.

Mama's plans for Birdie to marry well and one day lead New York society would prevail.

"The footmen are under strict instruction to bring all posts and packages to me," Percival said. "If I'm not available they are to leave them in my room. Surely they'd not disregard me."

"Unless Mama intercepted."

Percival's expression softened. "Miss, I know you believe she means you harm, but I sense she has nothing but goodwill toward you."

"Yes, her *good* will. Make no mistake."

"She'd not steal from you."

"Are you so naïve to her ways?" Birdie started for the stairs before a servant came through. "She'd strip me down to my corset and send me to a Vanderbilt ball if it meant having her way."

Percival pinched his lips, sending his laugh to his eyes. "You do her a disservice, miss." He motioned to the library. "She and your papa await you in the library."

"What?" She spun around to the man who had tucked her into bed when she was a child and Papa was away. The one who had cradled her against his barrel chest when William died. "What for?"

"I've no idea, but your mama sent Fatine to find you. I caught her in time and sent her on another errand."

"How long have they been waiting?"

"Not long. I told them you were rousing from your sleep and sent them tea and sandwiches."

"Isn't it a shame a grown woman has to have her butler run interference? Why should I hide my actions and ambitions from Papa and Mama? Would William be so timid? Would he have to enact a fainting spell to get out of the house? No, indeed not."

"He was the heir. You cannot know what your parents might have objected to in his choices. You are their hope now, Miss Birdie. Their heiress. Have a care to their desires for you."

"Most certainly. If they will have a care to mine." Birdie took the long corridor to the master library, passing under her ancestors' portraits—Shehorns and Candlers who built the empire her father now managed. She breezed into the grand, warm room, as if she were right on time, her countenance firm.

"Good evening, Mama, Papa."

Mama stood with an inspecting eye. "Are you well? What happened this afternoon?"

"I believe the fire was too hot. But yes, I am well." She kissed Mama's cheek and perched on the edge of the chair farthest from the fire.

Papa looked up from his desk where he read the *Evening Post*. "I see your University Settlement Society is at it again. Fighting John Astor over his tenements."

"Of course. Those dwellings are deplorable. You'd not let your prize mares eat their oats in a single one, Papa. They are cramped, insect-infested, and many of the rooms are windowless with no escape from the cold, the heat, or God forbid, a fire."

"Hmm," Papa muttered.

The society clashed with the men in Papa's class by demanding better living conditions for the poor, expressly in Hell's Kitchen. However, when one of their peers, Isaac Newton Stokes, became involved, Papa became a little more sympathetic to the plight of the immigrants.

Mama set aside her needlepoint, scooting to the edge of her chair. "We have some news, Birdie."

We have news might mean anything. A new house. A yacht. Yet another grand tour. This time to Australia. Or, as once in the past, word of her brother's death.

She was young, a mere fourteen, when William died. She adored her big brother, five years her senior, gregarious and handsome, strong, with a mop of blond locks no hair tonic could tame, a teasing glint in his blue eyes. Every girl in society wanted him.

"... *influenza ... on his trek through the Wild West.*"

Remembering William made her long for him. How different things might be if he still breathed.

"It's the best kind of news." Mama beamed at Papa. "You are to be married."

"What?" She was on her feet, trembling, reaching to the chair's arm for support.

"I think my statement was clear enough, Birdie."

"Married? To whom? I've no suitor. No love interests." She glanced at Papa. *Don't let her do this.* The fire crackled as if to join the conversation.

"Alfonse Van Cliff," Mama said, rising to pour a cup of tea.

The Van Cliff and Shehorn families had been friends and business partners of one sort or another since their ancestors sailed from Holland to New York in 1785.

"Alfonse? You must be joking. He's a notorious flirt. Insufferably full of himself." Though William had befriended him, finding Alfonse charming and witty, Birdie merely tolerated him.

"Schoolboy immaturities," Mama said, waving off Birdie's concern. "Alfonse has grown into a fine, mature man who is of no insignificance to commerce and society. He's worth a considerable fortune. Combined with your dowry, you two will quickly rise to the top."

"Top of what, might I ask?" She was trapped, being shoved into a life of her mama's design.

"You know full well, Elizabeth Candler Shehorn."

Birdie flushed with shame. Mama, using her full name as if she were a child . . .

"Papa, are you in agreement? Didn't you raise me to think for myself? Wasn't that your wish when you sent me to Wellesley?"

"I told you such a venture would cause us angst, Geoffrey." Mama's steely glance bored into Birdie.

Rising from his desk, Papa took up his pipe.

"Here, Geoffrey, let me." Mama scooted across the room to light Papa's pipe. Birdie collapsed against the chair cushion, her heart beating so fast her lungs could not properly draw a breath.

"Birdie, we leave for the Van Cliffs' in the morning." Papa stood by the fire, puffing his pipe, smoothing down his muttonchops.

"Yes, for New Year's Eve. Fatine and I have sorted out my costumes." Together they'd selected no fewer than fifty gowns for this seven-day event.

"Alfonse will have a question for you." Papa regarded her, smoke swirling before his face. "You will answer yes. Stow and I have settled the financial arrangement. Alfonse is agreeable. He's very fond of you. The two of you are considered a good match by all."

"Except by me." Birdie restrained her voice, holding steady on the edge of the seat cushion, battling a mounting dread.

"Birdie, for the love of heaven," Mama said with an angry sigh. "What is your objection? We are fortunate Alfonse has not already married. You are approaching your twenty-third birthday. Do you wish to be an old maid? Finding yourself one day stuck with an old curmudgeon like a Lowell Speight?" She shivered.

"I see no difference between the two scenarios. Mama, Papa, I do not love nor regard Alfonse. I find him arrogant, conceited, and disagreeable. Wasn't he to marry Lillian Hayes?"

"She chose a German prince." Papa spit the words. He took no delight in European aristocrats marrying American heiresses, moving hard-earned American dollars into their failing economic and social structures.

"Alfonse is confident. As a young man of his means should be." Mama had an answer for everything. Birdie knew better than to enter the ring with the champion.

But this was her life. Her heart.

"I won't do it." She rose again and moved around the heavy, ornate furniture toward the door. "I will not marry him."

"The arrangements have been made." Mama's bitter tone stabbed Birdie. "You decline him now and we will be shamed. Made to look the fools."

"You should've taken it into consideration before you spoke for me."

"Geoffrey, are you going to allow her to speak to me in such a tone?"

"Leave her be, Iris. We've made the arrangements. Now it's up to Alfonse to woo and win her. If he's half the man we believe, he'll see to it in short order."

Mama did not challenge him, though Birdie had no doubt there were more words behind those pinched lips. In moments such as these, Birdie wondered if Papa shared her suspicions about her mother, about whether the woman was as honorable as she led the world to believe.

"I've a fall wedding in mind. Birdie, see to it you're responsive to his affections." Mama returned to her needlepoint. "Did you hear Rose Gottlieb is to be engaged? Mrs. Gottlieb is giddy with excitement but she will not give up the suitor until the official announcement. We shall all wait to see who has won the lovely Rose."

There was nothing more to be said. Trapped without any means of her own, Birdie must submit to Papa and Mama's arrangements.

Running up the stairs, she burst into her room, falling on the settee in tears. *No, no, no.*

If only . . . if only . . . Mr. Barclay had regard for her novel and offered her publication. Having her own means would loose her from Mama's control. Even if it meant sharing a house with her friends in the University Society—well below any woman of her social standing—at least she'd be free.

Freedom. Such a beautiful existence.

She could not contain her tears. Weeping for her lost book, her lost love, her impending marriage, Birdie slipped to her knees, the pain of her heart forming desperate prayers.

As her words left her lips, a sweet, light breeze swept through her room. Rising up, Birdie glanced toward the window, drying her cheeks with the back of her hand. Had someone raised the sash?

Finding the window closed, she sat back down, the air stirring and swirling about her again, settling over her with the melody of a mystical song. One she heard often in her darkest hour.

Do not be dismayed, do not be dismayed, you don't have to worry or be afraid.

SIX

ELIJAH

Making his way down to dinner, cane in hand, he ran his free hand along his dinner jacket lapels. At the bottom of the stairs, he straightened his tie and smoothed his hair.

He'd not seen her yet, but he heard the Shehorns had arrived. He wanted to look sharp when Birdie clapped eyes on him for the first time in over four years.

The notion of being near her caused his pulse to pound. His thoughts spun round and round. *Gather yourself, chap, you've a duty to your family. Not your heart.*

He'd sailed to America for a specific purpose. To this he must remain true.

"There you are. Making a grand entrance, are we?" Alfonse greeted him with a jaunty grin. "Everyone's in the salon. The Shehorns, Vandergriffs, and Martins, all with beautiful daughters. It's a feast for every man's eyes."

"Then I am blessed. After this weekend, I must have eyes for only one." Rose Gottlieb. "Do tell, is your future intended among the lasses tonight?"

"Let's not focus on matters so serious. Betrothal and marriage are for the new year." Alfonse clapped Eli on the back as they breezed through the salon door, his blond head high, his voice full of charm. "Good evening, everyone. May I present the Earl of Montague, Elijah Percy."

The guests offered slight head bows and practiced curtsies. Eli greeted each one. Alfonse was right, the lasses were beautiful. But he desired to see only one. Birdie.

Mrs. Van Cliff stepped forward to introduce the guests. "Mr. and Mrs. Geoffrey Shehorn. Their daughter, Birdie, is also with us this week."

"My friends, the Shehorns. It's a pleasure to see you again."

"The pleasure is all ours, your lordship." Mrs. Shehorn curtsied. "We're delighted to see you. How do your parents fare?"

"Very well, thank you."

"I see you brought some of the war home with you." Mr. Shehorn motioned to Eli's cane. "But if that's all you suffered, then you fared well."

"I consider myself blessed."

A crack of light across the way drew his eye as an interior door opened and *she* entered with Trudy, more stunning in posture and poise than he remembered.

Birdie.

It was all he could do not to toss his cane and leap over furniture or shove past the others to take her in his arms.

She did not see him as she moved about the room greeting the daughters of the Vandergriffs and Martins.

Elijah downed a splash of port handed to him by Alfonse, watching her, feeling as if his heart beat outside of his chest for all to see.

Besides beauty, she exuded warmth and kindness. Her expressions transcended her external appearance to reveal the woman inside. He yearned to take her aside and speak with her without interruption. To hear how she fared. Did she ever write the book she spoke of in whispers four years ago?

Blast it all! Why had they stopped their correspondence?

There, she saw him, catching his stare. "Lord Montague." How he loved to hear her speak his name. "My goodness! You take my breath away. No one informed me you'd be among the guests." She glanced back at Trudy. "You never said."

She crossed the room, the electric lamps catching the auburn highlights of her chestnut hair, and slipped her gloved hands into his. Alfonse could have every other lass in the room. Eli would take this one. All to himself.

"Birdie, how lovely you look. Even more so than the last time we met."

"You're too kind."

"How do you two know one another?" Alfonse said, bursting in, soaking up Birdie's aura.

Birdie frowned at him. "Begging your pardon, Alfonse. I believe I was speaking to Lord Montague."

Eli. She must call him Eli when they were alone.

"We met years ago on a grand tour. Birdie's first, I believe," Eli said.

"You remembered. How sweet." She slid closer, giving Alfonse the edge of her shoulder. "Whatever brings you to New York? Don't tell me it's the season."

"He seeks a bride." Alfonse. Must he be so brazen?

"A bride? Do tell." The thin, watery sheen in her eyes polished her surprise. "What a lucky young woman."

No, no, no, this was not how he wanted to tell her. He'd deal with Alfonse later. Birdie deserved to be treated with care. While they had no understanding, they'd expressed feelings for one another that summer afternoon, walking across the Hapsworth Manor meadow where he nearly kissed her. Would it not have been the sweetest of kisses?

"There's nothing of interest to tell." Which for the moment was true. "I'd much rather hear of you."

"I too have nothing of interest to tell." Her gaze skirted past his cane. "You were wounded."

"He won the Victoria Cross," Trudy said.

Must everyone eavesdrop on their conversation?

"Mercy, what heroics earned you such a distinguished honor?"

"Yes, Lord Montague, do tell." Mrs. Shehorn, adorned with pearls and a diamond tiara, came alongside her daughter. "Regale us with your heroics."

"I'm afraid modesty does not permit me." Eli stepped back with a tip of his head. It was clear Mrs. Shehorn did not want her daughter alone with him.

Had Birdie confided in her of their near-kiss? Of their past affection? He thought it unlikely, because that summer Birdie spoke often of her mother's cool distance.

At this point, the senior Van Cliff took to the middle of the room. "May I have your attention, please? Lorena and I are delighted and honored to have you all with us this New Year's. Our home is your home." The guests responded with bold appreciation. "We'll have dinner in a moment, after which we'll adjourn for a myriad of activities. For us older set, we've employed a small orchestra for ballroom dancing. For the younger among us, I've asked the groomsmen to prepare the sleighs. The snow is packed well under a full moon and a galaxy of stars. We see much more of the heavens in the Berkshires than in the city. Should any of the young ones, or old, have the gumption to skate, the pond is decidedly frozen. We've distributed lanterns and skates of every size for your enjoyment.

There's nothing like exercise to ensure health, happiness, and a good night's sleep. A quartet from the orchestra will accompany the skaters. What's skating without music, I say?" The guests exclaimed their delight. "However," Mr. Van Cliff said, "I must request everyone's presence in the main hall at eleven fifty-five to bring in the New Year together. Nineteen hundred and three! We shall toast it with cheers and champagne. What say you all?"

"Hear, hear! Well done, Stow." Mr. Shehorn raised his glass. "But we expected no less from a Van Cliff. We shall celebrate in grand *American* style." Mr. Shehorn cut his glance toward Eli.

He'd heard America's wealthy had tired of their daughters marrying European nobility. He needed not the mind of Sherlock Holmes, nor even Watson's, to figure Shehorn among them.

Upon Van Cliff's conclusion, the butler entered, announcing dinner. But Eli was hungry only for conversation with Birdie.

As the elders of the party moved toward the expansive dining hall, the younger guests lagged behind. Eli joined Alfonse, who spoke with Birdie and Kathleen Martin by the fire.

"Ah, my lord," Alfonse said. "Your modesty has me curious. What did you do to earn such an honor?"

"Please, tell us." Birdie gestured around the room. "The others have left." Her expression softened him.

"Well . . ." He cleared his voice, retreating back to that day but viewing it from an emotional bird's nest, high above the true reality and horrendous details. "To be sure, I'm one of thousands of men who fought with life and limb for queen and country. I'm not special."

"But you must have saved a man's life or done something of equal valor to receive such an honor." Alfonse baited him with a teasing glint in his eye. He really observed no personal barriers, did he?

"Yes, I saved a man's life." Eli nodded, ending the story. Recounting the details caused him a certain anxiety. "As would any of you, given similar circumstances. Now, I believe we've been called to dinner." Eli urged the ladies forward.

"Posh, my good man." Alfonse with his horrible British affect. "You must recount the whole story."

"Alfonse, leave him be. Perhaps he doesn't wish to relive the events." Birdie's compassion filled her hazel eyes. "Don't let this coward bully you, Lord Montague."

"Coward?" Alfonse stiffened. "I don't think such a name is fitting, Birdie. Just because—"

Birdie slipped her arm through Eli's, which practically rendered him powerless. "Keep your humor about you, Alfonse. We are all cowards in light of Lord Montague and the men who fought for their country. Now, shall we go to dinner? I am famished."

Eli pressed his hand over hers, their gazes barely meeting as they filed out of the room behind Alfonse and Kathleen.

"Miss Shehorn," Eli ventured, a hoarse whisper in his throat. "Would you accompany me to the pond for skating after dinner?"

"I'd be delighted, Lord Montague. But can you skate with your knee?"

"I believe I'll give it a go, yes."

Because with Birdie Shehorn by his side, Elijah Percy believed he could do just about anything.

Even forget his duty.

SEVEN

TENLEY

She awoke with a jolt, sitting up in the shadows. Beneath her, the bed springs squeaked, and across the way, a golden light peeked around venetian blinds.

Focusing on the furniture in the room through the dim light, Tenley collapsed back down to her pillow, kicking off the thin layer of covers.

She was in Florida. Cocoa Beach. She'd arrived late Sunday evening, close to midnight, taking a taxi from Melbourne International to Blanche's Grove Manor on A1A.

Blanche texted she was going to bed.

Key under the mat. Your room is at the top of the stairs.
First door on your right. Library to the left. Can't miss it.
Through the French doors. See you in the daylight.

Rolling over onto her side, Tenley reached for her phone. Seven o'clock. With a sigh, she cradled her phone to her belly, stretching across the cool sheets, wondering if she should call Holt.

They had a fight to end all fights yesterday afternoon as Tenley packed.

"*She's manipulating you, Ten.*" *He took the tops she'd just put in her suitcase and stuffed them back in the dresser drawer.* "*She's lived without you for over twenty years and suddenly you're her only hope?*" *He snatched up her hands.* "*You're shutting down your writing for her. She's a dream killer! Why can't you see that? Come to Paris with me. Write, be bohemian.*"

"*I know, I know, this makes no sense.*" *She freed herself from his grip and gathered her tops from the drawer.* "*But she needs me, and for reasons I'm sure Freud himself might not understand, I have to go. This might be my last chance to have a relationship with her. She's fighting cancer, Holt. I've already lost my father. You have your parents and grandparents and siblings. I've got no one.*"

"*You have me. And Paris.*"

"*Paris, for all its glory, did not give birth to me.*"

He cocked a sly grin. "*Let it give birth to your next bestseller.*"

"*Yeah, and can we just ask about that? How does a first-time novelist under the age of thirty have a runaway hit?*"

"*You're talented.*"

"*Or my last name is Roth.*" *She reached for Holt, pulling him to her.* "*I have an idea. Why don't you come to Cocoa Beach after the symposium and I'll be as bohemian as you want.*" *She added a sultry tenor to* bohemian.

"*I'm going to finish my screenplay in Paris, Tenley.*" *He broke away from her, hands on his belt, staring at her suitcase.* "*Frankly, I can't believe you're choosing Blanche over me.*"

"*I'm not choosing her over you. I'm choosing . . .*" *What was she choosing? Really?* "*A last chance to have a relationship with my mother. I'm choosing compassion. Human kindness.*"

"So, what about this?" Holt swerved around with her ring box. "You never wear it."

"It's so beautiful . . ." Tenley reached for the box, tucking it into her suitcase. Holt roped his arms about her waist.

"Just like you." His kiss came swift and greedy, leaving Tenley no room to respond. When Holt broke away, Tenley pressed her fingertips against her lips.

"I-I'd better finish packing."

"Can I ask you something?" Holt folded his arms, watching. "Why do you want her approval so much? She doesn't deserve your devotion, Ten."

"No, but most of us don't deserve any kind of unmerited devotion." Another Grandpa saying. Something about God's unmerited favor, Jesus and the cross, blood and dying. Tenley never understood it all, so she tuned him out. But lately she found that repeating Grandpa Roth's wisdom came easily, as if she'd been listening after all. "We'll make it work, Holt. This long-distance thing. We'll e-mail, call, text. It might be fun, missing each other."

With a sigh, he headed from the room. "Fine, go to Cocoa Beach. But don't hold your breath for me to understand."

But she had held her breath, sharing little ideas the rest of the evening—"When I'm sixty, I think I'll be glad I spent this time with my mom"—with Holt only mumbling a reply.

She kissed him good-bye at the apartment and cried the entire cab ride to LaGuardia.

The deed was done. She was in Florida. Nothing to do but get on with it.

Flipping on the bedside lamp, she adjusted to her new world. Her room was quite large with dormer walls and a private bath.

The closet was dark, the walls running deep under the roof.

Finding a pull cord to a bare lightbulb, Tenley found two things—a man's red plaid robe and a pair of corduroy slippers.

Removing the robe from the hanger, she slipped it on, the threads releasing the scent of aftershave. It made her think of Daddy. Then she dug her feet into the slippers.

Inspecting her new Florida wardrobe in the dresser mirror, she moseyed into the hall, spying out the library.

It was beautiful. Large and spacious, with floor-to-ceiling shelves loaded with books. The windows framed the blue-green surface of the Atlantic and the golden edges of the rising sun.

Stunning. The room spoke of money, of care and details. If she didn't find inspiration here . . . Return to the passion she found writing *Someone to Love* . . . Then . . .

Tenley swerved behind her, peering toward the doors, searching for a place to set up. The desk in the center of the room, situated under a Tiffany floor lamp, appeared to be just her size. The dull, pale brown wood hinted of better days. The center drawer was accompanied by three side drawers on the right.

Tenley ran her hand over the smooth surface. This desk had been well used. *Life* happened at this desk. Four indents marked the center where perhaps a machine sat. A typewriter? An adding machine? On the front edge were soft worn grooves from where arms or hands might have rested.

Maybe Blanche was right. This place would be the inspiration she needed.

Adjacent to the desk sat a wood-frame, upholstered chair. Pulling it forward, Tenley sat at the desk. The chair was just the right height, and she had a bubbling sensation behind her heart.

"Are we going to be good friends, desk?"

Her confidence peeked from behind a dark wall. She could write another novel. Sure. The first one had just flowed. So this one would take a bit more time. But she was a bestselling, award-winning author.

All she needed was a change of scene and this adorable desk. While nothing stood out about the piece, Tenley felt its good bones.

She loved Grandpa Gordon's desk, but maybe sitting where he and Dad had written their brilliant bestsellers was just too much for a newbie like Tenley. What she needed was her own space. Her own desk. Her own writing traditions.

With a contented sigh, Tenley retrieved her laptop from the bedroom, inspired to set up and start dreaming.

Finding the nearest outlet—all the way against the wall—she pushed the desk and lamp into place and plugged in.

She switched on the light, and the lamp arched a Tiffany-colored rainbow across the desk. "Perfect."

She'd have to get the Internet password from Blanche, but otherwise she was set for a day of writing, a vibrant hum of inspiration in her chest.

The fragrance of eggs, bacon, and toast drifted through the library. Tenley's stomach rumbled.

She stared out the library's French doors. Light billowed up from the first-floor windows to the open second floor, and everything seemed so fresh and bright, even her weary soul.

"Tenley? You up?" Blanche called up from the first floor.

"Yeah, in the library."

"Come on down when you're ready. I've got breakfast cooking."

"I only drink coffee in the morning."

"Not today. You're having a hearty breakfast."

Yeah, well, she'd see about that. Inspecting the desk drawers, she found those on the side clean and empty. However, the middle drawer was wedged shut.

Hmm. Gripping the pull, Tenley leaned back, giving it a good tug, even anchoring her foot against one of the spindly, scuffed legs. The drawer refused to budge.

"Blanche, what's wrong with the middle drawer?"

"What?"

"The middle drawer? I can't open it."

Digging into her computer bag, she found an old receipt and slid it along the top of the drawer. It moved freely, unobstructed.

Was it nailed shut? Tenley dropped to her knees, inspecting the base. No nails.

"Breakfast!"

Bumping her head, Tenley crawled out from under the desk. She'd deal with the stubborn drawer later.

Taking her phone from the robe's pocket, she snapped a picture and texted it to Holt. He left today for France so he'd be up, on his way to the airport.

My new digs! Feeling inspired already. Miss and love you,
Ten

With a grin, she stretched across the desk, resting her cheek on the cool surface. "Let's write a book together."

This desk was indeed part of her journey. She knew it and believed for the first time she could write a great book here. Prove to herself, and the world, she was not a fraud.

"Tenley? Breakfast."

She gave the large, square library one last visual pass. Yep, this was her place. And she liked it.

She regarded the wall of bookshelves on her left. One section stuck out a bit farther than the others, and the shelves were rather empty save for a section in the middle.

Odd. Crossing over, she found a collection of Gordon Phipps

Roth books, slightly used hardback editions, and four rows of Dad's books, a mixture of hardback and paper.

"Blanche, you have Dad's and Grandpa Gordon's books?"

She took Dad's first book from the shelf. *After Dark, Light.* Ten years after it had been published, it was made into a movie and changed the course of their lives.

A struggling author existing from advance check to advance check became an "overnight" success.

They bought the big apartment in Murray Hill. Tenley quit her part-time job and became a full-time NYU student.

"So, you found your father's books." Blanche stood at the library doors, her tall, thin frame—older, wearier than the last time Tenley saw her—wrapped in a pink chenille robe, her blondish-gray hair twisted on top of her head.

"I'm surprised you have them." Tenley returned the book to the shelf. "Did you read his work?"

"Every book. I loved his writing. He was a talent. Like his great-grandfather."

"W-was that his desk?" Tenley pointed to the piece she'd shoved against the wall. "I don't remember it, but maybe you had it when you first got married?"

"That, my darling, is an antique. I know it doesn't look like it, but it goes back two hundred years." Blanche crossed over, sweeping her hand over the desk's surface. "It belonged to the couple who owned the house before my parents. A marquess and marchioness from England."

"Aristocracy? In Cocoa Beach?"

"Believe it or not." Blanche raised her arms and turned in a slow circle through a spill of sunlight. "You're standing where noblemen once stood."

"They lived here full-time?"

"Now that I can't tell you. I was only nine when my parents bought the place. My dad had just joined the space program. Helped launch the rocket that sent Neil Armstrong to the moon. Anyway, I remember my mother called her 'the marchioness.' Dad called him 'the real duke.'"

"Duke? Didn't you say he was a marquess?"

"Yes, but tell that to my dad. He was a big fan of John Wayne, 'the Duke,' you know. So he called the marquess 'the real duke.'"

"Ah, I see." Sorta. What did calling the marquess a duke have to do with John Wayne? Blanche must be leaving out something in the translation. "And this was their desk?"

"Probably. It wasn't my mother's. The middle drawer is stuck."

"Hmm." Blanche tugged on the drawer, leaving it be when it didn't budge. "Who knows? Probably swollen shut from the humidity. Are you hungry?" She started for the stairs. "I'm sorry I didn't meet you last night, but I'm rather wiped out by evening. And I've not even started with the chemo yet."

"It's no problem. I let myself in." Tenley preferred it, really. To see the house, adjust to her environment without facing her mother. "The key is on the dresser." She pointed to her room. "I'll get it."

"Keep it. It's yours while you're here."

In the kitchen, just off the open living room, Blanche set the table with white bone china and linen napkins.

"I never get to use my mother's set. So I thought, why not today?" She offered a weak smile. "For Tenley."

"I'm sorry you went to all the trouble. I don't eat breakfast."

"Well, you must. Look, I made eggs and bacon." She pointed to the frying pans on the gas stove. "Isn't breakfast the most important meal of the day?"

"Do you have any coffee? Or Diet Coke?"

"Neither." She winced. "We'll go to Publix after breakfast, get all you need and want. My first chemo treatment is tomorrow morning, so we're getting right to it. For now, can you fake a love for breakfast?" She motioned to Tenley's getup. "Nice robe, by the way. Belonged to my third husband, Roger. Nice man."

EIGHT

BIRDIE

On the edge of the frozen pond, Birdie watched Alfonse skate with Kathleen Martin, his arm tight around her waist, whispering something that made her laugh.

Behind her, the quartet played, the tips of their fingers protruding from their clipped gloves.

Servants bundled in furs huddled together by a fire, ready to assist the Van Cliff guests with skates or cups of hot cocoa.

It was quite lovely. Romantic even—if a girl enjoyed sitting alone while her so-called intended flirted with another. If Alfonse was aware of their arrangement, he pretended otherwise.

After dinner, Mama had yanked her into a quiet alcove and admonished her through clenched teeth, "Make your way toward Alfonse. Do not let that Martin swell steal his attention. Let him see he's made the right choice."

"What choice has he made, Mama?"

"Mind yourself."

Birdie rode to the pond with Alfonse and Kathleen, the sleigh bells ringing through the whispering night. Alfonse engaged her in trite questions when he wasn't engaging Miss Martin in conversation.

Meanwhile, dear, sweet Lord Montague had been detained by the men at the house. They wanted a true account of the Boer War. *"You were there. Let us hear what the papers did not tell us."*

On the pond, Alfonse and Kathleen whizzed past, their skates cutting into the ice, their movements in unison. The girl was lovely with a regal composure, her features in perfect harmony one to another, her dark hair curling about her face, her blue eyes fixed on Alfonse. She skated as if she were born to balance on two narrow blades.

Kathleen was an heiress of no small means. Though the Martins were new money—her grandfather had been dirt poor until his forties.

If Alfonse fancied her so much, why didn't he just ask for her hand? He appeared completely enamored with her and completely disinterested in Birdie. Which came as no surprise.

Birdie turned at the sound of sleigh bells. Had Lord Montague freed himself from the conversation of war? But alas, it was Trudy arriving with Lionel Vandergriff.

The two of them romped through the snow toward the selection of skates, Trudy clinging to Lionel's arm the same way Birdie had clung to Eli that final afternoon at Hapsworth.

Mama had arrived at breakfast, announcing, "We really must be going, Lord and Lady Ainsworth. We've bordered on abusing your hospitality."

After which Eli whisked her away for a walk across the meadow, stealing a few private moments for a private good-bye.

"I've grown quite an affection for you, dearest Birdie. I fear I'm going to miss you more than I can bear."

Oh how loudly her heart beat. "Surely not. You have so many friends here. Many a proper lady vies for your attention."

"*But they are not you.*" He brushed his finger along the line of her jaw. "*How did I become so lucky as to meet you, Elizabeth Shehorn?*"

"*I am not sure, dear Eli. But I daresay I am the lucky one.*"

Then he cradled her hand in his, taking a step toward her, his heart speaking through his gaze. He was going to kiss her! Oh, how sweet, love's first kiss.

She felt light and airy, wanted. But as he bent toward her, a footman—a rude, *rude* footman—rode up, declaring the carriage to the train had arrived. Birdie's parents awaited her.

Since that moment, something remained unsaid, undone, between them. Even after four years.

No sooner had she boarded their vessel home than her heart broke and spilled out, forming the pages of what would become *A View from Her Carriage.*

She envisioned his face as she waved good-bye through the carriage window, wondering if she'd ever possess her own heart again. One rarely had a second chance at first love.

"Is this seat vacant?"

Birdie jerked around and peered into *his* heart-stopping face. "Indeed it is, sir. I'm waiting for my good friend, Lord Montague."

"'Tis I, Birdie." He laughed, slipping down next to her. "Please, call me Elijah, or Eli. 'Lord Montague' is used in court or by the servants."

"Did the men tire you out with talk of war?"

"They were curious. I understand. Mostly they kept me from you."

"Eli, please." She glanced away, a fresh snow starting to fall. Lionel and Trudy were on the ice now, gliding around hand in hand. "I think they are in love. Those two."

"Then God bless them."

It was hard watching young lovers while sitting next to Eli. She was so close, yet so very, very far away. Seeing him brought forward the feelings she believed long-since faded.

In light of such emotion, whatever had possessed her to submit her story to Mr. Barclay? What if they'd actually published her book? Elijah might have read it and seen himself on the pages painted with Birdie's most raw and real affections.

Though she had changed their names from Birdie and Eli to Bette and Ethan, Lord Andercroff, the truth would be evident to those with eyes to see.

"Do you fancy a skate?" Eli said after a moment.

"Skating? I suppose. I'm not as strong on those narrow blades as Miss Martin or Trudy."

"Nor am I." He raised his cane. "But perhaps together we'll make one sound skater. Shall we give it a go?"

"Why not?"

They made their way toward the servants and, after choosing a pair of skates, sat on the nearest bench to lace them up.

"My brother, Robert, and I spent many a winter afternoon skating at Hapsworth," Eli said, wincing as he pulled on his left skate.

"Are you sure you're up to this? I wouldn't mind if you said no. I preferred the indoor sport of reading as a child. I only went out when Mama insisted."

"We can't let Alfonse and the others have all the fun. Hurry now, lace up your boot."

Mercy, how he set her heart racing. Could he hear its thunder? Feel the heat radiating from beneath her coat?

Eli stood, leaning on his cane, and offered Birdie his arm.

"I believe we are taking our lives into our hands."

Eli laughed, leading her onto the ice. "Then gladly. During the past three years I've faced hunger and cold, heat and pain, and stared death in the face. This? Sheer pleasure." Eli tapped his cane on the ice and slowly, carefully, they began. Birdie wobbled, gently clinging to him.

Trudy and Lionel sped past, racing from one end of the pond to the other, their quick starts and dramatic stops chipping the ice.

"Show-offs," Eli whispered. Birdie stumbled forward with a chortle.

"We'll just go at our pace."

"Slow and steady. Ha, did I just repeat my grandfather? At twenty-six I'm an old man."

"Well, you do have a cane."

His great, boisterous laugh rang out, drawing the attention of Alfonse and Kathleen, Trudy and Lionel.

Looping around the ice, Birdie fell into a rhythm with Eli, matching his steps, picking up one skate, then the next.

Besides the scent of the fire and the fragrance of the swaying fir trees, the perfume of the night, the cold and snow, filled her senses.

As did the subtle, woodsy scent that was Eli. She breathed in, trying to find the words that would capture this moment forever.

"What do you do with yourself these days?" Eli said, breaking the soft magic of her imagination. "You were off to school when we last met."

"I graduated from Wellesley in the spring. I'm home now, doing what girls like me do—"

"Heiresses?"

"Teas and parties. Making calls. Embarking on grand tours. Shopping in Paris. I do love my charity work, though."

"Didn't you aspire to be an authoress? A novelist?"

"I did. I do." She flushed as he leaned to see her face. "You remembered."

"Of course, of course. I recognized your flair for words when we exchanged letters. Birdie, why did we stop writing one another?"

"I've no idea, really."

Alfonse swished past on his own, knocking Birdie on the shoulder with a laugh. "Slowpokes."

"So, have you penned a great American novel?"

"No, I certainly have not." But she did pen one she could not locate. If Barclay didn't possess it, who did?

"What? I cannot believe it. You'll keep trying, though?"

She smiled at his tender encouragement. "Yes, I believe I will."

"Good. I demand a signed first edition *when* you are published."

"Enough about me, what of you?" She raised her chin. "What exactly brings you to America?"

"Family business."

"Is the family well?" When he peered at her, she sensed she was drowning in a warm pool of blue.

"Father is not. He's rather ill these days." Speaking of his father changed his countenance. "But drinking and gambling away the family fortune takes a toll on the best of men."

"Surely not, Eli. Surely not."

"I'm sorry to say. Plus with taxes and an ever-growing wage bill, the Marquess of Ainsworth is losing hold of his heritage and inheritance. I love my father, but he was never fit for the responsibility of Hapsworth and the surrounding village."

"You're angry with him."

He snapped his gaze to her. "Am I so obvious?"

"To me. Your friend."

"You're my friend. What a warm, delightful thought."

"Yes, isn't it?"

"Birdie," Eli said, inching her toward the bank and a bench under a large fir, away from the others. "How is it you are not married or betrothed? What is wrong with my American brethren that they cannot see your charm and beauty?"

"I was away at school. Too busy for betrothals and the like."

"But you've been home all these months." Eli sighed, shaking his head. "Forgive me, this is not my business."

"It is if you're my friend. Tell me, how is a young, handsome earl not betrothed or married?"

"I was away at war. Too busy for betrothals and the like." They were in their own world as they rounded the frozen pond and sat on the isolated bench.

"You mock me."

"Not at all." He squeezed her hand. "Do you want to know why they gave me the Victoria Cross?"

"If you wish to tell me, yes."

"We were under heavy fire, half starved, when I heard a couple of lads calling out. They'd fallen in the field. So I ran from my bunker to rescue them. On instinct." He tapped his knee. "I didn't realize I'd taken shrapnel until my batman saw the blood soaking my trousers."

"Those men were lucky you heard their cries."

"They'd have done the same for me."

"You are a good man, Eli."

"And how would you know, Birdie?" He scooted toward her, propping his arm on the top of the bench. "We spent a few weeks of the London season and a month of summer together, exchanged a few letters—"

"Because I know." She pressed her hand to his heart. "I've observed you, listened to you. You are nothing less than a hero."

"I do not deserve your high praise, but because it came from your lips, I humbly accept it with gratitude."

When Eli's gaze searched hers, Birdie trembled with expectation.

"There is the matter of the kiss," he said.

"Eli, you make me blush." A fresh snow drifted down upon them.

"It is New Year's Eve," Eli said, pulling her closer. "When it is perfectly acceptable for . . . for friends to exchange a kiss."

He was going to kiss her. Really and truly kiss her. On this cold, magical night. She leaned into him with every part of her being. His eyes searched hers. And she did not look away.

Just as Eli bent toward her, Alfonse appeared out of nowhere.

Birdie jerked backward, turning away, her lips tingling with anticipation.

"You two sitting this one out?" he said, grabbing her hand, pulling her to her feet. "We've not taken a turn around the ice. Eli, you can hobble along behind us, can't you?"

Before she could catch her breath, they were off, leaving Eli behind.

"What do you think you're doing?" His voice came low and demanding.

"I don't know what you mean."

"I see your parents haven't informed you of our agreement. We are to be married."

Birdie pulled her arm free from his. "I've been informed, yes, but I've agreed to nothing. I do not recall a proposal. How can I say yes, or no, if there is no proposal?"

"I was planning to ask sometime during the season."

"Until then you'd flirt with every pretty girl that passes your eye."

"Don't be jealous, Birdie. It doesn't become you."

"Jealous? You are very mistaken." She shoved away from him. "Leave me be. Poor Eli, you left him to his own devices."

"There's nothing poor about Eli . . . You do realize he's come here for an heiress. To marry for money. Rose Gottlieb."

She raised her chin, quaking beneath her coat. Rose Gottlieb? She was the darling of last year's debutantes. She was radiant and beautiful with raven hair against a creamy complexion. Demure and well bred, she would make a lovely, charming countess.

"Birdie?" Alfonse reached for her, his tone softer, his grip gentle. "Are you all right?"

"Yes, of course."

"So mind yourself. Eli belongs to another and you belong to me."

NINE

TENLEY

In five days, she'd taken Blanche to the doctor twice and the grocery store once, slept a total of seventy hours—who knew she was so tired?—drunk twenty cups of coffee and a twelve pack of Diet Coke, and ordered shoes, jeans, tops, dresses, and bedding off the Internet, shipping it all to her New York apartment.

When she ordered an antique armoire, the doorman called for an explanation, fearing her identity had been stolen.

She was out of control. She returned the armoire and imposed a hiatus on impulse shopping. Imagining her credit-card bill gave her heart palpitations.

In those same five days, she'd written exactly zero words. That's right, zero. Every morning, after tugging on Blanche's third husband's robe and slippers, she sat faithfully at *her desk* for six hours a day, thinking about words and stories.

Which, really, if she was honest, was how she started shopping in the first place.

Heroine . . . just who is the heroine of this story? What does she want? What's her goal? Is she rich, poor, in between? Is she smart, athletic? Hmm, I could do with a new pair of sneakers.

Things went downhill from there. The lovely little desk wasn't proving to be the inspiration she imagined. But she wasn't ready to give up yet. Nope. The sensation she experienced when she saw the desk was real.

"How's it going?" Blanche carried in a lunch tray—ham sandwich, chips, and a cold Diet Coke—and sat it on the desk.

Tenley gently closed her laptop, where *Chapter One* sat alone on a blank page. "You didn't have to bring me lunch. The chemo—"

"Is fine. For now." Blanche sat in an adjacent overstuffed club chair.

Tenley inspected her sandwich. She didn't typically eat processed meats. Or ham. Or anything in the pig family. She took a small bite.

Blanche fixed the edge of her robe over her knee. "If you want to talk about the story, I'll be glad to listen. Help if I can."

Tenley choked down her bite with a swig of Diet Coke. "Thanks, but I'm good."

"Your dad used to talk to me about his stories. We'd lie in bed at night, making up characters and dreaming up ways to make their lives miserable."

"Was walking out on your kid one of them?"

"No." She glanced away, adjusting her robe again. "But clearly you're angry with me about it."

"It's just a good way to make someone's life miserable."

"Are you miserable?"

"If I could get this book done, I'd feel better."

Blanche leaned forward with a sigh. "Let me just say this and get it out in the open. I'm sorry I left. I truly am, but I was suffocating with your father. When we met he was vibrant and handsome, with a good job at the newspaper. We were going to get a post in

Moscow or Berlin before he decided to clean toilets and ride the subway at midnight. For what? To get the pulse of the people? To find the everyman story? What about the pulse of his wife? I needed more from life, Tenley."

"Why didn't you take me with you? Or at least share custody?"

"I didn't know where I was going. I had no means to share custody."

"What do you want me to say? I forgive you? We went over this at Dad's funeral." Tenley bit into her sandwich.

"I don't want you to be angry with me. I appreciate you coming down. I know you had other choices and I get the sense it wasn't a pleasant good-bye with your fiancé. What's his name?"

"Holt."

"Holt? What is he, a cowboy?"

"A screenwriter."

"Ah. We have a thing for writers, you and I. Anyway . . . I am appreciative, Tenley. I want you to know how much." Blanche glanced away, her eyes misty.

"I-it's okay." Tenley set down her sandwich. "I can write in Paris another time."

She wasn't one to believe serendipity or fate had bent her road to align with a lesser, unknown course, but for a moment, very brief, she suspected her journey to Florida was about more than Blanche, more than chemo, more than writing a book.

"So, the book. Are you happy with it?" Blanche brushed her fingers under eyes.

"There's no book, Blanche. I have three months to deliver something I can't even imagine or feel." Tenley sat back with a sigh. "I'm stuck."

"Writer's block? Your dad had writer's block when he first started writing. Before you were born."

"Then there's hope. He snapped out of it. About twelve years later."

"Writing is a process. A journey." Blanche reached out, fingering the edge of Tenley's robe. "I bought this for Roger when we got married." Blanche's third husband.

"I never met him. How long were you married?"

"A year. We weren't meant to be."

"How'd you know?" Tenley reached for her Diet Coke.

Blanche shrugged. "He left."

For a moment, a brief moment, Tenley felt only compassion for her mother. Her selfish choices. Her search for something she couldn't find.

"As for you, just keep writing."

Tenley tapped the top of her laptop. "Keep writing? Don't you think I would if I had the slightest idea of what I was doing?"

Someone to Love had flowed. Like a spring river. But now . . .

Every inspired idea was a match strike, hot and bright but quickly fading.

"I remember your dad used to say that 'write what you know' was all wrong."

"I never heard him say that."

"He said one must write who they are."

"What if you don't know who you are?"

"Then that's what you have to discover." Blanche touched the edge of Tenley's robe again. "You should let me wash this."

"You don't have to do things for me, Blanche." Tenley ran her hand down the old, soft sleeve. She hadn't showered since Blanche's first chemo treatment, and so far, *this* robe over her pajamas was her main attire. Even for grocery store runs.

She was stuck in more ways than one.

After a second of silence, Blanche patted her hands to her knees, stood, and made her way to the door. "I'll come back for your tray. Meanwhile, just write who you are, Tenley. Write who you are."

Yeah, that was going to be a problem. Because she had no idea.

BIRDIE

"What do you think?" Papa said as they entered their Fifth Avenue manse after New Year's with the Van Cliffs. "Shall we build in the Berkshires, Iris? Stow will make the introduction to his architect."

Morning light spilled through the grand hall through the high and wide windows. It was a glorious and sunny January morning.

Mama gave him a coy smile. "Do whatever pleases you, Geoffrey."

Birdie handed her coat to Percival. They exchanged a glance. Mama would have her house in the Berkshires, make no mistake.

"I'm convinced. A home in the Berkshires would be lovely," Papa said. "The Van Cliff cottage was extraordinary. With electricity in every room. And plumbing. Didn't you find it convenient? I'll prepare a letter for this afternoon's mail." Papa patted Mama on the shoulder as he walked toward his den.

"Birdie," Mama said, stepping close. "You were quiet on the way home. How did you fare with Alfonse? Will we be announcing anything soon?"

"He could hardly drag himself from Kathleen Martin. So we did not fare well at all."

Papa paused at the library door, jutting out his chin, nodding. "He's working up to his proposal. I remember doing the same when I proposed to your mama, nervous she would refuse me."

Yes, a man would certainly have to build up courage to propose to Mama.

"Hardly, Geoffrey. You know I adored you. Birdie, however, gives Alfonse no encouragement. You must be welcoming and inviting. Surely I've taught you better." In fact, Mama taught her nothing except the pain of a riding crop. Her governess and nanny taught her about life and, daresay, love. "Come with me to the salon, Birdie."

"I'm rather tired. I'd like to go to my room."

She wanted to sneak away to her attic to pen her thoughts and feelings about Eli. He was in her life again, if only for a few moments.

After their evening of skating and ringing in the new year, Mama saw to it Birdie was occupied with the other women and scarcely left alone.

She had no more time with Eli. The Van Cliff guests departed bright and early this morning, hurrying back to New York for the start of the season, and Birdie missed a chance to bid him good-bye.

"You can lie down in a moment." Mama slipped her arm through Birdie's, leading her to the library. "I merely mean to review our calendar with you. Am I so much an imposition?"

"Of course not." Birdie followed her to the small salon off the foyer where Mama kept her calendar.

"I know Alfonse has yet to propose, but we'll want to sail to Paris the first of spring." A fire crackled in the small hearth and a tea service awaited them. "I'll write to Worth's to let them know." Mama opened her leather date book. "What do you think of sitting for a portrait while we're there? I remember how fascinated John Singer Sargent was with you when we met him two years ago. Yes, I think I'll write to him too."

Birdie reached for a sandwich and dropped to the couch. She disliked sitting for portraits. But a portrait was the least of her concerns. She must approach Mama with the truth.

"There won't be a need for a portrait or a trip to Worth's." Resisting Mama was futile, but she must try.

"Whatever are you talking about? Ah, Mimi Fish left her calling card." Mama gathered the stack of small decorated cards Percival arranged for her. "We'll have to call on her next Tuesday. Here's one from Alva." She continued to read aloud the small symbols of enormous social obligation. Vanderbilt. Payne. Whitney. Stuyvesant. "The season is upon us. How thrilling."

Birdie pressed her hand to her throat, tugging at the high lace dog collar of her dress. The fire was altogether too hot. She wanted to open the window and lean into the cold and thin sunlight.

"Pour some tea, Birdie. You look utterly flushed."

"It's warm in here." She moved to the settee farthest from the fire.

Mama put down the cards. "Now, to our calendar. I think an October wedding would be lovely."

"I'm not marrying Alfonse, Mama." Birdie held her composure. Any break in her countenance and Mama would invade with full force.

"What happened? Did he do something disagreeable?" Mama poured a cup of tea, slow and calculating. "Don't mind his harmless flirting. He's having a last hurrah."

"I do not love him. I do not want to marry him." Birdie reached for another sandwich. More for a distraction than hunger.

"Birdie, do open your eyes. See what is happening to Papa's and my friends. They are aging. I declare, Caroline Astor will throw her last ball in a few short years. She's fading from her position. Others have married off their daughters to European dukes and lords. We, you and I, are in prime position to rule New York society. Your marriage to a Van Cliff all but seals the deal."

Birdie swallowed her sandwich in one gulp. "Me? You cannot

possibly believe I am the next Mrs. Astor." Who would want to be such a snob? "You're right, Mama, society is changing. And it will have no room for the likes of us if we are not careful."

"Society will always have room for the likes of us. Who do you think they look to for style, fashion, decorum, and etiquette?"

"You may want to be the standard bearer, but I do not."

Mama leaned toward her. "With my very breath. Mrs. Astor took that role from my mother, shoved her aside. Created an elite society in which the entire Four Hundred could not match my mama's charm and class."

"Careful, Mama, these walls have ears."

"Hush, and you will not utter a word of our conversation."

"Not me." Birdie nodded toward the closed door. "You never know who might be listening on the other side."

"Then lower your voice." Determination filled Mama's voice. "I've groomed you for this moment. When Mrs. Astor retires, someone *will* take her place. And that someone is me and then you, Elizabeth Candler Shehorn. Marrying Alfonse is your first duty."

"Duty?" Birdie took up yet another sandwich. "I owe society no duty."

"You owe it to me." Mama's eyes narrowed, piercing Birdie with a visual sword. "You think four years at Wellesley makes you wise enough to know what it takes to make it in this world? Well, it doesn't. People are cruel and brutal. They'll as soon stab you in the back as kiss your cheek."

"Then why do I feel your blade in my back?"

Mama rose up, towering over her. "One day when your husband and children have opportunities no one else in the world has because of your place in New York, thus American society, you will thank me. When governors and presidents, kings and popes invite you to dine with them, you will *thank* me."

"I've no desire to dine with presidents. Or kings. And I will not be a party to some sort of vendetta against Mrs. Astor. I have no quarrel with her other than she created this elite society in the first place. Wouldn't we all be better off choosing our own friends, giving our money to the poor, improving neighborhoods? Papa's wealthy ancestors certainly thought modesty and sobriety were superior to lavish parties and ostentatious dwellings."

"We'd be living in dreadful brownstones in Murray Hill were it up to your Papa's relations. Is this about Lord Montague? Your resistance?"

"Lord Montague?" Birdie pushed up from the settee, turning away from Mama. She must not allow any hint of her affection to show. "My resistance is to your constant hand on my life. I want to make my own decisions. Choose my own husband. My own pastimes."

"Choose your own way?" Mama cackled. "Is this the thought of young women today? Your friends. How misguided. You will choose the way I tell you. As I my grandmama chose my way. It is proper and right."

"But you *wanted* to go Grandmama's way. I do not want to go yours."

"What I wanted, what you want, is neither here nor there. It is the way it has always been, and until you walk out of here a married woman, the way it will always be. If you have any ideas of Lord Montague, dismiss them. You know he is pledged to another."

"Yes, I know. Rose Gottlieb."

"Then do not do to her what Kathleen has done to you."

"Kathleen has not wronged me. Alfonse is the one with the wandering eye. And Eli is merely my friend—"

"Eli is it? You use your Christian names?"

"—and Rose will not deny him any friendship, I'm sure."

"Don't presume what Rose will endure." Mama refreshed her tea, tinging her spoon against the side of her cup, her jaw taut. "You must accept your future, Birdie. The sooner you do, the happier you'll be."

Debating Mama wearied her. She'd said more than enough for one day. The heat in the room had grown to an unbearable degree. Birdie rose. "Please excuse me, I'm going to lie down."

"Are you in love with him?" Mama's hard, direct question arrested Birdie at the door.

She hesitated, then sighed. "I don't know." Why must she weaken and expose her vulnerabilities to Mama? It only served to give her the upper hand.

"Since Hapsworth four years ago?"

"We had a lovely rapport. Enjoyed one another's company."

Mama crossed over to her. "Listen to me. Let go of whatever girlish intentions you entertained, Birdie. Not for my sake if you're so determined, but for your own. For his. Lord Montague must return home with an American fortune. The Gottliebs are prepared to exchange a generous dowry for an ancient family name. He must marry Rose. Because the Ainsworth family's financial redemption will never come from us."

TEN

JONAS

He'd spent his last few dollars buying an antique desk. One he hoped to restore and sell so he could jump-start his furniture business, putting the last year and a half behind him.

It was luck or divine intervention—he'd accept either one—the day he ran into Blanche Albright at Publix. Out of the blue, this friend of his mother offered to sell him her antique desk and chair for a song.

After inspection and research, he determined the classic English cherrywood piece in restored condition would bring four times what he paid for it.

Even better, he most likely had a buyer for the desk. Mrs. Shallot mentioned she was interested. The desk sale would be his seed money to start over again.

One good word from her, and he could leave Tug's cabinet-making shop and launch out on his own, crafting his own designs again.

It took him a couple of months to gather the one grand Blanche asked for the piece, but he'd done it. He ate a few more

PB and Js, shut off the air, and opened the windows, letting the breeze swish through his 1960s fixer-upper on the Banana River.

As he turned his truck into Grove Manor's drive, his buddy, Rob, let out a low whistle. "I've driven by this place a million times. Always wanted to look inside."

"I used to dream of owning it." Jonas parked in back and pushed through the low white gate toward the kitchen door, Rob following.

Rapping on the back screen, he peered through the fine weave. "Miss Blanche? It's me, Jonas Sullivan."

"And Rob."

He made a face at his friend. "And Rob."

"Hello, Jonas. And Rob." Blanche shoved open the screen door. "Come in, come in. What can I do for you boys?"

Jonas flipped his Florida State cap around, bill to the back. "If you don't mind, I've come for the desk."

"The desk?" Recognition hooded her eyes. "Oh, the desk. The one in the library."

"We talked about it at Publix? You offered to sell it to me with a chair."

"You want to take it now?" Her smile wavered as she glanced toward the second floor.

"If I could." He pulled a check from his pocket. "I've got the money right here."

"Well, you see, my daughter is using it. She's a writer, you know."

"Your daughter? Well, okay, I can probably find her something else to use if she really needs a desk." Last year he'd picked up a junker for his own use from a Cocoa Beach city hall auction. Kept it in his work shed.

"I'm sure she can make do. There's a comfy chair up there. Go on up."

Light spilled over the stairs from the skylights, glinting off the polished hardwood and creating a surreal floating sensation.

On the second-floor landing, Jonas walked toward the library doors, pausing when he saw her at the desk, her cheek resting against her hand.

She was draped in a worn, faded red-plaid robe, her head bobbing with sleep, the knot of chestnut hair snapping up and down.

"Hello?" Jonas rapped on the door frame. "Sorry to disturb but—"

The woman jerked around, her midnight-blue eyes wide with surprise. Beside him Rob whispered, "Whoa."

This was Miss Blanche's daughter? She was a mess. A *gorgeous* mess.

"W-what? Who are you?"

"Jonas Sullivan." He moved inside, offering his hand. "This is Rob."

"Me." Rob moved around Jonas to shake her hand. "I'm Rob."

"Very nice to meet you, I'm Rob."

Jonas shot Rob a glance. He liked this girl. "We've come for the desk. And you are . . ."

"Tenley. You've come for the desk?" She slipped her elbow over the smooth surface. "This desk? The one I'm using for writing?"

"Looked more like a mattress a few seconds ago. And yes, that's the one. The chair too."

"This chair, the one I'm sitting in?"

"Yes, the one you're sitting in." He turned to Rob. "Let's clear away this chair and that chest in the middle of the room, make a path to get this out. You think the staircase is wide enough?"

"I think so but . . ." Rob produced a pocket measuring tape. "Let me make sure."

"Hold it." Tenley was on her feet, very much awake. "You're

not taking this desk. Does Blanche know about this?" She moved toward the door, revealing long, lean legs beneath the robe, and leaned over the railing. "Blanche, two thieves are trying to take your desk."

"She knows. After all, she sold it to me." Jonas produced his check as Rob returned, stretching his measuring tape across the desk.

"We can just make it. If we're careful around the corners."

"Blanche?" Tenley stared at Jonas, arms folded. "Did you sell my desk and chair to this guy?"

"I did. A few months ago. In light of recent events, I forgot."

"What recent events?" Jonas peered from Tenley to Blanche.

"Cancer," Tenley said. "She's had surgery and just started chemo."

Jonas moved to the railing, leaning around Tenley. "Miss Blanche, I'm so sorry. Does Mom know?"

"She does, but I told her not to make a fuss. I have my girl, Tenley, with me."

"Well, you let us know if you need anything, you hear?"

"Will do, Jonas. I appreciate it."

"In the meantime, he can just leave, right?" Tenley said. "Without my desk."

He flashed his folded check again. "Got the money right here."

"Then the sale is not complete." She snatched the check from his hand. "Oooh, so sorry, Jonas Sullivan, but we don't accept personal checks here at Grove Manor." Tenley shoved the check at him. "Bye-bye."

"Yeah, you do take personal checks and I'm taking the desk. Blanche knows how to find me if it bounces. Which it won't." He slipped the check into his pocket. "Rob, let's go."

He liked this girl. She was raw, funny, and beautiful, yet a bit lost and forlorn.

However, the last time a beautiful woman caught his attention, it cost him everything.

Back at the desk, Jonas removed Tenley's laptop and phone. "You want to get the front, Rob?"

They'd taken two steps when Tenley flew at them. "Wait!" She flung herself over the desk with a wail, gripping the sides. "I *need* this desk. You don't understand. It's my friend. My *people.*"

"Your people?" Jonas and Rob lowered the desk. "Tenley, this is wood." He knocked on the desk's surface, then pinched the soft flesh of her hand. "This is people. Flesh and blood."

She rose up, planting herself in the middle of the desk. "Jimmy Fallon called. Wants to know if you can do the show for him tonight."

"Clever, but I heard he was asking for you."

"You can't take this desk." Arms folded, chin set, Tenley let gaze bore into his.

"Oh, I'm taking this desk."

"Blanche!"

Rob glared at Jonas behind Tenley's back, tipping his head toward her. *Let her have it.*

Yeah, okay, if he was objective he could see how this standoff was ridiculous. But ever since Cindy and Mason ran off with his designs, his money, and his heart, he'd done nothing but work and pay off debt.

He'd cut off cable. Hoarded leftovers from family dinners. Worn faded jeans and beat-up work boots.

So saving a thousand dollars for this desk meant he'd emerged from the darkest season of his life and something, *something,* was finally going his way.

"Tenley, what are you doing on the desk?" Miss Blanche stood in the library doorway. "Let the boys have it. You can use the one over there in the corner."

"It's a child's school desk."

"I've got one you can use," Jonas said. "But this antique is going with me."

"Afraid not, Cocoa Beach."

"Well, you have me there. I don't know where you're from."

"New York."

"Figures." Jonas gently pushed Tenley off. "Ready, Rob?"

"Okay, wait. Wait!" Tenley blocked the exit, a crazed look in her eye. "I have this deadline, you see, and it's not going very well. Forget that, it's going horrible. But this desk . . ." Tenley knelt beside it so Jonas motioned for Rob to set the piece down. "This desk gave me a spark of inspiration the moment I saw it. Like I could write in this room, at this desk." She sank down to the floor. "Like I wasn't a hack."

"So this desk is your good luck charm?" *Thank you, Rob.*

"Yes, yes, my good luck charm. My muse." Tenley jumped up, leaning over the desk toward Rob, the robe hanging off her shoulders. "So, you'll leave it?"

Jonas caught Rob's expression. The one he wore when a girl got the better of his senses. "When's your deadline? Jonas, you could always—"

"What if I bring you another desk?" Jonas refused to be bested by another pretty woman. If he hadn't learned his lesson, he was a fool.

"What if you leave this desk?" She turned to Rob. "My deadline is in July."

"Shoot, that's only a few months away, Joe," Rob said.

"Right, Joe." Tenley this time. "Only a few months away."

"I'll bring you another desk. Rob, you get that end."

"Wait, wait . . . I'll pay you."

"Tenley, please." Blanche slipped her arm around her daughter.

"There are other desks and chairs. Look, there's an old, inspiring recliner by the window. Use it. Jonas, I'm so sorry."

"It's all right, Miss Blanche." Jonas reached into his pocket for the check, offering it to Blanche. "Rob, watch the banister."

"I'll pay you double what you paid Blanche."

"I've already got a buyer, Tenley. Sorry. I'll bring you another desk."

"But that one spoke to me. It said *writer*." Tenley leaned against the railing as Jonas and Rob started down the stairs. "The middle drawer doesn't even open."

"I'll fix it."

"I can't believe you won't leave it a few months."

"Rob, careful around the landing. Got it?" Jonas glanced up at Tenley, descending with the desk, setting it in the foyer by the front door. "A desk doesn't help you write. It's an object. You either have it or you don't."

"Says the man who had to wear the same cleats for every baseball game he ever played, and if he couldn't find them . . ."

Tenley hammered down the stairs, hopping on top of the desk, the robe falling away, revealing her toned, smooth leg. "Tell me more about these lucky shoes."

"They weren't lucky shoes. They just fit me the best."

"What? They were the cleats you wore when we won the state title. Don't listen to him, Tenley. He believed he couldn't play without them."

"You want to button it up, Rob?" Jonas bent for a good grip on the desk. "Get off, please. I'm taking this with me."

Tenley crossed her arms. "Fine, where it goes, I go."

"Suit yourself. But it's going to be awfully hot in my workshop. Get the door, Rob."

Rob lifted his end and they headed out the door. When they hit the veranda, Tenley slid off, surrendering.

"Take it." She leaned against the side of the house. "You're right. It won't make any difference."

Her tone, her expression drove through him, straight to the soft spot in his heart. "Hold up, Rob." Jonas turned to Tenley. "What do you think the desk will help you do?"

She moved to the porch rail, leveling her blue gaze with his. "What did you think those lucky cleats would do? It doesn't have to make sense, does it?" She tugged on her hair, knotting it even more. "To be honest, all I've done so far is buy stuff I don't need."

She apologized with her eyes as wisps of her hair floated about her face.

"A desk isn't going to help you write a novel."

"I thought it might be my author quirk. You know, the thing I had to have to write. Virginia Woolf wrote at a standing desk. Truman Capote wouldn't start or end a book on a Friday. But you're right, nothing can help me write a book." She turned to go inside.

From the doorway, Miss Blanche mouthed, "Writer's block."

Oh boy . . . He regarded Tenley, then the desk. He'd been there. Stuck. Looking for anything, anyone to help him, developing more superstitions and game-time routines. "You really think this desk will help you work?"

She shrugged, pointing toward the scuff marks. "Looks like a typewriter sat there for a long time. There are ink stains in the right side drawer. I thought maybe, you know, it'd been someplace I hadn't." She shook her head, heading inside, the robe flowing around her legs. "This is so stupid. Nice to meet you, Cocoa Beach. Sorry I was so crazy."

Dang it. The familiar twist in his chest told him she'd won. "How much do you have written?"

She paused at the door. "Some."

"How much is some? When I went into the library, you were sleeping."

"I prefer *meditating*."

Jonas exhaled, motioning to the house. "Let's take it back up."

"You couldn't have figured that out before we carried it down?"

"Cocoa Beach, really, it's not necessary. Take it. Do whatever you were going to do with it."

"Restore it and sell it."

"Go for it."

"It can wait . . . Where are you from, again?"

"New York."

"Okay, it can wait, New York."

She followed them as they hoisted the desk back up to the library, setting it where she instructed. She was demure and conciliatory.

"I'll dedicate the book to you," she said.

"That's the least you can do. Are we good here?" He motioned to the desk.

She nodded. "Pick it up the first of August."

"This your first book?"

"My second."

"What do you write? Maybe I've heard of it. Maybe I read it."

"Romance. *Someone to Love*, and I doubt you've read it."

"Did it sell well?"

"Spent twenty-two weeks on the *New York Times* bestseller list."

Then what was her problem? Why the writer's block? "I never heard of it, but I'll ask my sisters." Jonas started out of the library. "Good luck, New York. See you in three months. And seriously, if your mom needs anything, tell her to call Ailis Sullivan."

She met him at the library door. "Thank you. Really. I know I must seem like a freak." She made a funny face and he laughed.

"Rob was kind to me. It wasn't just the cleats. If I won a game, I'd refuse to wash my uniform. I've been to freakyville." Jonas pointed to the desk. "Good luck."

He left her standing in the last light of evening gracing the window, the glow burning her image into his soul.

Rob followed him without a word until he clapped his door closed and Jonas fired up the engine.

"She got to you, didn't she?"

He glanced at Rob as he shifted into reverse. "Nope."

Rob propped his elbow on the door. "Oh, she got to you all right. That desk was the spark for launching your own business again. But you let it go."

"Only until August." He'd left the check with Blanche so he was paid up.

"I'm proud of you. I thought Cindy had taken romance out of you for good. Two years and counting." He smacked Jonas on the shoulder. "Welcome back, man, welcome back."

"I'm not back. Just doing a girl a favor. But I'm definitely not *back*." Nope, he wasn't, not even a little bit.

ELEVEN

BIRDIE

Mrs. Astor's opening ball of the season had been a success. Birdie danced until dawn, careful to keep her distance from Alfonse and Eli.

Alfonse, so as not to encourage him. Eli, so as not to encourage herself. She'd spied him with Rose Gottlieb and could not deny they made a handsome pair. Nor that the sight of them together pierced her heart.

"Fatine," she said when her maid came to clear away her breakfast dishes. "Is Mama about?"

"I believe she's still sleeping."

Good. She would not come looking, wondering if Alfonse proposed. Birdie wanted time to herself to begin another story.

From her room, down the corridor to the attic door, Birdie escaped up the stairs, stepping into the cold shadows.

Fumbling with cold fingers, she lit the gas lamp on her desk, spreading her hands to its tiny warmth.

From the discarded settee, she retrieved Great-Grandmama's afghan and covered her legs.

This was her private sanctuary. The place Mama's ambitions never reached. Birdie was safe here with her shadows and books, with her pen and paper, with her thoughts and dreams.

The desk came from a family friend, Mr. Van Buren, who delivered it to the house when Birdie was nine.

Papa had sailed to Europe for business and Mama liked to have her friends for late suppers after Birdie and William had gone to bed.

But they ducked away from the nanny and peek at the arriving guests through the upstairs banister.

On the night Mr. Van Buren came, they watched from the second-floor landing, peering into the foyer through the spindles, listening as he explained his gift to Mama.

"For Birdie," he said. "You said she enjoyed writing stories and reading."

"Mack, you shouldn't have." Mama held her chin high, regarding Mr. Van Buren down her nose. "How will I explain that to Geoffrey?"

"Tell him it was a gift."

"From whom? None of our friends would buy such an ugly desk." Mama glanced over her shoulder. "Come to the library before we are found."

William peered at Birdie. "What do you think that was about?"

"I don't know. Want to spy on them?"

William grinned, shaking his head. "You remember the last time Mama caught you eavesdropping."

"Yes, and you didn't rescue me at all." Birdie shuddered at the memory of Mama's sharp spanking.

"I dare you, then." William jutted his chin toward the library door. "Find out what they're saying and I'll give you all of my penny candy."

"All of it?" William never shared his candy.

"All of it. But you can't get caught by Mama or any of the servants."

Birdie started for the stairs, her pulse racing. Then stopped. "I can't."

"What? Chicken?" William was the Shehorn heir, the favored son of the family, a champion at everything. She was the little sister. The lurker in the shadows.

"You have to give me all the money in your piggy bank too."

"Done." William's grin was evident even in the darkness.

Step by step, Birdie descended, not daring to breathe, and cracked open the library door . . .

Birdie stared at the desk, her focus coming clear on the middle drawer. Well, she must get to work while she had the time. She retrieved her writing pad and pen, gazing toward the light falling through the window.

Mama banished the desk to the attic, where it sat alone under the cold eaves. It wasn't until years later, upon the anniversary of William's death, that Birdie discovered its hiding place. She'd gone to the attic to reminisce of their rainy summer afternoon playtimes— when she and William had the run of the long, wide room.

"Miss Birdie, are you up here?"

Birdie whirled to see her maid, Fatine, at the head of the stairs. "How did you find me?"

Fatine gripped her hands at her waist. "We've all seen you sneak up here from time to time. But don't despair, your secret is safe with us."

"What do you need?"

"You've a gentleman caller. Mr. Van Cliff."

"Here? Now? Did he say what he wants?" Birdie did not wish to see him. She wished to be alone, to write.

"It's not my place to ask."

"Of course. Please tell Mr. Van Cliff I'll be along."

"Do you want to change?" Fatine gestured toward Birdie's day dress. "Your new blue frock is beautiful on you."

"What I'm wearing is fine." Birdie smoothed the cream-colored wool of her skirt. She didn't care to be appealing for Alfonse.

Alfonse stood as Birdie entered the drawing room, the southern windows behind him full of January light. "I hope I'm not disturbing you."

"And if I said you were?"

His eyes lit with amusement. "Then I'd beg your pardon and see myself out."

"Alfonse, my apologies for my daughter's words." Birdie spun to see Mama in the far corner with her needlepoint. "Birdie studied clever retorts at Wellesley. She likes to practice them on the unsuspecting."

"Not true, Mama." Birdie smiled. "I practice only on the suspecting."

"Birdie, have a care. Alfonse, won't you be seated?" Mama focused on threading her needle. "Percival is bringing coffee."

Birdie remained standing. "Actually, I'm in the middle of—"

"Sit down, Birdie. Whatever you were doing can wait."

She sighed, debating her mother's command. Then sat.

"I hear you're building in the Berkshires." Alfonse perched next to her on the sofa, his eyes roaming her face.

"Papa and Mama are, yes." Birdie shifted to one side, finding Alfonse's intense attention disarming.

"It pleases me"—Alfonse inched closer, cupping his hand over hers, his skin hot and clammy—"that you like our little neck of the woods."

"Like I said, it will be Papa and Mama's home." Birdie pulled her hand free, cradling it in her lap. "Why have you come to see me?"

"To . . . to see how you fare. You were beautiful at the Astors' ball last night. Your red gown was becoming."

Percival entered with the coffee, pouring each a cup.

"How about a game of bridge, Alfonse? I'll rouse Mr. Shehorn to partner with me. Birdie, shall you and Alfonse make a team?"

It was a statement more than a question.

"I'd love to but I'm otherwise engaged tonight. Perhaps another evening." Alfonse shifted his attention to Birdie. "I came to see if Birdie would like to attend a lecture with me. At St. Paul's Sunday evening. On the history of the Great Awakening. We discussed this spiritual phenomenon once, and I thought you'd find the session enlightening."

"A lecture on the Great Awakening? Who shall be our chaperone?"

"Lord Montague has agreed to go along. He's interested in the spiritual phenomena of that time. Of course Whitefield was his countryman."

"Lord Montague?" Birdie smiled over her coffee at Mama. "How delightful. I'd love to attend."

Mama pressed her lips together and drove her needle through her canvas. "I should think he'd have more pressing things to attend to. What with pursuing Rose Gottlieb. Does he intend to invite her along as well? Mr. Shehorn and I would be delighted to chaperone, Alfonse."

"Mama, I wouldn't dream of disturbing you and Papa. Not with the season just beginning," Birdie taunted. Mama hated preaching. She attended church only to be seen by people, not God.

"Think nothing of it. It would be a joy to hear this speaker." Mama's voice fell as if she could hardly believe her own claim. "I too have been fascinated by the Great Awakening."

"I'd never place such an imposition on you, Mrs. Shehorn,"

Alfonse said, clueless to Mama's maneuvering. "Elijah is eager to come along."

"Then it's all arranged. Why don't we have a light supper here before we go. What do you say, Mama?"

"If you wish." Mama smiled politely, but she was not happy.

Oh, Mama, can't you trust me? Let me fly a little?

"The lecture is at eight," Alfonse said.

"Then we'll have supper at six. Though I won't be hungry at that hour."

Alfonse bid them adieu, bowing to kiss Birdie's hand. "I'll look forward to Sunday evening."

When he'd gone, Mama set aside her needlepoint. "You think you've pulled one over on me."

"Why would I think such a thing? Alfonse arranged this outing."

"You watch yourself. Lord Montague belongs to Rose, and if you interfere, you will drag all our names through the mud. And be more receptive to Alfonse. He's trying to court you."

Birdie moved toward the library door. "You don't want me to make it easy on him, do you?"

"Indeed I do. You will marry him, Birdie Shehorn. I'll have my way. Make no mistake."

Elijah

The cable from Mama reminded him he was not here to pursue his own interests or desires, but to secure his family name and heritage.

In his Holland House room, Eli read Mam's cable for the third time before dropping it in the fire, Mama's words reading the same each time. Direct and succinct.

"Remain steadfast. Remember your duty."

She used the words of his heart, addressing him as a solider. As a captain in Her Majesty's army, Eli understood duty. Lived and breathed it. How much more must he be devoted to Hapsworth and his family name?

Centuries of Ainsworth marquesses performed their duty, man after man securing the Percy position as a British peer.

But it seemed to Eli that as he stood atop the Ainsworth ancestral mountain, he was unsure of the ground beneath his feet.

The implicit urgency in Mama's note lingered in his belly. Did he have the courage to propose to a woman he did not love? Even more so, could he ask her to marry a man who did not love her?

Blast that weekend in the Berkshires. He had it all sorted out in his heart and mind until he saw Birdie.

Then all his resolve melted, and he cared very much that his marriage might not know love.

Benedict entered from the adjoining room, handing Eli a cane more suited to an evening out. "Do you need anything else, sir?"

"No, thank you. What plans have you for this evening?"

"I thought I'd take in the Great White Way."

Eli made a face. "And what, pray tell, is the Great White Way?"

"What they're calling Broadway these days, sir. Are you sure you don't need me for anything? I feel guilty with so much time on my hands."

"Consider it payback for the war." Eli handed him a ten-dollar bill. "Have dinner on me."

"This is too generous, sir, but thank you."

A knock sounded, and Benedict opened it to Alfonse, who stood on the other side sporting his dashing grin.

"Evening, Benedict. Eli, shall we go?" Alfonse picked up the cable envelope. "Everything all right back home?"

"Yes, just a greeting from Mama." Benedict helped him into his coat, then handed him his hat and cane. Eli reached for the envelope, tossing it into the fire.

It was one thing for people to know his family needed money. It was quite enough to leave about evidence that he was seeking a profitable marriage as a way of reconciling their debts.

"When you write home, give your parents my regards." Alfonse started out the door, then paused. "Might I ask you a pointed question, Eli?"

"I'm an open book."

"Is there an affection between you and Birdie Shehorn?"

"She's a friend." Eli glanced away, popping his hat onto his head. "Why do you ask?"

"Mere curiosity. Nothing more?"

"Nothing more."

The more he declared it, the more he would believe it. He was a gentleman of the highest regard, and he must remember why he came to America.

TWELVE

TENLEY

She'd settled Blanche with a cup of soup and crackers in bed, the TV remote on hand. "How do you feel?"

"Like death." They'd gone in for another morning chemotherapy session, then Blanche slept away the afternoon.

"The doctor said you'll feel better in a couple of days." Tenley powered on the TV, surfing to a rerun of *Blue Bloods*.

"But first I have to feel like this." Blanche scooped her soup, sniffing, curling her lip. "What is this?"

"Chicken soup. Just like you wanted."

"It smells horrible." She shoved it away. "I thought you were going to make homemade."

"I told you I don't cook." Tenley moved the soup forward on the tray and pointed to the bell on the bedside table. "Ring if you need me. I'm going to clean up the kitchen, start a load of laundry, and maybe write a little bit."

"Wash that robe." Blanche flicked her hand at Tenley's getup.

"I can't, I'm wearing it." She had started to wear it to the hospital, but Blanche refused to go if she didn't change.

"Didn't your mother teach you any better?"

"As a matter of fact, no."

They'd fallen into a rhythm, facing the breaches in their relationship with a bit of sarcasm.

As for the robe, it felt the same as the desk. Like it was part of her somehow, and her journey to figure out if she was going to succeed or fail.

Call them security blankets, but she was clinging to the robe and desk.

"Oh." She paused at the door. "Remember to drink your water."

"I heard the doc, Tenley. They zapped a few cells, not my hearing."

"Just making sure."

Blanche slurped her soup, trying not to make a face. "Thank you, Ten, and I mean it."

"Y-you're welcome."

"I read your book, you know." Blanche's voice cracked and faded. "*Someone to Love.* It was good. You've got talent."

Tenley fell against the door frame. "It's just a romance. Nothing to wow the literary world."

"Yet you won the Phipps Roth Award. Don't you know? All of life is about a romance." Blanche crumbled a handful of crackers into her soup.

"Did you find romance in all your marriages, Blanche?"

"I made a lot of mistakes. Don't be like me. Find a good man and *cling* to him."

"I found a good man." Holt. She was missing him this week and had sent several texts during Blanche's chemo session, but he had yet to respond. "But I'm here with you instead of in Paris with him."

"The cowboy?"

"The screenwriter."

"The one in France who never calls?"

"He calls."

"When?"

"When you're not paying attention."

Blanche waved her spoon at Tenley. "I'll tell you a good man. Jonas Sullivan. If I were twenty years younger—"

"Twenty?"

"Rats, the girl can count. Okay, thirty."

"Did you really leave Dad because he wanted to be a janitor and experience life?"

"That was my reason back then. But in hindsight I think I was just overwhelmed with motherhood. Probably had postpartum and didn't know it."

"For nine years?"

Blanche sniffed a scoop of her soup, made a face, and took another bite. "I wasn't cut out for it, Tenley. I was afraid of breaking you or ruining you in some way."

"Remember my eighth birthday? You threw me a big party somewhere, I can't remember, and we had a pony ride and ice cream. I thought I was the luckiest girl in the world. A year later, it was just Dad and me eating a Happy Meal."

"I never stopped loving you." Another slurp of soup and Blanche shoved it aside.

"Well, it sure felt that way when I was nine. Are you finished?" Tenley motioned to the tray. "I'll leave the crackers. Get some rest."

"You were fine, Tenley. With your dad. Look at you, accomplished and beautiful. Though you apparently didn't inherit my fashion sense. Are you really going to wear that robe every day?"

"It goes with the desk." Tenley paused at the door. "You're right, I was fine with Dad. But neither one of us was fine without you."

Dropping the tray in the kitchen, Tenley muffled a determined sob behind her hand, holding back her tears.

The quips and confessions of forgiveness enabled her to have a relationship with Blanche, and she was grateful. Surprisingly so. But at the end of the day, the woman was part mother, part stranger, and Tenley had to weep for the lost years.

Pushing through the kitchen door onto the veranda, Tenley faced the beach and the breeze, wiping her cheeks with the sleeve of her robe. The light of the pink and orange sunset trailed across the fading blue sky.

She snapped a picture and sent it to Holt.

Miss you, babe. How's it going?

To her delight, he responded immediately.

Amazing!

She waited. *And?* But her phone remained silent. *Forget this texting business. Phones are also for vocal conversation.* Pressing the phone to her ear, she sat on the steps waiting for him to pick up, the cool current of the beach breeze swirling under the porch eaves.

Disappointed when his voice mail answered, she left a message. "Holt, hey, it's me. I miss you. Call me if you can. Feels like forever since we talked. Glad everything is amazing in Paris. Blanche had another treatment today. She's doing well. Me too, you know, in case you were wondering. Love you."

She hung up, cradling her phone in her hand, listening to the sound of the waves just beyond the palmettos.

Holt, where are you? What's going on? A blip of anxiety met with her longing for him, and doubt seeped in.

She should've gone with him. Shouldn't have made room for him to doubt her love. She should've told him, "Yes!"

Tenley clapped her right hand over her left. She should wear her ring. Snap a picture for him.

Her legs twitched. She needed to move. Go. Do. Something. Anything. From the corner of her eye, she saw an old beach cruiser leaning against the house. A bike ride. That's what she needed. A ride on a bike.

Pocketing her phone, Tenley bumped the bike off the porch and headed out, her hair falling freely from her ponytail.

She sailed down A1A, her robe flapping behind her, away from the pedals and chain.

Motorists swerved past, swearing at her with their car horns. But Tenley pedaled on with no notion of a destination. Sweat beaded on her skin though the wind pressed against her with a sharp coolness.

Holt. *Pedal, pedal.* Blanche. *Pedal, pedal, pedal.* Cancer. *Pedal, pedal, pedal, PEDAL!* Book deadline. *Pedal.*

The wheel slipped off into the berm, bogging down in the sandy soil, jerking the bike to one side. Tenley wrestled with the handlebars to keep upright.

"Hey!" A truck pulled alongside her. "What are you doing?"

Eyes fixed ahead, she bore down, pedaling through the sand and grass, sweating. *Ignore him. Just keep moving.*

"Tenley, it's me, Jonas. The desk thief. Pull over."

She pedaled faster. "You said I could keep the desk until my book is done."

"Get to the Publix parking lot before you kill yourself." He crept along the lane next to her, protective, the traffic behind him protesting with horn blasts. "You look like the Wicked Witch of the West with that robe flapping behind you."

"Careful or I'll send out the monkeys." The bike wavered, the wheel skimming against the asphalt and a tuft of grass.

"Pull over."

"I'm fine."

But when the bike slipped one last time and she nearly toppled into a light pole, Tenley banked into the parking lot.

"Where are you going in such a hurry?" Jonas parked, then walked around the truck toward her, motioning to her robe. "If this got tangled up in the chain or spokes . . . Is something wrong? Is your mom okay?"

"Is something wrong? Ha! Yes, everything is wrong. Blanche is fine. A little sick. Sleeping."

"Everything can't be wrong. It's physically, spiritually, and cosmologically impossible."

"Great, a literalist." She whirled away from him, pacing in a small circle, her slippers skipping against the pavement. "Well, I'm a novelist and we live in hyperbole."

"Good to know." He leaned against his truck, arms folded, watching her through narrow eye slits. The strength of his arms pumped against his blue-green T-shirt.

"It's just . . . I'm here and *he's* there, you know?" She flipped her hand toward the east. "Probably writing an Oscar-winning screenplay with Nicolette Carson. What am I doing? Opening canned soup and staring at a blank page. I mean, I'm so pitiful I begged you to leave an old desk, citing its creative powers—"

"You never said it had creative powers."

"Hyperbole, friend. Stay with me." She paced, exercising the anxiety from her bones. "I made a fool of myself in front of strangers."

"A fool? More hyperbole?"

"No, literal now. Keep up."

"I can see why writing might be hard for you. Sometimes you're literal. Sometimes you're hyperbole."

She stopped, her gaze toward him. "Do you think that's it? Really? Am I too . . . conflicted?"

"Tenley, I have no idea." He raised his hands in surrender, shaking his head. "I was kidding . . . I thought we were bantering."

"But you make a good point. What if I'm a one-hit wonder?"

"At least you had a hit. And it was a wonder."

"Very droll. But I can't make a living as a one-hit wonder. And be honest, don't we all pity the one-hit wonders? We say, 'Whatever happened to that *Gone with the Wind* chick?' Or 'Was *Frankenstein* a book? I loved the movie.'"

"A commentary on our educational system. But Tenley, come on. Margaret Mitchell and Mary Shelley? If the plight of a one-hit wonder is an everlasting story . . ."

She grabbed a fistful of his shirt. "I write romance. No one remembers a romance."

"Jane Austen might disagree."

"Good point again, Cocoa Beach." She released him, stepping back, regarding him. "You know a lot about literature."

"I don't own a TV."

"What?"

"Time waster. I'd rather sit and think, or read. Put on some music."

"You don't watch sports?"

"Well now, that's different. Football season is a family holiday. I watch at the folks' house. College mostly." He flipped his hat around to show her a Florida State Seminoles emblem. "I played baseball for FSU."

"My fiancé is a Giants football fan. Rabid."

"Y-you're engaged?"

"Ah, we've come full circle. Yes, sort of." She winced, glancing at her hand. "He proposed, but I didn't exactly say yes."

"More of the literal-versus-hyperbole thing?"

"Maybe."

"So he's the one writing an Oscar-winning screenplay? With Nicolette Carson?"

"He's at her symposium in Paris."

"Paris? When he could be in Cocoa Beach with you?" He reached for her left hand. "Was he too cheap to give you a ring?"

"Holt Armstrong? Not on your life. He gave me a gorgeous, ginormous rock." She cupped her hand over her ring finger, exaggerating her point. "I just . . . can't . . . don't want to . . . ruin . . . " Sigh. "It's not me."

"Know what I do when I'm confused or wrestling with something?"

"Ride a bicycle down an insanely busy road in your robe?"

"No, but that is a future option." He hoisted her bike into the truck bed. "I stop thinking about it. Cut loose, have some fun. Maybe say a prayer." Opening the passenger door, he gestured for her to get in. "When was the last time you did any of those things? Come on. Get in."

She stared at him, stunned by his confidence, wide-open personality, and presumption she'd get into a truck with him.

"First of all, I can't remember the last time I did any of those things, and second of all, I don't climb into trucks with strange men."

He pulled a face. "I'll grant you *strange*, and indeed, I am a man, but you know me. My mother knows your mother. It's fine. Should we call Miss Blanche and ask her if it's okay?"

"Where are we going?" She was starting to like him and his sun-kissed cheeks rising above his evening beard.

"My parents'. It's Wednesday-night dinner."

Tenley softened her posture. "A family dinner? How many? You, your parents, and . . ."

A large-family dinner was on her bucket list, drafted after hours and hours of watching Christmas movies on her own while Dad worked or traveled. Her part-time nanny, ol' Mrs. Eddleman, tried to watch but fell asleep during the opening credits.

The large-family scenes drew her like a kid to candy. *Ooo, what does this taste like?*

"Four brothers. Two sisters. Two sets of twins. Identical. Sisters are twins, also the youngest brothers."

Tenley reached to the truck for support, hand to her heart. "There's nine of you?"

"About eighteen when the friends, boyfriends, and girlfriends show up. But most Wednesdays we're not that many."

"Shew."

"More like thirty."

"Thirty!"

He grinned. "Exactly. Fun, laughter. Now get in."

"You know, I really should get back to Blanche." She glanced at her bike in the truck bed. While the idea of a large, loud, laughing family gathering fascinated her, the reality of sitting down with one overwhelmed her.

"Maybe another time." She jerked her thumb toward the house. "I should get back."

"And write?" He dropped his arm over the top of the door, leaning, motioning for her to get in. "Sometimes the muse needs a break. I promise you'll have fun. The house is—"

"There is no *fun* in *deadline*."

"—on the river. You can sit on the dock and watch the sunset. Go kayaking if you need some solitude."

"Thanks, Jonas, really, but—"

"Tenley, listen, I know what you're going through. I used to own a furniture business. Designed and built my own. When I started, I had ideas coming out my ears. I lived, dreamed, breathed furniture design. Couldn't get enough. But the moment I started the actual work, putting the design on paper so to speak, nothing worked. I hated everything."

"Then you know what I'm going through."

"One day my dad gave me wise counsel. Step back, take a break, find a fresh perspective. Go for a run or swim, read, take a long drive, whatever. But let go."

"My dad used to say the same thing. He'd be on deadline, frustrated, and just quit. Do something different."

"So you know, the trick is to take a break."

"Jonas, I've been taking a break. That's why I'm in a bind. I'm down to the final three months."

"Well, tonight isn't going to make any difference. Get in. You need to step out of yourself for a few hours. So your dad was a writer? Would I know him?"

"Conrad Roth."

He grinned. "Of course, of course. My dad has one of his books by his chair." He gave her a pleading puppy-dog face. "Now you *have* to come home with me. They'll kill me if I don't introduce you to them."

Tenley exhaled. "Fine. Besides, you stuck my bike in the truck bed." She climbed into the passenger seat. "We need to go by the house so I can—"

"You don't need to change. We're casual at the Sullivan house."

"I was going to say check on Blanche." Tenley leaned to see her reflection in the side mirror. "But if you think I need to change . . ."

"I don't. Nope, not at all." Jonas moved onto A1A.

"Then why did you suggest I might?"

"I have sisters who are always changing their clothes." He gave her a once-over. "But you look great. The robe is so . . . you."

She burst out laughing. "Liar, liar, pants on fire."

"Besides, we don't have time for you to change. I'm starved and want to get there before the snack foods are scarfed up."

At Grove Manor, Blanche slept with deep, even breaths. Tenley refilled her water glass, covered her with a blanket, and left a note—the most cohesive thing she'd written since arriving in Florida—on the monogrammed stationary she found in the nightstand drawer.

Back in the truck with Jonas, she said, "Thank you."

"For not running you off the road?" He swung the truck around, heading down the drive. "Can I tell you something, Tenley?"

"Now you ask?" She slumped down, wrapping her robe tighter, digging her feet into the slippers. "Go ahead."

"Don't take this the wrong way—"

"Uh-oh. Nothing good ever started with 'Don't take this the wrong way, but—'"

"I don't know about your fiancé, but if you were my girl, I know where I'd be."

"Yeah, where's that?"

"Anywhere you were."

THIRTEEN

BIRDIE

Bundled against the cold, Birdie walked alongside Elijah as he escorted her down the walk. Alfonse remained in the nave talking with an old chum from Harvard.

The quiet night settled around them as they strolled under the gaslights toward a private brougham.

"Penny for your thoughts?" Eli said.

"I'm not sure they are worth that much but yes, I was considering all we heard tonight." The lecturer, a young man straight from Princeton Seminary, spoke with an eloquence and passion Birdie had never heard from a sermon lectern. Her reverend spoke softly, so as not to tempt the headaches of those who drank too much and stayed up too late.

"He knew his subject matter," Eli said, pausing to pull on his gloves. "He seemed a sincere chap."

"Do you believe people shook under the unction of Whitefield's preaching?" For Birdie, church seemed to be more of a social occasion—a time to show off a new frock or chat with friends—than an opportunity to encounter a God she could not see or touch.

But the lecturer had suggested true faith required more than learning catechism and taking first communion. Several times he implied the power of the Holy Spirit was available to the common man, to those who believed in Jesus and the cross. That faith was not just a simple assurance of an eternal heaven.

"There are many accounts of it, both here and in England. So yes, I believe. I see no reason to doubt."

"Shouldn't we doubt? Question? Is God really some angry being waiting to punish us?" Birdie shuddered at the idea of Edwards's angry God.

She grew up with an exacting, demanding mother and a distant though kind father. She'd not serve an Almighty who exhibited the same attributes. She'd not spend so-called eternity being made to feel imperfect and inadequate.

"Is that what you heard tonight?" He laughed low. "I heard of a God who loves us so much He spared not His own Son to make a way for us to know His pleasure and love." He patted his chest. "The notion warms me, really. I feel a bit of my daily burden eased."

She slipped her arm through his. "Then pray I come to understand."

"Always, my friend." Elijah stopped and turned to her. "Our time in the Berkshires and here tonight reminds me how much I enjoy you. I've missed you."

"And I you."

He brushed the tip of his glove under her chin. "Do you remember your last day at Hapsworth?"

"How could I forget? We walked across the grounds toward the fields. It was a beautiful yet sad day."

"We almost kissed." His gaze swept her face and crossed her lips.

"Eli—" She mustn't reveal her feelings or encourage him in any way. If not for his sake, her own. The path of Eli led to a dead end. "Alfonse will be coming."

"But do you remember?" He leaned toward her, his question more than mere words. It was almost an invitation.

"Of course. B-but Eli, four years have passed." She stepped back, away from his warmth and whispers, Mama's stern warning rattling through her. "You and Rose are to be engaged."

"I've made no offer, Birdie. I am still a free man. She is a free woman." Eli slipped his hand into hers. "When I sailed here I had no idea you were also a free woman. Love, just say the word and I'll—"

"There you are." Alfonse joined them, clapping his hands together. "I thought you'd gone on without me. May I introduce Farnsworth, my friend and colleague. Farnsworth, I present Lord Montague and Miss Birdie Shehorn."

"Pleased to make your acquaintance." He bowed to Eli and kissed Birdie's hand. "She's everything you claim, Alfonse." Farnsworth smiled at her, the gaslight catching the twinkle in his eye. "I can see she will make you a beautiful wife. An intellectual one at that. I could not get my fiancée to attend this lecture."

"Fiancée?" Eli said, moving away from Birdie. "You're engaged? Birdie—Miss Shehorn, you never said."

"We've come to an understanding." Alfonse puffed out his chest. "Eli, remember I mentioned my situation to you in the Berkshires. Farnsworth was asking if—"

"Begging your pardon, Alfonse, but we've come to no understanding."

"All but, darling. Your father has settled the financial arrangements."

"I am not"—shaking so, she struggled to speak—"an item to be sold to the highest bidder. Mr. Farnsworth, I don't know what stories Alfonse has been telling you, but we are *not* engaged. He has not even proposed." Birdie turned for the brougham. He'd gone too far. Too far.

"Birdie, wait—" Alfonse took hold of her arm but she snatched it away. "Do not walk away from me."

"Take another means home, Alfonse. This brougham is mine. You have no right to speak for me." She pressed close, lowering her voice. "Never, ever do that again."

As the driver chirruped to the horse, Birdie peered out the carriage window, once again seeing Eli's face as she was carried off, their conversation, their kiss, thwarted just like the longing in her heart.

A week had passed since Alfonse's misstep in front of St. Paul's. He'd showered her with flowers and chocolates, even sent a quartet to the Candler ball to sing to her.

Which mortified her.

He called on her Friday afternoon, but she refused him. She decided not to attend the opera or the Whitney ball. Much to Mama's despair.

"You are ruining our reputation."

"Because I choose not to attend a party? Then what sort of reputation do we have to begin with?"

However, staying away from the parties meant she'd not seen Eli, and she was desperate to speak with him. She meant to convey her regrets over Alfonse's announcement and over the fact that she'd not mentioned the discussions to Eli herself.

She'd written to him but burned the letter in her fireplace. Perhaps, in some mysterious way, Alfonse's blunder was a blessing. Eli had a duty to Rose, and Birdie had no right to any of his affections.

Monday afternoon when she came down to lunch, Percival passed her a note from Alfonse.

May I please call on you this afternoon?

"Who's written you?" Mama asked over her cup of tea.

"Alfonse." Birdie tucked the letter under her plate.

"What has happened between you?" Mama glanced at Papa. "Do you know, Geoffrey? He's sent candy and flowers . . . and that quartet at the Candlers' . . . Birdie, everyone was talking about it."

"I'm in the dark as well, Iris." Papa snapped his paper in half to read the financial pages. "Let the children work it out for themselves."

"Then for heaven's sake, Birdie, forgive the man. Get on with it. He'll never propose otherwise. Geoffrey, have you heard from your man about passage to Paris this spring?"

Never propose? What a delightful notion. Birdie thanked the footman for pouring her tea, then sweetened it with milk and sugar.

Yet, if she didn't forgive him, only heaven knew what he'd do next. She'd just finished a meat pie when Papa passed her a folded section of the *Herald*.

"Look here, Birdie." Papa tapped the article above the broadsheet's fold. "Gordon Phipps Roth has a new book coming this summer. Is he still your favorite author?"

"One of them, yes. How delightful." She set aside her fork and knife. "Did I tell you I saw him?" She stopped, realizing her error. Papa would want to know where, and Mama would want to know what business she had with Barclay Publishing.

"You did not." Papa sipped his coffee with a pleased expression. "Where did you see him? A lecture? I hear he's quite entertaining."

"He should be," Mama said. "He's s storyteller."

"I saw him at Delmonico's." Which was true. Sometime last year. And from a distance. "While lunching with the University Settlement Society."

"Perhaps when his book releases we can have him to dinner."

Papa checked his pocket watch. "The Courtneys are good friends with his sister, I believe."

"That would be lovely, Papa." Birdie scanned the page, taking in the author's photograph, his wild hair tamed enough for the expression in his eyes to peek through.

New Phipps Roth Novel to Be Released This Summer.

The renowned Gordon Phipps Roth has done it again. His latest masterpiece from Barclay Publishing, The Girl in the Carriage, *about a young society woman's adventures at the dawning of a new century and the love she left behind—*

What? Birdie snapped the paper closer. *A young society woman's adventures . . . dawning of a new century . . . love left behind.* "It can't be."

"What are you mumbling about, Birdie?" Mama said. "Speak up so we can all hear. I've trained you better."

. . . the first book from Phipps Roth in over four years has delighted critics. 'Welcome back, Phipps Roth, we've missed you. A stellar fifth novel,' said the New York Times.

Birdie scanning to the end. Surely the great Daniel Barclay would not use another author's idea. Or worse, story. This must be some sort of mistake. A rare and odd coincidence.

But the churning within warned her otherwise. She pushed away from the table, crumpling the paper, not caring the black ink smeared her cream-colored sleeve.

"If you'll excuse me."

Papa rose from his chair. "Finished dining already?"

"Yes, I've something to tend."

Mama eyed her as she left. "I hope it's to accept Alfonse's apology. Surely he's been punished enough for whatever egregious thing he perpetrated."

"Of course." But her thoughts were far away from Alfonse. At the dining room door, she paused. "Mama, can you recall a package delivered to me over the summer? August, I believe. About this big?" Birdie set the paper on the table by the door and indicated the size of her manuscript. "It arrived by courier."

"I was away last August. As were you. And Papa. Why do you ask? Percival handles all packages."

"Yes, of course. The Grand Tour. Egypt. What about September?"

Mama narrowed her gaze at Birdie, using her mama-powers to investigate beyond the question.

"No, Birdie, and I don't like your implication. Check the servants' closet downstairs. Sometimes packages are stored there when we are away."

"Papa, do you know of a package?" Birdie asked.

"Listen to your mama and check with the servants."

Down the back stairs, she descended into the world of the other class, nearly crashing into one of the kitchen maids.

If Barclay didn't have her manuscript, and Birdie didn't have it, nor had Mama come across it and hidden it, then where was it and why was the description of Gordon Phipps Roth's new book identical to the story she had written?

One of the maids approached. "Can I help you, Miss Birdie?"

"Where is your closet?"

She pointed, eyes wide, to the end of the hall. Jerking open the door, Birdie dropped to her knees, searching among the muddy boots, finding nothing but a dark hole.

"You'll need this." The maid passed a lamp over her shoulder.

"Thank you." Birdie shoved aside coats and cloaks, mufflers and shawls. Nothing. Shoes lined the floor while hats and gloves lined the shelves.

Shutting the door, she passed the lamp back to the maid.

"Is there anything I can help you with?" the girl asked.

Tenley peered at her for a moment. "You're new, are you not?"

She blushed. "Started New Year's Day."

"Then you wouldn't have knowledge of a package delivered last summer."

"No, miss, I'm sorry."

Trailing up to the attic, Birdie sat at her desk, considering the news. What was she to do?

Confront Barclay again? With what proof? She should let it go, work on a new book for herself and anticipate the next masterpiece by a beloved author.

An idea formed.

Lighting the lamp, she shoved aside all second thoughts, quickly withdrew a sheet of stationery from her desk.

FOURTEEN

JONAS

He hadn't thought this through. Bringing Tenley to the house would raise questions. Lots of questions.

He'd not brought a girl home since Cindy. And before that, it was Jenny, from his senior year of high school.

He'd lead with facts—*I found her on the side of the road.* That'd steer them away from notions of "Jonas brought a girl home."

With a slight glance at his guest, he wondered if he should just head up to Courtenay Parkway and find a nice riverside restaurant.

Home was a crazy place. The Sullivans were a blue-collar people. Salt-of-the-earth types. Nothing fancy. Just large, loud, and loving. Accepting of everyone.

What type was Tenley? Raised by her father, a famous author. Down to earth? Privileged? The darn robe really gave him no clues.

At the next light, he turned toward his parents' home, easing down the street lined with cars. Tenley's opinion of his family was moot. She was leaving in a few months. End of story.

She leaned forward as he circled the cul-de-sac to double park next to Dad's truck. Looked like everyone had come out for this one.

"All these cars aren't for your family dinner, are they?" She counted softly. "... eight, nine, ten ... thirteen ..."

"No, of course not. The blue VW belongs to the neighbor."

"Oh my gosh, all these cars brought people to your house?" She gripped his arm. "Give me the skinny. Are we talking the Munsters or the Middle?"

"Yes."

She fanned her face. "I can do this. Easy, right? I have a master's degree from NYU. I live in Manhattan for crying out loud."

He liked her. The honest way she hid from life.

"Ready?" He opened his door. "We'll just walk in, say hi, and act like you've been here before."

"But I haven't."

"Thus the acting." He hesitated before stepping out. "I should warn you, though, you're a girl and I'm a boy—"

"Forgive me, Jonas, but I've been underestimating your keen discernment."

"—and I don't usually bring your kind around."

"My kind? Crazy writers? Girls wearing a red-plaid man robe and slippers?"

"All of the above. Mostly, beautiful girls. So if the fam pesters you about us, and there is no us, just tell them to back off. Give it to them plain."

"You think I'm beautiful?" She teased with her grin. "That's so sweet. I could tell them we've been secretly in love since—"

"They won't believe you." He stepped out, walking around to meet her. *Beautiful*. The word just *had* to slip out. Well, she was beautiful.

"Why won't they believe we're secretly in love?"

"Because they know me."

The house at the end of the walkway was built in the fifties.

The sprawling live oaks were even older, their thick roots threading through the lawn.

The Sullivans were not lawn people. They were people people.

"You've never been in love? Never dated? How many girls have you kissed?" She skipped up the walk beside him, her slippers slapping the cracked concrete.

"Ha, that's for me to know and you to find out."

"A challenge. I accept. I can ask your sisters. Oh, I forgot to tell you, I don't eat red meat."

He paused at the door, the sounds from inside already vibrant and loud. "No steak or hamburgers? No pot roast or corned beef?"

"Or chicken." He wouldn't voice it, but she already seemed freer than she had been in the Publix parking lot.

"Not fried or roasted? Girl, do you know what you are missing?"

"Also, nothing starchy or yellow."

"Fruit?"

"Yes, fruit, as long as it's in its original form."

"You're killing me, New York. What do you eat? Lettuce? Beans? Grass? That's about all that's left."

"Depends. What kind of grass?"

"Augustine." He motioned to the healthy side of his parents' front lawn.

"Um, no."

"So it's hot dogs and Twinkies?"

She grinned. "Not even when I was two."

"I give up. How do you survive?"

"Diet Coke, coffee."

He reached for the doorknob. "Oh, *that's* healthy. Artificially colored caffeine flowing through your veins with artificial sweeteners."

"I'm well preserved."

Wearing that ratty robe and clown-size slippers, she was getting under his skin, awakening dormant longings.

"Let's go see if Mom has some coffee brewing. Ready?"

"Yes, no, wait." She leaned against him, took off her socks and slippers, wadded them up, and stuffed them into her pockets. Her gaze met his. "I didn't want to look weird."

With that, he opened the door, leading Tenley into a round of greetings.

"Joe's here."

"Mom, Jonas just came in."

"Jonas, did you get my text?"

But Mom cut through them all. "My prodigal returns." She crossed over with her arms open for an embrace, her smile white against her tan face.

"Prodigal? I missed one week." He kissed her cheek, then shook Dad's hand. The man was still youthful and lean, kept in shape by decades of hard work.

"Jonas." Mom flicked her gaze to Tenley. "Who do we have here?"

"Tenley Roth. She's Miss Blanche's daughter. Tenley, this is my mom, Ailis, or Mom, as everyone calls her. And my dad, Fergus."

"Well, welcome, welcome. Blanche has talked so much about you." Mom wrapped Tenley in a hug and mouthed to Jonas, "She never said a word!"

"Really?" Tenley leaned limply against Mom. "We're not that close. I'm surprised."

"But what mama isn't proud of her beautiful daughter?" Mom rocked Tenley back and forth. *Easy there, Mom. Let go.*

"Her father was Conrad Roth. The author."

"Well, of course, we knew that. We loved your father's books. So sorry about his untimely death."

"Th-thank you. S-sorry to barge in on family night." Tenley

glanced down at her robe. "I was working . . . then riding a bike . . . Jonas kind of kidnap—"

From the Florida room, his sister Erin entered, her chatter dying when she spied Tenley.

"Jonas? Who is this?" Erin shoved past Mom. "You look exactly like my favorite author, Tenley Roth."

"Because she is Tenley Roth."

"No way!" And . . . the party went postal. "Elaine, Elaine, get in here. You are never going to believe what Jonas brought us as a graduation present. Tenley Roth!"

"No, no, Erin, she's not your graduation . . . I found her on the side of the road. Really."

But when Elaine came, in the E's, as Mom called them, were practically hysterical.

"We love, love, loved your book."

"We started a book club just so we could talk about it."

"I have the hardback, the paperback, and the e-book."

Standing there in her robe, that ridiculous robe, with the socks and slippers bulging from the pockets, Jonas saw a glint, the sparkle of a buried gem, in Tenley. He saw a woman worthy of love. Deserving of a man who would give her himself.

"I just can't believe you're here," Erin said. "This is unbelievable."

"Tell me, what did you like most about the book?" Tenley finally got a word in.

"Ezra." The E's made one bold, unified declaration.

Tenley nodded. "Of course, he's everyone's favorite. Probably the key to the book's success. He's a true hero."

"Elaine updated her online dating profile to say, 'Read this book for the kind of guy I want.'"

Elaine nudged Erin. "You wrote that because you were too chicken to put it on your own profile."

Jonas stepped into the conversation. "Can we go back to where you two have an online dating profile? Does Dad know about this?"

"Jonas, Tenley, y'all want anything to drink?" Dad, the master of ceremonies for the Sullivan clan, approached wearing his apron and chef's hat. "Soda, water, iced tea . . ."

"Diet Coke?" Tenley asked.

"Coming up. Jonas, take the girl out back, save her from the E's. Let her see the deck and the river. It's a lovely night. I'm about to put the meat on the fire. It's been marinating all day." Dad handed Tenley a bedewed Diet Coke can. "Are you allergic to anything, Tenley?"

She popped the top. "Life?"

Dad's bursting laugh bounced through the kitchen. "Aren't we all, darling? Aren't we all?"

Grabbing a cold Coke, Jonas led her out back.

"Why's your dad laughing? Does he think I'm kidding?" Tenley sipped her Diet Coke as Erin rammed a paperback into her gut.

"Can you sign this for me, please?"

Elaine followed with a hardcover. "I've read it three times. But I'm reading it again at night before I fall asleep."

"Careful now, you'll find all of my mistakes."

"Never. Ezra gets better every time."

At the picnic table, Jonas hovered nearby as Tenley talked to the E's and signed their books.

She already fit in. Not because of the E's crazy obsession but because she was . . . Tenley. Save for the introductions, it felt like she'd been here a hundred times.

An eclectic circle of lawn chairs surrounded the picnic tables, and from Dad's mounted speakers, bossa nova music filled the air.

Jonas surveyed the yard, his brothers on the dock fishing, friends arriving with foil-covered dishes, the breeze dragging a cool evening and brilliant sky over them. This just might be a piece of heaven on earth.

He glanced at Tenley, liking that she was part of the scene. Only trouble was, he wasn't fixed for a relationship. He had a lot of goals before "settling down."

But Tenley wasn't a permanent member of Cocoa Beach. She was merely a hitchhiker on her way to another part of the galaxy.

"When's your next book out?" Erin said, cradling her copy of Tenley's book. "I was just on your website but there's no update."

"The spring." Tenley peeked up at Jonas. *Don't say anything.*

"She's writing the book over at Grove Manor," he said.

The girls let out a small gasp and peppered her with more questions.

"What's it about?"

"We'd be happy to read an early copy for you."

"Enough." Jonas shooed them away. "Leave her alone."

"Fine, but I need a selfie. For Instagram." Erin motioned to the upper deck Jonas had helped Dad build. "Let's go to the top deck. The river view is so beautiful."

Fifteen years ago when they moved in, the 1950s home on the river was a dump. The neglected terrazzo floors were cracked, and every last one of the appliances was the original.

But it was theirs, and after having lived in rental after rental and even in their car for a time, owning their own home made the Sullivans feel like royalty.

First chunk of free change he had, Jonas bought the lumber and built the deck.

"Lead the way." Tenley smiled at Jonas, waving good-bye, her robe flapping and scraping over the top of the grass. "I'm off with my *people.*"

"I thought the desk and chair were your people."

"Do you remember everything I say?"

Jonas returned to his seat on top of the picnic table. The youngest twins, Caleb and Josh, caught a fish. His brother Julius had just arrived, his tie askew and collar unbuttoned. Brother Cameron coached football at Astronaut High. He'd be late.

"Where'd you find her, son?" Dad sat next to him, grill tools in hand. "Couldn't you have given her a chance to clean up?"

"She was riding a bike down A1A." Jonas took a sip of his drink. "I've never seen her in anything else. She wanted to change but I told her we were casual."

"What's in her pockets?"

"Men's slippers and socks."

Dad whistled. "You know, Blanche has never mentioned a daughter to your mom."

"I don't think they are very close. Tenley calls her Blanche."

"So does this mean you're back in the dating game?"

"Nope. Just helping a friend, Dad."

"A very pretty friend." Dad tilted his head to one side, gazing up at the E's taking selfies with their favorite author. "But I'm still trying to figure out the outfit."

"She's got writer's block. I think she's trying to find some sort of mojo. Wear the same thing every day. Wouldn't let me take a desk Blanche sold to me. Said it inspired her to write."

Dad hopped up when Caleb and Josh tried to throw their fish on his fire. Julius stood on the patio with a couple of buddies from high school.

Jonas gazed at Tenley talking with the E's on the upper deck. Maybe, if he were interested in love again, she'd be the one to lure him in. But . . .

She was engaged. Ring or no ring, there was a man in her life with whom she'd made a commitment.

Steer clear, man.

From the porch, Mom rang the dinner bell. Dad blessed the food in his big evangelist voice, then Mom held everyone back, inviting Tenley forward.

"Tonight, you're our guest. But ever after you're family and you'll have to fight the horde like the rest of us."

Mom shoved a plate at her along with a napkin roll and led her down the food line, exhorting her to eat everything she claimed she didn't like.

"We buy our beef from a rancher. You can't beat it. We've got potato salad here and, oh, my grandmother's baked beans recipe. It's better than kissing."

Jonas followed, every step or two encouraging Mom to go easy on Tenley. He filled his plate, grabbed a couple of water bottles, and led Tenley to chairs at the edge of the river.

"You don't have to eat all of that," he said, balancing his plate on his lap. "Food is Mom's love language."

"It's okay. It really does smell good." Tenley stabbed at her potato salad then gazed toward the river. "It's beautiful out here."

"Can I ask why you call your mom Blanche?"

She swallowed, pointing to the potato salad. "This is good. Blanche? She left when I was nine. I didn't see her very often, and when I was a teenager, I thought I'd *show her* by calling her Blanche. But she didn't care. Thought it was hip."

"You're closer now? That's why you came to help her?"

"We're not closer but I came anyway. She said she didn't have anyone else."

"And your fiancé went to Paris?"

"Yep. And I came here. I'm a saint, right?" She sat back, eyes fixed on the ripple of the river, and wiped her fingers with her napkin.

"To Blanche, I'm sure." He hesitated, then asked, "Why didn't your fiancé come with you?"

"Well, Paris with Nicolette, writing scripts . . . Tough competition."

"You said you don't wear your ring because it's 'not me.'"

"Seriously, are you going to remember everything I say? If you are, I'm not sure we can be friends."

"Just wondering why it's not you."

"I don't know." She scowled and shoved another forkful of potato salad into her mouth, then swiveled to face him. "Look, Jonas, I know we just met and we're exchanging information—which by the way I have nothing personal on you *yet*—but I don't owe you an explanation about my engagement or the accompanying ring."

"Nope, you don't." He stared toward the water, considering his next move. Should he say what was on his mind? Just go there? "But I'm kind of thinking you owe yourself one."

FIFTEEN

BIRDIE

The private brougham arrived at the Barclay Publishing offices on Broadway shortly after three.

The blustery wind pushed her toward the doors, and when she stepped into the foyer, she found Eli waiting for her.

"Good afternoon." She nodded to the lobby porter and removed her gloves, distracting herself from the jittery sensation Eli's presence inspired. "I hope accompanying me has not inconvenienced you in any way."

"Certainly not. I gladly offer you my moral and emotional support."

The day she'd read the Phipps Roth article, she'd also written to Eli, explaining her dilemma, asking for his support on her mission to see the publisher. She longed for moral support. Someone to believe her. Eli had always encouraged her writing aspirations.

Though he did not know he was the inspiration for *A View from Her Carriage*—and she had no plans to tell him—she felt he could be trusted with her rather scandalous suspicion.

His reply came within the hour.

"I'll gladly accompany you."

"Are you feeling brave?" he said, smoothing his dark hair from his face.

"Not at all. Mama instilled in me a healthy fear of all authority."

"You are not accusing the publisher, correct? Merely inquiring."

The lobby porter stepped forward. "Would you prefer the elevator or the stairs?"

"The stairs. Those closed boxes give me shivers."

"Indeed, miss."

So Eli escorted her up the stairs. "May I speak honestly, Birdie? You do realize it's highly unlikely Phipps Roth's book is yours."

"I'm well aware. But Eli, I cannot help but wonder. Will it hurt to inquire? No matter how preposterous?" Birdie paused on the second-floor landing. Did Eli agree with her? "His book description is so like mine. I wonder if somehow my story, which Barclay was in possession of for some six months, might have been conveyed to Phipps Roth in a conversation, and the idea took hold."

"I've heard it said there really are no new ideas."

"As I've heard, but the description of Phipps Roth's book so mirrors my own. Do you think I shouldn't even bother Barclay? Will I shame myself and the Shehorn name by approaching him? Although if history holds course, he may very well refuse to see me."

Eli looped his arm through hers. "We're here. Let's speak to the man before you go on sorting it out in your head."

When they entered the Barclay Publishing offices, Mrs. Petersheim came around her desk. "Miss Shehorn, good afternoon. What are you doing here?"

"Is Mr. Barclay available? I need only a moment of his time."

"He's very busy." She propped her hands on her ample hips, her expression set. "I'm not sure he can see you. Perhaps I can relay a message?"

"My conversation is of a private matter. May I introduce you to the Earl of Montague? Lord Montague, Mrs. Petersheim."

"Your Majesty," she whispered with an awkward curtsy.

"I'm not royalty. Lord Montague will do. Mrs. Petersheim, you would be doing me a great service if you'd alert Mr. Barclay to our presence."

Birdie was nothing short of genius to bring him along. How splendid! His good looks were rivaled only by his good charm.

Mrs. Petersheim vanished in a flustered flurry, disappearing behind a frosted glass door.

"I tip my hat to you, Lord Montague." She inclined her head, touching the brim of her hat. "Well done."

"Being a peer does have its advantages." He laughed low, only for her. "Even in America."

Birdie inhaled the earthy fragrance of his scent, longing to remember everything about him. The way he smelled, the grip of his hand around hers, the distinct sculpture of his face.

"I-I wish things were different," he said. "With us. You're blushing. Am I out of line? It's that I find no time to speak with you."

She turned away. "Eli, please, we are in an office building. What do you expect me to do or say?"

"That you feel the same way." He sighed, stepping back, turning his hat in his hands. "I'm being foolish. I am bound to do my duty with no regard to my heart."

"My obligations are only slightly less strenuous." She glanced around, offering him a smile. "We are a tragic love story in the making. If only we'd lived in another time . . ."

"I can't imagine a time when laws or society or peerage do not dictate the lives of their children. Who should marry whom. Who inherits and who is left in the cold."

Mr. Barclay's door clattered open. "Miss Shehorn, Mrs. Petersheim informs me you wish to see me."

"Yes, sir, indeed." Blessed! He did not try to escape. Birdie rushed into his office, leaving Eli's confession on the reception floor. What more was there to say?

"Five minutes," Barclay said. "Not a moment more."

"You are more than generous."

The three of them gathered in the center of his office. "May I introduce Lord Montague, Elijah Percy."

Barclay clapped Eli's hand in a hearty shake. "We're thinking of opening an office in London."

"A splendid city. Let me know if I may assist in any way." Eli reached into his pocket and passed Barclay his card. "Now if you could assist Miss Shehorn."

He'd taken command of the conversation. Bravo, Eli!

"Another manuscript go missing, Miss Shehorn?"

She laughed, trying to dislodge her own unease. "I have a question about Mr. Phipps Roth's new book." From her reticule, she retrieved the three-day-old article.

"What sort of question? I'm sure we don't need your permission to publish a book." He refused the article she offered, turning back to his desk. "Can you get to the nature of your visit? I've work to do." Mr. Barclay tapped his fingers on a bundled manuscript, then aimed a steely gaze at Birdie.

"Of course, you are a busy man." Birdie unfolded the article. "I-it's just that . . ." She peered at Eli. If he appeared to doubt, she'd turn for the door. But he nodded, smiling, urging her on.

"Miss Shehorn, please state your business." Mr. Barclay sat down, reaching for the manuscript and his red pencil.

"It's simply, Mr. Barclay, the description I read sounds very familiar to me, and I was wondering . . ." In an instant, Birdie could see the scene unfolding before her mind's eye. She, a young heiress, all but accusing a respected New York businessman of what? Cheating? Stealing?

Did her arrogance lead her to believe her idea was so exceptional Barclay would risk his reputation and livelihood to apprehend it?

Mama's voice droned through her head. *"Consider your reputation, Birdie. What you do reflects on all of us."*

"Wondering what?" Mr. Barclay looked up from his work. "Do go on. I'm curious . . ."

Eli stepped forward. "She found the description to be very simi—"

"Enchanting. I found it to be very enchanting." She stuffed the newspaper clipping into her reticule. "I wonder if I might have an advance copy to read, perhaps lend my support."

"Birdie?" Eli said. "Did you want to sort out another matter with Barclay?"

"No."

"Are you sure?"

"Miss Shehorn, do you mean to tell me you came all the way down here merely to lend your support to Gordon's new book?"

"Yes, that's exactly what I came to say. I'm a devoted fan."

"I'd have preferred you to write a letter."

"I wanted to show my full enthusiasm." She posed with a proper New York–heiress posture.

Mr. Barclay walked around his desk toward the door. "How kind of you. I'll keep your offer in mind. Now if I could bid you a good day."

"Thank you." Maintaining her decorum, Birdie hurried for the open door. "I'll write to you for a convenient time to host Mr. Phipps Roth. Please give him my best."

"Oh, Miss Shehorn." Barclay stopped her in reception. "I take it you've found your missing manuscript?"

"It was right where I suspected all along."

Mr. Barclay bid them adieu, and Eli walked Birdie to the stairs.

"Birdie, love, what happened in there?"

"I couldn't, Eli. I couldn't." She collapsed against him, gripping his soldier-trained shoulders. "The moment I was about to speak, I realized I was about to ask the man who'd given the world Gordon Phipps Roth, and so *much* great literature, if he somehow *took* my work. I felt like such a fool, like the spoiled heiress he believes me to be."

He kissed the top of her head, then her temple. "I'm proud of you, my little bird. If you're sure."

"I want to write my stories, Eli." She glanced up at him. "Desperately. It's the one occupation that is mine. No Mama. No Papa. No Shehorn name or expectations of a girl in my station. I'm in command of my life for those brief moments I put pen to paper." She turned away from him. "But do I want to find myself in a fight with the man who might help me realize my dream? And truly, would Gordon Phipps Roth stoop to copy another's work? I daresay I would not. I suppose I'm not making any sense."

"Love, you are making the most sense of anyone I know." Eli took her in his arms, his eyes searching hers. "How I wish I could kiss you."

"Eli, I am so grateful for your friendship and that you accompanied me here today, but . . ." Birdie released herself from his hold. "Let us be honest. Our time came and went. You are to marry another. So please, never speak of kissing me again."

TENLEY

She woke up tired. Weary. Having wrestled through the night with words. Giant, ominous creatures that crushed her into the sandy soil of Cocoa Beach.

Failure. Blocked. Loser. Reject. Cheater.

Shooting upright in bed, kicking aside her covers, she noticed her skin prickled with perspiration. Exhaling, grateful to be awake, she plopped back onto her pillow and listened to the sleeping house, the AC quietly kicking on.

When words became a writer's nightmare, the writer was in trouble. Tenley Merry Roth was in deep doo-doo.

Schlepping to the bathroom, she slurped water from the faucet, then peered at her reflection. The ratty topknot on her head bounced forward toward her puffy face. She'd fallen asleep in the robe, *her* robe, wearing the pajamas she'd worn for the past two days.

Her socks and slippers lay haphazardly at the foot of the bed beside a growing pile of dirty underwear and socks. The only clothing she managed to change.

Some things just couldn't be compromised.

But it wasn't just writer's block that bothered her. It was Jonas and his freakishly large family and how they had accepted her at *hello*. How his dad laughed at her allergic-to-life quip.

The Sullivan house overflowed with music and laughter. The boy twins built a fire in the fire pit and sat around with their friends laughing over . . . nothing. Just laughing.

The Sullivans were a subcommunity in the community of life. And she wanted to belong. How crazy was that?

By the time Jonas drove her home a little after ten, Tenley felt like she'd seen life in color for the first time since Dad's funeral.

How did she not know she'd lived in shades of black and white and sepia?

The real complication came with Jonas. Sweet, cute, sexy Jonas.

Tenley flopped down on her bed, reaching for her phone. Three a.m. Rolling onto her side, she tried to drift off, but her mind relived her good-night with Jonas.

"Thanks for running me off the road."

"Anytime."

"You were right. Meat is good."

"Glad you liked it." He gripped the steering wheel, nodding his head, awkwardness moving in between them.

"I'm sorry I snapped at you about my engagement ring."

"You're right, it's not my business. We've known each other, what, less than a week?"

Then why did it feel like always? As if she'd known him forever but just now got to see his face. *"Good night, then."*

"Good night, Tenley."

She tossed from side to side, the tone of his voice sinking through her. He didn't say, "See you soon," or "Dinner next week? Same time and place?" or even ask for her number.

Why did she care? She was *engaged*!

Sitting up, she popped on the bedside lamp and dialed Holt. Three a.m. meant nine in Paris. He'd be awake. When he answered, she grinned and exhaled.

"Tenley?" Sleep thickened his voice. "What are you doing up?"

"Had a bad dream." She leaned against the wall and stretched out her legs. Dad had always talked her through her nightmares. Nightmares, he'd say, were the devil's tools.

"Just a dream," Holt said. "Doesn't mean anything. Go back to sleep. Or do some writing."

"I wrestled these giant, ugly words." She shivered and wrapped the robe around herself. "They were powerful and strong. I couldn't defeat them."

"Words? Probably because you're supposed to be writing." His voice ebbed and flowed, dropping off, then forcing through with a heavy sigh.

"*Failure, cheater, block*? I'm supposed to be writing those?"

"Sounds like one of your dad's books. A thriller."

"Some people say dreams reflect life."

Instantly the word *cheater* flashed through her mind. *Cheater*? Yes, of course. She was cheating on Holt by hanging out with Jonas.

"Or you're just worried about your deadline. Take a sleeping pill. Go back to sleep."

"Holt, I had dinner with a new friend last night. Well, not just him but his entire *Eight Is Enough* family and their friends."

"Great, great. Look, Tenley, I was up late working. Do you need anything else?"

"His name is Jonas, but you don't have to worry or anything. He's not my type." Yeah, just lie to the man and *yourself.* "He's a furniture designer."

"I'm not worried. How much have you written?"

"Nothing. What about you?"

"Finished the first rewrite of our script."

"Our?"

"Yeah, Nicolette and me. Didn't I tell you?"

"When would you have told me? We haven't talked, Holt."

"Nic stayed on in Paris after the symposium. She liked my screenplay of the midwestern boy showing up in Manhattan as green as the spring grass, and we've been rewriting. It's funny, Ten. Really funny. I'm proud of it."

"Funny like teenage-boy funny? Or funny as in poignant and ironic?"

"A bit of both."

She tugged on a loose thread waving up from the robe's pocket seam. "Send it to me. I want to read it." *Don't freeze me out.*

"Yeah, okay. I'll check with her. We're keeping it tight since Nic's name is on it."

"Since when did you start calling her Nic?" She resisted a stab of jealousy.

"*Nicolette* gets cumbersome."

"A-are you having fun?"

"Paris in spring? What do you think?"

"I wish I was there." Tenley yanked on the loose thread dangling from the robe's sleeve.

"Yeah, Ten, me too." Holt yawned. "Call me later, okay?"

"You can call me."

"Okay, I'll call when I get up. Get some sleep, babe."

She smiled with the vibration of being called *babe.* "I love you."

But he'd already hung up. "Love you too, Tenley," she said to the air, to the bed, to the wad of dirty laundry.

With a yawn, she turned off the light. As she drifted off, a thump from below became a bloodcurdling scream.

"Tenley!"

Blanche? She kicked out of bed and darted across the creaky hardwood to the banister. "Blanche?"

"Well of course Blanche. Who else would it be?"

"Why are you screaming?"

"I fell . . . my wrist. I think it's broken."

"Broken?" Tenley darted down the stairs to Blanche's bedroom. Snapping on the light, she found her mother crumpled on the bathroom floor. "What happened?" She knelt beside her, aiding her to an upright position. "Can you stand?"

"If I could, would I have had to call you?" She winced, holding her wrist against her side.

"Careful, I could always go back to bed and leave you here."

"I wanted a stupid drink of water so I came in here. It's that ridiculous rug. Look at it, all twisted up and mocking me."

"Let's not blame an innocent rug. Why didn't you turn on a light?"

"'Cause I know this bathroom. Don't need one." She winced again, doubling forward. "It hurts like a—"

"All right, let's go."

"Where?"

"ER." Tenley hooked her arm under her mother's and drew her forward. "Use your left hand to push up."

"The ER? Come on, it's not as bad as all that."

"Your complexion is green."

"That's from the chemo."

"We're going. If I have to help you pee for the next few weeks, I want to make sure you're really hurt."

"Pee? Oh, law, I didn't think I could sink lower than cancer and chemo."

After helping Blanche don her robe and slippers, the two of them headed out, Tenley grabbing the keys to Blanche's Mercedes off the hook by the garage door.

"Look, we're the robe-and-slippers sisters." Blanche laughed between low moans.

"Finally we have something in common. Can you buckle yourself in, or do you need me to help?"

"I can do it." Blanche took the strap Tenley offered and stretched it across her body. "So you went to the Sullivans' last night?"

"You saw my note?"

"How'd that happen?" Blanche winced as she buckled in.

"I went for a bike ride and ran into Jonas."

"Literally?"

"Yes. I'm dead, but my ghost came back to help you." She raised the garage door with the remote and backed out.

"So, you and Jonas, sitting in a tree, k-i-s-s-i-n-g?"

"I'm engaged, Blanche." Sorta. Eighty percent.

"So you say. Please don't tell me you were wearing that robe last night."

"With the socks and slippers."

"I'll call Ailis later and apologize." She winced, holding her wrist, her complexion pale in the dashboard lights.

"No need. I took them off and stuffed them in the robe's pockets."

"Better yet, I'll send her flowers. Remind me."

When the Cape Canaveral Hospital sign came into view, Tenley pulled around to the ER and helped Blanche inside.

"Don't get old, Tenley. It stinks."

"Youth isn't all it's cracked up to be either."

"Then you're doing it wrong."

She aided Blanche to a waiting room chair, aware for the first time how frail her mother was, feeling every rib under her palm. Collecting Blanche's information, she signed her in, giving the admitting attendant details on her health.

"She's a cancer patient . . . on chemo . . . fell . . . maybe broke her wrist . . ." When she returned to the chairs, she gave Blanche the wait time. "About five minutes."

"I can wait five minutes." Blanche looked over at her. "So, tell me about your cowboy."

"Screenwriter."

"When did you fall in love with him?"

When did she . . . "What?"

"When did you know he was the one? Did he make your heart sing? Make the hair on the back of your neck stand up?"

Really? This was where Blanche wanted to go while sitting in the ER at three thirty in the morning? "My life's not a romance novel, Blanche."

"Still, at some point the boy had to make your stomach flip-flop."

"Did Dad make your stomach flip-flop?"

A slow smile spread across her face. "Indeed he did. And more than my stomach."

"Okay, that's enough."

"So you and this Holt . . . when did you fall in love?"

"I don't know . . . midnight at Starbucks over coffee and chocolate croissants. We both wrote there at night and started noticing each other. I was working on my master's thesis and he a screenplay. When Dad died and I started writing *Someone to Love*, things changed between us."

"He was there for you."

"Yeah, he was." What a nice reminder. She forgot that sometimes. "We started dating a year ago. When I moved to a new place. He came with me."

"Is he smart? Funny? Handsome?"

"Yes, and he's from a well-to-do family. So he's not mooching off me."

"Does he love you? That's really what I want to know."

"He proposed, didn't he?"

Blanche reached up with her good hand, tweaking Tenley's chin. "That doesn't mean he loves you." Her tired blue eyes contained no guile. Just a surprising affection.

"I think he does, yes. But then again, you loved Dad and look how that turned out."

Blanche turned aside with a huff. "I was too restless for my own good."

"Then when you finally settled down, how come you never came back?"

She shook her head, holding her wounded wrist to her chest. "He wouldn't have wanted me. Married two more times, neither of them lasting more than three years." Regret watered her confession. "That's a lot of heartache, Tenley. Don't do what I did."

"He would've taken you back, Blanche. We both would've."

"I don't think so. He never even hinted such to me."

"When I was writing *Someone to Love*, I think I had you two in mind." She misted with emotion. "Joely and Ezra were you and Dad. I was so overcome with melancholy I think I wrote the romance I wanted you two to have."

"You saw me as Joely?" Blanche pressed her good hand on Tenley's arm. "How generous."

"You really read the book?"

"I told you I did."

"And you really liked it?"

"As I said. Loved it. You're very talented."

"Well, maybe. And don't give me too much credit. I was just trying to deal with my grief."

"So, I was Joely?"

"In theory. Probably a little bit me. We were the woman Ezra loved. The one he wanted to give the best. Ezra was everything great about Dad. Hyperbolically speaking, of course."

"Naturally. Your dad was a good man."

Tenley stood up and stretched, jamming her hands into her pockets. "He never went on a date because he put me first. His boss at the janitor job wanted to promote him, but he turned it down so he could be home every night, cooking supper, asking me about my day—preteen girl stuff, of which I'm sure he cared little—helping me with my homework, throwing in a load of laundry, washing up the dishes, answering school or PTA e-mails, arranging for me to visit friends. Guess he was getting his dose of the everyman. He'd prep for the morning while I took my bath. About eight, he'd sit down to write and I'd curl up in the big chair by his desk to read, falling asleep in the first five minutes. He'd scoop me up, kiss my forehead, and tuck me into bed, singing 'Jesus loves you, this I know, for the Bible tells me so.'" Tenley glanced at Blanche. "That's the man you left."

"Rubbing salt in my wound won't change who I was or what I did, Tenley. I can only try now to make it right."

"I'm not rubbing salt, but . . . he loved you. Looking back, I can see it. Feel it."

"I'm sure he didn't after I left."

Tenley returned to her seat with a glance at the reception desk. The nurse should be calling Blanche in soon. Funny, the conversations that the wee hours inspired the heart to speak. Like grief, even a small crisis forced honest insight.

"Every once in a while I'd wake up, see the den light on, and sneak out of bed. I'd curl up in the big chair with my pillow and blanket while Dad tapped away on his computer. Without looking up, he'd lean over and pat my leg. 'Everything all right, Ten?' Then he'd go back to work." Tenley pressed her hand to her forehead, understanding highlighting her memories. "He worked so hard. By the time his first book was published, he had ten more stacked in the closet. And I think, Blanche, he was trying to answer a longing—"

"Blanche Albright." The nurse stood at the edge of the reception chairs. But neither Blanche nor Tenley moved.

"Answer what longing, Tenley?" Blanche clung to her arm.

"For you. I think, deep down, he was always longing for you."

SIXTEEN

ELIJAH

By January's end, Eli was both energized and exhausted with the whirlwind season. Opera performances were followed by magnificent balls, midnight suppers, and weekends in the Hamptons at the Gottliebs' estate.

After Birdie's direct admonition that she would never be his, he picked up his sword, so to speak, and faced his duty.

Nobility appealed to the Gottliebs and New York society, and it seemed every lady of esteem desired an English earl at her table.

He also earned the respect and envy of the men for escorting one of the city's most beautiful and beloved daughters. Rose was, after all, a rose—alluring and fragrant with a porcelain complexion, raven hair, and eyes the color of the deepest sea.

Standing among the men in Alva Vanderbilt's enormous, glorious ballroom, Eli caught sight of Rose among the women, hiding coyly behind her fan.

He'd grown to enjoy her this past month, refining his affections for her. He'd yet to propose, but they both seemed to be enjoying the chase. The ritual of dating.

His pursuit. Her retreat.

Nevertheless, the senior Gottlieb, Franz, suggested the entire family travel to Hapsworth in the spring to meet Papa and Mama and introduce Rose to London society as the future Countess of Montague.

"She can get acquainted with you and your family at Hapsworth and adjust to her surroundings and future home with her family in tow for comfort."

The news delighted his parents. It meant the match was progressing nicely.

Alfonse maneuvered along the perimeter of the ballroom, kissing every female hand offered him. He was a flirt to be sure. How could Birdie's parents match her to him?

A porter passed with a tray of drinks, and Eli helped himself as he scanned the room for Birdie, searching for her mass of auburn hair or a glance from her wild hazel eyes.

For the life of him, he could not rid her from his mind. Efforts to dislodge her in the morning were overcome by the evening as he entered the Metropolitan or some magnificent ballroom.

He'd fail his mission were he not careful. To be sure, Rose delighted him in so many ways. Charming and winsome, she was at ease in every situation. Her mother had trained her well. He'd also found her to be a quick wit and skilled storyteller.

So what commanded his affection for Birdie? The unmet kiss? Was it as simple as lust? A young man's yearning to taste the forbidden? Surely he had more mastery over his senses and desires.

"Taking in the view, I see." Alfonse clapped him on the shoulder and nodded toward Rose. "You're a fool if you don't fall in love with her. She's the most beautiful woman in the room."

"Might I say the same of you? If you don't fall in love with Birdie Shehorn, you're a fool's fool."

"What makes you think I've not fallen head over heels?" Alfonse cocked a confident grin. One Eli knew well.

"Because you kissed the hand of every lass as you entered." Eli spotted Birdie across the ballroom with her parents. How lovely she looked, wrapped in silk and fur, diamonds sparkling around her neck and in her hair.

"Surely you joke. Is that not a gentlemanly thing to do?"

"Then tell, where is your future intended?"

"She's . . . well . . ." Alfonse scanned the room, adjusting his bow tie, smoothing his hair, catching the eye of every lass in his line of sight. "She's—"

"There." Eli pointed to her, then shoved his friend toward the shadows of the room's edge. "Listen to me, you stupid chap. You will never in your life come across any treasure as great as Birdie. More than your wealth and riches, more than your clubs and sports, more than a stable of prize horses or houses in the Berkshires or yachts to sail the highest seas. She will be your greatest joy and comfort in life. So please, be a man." Eli popped his shoulder. "Draw yourself away from silly distractions. If I hear you've wronged her, I might sail from England to land a fist in your ugly mug."

Alfonse regarded him with a stern, dark gaze. "Eli, you make me suspect you're in love with her."

"My affections belong to Rose." His answer held the required confidence. "But Birdie is a friend. And I know a good, worthy woman when I see one. What do you need with all your frivolous flirtations? Grow up." Had he sold his bit? Hidden the truth?

"I see the war has made you forthright."

"When you must point a weapon at another man's head before he points one at yours, there is little time for diplomacy."

"Then I heed your advice. You're a true friend. You're right. Birdie is special, is she not?"

"More than any woman in the room."

"Save for Rose."

"Of course."

"Have you proposed?" Alfonse said, waving at Birdie when she looked their way. "I was going to wait until the end of the season, but perhaps I should propose sooner."

"I've not proposed yet, but I have a day in mind." Valentine's Day. A day that came supplied with romance.

The orchestra struck up a quadrille and Rose appeared before Alfonse, holding up her dance card.

"Alfonse, I believe this dance is ours." She nodded at Eli. "I hope you don't mind."

"I am bound by the rules of the dance card." He tipped his head toward her. "You look beautiful, Rose." Raising his cane, Eli leaned to see her bedazzled card. "Tell me, which are mine? I hope they are all waltzes."

She gave her dance card a coy review. "We shall see." She linked her arm through Alfonse's with a backward glance at Eli. "We shall see." The game of chase and retreat continued.

Leaning on his cane, Eli watched the dancers. The women swirled past in lovely costumes adorned with gold and diamonds. Not to be outdone, the men glittered with gold watches and diamond cuff links.

Rose and Alfonse danced the reel with grace and expertise representing everything this New York society treasured—youth, gaiety, wealth, and beauty.

For a moment, Eli rued his cane and the price of the war. Wouldn't he love to glide around the floor with his future bride, the envy of all?

His advice to Alfonse rebounded through him. He also had a

gem of a woman. One to be honored and cherished. He must dedicate his every affection to her.

Contented, making peace with his future, he turned to see Birdie standing near, listening with focus as charmless Hubbard McGlen prattled on.

He stepped toward her, his resolve to forget her shredding like dry winter wheat. "Good evening, Miss Shehorn."

She turned. "Lord Montague . . . hello. Mr. McGlen, may I introduce Lord Montague."

"Yes, indeed, we've met." The man tipped his head toward Eli. "It's a pleasure to see you again."

"And you, sir."

The quadrille ended and Rose took up with another partner, as did Alfonse. McGlen made his way toward the older men by the punch bowl and Eli was alone with Birdie.

"You've no one on your dance card, Birdie?" He reached for the gold-embossed piece swinging from her wrist. "I see this dance is mine."

She glanced at the card, keeping her gaze low, away from him. "It's another reel. You don't have to—"

He caught her by the arm and led her down the hall, ducking inside the first open door.

"This must be the smoking room," he said, easing the door closed, the atmosphere heady with tobacco.

"Eli, what's all this clandestine tomfoolery?" Birdie remained near the door. "I should go." But her feet remained planted.

"I just wanted a quiet moment." He sat on the settee, patting the cushion next to him. "May I say how beautiful you look?"

His heart thundered as he spoke, while his head rebuked him. Being in her presence invigorated him. It was more than wanting to taste her sweet lips. He wished to hear of her day, ask her thoughts, ponder life with her.

"Eli, is this wise?" She hesitated, then joined him on the settee.

"Perhaps not, but at the moment I don't care." He peered at her through the low glow of the chandelier's electric light. "How are you? What have you been doing since that afternoon at Barclay's?"

"Well. Dreaming of a new story to write." Raising her chin, she stared toward the fireplace.

"And Alfonse?" Eli stood, pacing to the fire. "He plans to marry you."

"Is that why you brought me here? To champion your friend? Eli, do what you must for your family and the Gottliebs, but leave me to my own choosing."

He returned to the settee, taking her hand in his. "Why must duty require me to break my own heart?"

Her eyes glistened, reflecting the light of the room. "We live in a world of fortune and luxury, yet how poor and sad we are at times."

"I don't want to be sad. But I'll take poor if it's with you." Eli gathered her in his arms. "I can't help but wonder if you and I were pledged together—"

"You are speaking things that cannot be." She shoved away from him. "I cannot let you break Rose's heart. It's easy in passion's moment to say you don't care about poverty, but you will when we are living on nothing but—"

"Love."

"—a meager allowance. You will have regret. How would you support us?"

"I'm a captain in Her Majesty's army. I can take a permanent position. You, well, you could write your novels. We'd get by, Birdie."

"You and I have never known 'getting by,' Eli." She refused to look at him, tugging at her gloves and straightening the folds of her skirt. "You belong to Rose. It has taken me weeks to not think of you every waking moment." She stood. "We should go. Remember, Rose and Alfonse are our friends."

"Of course, you are right." In the amber firelight, he could see the pulse of her heart in the delicate lines of her neck. "I think I could love you with every ounce of my being." He reached for her, nudging his nose against her cheek, her warm breath sweet against his skin.

"Eli—" He feared she'd pull away, but trembling, she leaned against him and he knew nothing but her.

There was neither darkness nor light, debt nor wage bills, Hapsworth repairs nor taxes. In this moment there were no arrangements or obligations.

Just the sweetness of holding the woman he loved.

Taking her hand, he pressed it against his chest. "My heart beats for you."

Her eyes searched his as she raised his hand to her heart. "And mine for you."

Gently, his lips touched hers and he knew his mistake. One would never be enough. She tasted like honey, dripping and sweet.

"Eli—" Raising her hand to his neck, Birdie wove her fingers into his hair and clung to his second kiss, her passion sinking into his skin.

"I'm yours, my love." His lips trailed the slim corridor of her neck.

She'd just expressed a loving exhale when the parlor door banged open, sending a large swath of light over the young lovers. The formidable Mrs. Shehorn stood in the doorway, her countenance as stone.

"Elizabeth Shehorn, Alfonse is searching for you. Lord Montague, your fiancée is likewise looking for you."

He cleared his throat but took Birdie's hand, hiding it in the folds of her skirt. "Thank you, Mrs. Shehorn. We'll be along."

She laughed. "Haven't you done enough damage, Lord Montague? Birdie, come with me this instant."

Birdie squeezed his hand, then slipped free, disappearing into the light and music beyond the door.

Mrs. Shehorn regarded him and Eli braced for her rebuke. "If you love her, leave her be." She slammed the door behind her.

Shaking, Eli dropped to the chair, the heat from the fireplace failing to warm him. The kiss. He was lost in it, tasting her lips, feeling her form against him.

He may never find his way free. He loved her now more than ever.

"You've mucked yourself up now, Lord Montague."

Eli jumped up, scanning the room. "Who's here?" The light of a match flared just beyond the draperies, highlighting the astute features of Geoffrey Shehorn. "I came in here for a smoke and some quiet. Then you two came in. I didn't realize it was my daughter until the intimacies had started." His cigar glowed in the darkness, sending the scent of burning tobacco through the room. "She can't beat her mother, Eli. She knows it. I know it. Everyone knows it. Except maybe you." He tapped his ashes in the nearest gold and silver ashtray. "Iris will have her married to Alfonse Van Cliff by year's end. She'll settle down into the life of an heiress, married to an heir to one of the biggest fortunes in the world. Day by day she'll become a leader in society just as her mother foretold. She'll bear children and ensure the Van Cliff–Shehorn dynasty."

"Sounds like a prison of sorts."

"I'm sure you're familiar with its bars." Shehorn sat in a chair, crossing his legs and loosing the button of his tuxedo. "Everyone knows why *you're* here. To prop up your land and title."

"The match was brokered for me by my aunt and mother while I was in Africa."

"We may be in a new century, Lord Montague, but our ways have not changed. Birdie will marry Alfonse. She talks of writing and being on her own—with my money I'm sure—but her mother will win. Mrs. Shehorn always wins."

"You don't give Birdie credit. She knows her own mind."

"Yes, but she's no match for her mother."

"And you won't help her."

He puffed on his cigar, laughing low. "I oversee millions of dollars, yet one stout and stubborn woman oversees me. She is the master at home, I her servant."

"Don't you care whether Birdie marries someone she loves? Who loves her?" Eli poured the man a glass of port, then sat in the adjacent chair.

"My ancestors wanted nothing to do with the Old World. Your world." He puffed on his cigar, then sipped his port. "The one with class divides and royalty, aristocracy. They believed all men were created equal. But today, we seek royal unions. We're marrying our daughters to dukes and counts. Princes. Our Knickerbocker grand-fathers are turning over in their graves."

"I'm sorry you find our lot so distasteful. But I do love your daughter."

"Lord Montague, you're a good man. I like you." Shehorn stamped out his cigar, leaving the smoldering stick in the ashtray, and drained the last of his port. "But if you make a play for Birdie, she'll be cut off. There will be no wedding settlement. There will be no inheritance."

"Even if I take no settlement for myself or Hapsworth, you'd disinherit your only child?"

"Good, you understand me." Shehorn stood, squaring his tie, buttoning his coat.

"So she's to be trapped in the cage of your will."

"Trapped? I prefer to call it safe." He motioned for Eli to follow him. "Now, you heard my wife. Your future fiancée seeks you."

SEVENTEEN

TENLEY

Dropping down to the beach, she dug her toes into the cool sand and lifted her face to the sunrise, the dampness in the air soaking into her skin.

Overhead, seagulls flew in random formation, cawing, swooping down to see if she carried any treats.

She did not.

Four hours in the ER with Blanche and they were home. She'd fractured a bone in her wrist, so the doctor wrapped her in a cast, warning them to be patient, because chemotherapy slowed the healing process.

Digging up a fistful of sand, the grains sifting through her fingers, Tenley felt a bit fractured herself.

Blanche had performed an X-ray of sorts with her waiting-room questions. When did she fall in love with Holt? Did he love her?

She'd assumed those things. They lived together. Did life together. Holt proposed. Wasn't that love?

Though she'd never said yes. She didn't wear his ring. Was that the problem?

Pulling out her phone, she messaged Holt. One word. Yes. Her finger hovered over the Send icon.

Jonas. There. She admitted it. She liked him. The way he cared for others and filled out a pair of Levi's got under her skin.

She shot up from the beach and shouted at the waves. "I did not come here to meet anyone. I came to write. Do you hear me? Write. And take care of her . . ." She gestured toward the house. "So don't try to sneak in some twist to this simple plot."

Yeah, like the wind and waves cared? But it felt good to get it out.

The snap of the wind caught the edge of the robe and it flapped behind her. Tenley deleted the text to Holt and turned toward the house, the seagulls chasing her, crying out.

Don't . . . don't . . .

The Atlantic beat against the shore.

Be dismayed. Nor afraid.

The seagulls and the sea sang her song. Tears slipped across her tired eyes, but as she walked under the ivy-covered trellis into Blanche's backyard, she was smiling.

JONAS

He sat in his usual spot at Simply Delicious Café & Bakery, across from Rob and Marvin, eating a breakfast of eggs, bacon, French toast, and coffee.

The trio had eaten here every Monday morning since he came home from college, injured and lost without baseball. A torn rotator cuff ended his pitching career.

Rob and Marvin got him through, helping him gain an identity outside of baseball. They listened when he started dreaming of designing furniture. He had to do something with his hands. They stood by him when Cindy ran off with Mason, taking his heart and his dreams.

"Have you seen Miss Blanche's daughter?" Rob asked, holding up his coffee cup for Nita to refill.

"She came to Wednesday dinner last week."

"You asked her out?"

"Nope. She was riding a bike down A1A. I rescued her from killing herself. I was on my way to the folks', so I had her tag along."

"What's this?" Marvin said. "I haven't heard of a new woman in your life."

"She's not in my life." Jonas dripped syrup over his French toast. "Listen, we need to get on the Holmes order as soon as we get into the shop."

The three of them worked for Crammer Custom Cabinets, the job Jonas landed after Cindy and Mason stole his money and designs.

"I don't care about the Holmes order," Marvin said, leaning on his elbows, his broad arms too big for his shirt. The man had been a superstar wide receiver for Alabama until a torn ACL took him out of the game. Ended his hopes of going pro. Cabinet work tided him over while he finished his degree at UCF. "Who is this chick?"

"She's crazy, man," Rob said. "We went to get a desk from Grove Manor and this girl said it was 'her people.' Begged Jonas not to take it."

Marvin shook his head. "Mm-mm-mm. But he did anyway, didn't he? He wanted that desk to jump-start his new business."

"Nope, he made me haul it back upstairs."

Marvin sat back, disbelieving. "Uh-oh. Is there a crack in your romance armor?"

"Nope. By the way, she's engaged."

"Too bad. Is she pretty?"

"You can see for yourself." Rob motioned with his coffee cup. "She's at the front door. Tenley, hi, remember me?"

"Oh brother." Jonas sank down in his chair. He'd just worked her out of his system over the weekend.

"Rob, right?" Tenley stood at the end of their table wearing, no surprise, a robe and slippers. "Hey, Jonas."

"Tenley, what are you doing here?"

"Looking for coffee."

Marvin offered his large, dark hand. "Marvin Strover, nice to meet you. Pull up a chair and join us." Under the table, a large booted foot kicked out the chair next to Jonas.

"I don't want to interrupt. I can sit over there." She pointed to a lonely two-top in the corner.

Rob hopped up, holding out the chair. "Please, sit. You're not interrupting."

Nita paused as she passed, setting down a menu and napkin roll. "Coffee?"

"Please." She held up the white Corelle coffee cup. "You got anything larger? Maybe a small soup bowl?"

"Don't worry, honey. I'll keep you topped off."

Jonas made a face, passing her a menu. "How is your stomach not a barren wasteland?"

"I don't know. Maybe it is." She sipped her coffee, eyes closed.

"You need to eat if you're going to guzzle coffee."

"I don't do breakfast."

"Toast and eggs are pretty good, but I'm not sure they're certified organic."

"Shutty uppy." Nevertheless, she glanced at the menu. "I'll have eggs and toast. Are you happy?" She set the menu on the edge of the table.

"I speak for your stomach . . . yes. So, how's the writing? How's Blanche?"

"She broke her wrist last Thursday. Otherwise she's fine. We have another chemo treatment tomorrow."

"She broke her wrist?"

"Fell in the bathroom."

"I'm telling you. If you need anything, let us know."

"Thank you."

"And writing?"

Tenley turned to Rob and Marvin. "So how do you two know Jonas?"

"High school."

"Here's to good friends." She saluted them with her coffee.

"Going on fifteen years," Rob said.

"You're avoiding me." Jonas leaned to see her face. "How's the book? Has the desk helped?"

She draped her arm over the back of her chair and turned toward him. "Not at all."

"Then can I come pick it up?"

"Sure, why not?"

"Okay then. I'll stop by this week." But he wasn't confident in her answer. He tried to read her expression, determine her sincerity. Was she serious or being defeatist?

She flicked her hand at him. "I'm not sure about anything."

"I loved writing in high school," Marvin said. "It was my best subject."

"Is writing a subject?" Rob said. "'Hey, Marvin, what class do you have next?' 'Writing.'"

"Okay, then English, wise guy."

"As I recall, you spent most of English class writing love letters to Michelle Jackson, who was *way* out of your league." Rob exchanged a glance with Tenley as if she were a part of their personal history. It sat well with Jonas that his buddies included her.

"At least she knew how I felt. As opposed to Jana Alcott, whom you *still* admire from afar. And by the way, Michelle danced with me at our ten-year reunion."

"Pity dance if ever there was one."

"Pity dance? You'd kill to have a pity dance with Jana."

Jonas roped his arm over the back of Tenley's chair. "What we have here is Darryl and his other brother Darryl."

"Darryl?" She made a face. "Who's Darryl?"

"*The Bob Newhart Show.* Larry and his brother Darryl and his other brother Darryl. Come on, you know it."

"Clueless here, Cocoa Beach."

"What? This is a crime against good television. It's the series where Newhart ran a New England country inn. His neighbors were these crazy woodsmen . . ."

"Still clueless."

"Come on." He raised his cup to Nita for a refill. "The final show of the series is television history. Classic." Jonas laughed. "Mom called the youngest twins, Joshua and Caleb, Darryl and Darryl until they were ten."

When Nita returned Tenley ordered eggs, then pointed to Jonas's French toast. "That any good?"

"The best."

"Okay, bring me some of that but with sugar-free syrup."

"Diet Coke, coffee, and sugar-free syrup, and you're worried about red meat?"

"Should I ask your friends about your quirks?"

"So, sugar-free syrup? Is it good? I'll have to try it."

Her eyes laughed at him, and he hated how it warmed him. Made him happy. *She's engaged, man!*

Marvin interrupted, thank goodness, leaning her way. "What's with the robe?"

"I have no idea. I just like it." She wrapped the edges around her, covering her shorts and T-shirt. How did she do that? Just walk right in and find a seat in his heart? "Another quirk, I guess. So if this *Bob Newhart Show* is a classic, how come my dad and I never watched it? We consumed a lot of classic TV. *I Love Lucy*, Dick Van Dyke, *Star Trek*."

"What are you doing tonight?" Jonas said, a germ of an idea sparking. "We were just talking about watching it."

"No we weren't," Rob said. "What're you—"

"Yeah, yeah, I remember." Marvin slapped Rob on the arm. "We were going to tell you. But, um, man, something came up with me. I can't make it."

"We're having a *Newhart* marathon?" Rob made a face. "Who made that call? How about *Longmire* or—"

"Rob, I just got a text from Boss Man." Marvin scooted away from the table, dropping a twenty and a couple of ones on the table. "Said we needed to make a stop before going to the shop."

"I didn't hear your phone go off."

"It was on vibrate." Marvin tapped him on the shoulder. "Let's go."

"Let me finish my coffee. And I have to pay."

"I got you." Marvin yanked Rob's coffee from his hand just as he took a sip. "Boss Man said hurry. Jonas, we'll see you later. Tenley, nice to meet you."

"Where are we going?" Rob snatched up his hat and followed Marvin out the door, and Jonas was alone with Tenley.

"Well, that wasn't obvious," she said, smiling as Nita set down her breakfast.

"They're a couple of idiots." He sighed, shaking his head. "No big deal but do you want to watch *Bob Newhart* tonight? I'll bring the DVDs."

"At Grove Manor? We'll have pizza delivered. I think Blanche might enjoy it." She doused her French toast with syrup and cut a broad piece.

"Seven o'clock?"

"Mmm . . . Jonas, this is good."

"Told you." He smashed a twenty in Nita's hand as she passed and indicated it was for his meal and Tenley's, then grabbed his keys, scooting away from the table. "Sorry to leave you sitting here alone, but I need to get to work."

"I'm not alone. I have coffee and eggs and this amazing French toast."

"Have a good day. Write a lot. You can let me know later if you really want me to take the desk."

"I already know. Take it. It's not doing me any good."

He hesitated, discerning her attitude. "You know, it's not the desk you need to write a book. You just need you. You have everything in you to do what you need, Tenley. So don't worry or be afraid."

Her gaze flipped to him as she lowered a forkful of syrupy toast. "What did you say?"

"That . . . you know . . . you can do it."

"No, that last part?"

"Don't worry or be afraid."

"What made you say that?"

He shrugged. "I don't know. Just felt like the right thing to say. Why? You look a little pale."

She wiped her fingers with her napkin, sitting back with a slow smile. "H-have a good day, Jonas."

In his truck, he slammed the door and cranked the engine, his mind and heart full of Tenley Roth. The way she moved, her quips combined with the underlying insecurity she tried to hide. And that robe. That stupid robe.

Driving A1A to the shop, he contemplated his options. Cancel tonight. Send Rob and Marvin for the desk.

Keep their plans but reinforce the breach in his walls that was letting her in.

Or just let go and *feel* something for her even if it meant he'd lose in the end. Because if he couldn't love without having something in return, then he was nothing.

And for Tenley, he wanted to be something.

EIGHTEEN

BIRDIE

Dancing under the cascading light of a French chandelier over a polished marble floor, the guests wove the ballroom of the Delafields' Fifth Avenue mansion with gold and red.

At the St. Valentine's Day dance, the men donned custom-made gold tuxedos while the women glided about in red gowns trimmed in diamonds.

As the newest members of New York's upper class, the Delafields were eager to impress.

Birdie entered the grand ballroom wearing a new gown of the richest red and smoothest silk, a diamond bracelet over her gold satin gloves and a ruby tiara in her hair.

In truth, she'd wanted to stay home from this party, but Papa and Mama refused to let her.

"Alfonse will be waiting to escort you. He sent you the lovely flowers."

Yes, by all means. Surrender her affections for a bouquet of flowers.

What disturbed her more was Papa. Ever since the Vanderbilt

ball, he'd changed. His interest in Birdie's social life moved from casual to calculated.

Did Mama tell him she had discovered her alone with Eli? Had Alfonse or Mr. Van Cliff spoken to him?

Could he see the blush on her cheeks when her thoughts wandered to the kiss she had shared with Eli? At times, she could still feel the tender wetness of his lips against hers. She ached so to see him, and she had filled page after page with words of her longing for him.

Meanwhile, her parents made the case for Alfonse. This past week Papa invited her to a luncheon, and she arrived to find Alfonse at the table. Then yesterday he announced he'd booked passage to Paris so she and Mama could shop for her trousseau.

Battling Mama was one thing, but adding Papa to her struggle overwhelmed her.

"I see Alfonse." Mama gently pressed Birdie's back, passing over her dance card. "There he is talking to Rose Gottlieb. Isn't she a beauty? Her recent engagement shows. I do believe she and Eli have found love."

Birdie opened her fan and hid behind its ornate design, fighting a sting of tears.

Eli and Rose had announced their engagement this week. They topped the society page of every newspaper with a raving article and a dazzling photo of Rose.

While Birdie had anticipated the news, the reality hit hard.

But never mind. Eli might be engaged, but she was free, and tonight she'd be lively and gay.

"Look at this marvelous display, Mama. Is there a more handsome set of people anywhere on the earth?"

"I believe there is not." She wrapped her arm around Birdie's. "Alfonse is making his way toward us. Isn't he handsome in his gold tuxedo? You must realize what a good match he is for you."

Alfonse bowed before them. "May I have this dance?" Sweeping her into his arms, he turned her in an eloquent waltz. "You are lovely. Red suits you. But white will suit you more."

"White is not my color. I prefer black. Or blue." He was fishing, trying to elicit a response. But if he wanted to know her thoughts on marrying him, he'd have to ask outright.

Over his shoulder, Birdie saw Eli dancing with Rose. She *was* stunning in red with her dark hair and pale skin.

Eli caught her eye and smiled.

"I must tell Eli and Rose congratulations."

"They seem most happy," Alfonse said in time to the music.

"Are you happy, Alfonse?"

"Happy? Of course. I've nothing to be unhappy about. Why do you ask?"

"Can't I ask a simple question?"

"Then turnabout is fair play. Are you happy, Birdie?"

"I suppose. Happiness is a choice, and I choose to be happy."

The music changed, and the orchestra played a jaunty quadrille. Daniel Wentworth came to claim her. Birdie enjoyed Daniel, a portly young man with too many chins and an easy laugh. Yet an exceptional dancer.

Moving through the rhythm of the reel, taking one hand, then another, crossing over and back again, warming to the joy of dancing, she felt her hand clasp into *his*. Elijah's.

How resplendent he looked in gold with his black hair slicked in place, exposing the high curves of his ruddy cheeks.

"Miss Shehorn, you look wonderful."

"Same to you, Lord Montague."

Too soon the dance moved her down the line back to Daniel, then to Alfonse, who danced with Helena Struthers, a sought-after debutante. Birdie had seen him with her before, talking in low tones, whispering into her ear, making Helena laugh and pat him with her fan.

Alfonse was a handsome, imposing figure, with eyes the color of a bright sky. No wonder the ladies loved him. But could Birdie? And could he resist the adulation of others?

When the dance ended to resounding applause, Alfonse caught Birdie by the waist. "Let's have our photograph."

"Our photograph?" Wouldn't such a permanent thing encourage him?

"Come. It will be fun. After all, the Delafields went to all the bother of hiring a photographer."

Choose to be happy . . . "All right, if you wish."

He offered her his arm and led her up the grand curved staircase with the lion's-head newel posts to the second-floor salon, where the Delafields' photographer had set up a makeshift studio.

They found themselves entering a queue until a liveried servant came around, issuing them a gold nugget engraved with a number.

"Please enjoy the fire and a glass of champagne while you wait."

Alfonse tapped his glass against Birdie's. "To us."

She watched him a moment. Was he the sort she'd dream about at night, creating stories in which he was the dashing hero? Was he *her* knight in shining armor? The one she imagined as a young girl?

No. Simply no. Try as she might, she just could not hurdle the barriers in her heart.

"Are you going to propose?"

He choked on his champagne. "That's rather bold, Birdie."

"I've been told you are but you've not gotten around to it. So are you?" Really, she wanted to put them both out of their misery.

"I've plans, yes. Everything is arranged."

"What is the delay?"

He shied away from her with a glance toward the photographer. "I'm waiting for the slightest hint of a yes."

"I'm waiting for the slightest hint of an ask."

The room steward called a number. "Five."

Alfonse raised their nugget and moved with Birdie toward the photographer, where Elijah and Rose were posed, smiling.

"Shall we give them a run for their money as the couple of the season?" Alfonse said. "Upstage their engagement with our own?"

"It's not a competition, Alfonse."

"No, but competition always adds a bit of fun."

Elijah and Rose completed their sitting, and as the photographer prepared his next film, Birdie and Alfonse greeted the newly engaged couple.

"Happy Valentine's Day." Eli shook Alfonse's hand, nodding toward Birdie.

"Rose, you are a vision," Birdie said, leaning toward her with a kiss. But when she tried to draw back, Rose hugged her, not letting go.

"I can't . . . " she whispered, her fingers digging into Birdie's shoulders. "I can't." When she stepped away, her eyes bore the unmistakable sheen of tears.

"Miss Shehorn, I meant to give this to you at an earlier time. I've been carrying it around for a fortnight." Elijah retrieved a newspaper clipping from his chest pocket. "A clipping from a publisher seeking stories."

Birdie scanned the headline with a glace toward Rose. "A writing contest?"

"Birdie, the photographer is waiting on us." Alfonse gave her a gentle push.

"Scribner's Sons is seeking stories that might engage a child in understanding Christ's gospel," Eli said. "Surely you could pen something simple but true. Perhaps a story from the pages of the catechism."

"How did I miss this?" She pressed her gloved hand on Elijah's. "Much obliged."

"It was buried in the back of the society section."

"Could there not be a clearer metaphor?" Birdie turned over the cutout to see a photograph of Rose's face. She glanced up at him, their eyes meeting. A metaphor indeed. "Pardon me, but I've not congratulated you on your engagement."

"Thank you." He nodded with a side glance at Rose. She'd linked her arm through his, holding on to a trembling smile. "We're talking of an August wedding."

"Yes, August." Her words quivered.

Rose, darling. Whatever is the matter? Birdie's heart longed to comfort the poor girl. What frightened her? Surely not Eli himself. There was no one like him. How could she not be madly in love?

"Your turn, Mr. Van Cliff." The steward urged them toward the photographer.

With a backward glance at the newly engaged couple, Birdie caught Rose looking back at her, pleading.

"Rose seems to be happy," Alfonse said, aiding her onto the photographer's set. "We had a good chat earlier. She's beaming with love."

"What makes you say so?"

"She said as much."

Birdie posed with Alfonse, his arm too familiar and too tight around her waist. As for Rose, Birdie knew what the men did not. She was playing her part. Doing what society—and her parents—expected.

The photographer snapped the photo, and when they were

through, Alfonse led her to the balcony overlooking the ball-room.

"Take a look around, Birdie. This is our world. We are the hope and future of New York society and thus the world."

She watched the dancers swirl about the floor, searching for Rose and Eli. "Perhaps we think too much of ourselves."

"Mark my words, you and I will shape the next generation."

Perhaps. With her words and stories. But never as Mrs. Alfonse Van Cliff.

TENLEY

By Monday afternoon, she'd written several hundred words. Actual, real story words.

Just to get the juices going, she closed her eyes and typed, her heart spilling through her fingers. The spontaneous inspiration was lovely but short lived.

The writing was a creative match—fast and hot with a quickly dying flame. One couldn't cook a meal with a match. Nor could one write a book.

But she was desperate, so she chased the flame.

Téa Jones was going on a date whether she wanted to or not. Those were the rules. Not that she followed the rules, but once in a great while she conceded they were good for something.

She'd back out, but she'd bet her best friend, and she'd never let Allie win. No sir. Trouble was, she never counted on Joshua Huntington calling and asking her to dinner at Longdoggers Beachside and a movie.

Josh Huntington, the high school track star who never looked her way, ever, wanted to share a jumbo popcorn and an armrest with her at the Bijou?

Slipping into her heels, no boots, no flip-flops for a casual night, she felt a fear that made her want to dive for her phone and text him to cancel.

Because . . . Because why?

Why do not you want to go out with him, Téa Jones? You scaredy cat, you two-dimensional, flat . . . jj fdka fi tia fkahufhiukjas jha ida huiteha fdah ka.

Tenley slapped the keyboard, pushing away from the desk, which, by the way, Jonas could most *definitely* have. She'd made a fool of herself over nothing.

Doubt blew out her flame. She'd just written the most honest words she'd written since *Someone to Love* but couldn't think of another thing to write.

Write who you are . . .

Well, what if you're lost? And a big fat nothing?

As she uncurled from her chair, stretching away from the negative vibe, her gaze landed on the stuck middle drawer. She gave it a tug. It still didn't budge.

"Why won't you open? I may be stuck, but you're not going to be." She *would* open this thing and see what was inside. Besides her tiny slip of paper. She may have no command of her muse, but this drawer would yield to her will.

Dropping down onto the chair again, Tenley gave the knob a firm yank. The desk tipped toward her, but the drawer did not open. Getting a better grip on the pull, she propped her feet on the legs and tried again.

Nothing.

She bent to see underneath, but everything looked normal to her untrained eye. No weird nails or screws holding it shut.

Tenley tugged again. Nothing. She went to the second-floor railing. "Blanche, what's up with this desk?" Leaning over the railing, she listened for an answer.

A thump resounded from below. "Blanche?"

Tenley bounded down the stairs into her mother's bedroom. "Don't tell me you broke your other wrist."

She found her mother on a stepladder in the closet, searching the top shelf with her good hand.

Tenley pressed her hand against Blanche's back, holding her steady. "What are you doing?"

"Looking for something." Blanche toppled another box to the floor.

"Stop, you're going to get hurt. What do you need?" Tenley coaxed Blanche over to her bed, then peeked into the closet, finding a row of boxes along the wall.

"I was looking for something to give to you. It's in one of those boxes."

"But you don't know which one?" There must be a couple of dozen. Not large, but large enough.

"I think it's a pink hatbox."

Tenley scanned the top shelf and the built-in shelves. "There are five pink hatboxes. Did you really wear that many hats?" She reached for the first one, tipping it over the shelf edge with her fingertips.

"That was my British phase."

"You had a British phase?"

"I briefly dated a low-ranking aristocrat."

Tenley peeked around the closet edge. "How did you find time to love so many men?"

"I had nothing else to do."

"Maybe come home and raise your daughter." Tenley set the first pink box on the bed, then took out the rest, lining them up.

"So we're back to that."

"Did we ever leave it?"

Averting her gaze, Blanche popped the lid from the box to find a pink hat with a pink feather plume. "Nope." On to the next.

"What are you looking for?"

"You'll see when I find it."

Blanche lifted the lid of each box as Tenley put them on the bed. "That's the last one. And next time you want to visit the closet, call me. How's your wrist?"

"Fine, fine. Ah, here." The fifth pink box revealed a tin canister and a collection of disorganized photos. "Look here at this old reel-to-reel. I'd forgotten I stuffed it in here." Blanche tossed the tin aside and dumped out the photographs.

"What are these?" Stretching across the bed, Tenley shuffled through the black-and-whites and faded color photographs of smiles and faces she'd never seen.

"That's my mother." Blanche tapped the top photograph. "Wasn't she a beauty?"

Tenley regarded the black-and-white image of a woman in her twenties. Judging by the hairdo, it was taken in the '50s. She *was* beautiful with her almond-shaped eyes, high cheeks, and full lips.

"Did I ever meet her?"

"When you were a baby. She died when you were two. Smoker her whole life. Don't smoke."

"No worry. Can't stand the stuff."

Blanche leaned for a closer look. "You look like her."

"I look like her?" Tenley rose up to look into the bureau mirror, patting her knotted ponytail. This woman was beautiful. She was . . . rough, not showered, and—oh man, she'd sat with Jonas and his friends at breakfast. "I'm a mess."

"You wouldn't, if you'd wash your hair and change out of that dang robe. Shoot, even Roger didn't like it that much."

"What happened to Roger?"

"His secretary."

Blanche flashed up another photo. "This was my dad. In high school. Mom used to carry it in her wallet. Wasn't he a looker?"

Tenley sat on her knees. "Did I know him?"

"No, he died when I was fourteen. Look, here's another one. This is my great-grandfather, sometime around 1920, I think. Isn't he totally GQ? Look at the shine on those shoes."

"H-how did he die? Your dad . . ." There was so much Tenley didn't know.

"Heart attack. Forty years old. Mom was never the same. *We* were never the same." Emotion rose in Blanche's voice. "You know how you said Conrad was always searching for me? I think I've spent my life searching for . . . something. The shrinks would say my dad, and they'd probably be right. I never appreciated my mother. Nor my husband, and by husband, I mean your dad."

Tenley stared at the images of the grandparents she never knew, Blanche's remorse echoing through her.

She didn't want to live with the regret of not giving Blanche a chance. Even if she didn't deserve it. She wanted to blurt, "Then why didn't you appreciate your own daughter?" but held her tongue.

Tenley reached for another photo. A faded seventies Kodachrome. "Who's this? Looks like you there on the left."

"Yes, me and your aunt Reese."

"Were you close growing up?" Reese was pretty, like Blanche, with thick curls and an impish grin.

"Sometimes. She's four years younger so we never really had the same circle of friends, but when we were older we forged a friendship." Blanche sighed. "She never forgave me for leaving your dad. Or you."

"Yet she came to help you this spring?"

"Our relationship still walks with a limp. She's the one who suggested I call you."

"Why didn't she ever reach out to me? To Dad?"

"It's a fine line to walk when your sister leaves her family, Tenley. Then she married, moved west, and started her own family."

"What do you do with your regrets, Blanche?"

She gently touched the photo she held. "Try not to visit them very often."

"So, you have it all worked out? The choices you made, the hurt you caused won't affect you." Tenley tossed the photo of her grandmother back to the box. "I should get back upstairs." From the robe pocket, her phone pinged. It was Jonas. Texting to say he'd be by tonight as planned.

"Wait, I want to give you something. I pulled these boxes down for a reason." Blanche spread the pictures across the bed, spotting the one she wanted. "And no, I don't have it all worked out. You asked, and I answered. I don't visit regret often because there's nothing I can do about it. Here."

She passed a framed image to Tenley. Beneath the glass, the woman Blanche had identified as her mother held baby Tenley.

"My mother and you. I thought you'd like to have it."

Tenley dropped to the bed's edge. "Where was this taken?" The soft-focus background suggested a house. "How old am I?"

"It was taken right out there." Blanche pointed to the living room. "You were ten months old. Conrad and I came down for Christmas."

The image of herself in her maternal grandmother's arms sank through her senses into her soul and answered a longing she didn't know she possessed.

"Can I keep this? Dad and Grandpa weren't much for pictures." Tenley pointed to the pile on the bed. "Apparently you weren't either."

"I'm not an organizer."

"I do have one of Grandpa with Grandpa Gordon Phipps Roth. That one is cool."

"Is it hard being a descendant of such a beloved author? Not to mention your father's reputation." Blanche shuffled through the photos. "You can take any photo you want. Take the whole box."

"I don't know . . . it's not like I wake up every day going, 'I'm Gordon Phipps Roth's great-great-granddaughter.' Or 'I'm Conrad Roth's daughter.' He was just Dad to me."

"Maybe it's subconscious. Maybe it's why you're blocked. You're trying to live up to—"

"I hadn't really thought of that until now. Thanks. I was mostly worried about my own success, but now that you've added dear Dad and Great-Great-Grandpa to the mix, I'll be good and blocked."

"Sorry."

"Forget it. I really can't blame you or them. Only myself." Tenley sighed, glancing at the photo. "Thanks for this, Blanche."

She smiled softly. "You're welcome."

"I'd better get back to work. Jonas is coming tonight with pizza and some DVDs. *The Bob Newhart Show.*"

"Really? I loved that sitcom."

"Good. I'll meet you in the living room around seven. He's taking the desk too. Might as well. It's not helping me, and he wants it."

"Oh, Tenley, are you sure? You were so hopeful about it."

She scoffed. "Goes to show what I know. How can wood and varnish inspire a real novelist?"

Turning to leave, Tenley caught the edge of a thick gilded frame under a scattering of photos. She pulled it free, finding a regal-looking couple by a car on the beach, dressed in what would have been Sunday best in the forties. "Who's this?"

Blanche leaned to see. "Oh, that's the Marquess and Marchioness of Ainsworth. I'd forgotten I had that picture."

"So they really did live here?"

"Of course. Did you think I made it up?"

Tenley made a face, shrugging. *Maybe.* "Cocoa Beach in the forties had to be the exact opposite of aristocratic life in England." Especially landed gentry. Tenley flipped over the photo, looking for a date. Sure enough, 1947.

"She was a Gilded Age heiress. Her father owned land here and they built the house in the early '30s, spending winters here. They moved permanently right before the war, I think."

Tenley studied the image. The marchioness was beautiful, classic, in the way one expected of heiresses and aristocrats.

Yet she had a rebel air about her and wore an "I dare you" expression. The marquess was the definition of *dashing*, his hat pushed back on his head, a sporty grin on his lips, one hand tucked into his suit pocket and the other around his wife.

"They were in love," Tenley whispered.

"What?" Blanche said, lost in examining photos of her own.

"Nothing." Then, "Do you believe in true love, Blanche?"

She looked up, regarding Tenley for a moment. "Seriously? You're asking a woman who had four husbands."

"Well, do you?"

"Yes. But I think for some people it never happens."

"That's depressing. I-I mean if there's no such thing as true love, what's the point in life?" Tenley said, eyes fixed on the picture of the marchioness and marquess. "C-can I have this?"

"Like I said, take what you want. All of this is yours when I die anyway."

"You're not dying."

"Well, not today but someday."

"You don't have to leave it all to me, Blanche. How about your sister or her kids?"

Blanche's eyes shimmered when she looked up. "Because it all belongs to you. You're my heiress." She flashed a watery smile. "Now, see . . . you made my eyes water."

Tenley patted her arm. "Stop or you'll make my eyes water." She reached for the tin. "What's this?"

"An empty reel-to-reel tin. There used to be one of Reese and me as girls, but I don't know what happened to it or the projector. Roger was fascinated with it, so he might have hauled it off."

"Too bad."

Blanche handed Tenley another photo. "Your dad and me on our wedding day. Look at me with my big hair and Princess Di puffy sleeves."

It was strange seeing the two of them together, smiling, happy. Tenley added the photo to the collection in her hand. "Dad never said a bad word about you. Ever."

Blanche organized the photos. The small ones together, the large . . . "Thank you for that . . . though I gave him plenty of ammunition. You asked about regrets. One thing I don't regret is you."

"You had a funny way of showing it."

"I suppose I did."

Tenley held up the pictures, finding no response to Blanche's honest answer. "Thanks for these. But I'd better get back to the grind." She started out of the room, then hesitated. "See you at seven for Jonas, pizza, and Newhart?"

"See you at seven."

Back in the library, Tenley set the photos on the edge of the desk, studying the images behind the glass, feeling oddly connected to the people of the past, and feeling oddly connected to the woman downstairs.

NINETEEN

BIRDIE

The evening passed with great pains as the giant hall clock bonged eleven, then midnight, when Papa retired, and finally one. Mama, the ever-vigilant chaperone, dozed in her chair by the fire.

Birdie rubbed her hand along the back of her neck as Alfonse gathered the cards from the last round of two-handed bridge.

"Good night, Alfonse." She stood, reinforcing her intention.

"Good night?" He retrieved his pocket watch, checking the time as if he'd not heard the solitary chime. "The night is young. Were we at a ball, we'd just be sitting down to dessert."

"Let's save our energy for the Gottlieb ball tomorrow night." Birdie motioned to her mama. "I should send her to bed. Her maid must be weary with waiting."

"You made your case." Alfonse shoved his chair under the table. "But I shall miss your company."

He'd been trying the past week and a half to be more attentive. More charming. But his compliments were hollow, falling short of the mark.

Taking her hand, he walked to the grand hall, where a footman waited. "Bring Mr. Van Cliff's coat and hat, please."

"Are we going to decide soon?"

"Decide?" She pulled free, resting her hand on the curve of the banister, wishing the footman would hurry with Alfonse's things. "We know what we're wearing to the Gottlieb costume ball."

"Yes, of course. There, at last, my coat and hat." Alfonse slipped his arms into the sleeves as the footman held up his coat. "I'm going as a European prince. And you—"

"Joan of Arc. It's all settled. Let's not bring it up again."

"Why you want to go as a martyr is beyond me."

"She was courageous. Stood her ground. Remained true to her beliefs."

"Then I shall be the prince who saves you from the stake." Alfonse leaned toward her, brow arched, fingers catching her chin. "Your father would like to make the announcement before the end of the season. We've only a few weeks left."

"What announcement would that be?"

"Don't be coy. Of our nuptials."

"What nuptials?"

He whirled away from her, muttering a low expletive. "What do you want from me?"

"What do you want from me?"

"You know full well—"

"As do you."

His cheeks brightened as he jerked his leather gloves over his large hands. "Then I shall say good night."

When the door clicked closed behind him, she pressed her fingers to her lips, muting her laugh.

"Why do you torture him?" Mama came from the shadows.

"Eavesdropping, Mama?"

"He fears your rejection." She joined Birdie by the staircase. "You know what he wants. Just answer him."

"Answer him? He's never asked me a question. Yet he constantly speaks of marriage as if the deal is complete. While it may be in his mind, it is not in mine. Since everything has been decided for me, can't I at least have a question to which I can say yes or no?"

"I think that's his fear. You'll say no."

"Surely not. He's a Van Cliff. The halls of Clifton are loaded with portraits of Van Cliff men strutting and posing like wild stallions. A possible no from a girl he doesn't truly love should not cower him."

"You do paint a picture with your words." Mama yawned and patted Birdie's shoulder. "But don't be coy. Give him your yes, and love will follow. Either way, you and I sail to Paris the end of March for your trousseau."

They climbed the stairs in silence. Birdie had wished to sneak away to her attic tonight to write or read. Scribner's Sons had published the latest Henry James book, *The Wings of the Dove*. But the evening passed with cards and conversation.

"Mama?" She paused by her bedroom door. It was in these rare and wee, weary moments she could speak her heart to her mother. "What if I refuse him?"

"Birdie, please, it's late. Don't pretend. You are marrying him." Mama continued toward her room. "Now go to bed. Get some sleep. Don't read."

"Did you marry for love?" The question came from a deep wondering in her heart. Birdie had wanted to ask since she was a girl but never found the courage. "Or did you marry Papa for position and money?"

Mama stood at her bedroom door, her back to Birdie. "Why ask such a thing? If I had not married your papa, I would not have had William, my beloved son, may he rest in peace, nor you. Now good night."

"I want to know. Did you marry for love?"

Mama twisted the knob on her door and slipped inside. "Good night, Birdie."

In her bedroom, Birdie leaned against the door, clutching her hands to her chest. Love. Wasn't anyone willing to speak of love *and* marriage? What exactly was love?

The subject of sermons? Of the Christ on the cross?

Or the emotions that moved poets and writers?

Was it the sometimes distant, sometimes formal exchange between Papa and Mama?

Perhaps a stolen kiss? Or a surrender to illicit passion?

Could love bloom in a marriage arranged between families?

Or was love a choice? Did her feelings for Eli speak of love or girlhood infatuation? Could she just choose Alfonse and love him?

Her maid knocked on the door and Birdie stood aside to let her in. "Are you all right, miss?"

"What do you know of love, Fatine?"

"I'm only seventeen, miss. I don't know much, I'm afraid."

"Certainly. Well, neither do I."

Elijah

The hearth fire blazed, filling the leather-accented drawing room of the Manhattan club with warmth. The low glowing lights and the sound of men's voices were far from Elijah as he sat with Franz Gottlieb's lawyer and the one Father had retained to represent the House of Ainsworth. A Mr. Len Pile, who'd relocated to New York in the '90s.

"Everything seems in order." Pile reviewed the final draft of the financial settlement between the Gottliebs and the Percys. "Very generous of you, Mr. Gottlieb."

"Nothing but the best for our Rose. She's aptly named. As fine a woman as the flower, but mind you, Montague, she's not without her thorns."

Eli chuckled over his rising nerves. "Then I shall take heed." The moment of truth. Once the documents were final, he must keep true. He could not change his mind. It would be scandalous.

"With this agreement, you're locked in, Lord Montague." Gottlieb's lawyer, Mack Van Buren, reached for the gold fountain pen resting in the well in the center of the table. "Best learn to deal with the rose as well as the thorns. Shall we sign?"

Pile sat forward. "To be clear, the transfer of funds and the stocks will take time. We'll confirm when they are complete."

"We'll begin first thing in the morning." Gottlieb sat back, crossed his legs, and motioned for a porter to light his cigar. "By the time you and Rose sale for York, matters will have concluded."

This morning, passage had been booked for Elijah and the Gottliebs to sail to England at the end of March.

They'd spend time at Hapsworth before taking on the London season, introducing Rose to Eli's peers and society. Then Rose and her mother would travel to Worth's and arrange her trousseau. In November, they would marry in New York.

"I've no doubt of your sincerity and integrity." Eli reached for the pen, sensing Gottlieb's delight at granting his daughter the finest of everything. Somehow, Eli must fit into the picture, prove himself worthy.

Hearts and futures were on the line. Expressly his and Rose's.

Since the Valentine's Day ball at the Delafields', he'd mused over the image of Rose clinging to Birdie as they left the photographer's parlor, her eyes brimming for no apparent reason.

He inquired of her but she assured him all was well, then went on about how she and her mother were planning a trip to Worth's and sampling wedding cakes.

Yet, the other evening at the Gottliebs', he saw Rose sneak into a water closet during a break from the dinner party. He could've sworn he heard muffled weeping.

"Lord Montague, your glass." Pile nudged him, motioning to the glass of brandy the porter set in front of him.

"To Rose and Elijah," Van Buren said, standing.

Eli struggled to his feet, leaning on his cane, joining his future father-in-law and their lawyers. "To us," he said, tossing back his drink, the burn of the alcohol numbing his anxieties.

Soldier on, mate. Fulfill your duty.

News had arrived in England of their engagement, and the king and queen sent congratulations to Hapsworth.

"Montague." Gottlieb leaned in for a private conversation. "You'll find Rose up to the task."

"Of course." Eli offered a reassuring smile. "I've no doubt."

"I sense your wariness but she's strong and capable, well-educated, and as fine a beauty as you'll ever see."

"You're proud of her."

"She's my heartbeat."

"I'll do my best to be worthy of her." Elijah set his glass on the table, his knee aching as it often did in the evenings. "But life on a country estate is quite different from life in New York. The winter months are long and dreary. I'm still engaged in Her Majesty's service as a captain with the fusiliers and will travel from time to time."

"Rose is resourceful." Gottlieb brightened as he spoke of his daughter. "She knows the value of hard work. I made sure of it."

"What of being an ocean away from her friends and family?"

"She'll make new friends. She's always been keen with people, able to find the good in everyone. You've seen how lively she is at parties, the center of attention." Mr. Gottlieb arched his brow. "All we ask is that you let her and the children return home for the season every few years. We shall visit, of course."

"I insist you do." Eli sat back, waiting for the peace that came when one bypassed one's mind and trusted in the will of the Divine.

Gottlieb recognized a man who'd just entered the room and excused himself.

Van Buren watched Eli through curling cigar smoke. Approximately his father's age, the society lawyer was a dashing chap with a certain savoir faire.

"I envy you," he said after a moment. "You're young, handsome, privileged, and about to marry a wealthy, beautiful young woman."

"Did you miss your turn at the altar, Van Buren?"

Van Buren smirked, tugging at his bow tie. "More like I escaped."

"Certainly there was a fair maid who captured your heart."

"What makes you say so?" Van Buren motioned for the porter to bring another brandy. "Perhaps many a fair maid has captured my heart."

"I may not have your years and experience, but I'm quite certain there is always one young lady to steal—and perhaps break—a young man's heart along the course of his life."

Van Buren exhaled a line of smoke and sobered. "She was obligated to another."

"Love . . . a complicated business, is it not?"

"Especially when families and money, and titles, are at stake."

Van Buren retreated into silence, and Eli was grateful. He needed to be alone with his thoughts, pondering the deed that was done today.

Unwittingly, his thoughts drifted to Birdie. Was she happy with Alfonse? No announcement had come from the Shehorn household of their nuptials. Was there anything he could do for her before their paths parted?

"Van Buren." Eli leaned forward, waving off the swirling smoke. "What if you suspected a theft but had no real proof?"

"Then you'd have no real case. Why? What's been stolen?"

"I've reason to believe an unpublished manuscript."

"Who would want to steal an unpublished manuscript? Was it from someone famous? Mark Twain? Jack London?" Van Buren tapped ashes from his cigar.

"No, nothing so esteemed. This manuscript belonged to a friend. It's quite possible it was merely mislaid."

"I'm intrigued. What makes him think his manuscript might be stolen?"

Eli angled a bit closer, lowering his voice. "A publisher is producing a book very similar to my friend's title and story."

Van Buren arched his brow. "Which publisher?"

"Barclay."

Van Buren laughed. "One of the prize publishers in the city with a stellar reputation? Does your friend take opiates?"

"No, of course not. It's just my friend submitted *his* manuscript to Barclay and has never seen it again. Though there is a receipt showing the publisher hired a courier to return it. But the package seems never to have arrived."

"Without proof, you'd be laughed out of the publisher's office. No judge would waste his time. Besides, if your friend intends to keep writing, suing a publisher would be literary suicide." Van Buren stood, acknowledging someone else in the room, his interest in the conversation waning.

"So the thief wins?" Eli said.

"My dear man," Van Buren said as he stepped away. "A good thief always wins."

So that was it. Birdie lost her manuscript. So then she must keep writing and trying. He motioned for a porter, and when he arrived Eli asked for pen and paper. He'd write to Birdie to encourage her. Remind her of the call for stories he'd found in the paper.

He signed the note *Your friend, Eli*, then addressed the envelope. Soon he'd sail home with Rose and everything would change.

He'd no longer be privileged to inquire of Birdie's life and dreams. She'd belong to another, as would he.

"Take care, Lord Montague."

He glanced into the concerned expression of Stow Van Cliff, a pipe on the edge of his lips, a glass of brandy in hand.

"Do you have words of caution, sir?"

"He's unscrupulous. . . Van Buren. Only sees to his own ambitions regardless of what it costs others."

"You've gone head-to-head with him, then?"

"Back in the Tammany Hall days, yes. He was a young apprentice of Boss Tweed."

"Seems rather unforgiving to hold a grudge these years later."

"I would agree had his legal and political ambitions not cost me a great deal of money and stabbed me in the back at the same time."

"Are you shy on capital, Mr. Van Cliff? It seems to me you are faring rather well. Your son has made a good match and—"

"I see your point, Lord Montague. Now you see mine. A man's word and character is his bond. What has he left if he sells his soul for a buck? If he betrays his friends? Ask around. Van Buren has more enemies than friends."

"May I ask what he did to you?"

"In the early '80s, Geoffrey Shehorn and I were young men. We conspired together with a bit of investment from our fathers to export goods west, to help build the country. Van Buren used his political sway to engage us in a war of duties and taxes, lobbying for another company to take the trade route, while to our faces, he promised his support. We drank with him when we lost. He was our friend. We later discovered he'd invested heavily in the company that took the route."

"But you've recovered. Surely you forgive his ambition."

"I do not forgive. I'll never do business with him nor any of his acquaintances. Even sitting in conversation with him sullies a man's reputation. If he had sons, I'd see to it they never crossed my path. I do not trust him or any of his blood relations. He's the lowest of men to lie and cheat his friends." Van Cliff lowered his chin and bent toward Eli. "He has also been in more Fifth Avenue and Newport bedrooms than allowed any decent man." He arched his brow. "Do you hear me, son?"

"I'm not unfamiliar with the ways of the world."

"So be wary, Lord Montague. You've been warned." With a nod, Van Cliff backed away. "Check your pockets. He may have already stolen your watch."

The man rejoined his card game, leaving Eli to ponder his warning. He'd bear it in mind should Gottlieb suggest him for future dealings.

Across the room Eli caught Mr. Gottlieb engaged in a head-to-head conversation with Van Buren. Should he warn his future father-in-law? Surely he knew of the man's ways.

With a sigh and a growing heaviness, he glanced at the rich American men populating the room with their tailored tuxedoes and imported libations and wondered if any of them were happy. Genuinely happy. Were they in love with their wives and children? Did they possess enough of the material world or did they thirst for more?

Had they fallen into the trap of his lot in Britain—men who had everything yet gained nothing?

Be grateful, Eli. As for him, he may not have the woman of his heart, but he had a good woman, a beautiful woman. With her wealth and good family name, along with his title, they'd make something of themselves.

He reached for his glass of port, standing to join Gottlieb and Van Buren, listening in for any folderol and resigning himself to no more regrets.

The only way to *his* happiness was to firmly embrace his future.

TWENTY

JONAS

"Mom, where are the DVDs of *The Bob Newhart Show*?"

Mom came from the kitchen still wearing her shirt and jacket from the workday. "In the hall closet. Why?"

Jonas shrugged, heading down the hall. "I want to watch them."

"You just had a bright idea today to watch old *Newhart* DVDs?" Mom stepped out of her low-heel shoes, curling her toes into the carpet. "What's up?"

"Nothing." Ah, there, he found them. Top shelf. Buried in the back. "I just met someone who's never seen the show."

"Tenley?" The trouble with moms was they looked too close, saw too much, and read between the proverbial lines.

Jonas tucked the DVDs under his arm and closed the bifold doors. "Marvin, Rob, and I ran into her at the diner earlier this week. She didn't get my Darryl-and-other-brother-Darryl reference, so . . ." He sounded casual, right? Totally casual.

"And it's incumbent upon you to educate her?"

"She's a writer. How can she really portray Americana if she hasn't watched *The Bob Newhart Show*?" He started for the door before Mom dug any deeper. He knew the questions she'd ask, and he didn't have the answers. Well, he had one. "Don't get any ideas. She's engaged."

Mom frowned. "Really? I didn't see a ring."

"You don't have to wear a ring to be engaged." He kissed Mom's forehead. "Gotta go. See you later."

"You don't need a ring, but it's a good start." Mom held up her hand, flashing her wedding set. "This says I'm not alone. Someone walks with me, watches my back. It warns other men not to fall in love with me."

"Ah, Mom, didn't work with you. Every man falls in love when he meets you."

"Stop right there. Your fake charm doesn't work on me. Jonas, if Tenley loves this boy—"

"Mom, she's here to help Blanche and write a book. Not assess her life." He held up the collection of shows. "I'm just doing my part to educate her on classic American sitcoms. Besides, she's letting go of that desk I wanted from Blanche. I can pick it up and start restoring it. I'll sell it to Mrs. Shallot and have more seed money."

"You got it all worked out, don't you?"

He hesitated. "What's that supposed to mean?"

Mom stepped up, pretending to unlock his heart. "Cindy's been gone a long time."

Ah . . . "Good-bye, Mom." But Jonas carried her words in his chest. Felt a pang from her unlocking of his heart. Well, he'd lock it back up before he sat down to watch *Newhart* with Tenley.

At his truck, Dad waited by the driver's side.

"Going to watch *Newhart*?" He pointed to the box.

"What gave it away?" Jonas grinned as he tossed the DVDs into the truck, knowing Dad wasn't lurking around for small talk. "Tenley's never seen the show. Everything all right, Dad?"

The man shifted his stance and stared toward the river where the afternoon light dazzled.

"Can't seem to bring myself to say the words."

Jonas leaned against the truck, folding his arms. "You need money?"

"Your mother doesn't know I'm asking. I told her we were fine."

"What happened?" He'd helped out his parents before. Gladly. But he hated how it made him feel like a scrutinizing parent while his wise, hardworking father took the posture of an undisciplined child.

"Bills piled up. A little here, a little there. Last-semester expenses for the E's. Thank goodness they're mostly on scholarship. Caleb and Joshua are both playing football and have spring camp fees, plus a gym membership. It added up. We're still playing catch-up from your mom being laid off. Even though she's got a good job now."

The Sullivans had gone through a lot of hard times when Jonas was growing up, but Dad and Mom kept a roof over their heads—even when the sheriff kicked them out of their rental—and food in their stomachs.

They just never seemed to catch a break. One financial tension chased another. Just when they got ahead, one of them was laid off. Or the car broke down. Or the refrigerator broke. Or the pipes flooded. The list went on.

Mom deserved sainthood for the laundromat years.

"How much?" Because he'd been saving to get his business going again, Jonas had some money set aside to buy lumber and tools. Mason took half when he hightailed it with Cindy.

"How much do you have?" Dad's laugh fell flat. Too much truth in his question to be a joke. "To be honest, about a grand."

The last of his savings. Especially since he'd paid Blanche for the desk.

Jonas kicked at the tuft of grass boldly growing through the driveway cracks, a scripture he'd tucked in his heart years ago rising to the surface.

Do not withhold good . . . when it is in your power to do it.

"I have a grand, Dad. It's yours." How could he refuse his father, the man who raised him, the man who taught him about life, about Jesus? Taught him how to shoot a gun and bait a hook? Made sure he respected his mama, sisters, and brothers?

"Just so you know, we told the girls not to expect anything fancy for their graduation."

"Doesn't seem right. They've worked hard."

"But I can't borrow money from you and then throw them a big shindig."

"You're not borrowing money from me, Dad. I'm giving it. It's a gift. You don't owe me."

"Can't do that . . . We'll catch up and pay you back. I know you're trying to recover from your own loss."

"Forget it." He popped open the truck door. "Consider the money payback for twenty years of raising me."

"You did eat a lot." Emotion choked Dad's laugh. "I suppose you're wondering why I don't ask your brother Julius since he's an engineer and all. But—"

"It's our secret, Dad."

"I think Julius would lose respect for me, Joe. I really do."

"There's where you're wrong." He popped Dad on the shoulder, then pulled a twenty from his pocket. Last of his cash for the week. "Take Mom to dinner. Have fun."

"No, no, now. I can't, Jonas."

"Take Mom out to dinner on me." Jonas stuffed the bill into Dad's work-shirt pocket. "I'll deposit the thousand in your account in the morning."

From behind the steering wheel, Jonas watched his dad go

inside, his shoulders slightly hunched. Didn't he know he was the family hero? Even amid the struggle, the Sullivans could always count on him. Because he never quit and never gave up.

Jonas hoped to be just like him.

BIRDIE

By the midday light falling through the high windows, Birdie sat at her desk and smoothed her hand over the newspaper clipping Eli had given her.

It was his encouragement that drove her to consider answering the Scribner's Sons call for children's stories about Christ.

Picking up his letter, she read it again for the tenth time.

> Dearest Birdie,
>
> I hope this note finds you well. I sail for home soon, and in case I don't get to say good-bye, be well, my friend. Do not give up on your writing. You are talented, and in my humble opinion, the world needs to hear your stories. Until we meet again.
>
> Your friend, Eli

How was it he had swept back into her heart so quickly? She would miss him when he was gone.

Beneath her, the house was quiet. Mama napped and the staff went nimbly about their chores.

Lighting the desk lamp, Birdie took out several sheets of paper from the middle drawer. After spreading them across the desk, she reached for her ink pen.

She pondered a short story about Christ, an anecdote she remembered from Sunday school, but her thoughts drifted toward anxiety.

This afternoon Papa pressed her to give Alfonse an answer. He was not humored when she insisted she'd never been asked a question.

She agreed to answer him—which Papa understood to be her consent. Perhaps it was. Until she sat in the attic with Eli's short letter.

Just reading his handwriting and hearing his voice in the words awakened a desire Birdie never experienced with Alfonse. To love and be loved. She could sit with Eli for hours, talking, never thinking of another soul.

With Alfonse, she counted the minutes.

Besides, he'd never indicated any love or affection for her. His non-proposal only confirmed the lack. Staring at the flow of light drifting across the bare hardwood, Birdie closed her eyes. Was she to marry him? Was this . . . God's will?

"But I love another."

As she breathed out, her song whispered across her heart. The one she heard after nightmares. After William died. After one of Mama's spankings. Where it came from she did not know, only that she treasured it now more than ever.

Do not be dismayed, you don't have to worry or be afraid.

"Help me to understand, God."

A tree bloomed before her mind's eye. A beautiful, fruitful tree with birds singing in the leafy branches. Birdie watched the scene with her heart and imagination.

A woodsman appeared, a regal and royal sort of man, and swung a large ax against the tree.

"No." Birdie jerked forward.

Tell this story.

She knew at once it was about the Christ. The one called the Tree of Life, who was cut down for the sins of all men.

Scattering her papers across the desk again, her hand trembling as she dipped her pen, she began to unfurl the scene with her best words.

Once upon a time, there was a garden with a beautiful, powerful tree.

TWENTY-ONE

TENLEY

From: Queen.Brene@BarclayPublishing.com
Subject: Your Manuscript!

Tenley,

Just checking in to see how it's going. Did you see the sales numbers on the mass paperback? We're thrilled.

More good news. Sales-secured end caps (you know, at the checkout counter?) in two chain stores for *Someone to Love* as well as your *next* book for summer reading. You'll be sharing the spotlight with your great-great-grandfather and a special anniversary edition of *The Girl in the Carriage*, and a reissue of your dad's last book.

This is a huge win for all of us, Tenley. We really want to take advantage of your heritage and keep this wild momentum going.

That being said . . . No pressure, right? Are you on track for a July 31 deadline? Do you have anything I can use for the catalog and marketing promo? I don't want to pressure you, but we're cutting it close.

Let me know if you need me. I'm here for you,

Brené

From: Charlie@McGuireLit.com
Subject: Movie Option

Tenley,

Good news, kiddo! Gonda Films optioned *Someone to Love* and is ready to option your *next* book. I just need a description, a paragraph, highlighting the tension of the story, the happily ever after, and the takeaway.

I'm saving the offer until the paperwork is complete but you'll want to be sitting down when you read it. ;p

You know Gonda directed *King Stephen I* with Clive Boston? Which won the Oscar for best picture.

So, send me what you have on book two. Hope it's coming along. Your career is off to a great start. I'm here if you need me.

You've hit the big time!

Charlie

From: JeremiahGonda@GondaFilms
Subject: Welcome to Gonda Films

Tenley,

Welcome to our family. Even though we've not inked

the final deal yet, I wanted you to know how excited we are about *Someone to Love* and that we're eager to hear about your next book. We believe your voice and your stories are perfect for the kind of movies we want to make.

I've been talking to Chris Painter about playing Ezra. I think he's perfect for the part. And Nicolette Carson has been dying to play Joely so we're in talks with her. More to come.

Hope all is going well with you. Looking forward to meeting face-to-face soon.

Jer

TENLEY

She closed her laptop, dropping her head to the desk. She spent the afternoon reading articles on how to write a novel, and downloaded an e-book on writing swoon-worthy romances.

It seemed so simple. Writing romance. Boy meets girl. Boy and girl fall in love. Something happens and they break up. Boy makes grand gesture and wins the girl's heart and ta-da, happily ever after. How hard could it be?

Hard. Really hard.

After the how-to reading, she looked up all her favorite authors, scoured the *New York Times* bestseller list, hunted down new and fabulous books that she might want to read someday, and came away with a paralyzing fear.

She was a hack. At twenty-nine, what did she know about

storytelling? About life? Her father hadn't published until he was almost forty. Gordon Phipps Roth published young but after six books took a sabbatical.

Could she take a sabbatical after one book?

She wanted to write something poignant and meaningful, not just a frivolous story about . . . *whatever.*

The first book, poured out in grief therapy, didn't have to have a point or some profound hook. It was all emotion, all about the larger-than-life character of Ezra, a memorial to Dad.

She wasn't thinking about whose blood flowed in her veins or how her writing linked her to a literary great. She just wanted to feel better.

A robin landed outside her window and tapped the pane. "What do I do, little bird?"

Thoughts of giving up were followed by flares of "No! Not yet." On the desk, she'd set the picture of the marquess and marchioness, along with the one of her with her grandmother.

The picture of Dad and Blanche's wedding day, she tucked into the frame of her dresser mirror.

Picking up the frame of the aristocrats, Tenley studied their expressions. "What kind of story did you live?" She could do research on them. But, ah, she wrote contemporary stories—

"Tenley?" Blanche stood at the library door, her long, thinning hair draped around her shoulders, a box in her hand. "Can you do me a favor?"

"Sure." She jumped up, helping her mother to the club chair by the Tiffany lamp. "You hungry? Want me to get more boxes out of the closet?"

"No, I want you to shave my head." Blanche pulled the lid from the box to reveal a set of dog clippers.

"Um, Blanche, those are dog clippers." Tenley straightened her robe on her shoulders, still bothered by her lack of achievement. The library was warm, too warm for the old garment, but she still couldn't part with it. "And I'm not shaving your head."

"Why not? My hair is coming out." She tugged at her bangs, freeing a wad of grayish-blonde strands. "It's depressing."

"Fine. Then we can go to a salon or barber."

"Please?" Blanche offered Tenley the clippers. "I won't ask for another thing."

"Ha! You can't make that promise."

"Of course not, I'm a chemo patient." She shoved the clippers at Tenley again. "It's a beautiful afternoon. We can go outside and take a few selfies. 'My daughter shaved my head today.'"

The doorbell chimed just in time. "Jonas is here."

"Jonas?" Blanche tucked the clippers into the box, smoothing down her hair. "Already? Do not open that door until I'm in my room. I may be old and losing my hair, but I still want to look nice for a handsome man." Blanche scurried past Tenley down the stairs and into her room, slamming the door.

At the door, Tenley invited Jonas in. "By the way, seriously, take the desk." She swung her arm toward the library, motioning for him to come in. "I'm a complete hack."

"You're not a complete hack." He set the DVDs on the living room table and raised a plastic bag for her to see. "I brought TV snacks. Pringles, M&M's."

"I thought we were ordering pizza." In the kitchen she opened Blanche's take-out drawer. "Do you like cheese? Thick or thin crust?"

"We are, but that doesn't mean we can't have TV snacks. I'll eat any pizza you order. Except anchovies." He stood at the edge of the kitchen, his T-shirt hanging over a pair of shorts, the fragrance of soap rising from his skin.

She ordered two large pizzas—one cheese, one pepperoni—and

set up in the living room. Jonas prepped the DVD player with *Newhart* season one and dropped to the couch next to Tenley.

"So, not a good writing day?"

"Not really. But I don't want to talk about me. How was your day?"

He made a face. "Had to help my dad with something, but it's all good."

"Are you sure? Why the face?"

He shrugged. "When I was a kid, Dad and Mom worked harder than anyone I knew raising a large family. Always kept a roof over our heads, food on the table, decent clothes on our backs. Mom's the queen of the hand-me-downs."

"I was an only child. I didn't have to share or wear hand-me-downs." Sitting back, resting her head on the back of the sofa, Tenley listened, absorbing his story, his voice, his presence. "But I was also alone a lot."

"Only time I had alone time was in the shower and sometimes not even then. Someone had to brush their teeth or use the toilet. Man, my parents made it work with seven kids. Then they hit a season where every time we turned around, one of them was getting laid off."

"So they got behind?"

"Yep. When I was fourteen, they were so late with the rent the sheriff came. Made us move out. Dad . . . I'd never seen him like that. Couldn't look us kids in the eye. We had to sleep in the cars for a week until the church helped us out. For the first time Mom wasn't telling Dad, 'Don't worry, we'll make it, Ferg.'" He lifted his chin. "Do you hear a buzzing sound?"

Tenley listened. "No. What kind of buzzing?"

Jonas shook his head, sitting forward with a low laugh. "Sorry, don't know why I told you that story."

"Because you're thinking of your dad."

"I guess." He glanced over at her. "I had to loan—well, give—him some money. He says he'll pay me back, but . . ."

"You're a good son." She rubbed her hand over the firm contour of his back, a spontaneous but intimate move. Drawing her hand away, Tenley motioned toward the library. "Why don't we get the desk?"

He glanced at her, ignoring her command. "Dad would be embarrassed if he knew I said anything."

"About what?" She made a face and he laughed, crashing back against the couch.

"Thanks for listening."

She held his gaze, a slow, rising heat wafting between them. "Anytime."

"Tenley, I just want to say—"

Blanche's bedroom door flow open. "Is it time for *Newhart*? Hello, Jonas." She wore a pair of shorts and a T-shirt with a colorful turban on her head.

"We're waiting for the pizza," Tenley said, pointing to Blanche's head. "What's with the turban?"

She plopped down to the club chair. "Let's just say one shouldn't use dog clippers on oneself."

TWENTY-TWO

BIRDIE

A fire blazed in the grand salon's hearth as she sat, alone, with Alfonse. Birdie studied her hands, unsure what to do with them.

Five minutes ago the room overflowed with Mama and Papa and fifty dinner guests. Then Percival arrived, announcing that the concert in the ballroom, featuring the orchestra from the Metropolitan, was about to begin.

In a feat only Mama could have arranged, the guests bustled out and Birdie was left back with Alfonse.

"Here we are." Alfonse sat next to her on the fainting couch.

"Why are we here? I don't want to miss the concert." She started to stand but Alfonse took hold of her arm. "The others will wonder why we've hidden ourselves."

Alfonse exhaled. "Isn't it obvious, Birdie? I'm going to propose."

"No, it is not obvious." She leveled her gaze at him with a fresh boldness. "Well?"

She was feeling confident today. She'd finished her Christ story for Scribner's Sons and messengered it over to the publisher right away, certain they'd make an offer.

Even if they did not, the story impacted her. The truth of Christ as the Tree of Life lifted her spirits.

Alfonse dropped to one knee and took Birdie's hand. His touch was cold and clammy. On instinct she withdrew.

But Alfonse reached for her again. "Elizabeth Candler Shehorn, will you be my wife?"

Without any preamble or afterword, he slid a ring down her finger, the firelight catching the brilliance of the gold and diamonds.

"Alfonse, I-I . . ." Birdie held up her hand, finding it more difficult to refuse him than she imagined. "The ring is stunning."

"I commissioned it from Tiffany's just for you. It's not from the family. There will be plenty of heirlooms in our lifetime." He stood, bringing her to her feet, his long fingers trying to intertwine with hers. "Is that a yes?"

"Am I so shallow to accept a life of marriage due to the beauty of a ring? Do you have no declaration of love or affection?" Her heart plummeted. She'd thrown down the gauntlet. If he confessed his love, she'd be obliged to respond in kind.

"Birdie," he said, his smile wide and charming. "Our great-grandfathers sailed from Holland together. It's a wonder the Van Cliffs and Shehorns have not married before now."

"But this is about you and me."

"Yes, and our families have agreed. We're well matched, set to lead New York society. We shall have beautiful, intelligent, prosperous children."

"You make every case for marriage but love."

"You want love, Birdie?" Alfonse released her hands. "Then fine, I'll love you. After all, love is a matter of the mind. Not the heart."

"Then what am I to do? I feel love neither in my heart nor in my mind."

"You have to choose as I do. What do you think William would say? Do you think your big brother would discourage you from marrying his school chum?"

"My dear brother would tell me to follow my heart." Birdie slipped the ring from her finger and pressed it into his palm. "Alfonse, I cannot accept this. You deserve someone who loves you." She raised her eyes to his. "As do I. I want romantic, heart-palpitating love. The sort of love that moves a man to write romantic poetry and sing silly songs."

"You've read too many penny novels." He offered up the ring. "I've proposed, given you a ring, promised love. What more do you want? You must accept. Our fathers, *my* father, are expecting to make the announcement tonight. I cannot go in there and tell him I've failed."

"You have not failed. You've done your part. It is I who has failed. I'm the one refusing this arrangement." She gripped his arm, addressing him as a friend, not an awkward paramour. "Is this really what you want? Am I what you want? Do you want to live in a loveless marriage? I don't, I tell you. I have dreams for myself—and Alfonse, they do not include you as my husband. I'm sorry."

He snatched her in his arms with an aggressive grip. "Do you think this folderol deters me? This talk of dreams and love? I've a mission, a responsibility, and I will see it through." He waved the ring at her. "You want away from your mama? I want away from my father. This is the first step to our freedom, Birdie."

"Freedom? In a marriage without love and affection? What you speak of is more bondage than we already have."

"I see." He sighed. "Yet everyone else in our class is content to marry for name and money."

"Yes, and they're miserable. I've watched our peers in their loveless marriages, taking lovers or waiting until the children are grown to seek a divorce. No, my freedom is in here." She tapped her heart. "I'll make my own way."

"Your father will cut off your inheritance."

"Let him. I'll make my own way, penning novels." The confession vibrated through her. What a blessing to speak her plans out loud. As if they could truly happen. "Mark my words. You'll see my name on a book cover, in the front window of the shops."

Alfonse fell to the couch with a laugh. "You can't be serious. That's your master plan?" He gestured to the room. "You can't live like this on an author's earnings. You'll starve to death. This is our ticket, Birdie."

"No, Alfonse." She tapped her heart once more. "This is my ticket. Making my own way. I don't need this"—she glanced about the room—"to be happy. If I can choose my own path, my own husband, that will make me happy. I want my wedding vows to mean something, Alfonse."

"You've not heard the last of this. I won't be beaten." Alfonse made his way out of the room, slamming the door so hard the salon windows rattled.

Collapsing in a chair by the fire, Birdie whispered her fears to the One she'd meditated on the last few days. How could she marry Alfonse? He was as harsh and determined as Mama! Her wants did not matter.

"So, you rejected him." Birdie turned to see Mama in the doorway, the light from the hallway surrounding her dark silhouette.

"I did not reject him. I refused his proposal. There's a difference."

Mama's gown swished against the salon's furnishings as she crossed the room. Bending over, she inched her nose toward Birdie's. "You listen to me, young lady. You humiliated your papa and me tonight. It's been arranged and agreed upon. If you don't come around, you bring shame on us all. So when Alfonse proposes *again*, you accept him. Birdie, you *will* marry Alfonse Van Cliff."

TWENTY-THREE

TENLEY

Newhart changed her life. Was that sacrilege? She'd just not laughed so hard in so long.

She'd written nothing since Jonas hit Play on episode one of season one. Why write when there was so much good humor in the world?

At first she was unsure about the stuttering comic.

"Am I supposed to laugh or feel sorry for him?"

By episode five she was hooked, pushing Pause to marvel at the eighties high-waisted pants and big hair.

Instead of writing, she settled down in the afternoons with Blanche for a *Newhart* binge.

Two weeks and two chemo treatments with the end of May hurtling toward her. She had to start thinking about her deadline.

Tomorrow.

For now, she retrieved Blanche's mostly eaten dinner and leaned her back against the pillows.

Yesterday's chemo had not gone well for her. She battled fatigue and nausea, and Tenley spent all day cleaning up after her and running loads of laundry.

"Do you think I have cancer because I abandoned you?" Blanche closed her eyes as she settled into bed, sections of her badly shorn hair going every which way.

"What? No. Why would you—"

"God is punishing me."

"Blanche, I don't know much about God, but Dad talked about a God of love."

"He's also a God of judgment."

Tenley knelt next to her mother. "If I forgave you, don't you think God would too?"

Blanche smiled, eyes still closed. "I don't deserve your kindness."

"Yeah, well, we can debate that when you're feeling better."

In the kitchen, Tenley emptied the soup bowl and stacked it in the dishwasher, then bundled up the sleeve of saltines, storing them in the pantry.

A wad of early evening light spilled through the kitchen, beckoning Tenley onto the veranda. Leaning against the rail, she stared toward the beach, listening to the waves and wind.

Where had the last two weeks gone? How could she have squandered so much time? She tried to remember what she'd done with her days besides soaking up *Newhart*, and other than the days she tended Blanche, she couldn't think of anything.

Jonas came by a couple of times. Watched *Newhart*. But she couldn't use him as an excuse.

She'd urged him again to take the desk, but he seemed to have forgotten all about it. Truth be told, she wasn't sure if she wanted the desk for inspiration or out of her sight, giving her an excuse not to write.

I lost my people.

A salty sea breeze slipped through the palms and palmettos and whispered through the veranda.

Tenley exhaled, battling the tension of disappointment. She was letting not only her publisher down, but herself.

And Holt. What was going on between them? She'd not heard from Holt in over a week, when he'd texted some weird, nonsensical message.

Hi! lolololol
Hi back! What's going on? LOL

But he never responded.

"Holt, what are you up to?" Tenley sat on the veranda steps, picturing the man's intelligent expression.

It bothered her that he never answered. It bothered her even more that she hadn't noticed until now.

Snatching her phone from her robe pocket, she called him. It was just after midnight in Paris, but he would be awake.

"Tenley, hello." His slurred words were buoyant. "What's up?"

"Not much. Just missing you. What are you doing?"

"We're out, having dinner and drinks." A cackle punctuated his sentence.

Drunk Holt. She never liked him.

"Who's we?" The screenwriters who attended Nicolette's symposium should be gone by now. "Did you meet more screenwriters?"

The distant clanking of glasses answered.

"Holt? Hello?"

"Sorry. What did you say?"

"Who's we?"

"Nicolette and me."

Tenley heard a female voice in the background. "Hi, Tenley."

"Tell her hi."

"She said hi back." Holt's muffled voice slurred her message. "So, what's up?"

"You sent me a hi, lololol text a few days ago and then nothing else. I texted back but you never answered." Tenley positioned her back against the veranda post, voices and laughter from the beach piercing the seagrass and palmettos.

"I texted you what?"

She sighed. "Never mind. Just look at your phone later."

"Did Blanche croak yet? You can join me here." His voice rose and fell as if he couldn't control it.

"No, she didn't *croak* yet. What's the matter with you? She's doing well. And if she did pass away, I'd expect you here with me."

"Of course . . . absolutely. Don't get bent, Ten."

"Don't wish my mother dead."

"Like you haven't thought about it from time to time. How's the book?"

"Fine." Well, it would be. Tomorrow. And she'd never wished her mother dead. Ever. "Hey, I made a friend here. Jonas. Remember I mentioned him before? His mom is friends with Blanche."

"Yeah? What's he do?"

"Something with cabinets and furniture."

"She made a friend . . . Jonas." By the fade in Holt's voice, he was talking to Nicolette. "Hey, Ten, Nic wants to know if he's good-looking."

"Nothing to write home about." Because she was home. "Why? Does she want to meet him?"

"She wants to know if you want to meet him?" Holt's raucous laugh irritated her. "She said yes. But wow, you should see one of *People*'s most beautiful without makeup. *Scar-yyy.*"

"Oh, shut up. Like you're any better. Don't listen to him, Tenley."

The conversation tripped downhill from there, and Tenley

hung up with Holt laughing over something she could not see and he could not explain.

Slipping her phone back into her pocket, she wrestled with the unsettled sensation growing in her middle. The most important things in her life were in limbo. Her book, her relationship with Holt . . .

In the meantime, she needed a shower. If she skipped one more day she feared vermin might appear from the knot on top of her head. She was sure she heard the sounds of construction up there, the little varmints building a small city, houses, roads, schools for their offspring.

About to dash upstairs, she heard her phone buzz. She hoped it was Holt calling back with an apology and explanation. But it was Jonas's number on the screen.

"What's up, Cocoa Beach?" She smiled.

"How's Blanche?"

"Good. Sleeping. Chemo kicked her butt this time."

"What are you doing?" The sounds of the ocean rocked behind Jonas's call along with muffled voices and the distinct scratch of his phone against his shirt.

"Thinking of taking a shower."

"Do it later. Come out to the beach."

"The beach?" She stood, peering past the trellis and palmettos toward Blanche's clip of the Atlantic. "What for? Swimming? I don't do sharks, Cocoa Beach."

"Eating or swimming with?"

"Neither."

He appeared at the edge of the lawn, his sun-kissed hair waving away from his tanned face, the perfect canvas for his clear blue eyes. As he waved her toward him, she was helpless to resist. The varmints in her hair would have to wait.

"What's going on?" she said, phone still pressed to her ear.

More than his gorgeous self made her step off the veranda. It was his aura. The peace he carried with him.

He was the sun and she a weak, wandering planet, caught in his gravity.

"Do you like seafood?" He met her under the vine-covered trellis, the broad expanse of his chest beckoning her to fall against him and bury her burdens there. It was almost too much after that emotionally empty call with Holt.

"I love seafood." She lowered her phone, ending the call, and peered up at him. "Hey—" she whispered.

"Hey back." His hand brushed hers as he motioned down the beach. "Mom wanted to have a picnic for Wednesday night dinner."

Following Jonas, Tenley found the entire Sullivan clan setting up portable tables and chairs, unloading big blue coolers and trays of food.

Mrs. Sullivan waved. "Hope you're hungry, Tenley."

"I'm starved."

"Tenley, we saved you a seat over here," Erin said. Or was it Elaine?

Jonas nodded for her to follow, whispering, "Erin's in pink, Elaine in white."

"Back off, Sullivan, you're starting to read my mind." She tried to wink at him and he laughed.

"Got something in your eye?"

"No. I just can't wink."

"Stop. Watch." He stepped around in front of her, gazing down, smiling, then slowly, almost seductively, winked. Heart. Be. Still. "Like that."

"Y-yeah, like that." She tried again. He laughed again. Well, it was hard to wink when he was making her so . . . crazy. Like she wanted to grab hold of him and not let go.

"You can do it. Just practice." He walked her over to the family. After only one meeting, she felt oddly a part of this gregarious group, not like an outsider looking in.

Outsider. That was the way she looked at the world after Blanche left. She was a motherless oddball. It didn't matter half the kids in her class only had one parent. She felt isolated and lost.

"Mom," Jonas said. "Blanche is asleep."

"Well, good. She needs to rest. I'll make a plate for her in a bit and run it up to the house. Tenley, she can eat it whenever she wants."

Setting up and sitting down apparently required all the family to talk at once. Because that's what they did. Tenley no sooner got involved in one conversation than another one wove in. How the Sullivans managed to keep them all going was a mystery to her.

At last the plastic cups, plates, and forks were set out with a stack of napkins and food spread the length of the table. Shrimp, corn, and potatoes, with coleslaw and green beans.

"Low-country boil," Jonas said, leaning over her shoulder, snatching a taste of shrimp.

"I always wanted to try low-country boil."

"You've come to the right place."

"Fill your own drink," Mrs. Sullivan said, pointing to the coolers. "We've got sodas, water, and iced tea. Tenley . . ." She motioned to the men and the twins. "Get in quick or there won't be anything left. Joe, help her get some food before the vultures land."

"Really, Mrs. Sullivan, I don't need to—"

"Are we ready?" Mr. Sullivan grabbed her hand and one by one, the Sullivans linked themselves together around the table. "Let's bless the food."

When Jonas's palm met hers he winked, causing her to wobble and tingle.

Bowing her head, she saw her attire. And caught a whiff of her unwashed self, noticing for the first time a Blanche stain on the sleeve. She tried to slip her hand from Jonas's to rub it off, but he held on.

"I really should clean up," she whispered, digging her feet into the warm sand, tucking her stained sleeve behind her back.

"You're fine."

Up front, Mr. Sullivan prayed on. ". . . our blessings. You are so gracious and good to us."

"If you leave . . ." He tipped his bowed head toward his brothers. "There will be nothing left by the time you get back."

Upon the amen, everyone moved to the table.

Tenley released Mr. Sullivan's comforting hand and Jonas's reassuring one, and reached for a plate, shoving in with the E's. Jonas followed, introducing her to his brother Cameron, who'd been absent the night she ate with the family.

When her plate contained a sufficient amount of low-country boil and coleslaw, Jonas suggested two chairs in the middle of the long table.

She ate—so, so good—cocooned in the harmonic dissonance of a large family, where every sound was distinct yet blended. She could make no distinctions in the conversations yet somehow heard every word.

The Sullivans talked baseball, politics, and faith, the upcoming graduation of the E's, and the boy twins' expectations for fall football. They laughed at scenes from *The Bob Newhart Show* and debated whether the Florida coast would see a quiet hurricane season.

Note to self: Leave if hurricane approaches.

After every stomach was full, the boys got up a Frisbee game, running and diving on the sand. Mrs. Sullivan carried a plate up to the house for Blanche. The E's set up a volleyball game with their Dad and Jonas.

Tenley declined an invitation to play ball—her sport was reading—and sat on a beach blanket watching, fascinated by the large-family dynamic.

The twin boys kept changing the rules of the sand Frisbee game in their favor. Their big brothers challenged and taunted them.

The E's were uncoordinated at volleyball but never gave up. She laughed when Jonas tapped the ball over the net and hit Erin square on top of the head.

When the game ended, Jonas dropped down on the blanket next to her. "Having fun?"

The best. "Your family is crazy."

"Insanely." He offered her his hand. "Want to go for a walk? I need to create some room for another piece of cake."

She gave him her hand and he pulled her to her feet, releasing her as they started down the beach.

"You know how you told me your dad asked for—"

"Yeah . . ."

"And how you once got kicked out of your house?"

Jonas walked on, his bare feet kicking through the sand.

"At least you have this." Tenley gestured behind her, to the family setting. "You stayed together. As far as I can tell, you love each other."

"The folks made sure of it. Always found a way. It wasn't fun feeling like a charity case . . . I was embarrassed. I'd never invite my friends over. But now—"

"The Sullivans are the place to be on Wednesday night."

"I never thought of it like that, but yeah, we are." Jonas hooked his arm around her shoulder. "You miss your dad?"

"Every day." Holding up the hem of her robe, Tenley splashed through the surf. "Can I ask you a question?"

"Should I brace myself?"

"Why aren't you married?"

"Ah, the first pitch and she goes personal." Jonas mimed holding a bat and swinging. "Ball one. Next question."

"Looks like a strike to me," Tenley said. "Come on, give it up, Cocoa Beach. Why are you not married?"

"What makes you think I should be married, New York?" The breeze swooped between them, spraying a salty dew against their skin.

"Really? You are *so* the marrying kind."

"Really? Wow . . ." He laughed. "Do tell. What makes me the marrying kind?"

"Look around." She pointed back to the picnic, then at his sand-stained shirt. "You're a big brother, a doting son. You still attend family dinners and play games with your father, brothers, and sisters."

"It's family. What do you expect?"

"Why aren't you off in some big city chasing your furniture-design dreams? That's what most guys would be doing. Family, schmamily. But no, not you, Cocoa Beach. You stayed near home. You're devoted. Kind and sweet, clever."

"You're describing our old golden retriever."

She bumped into him, laughing. "You're telling me there's not a half-dozen women vying for your attention? I don't believe it."

"Nope." He stopped, gazing down at her. "Not even one."

"Then what's her name?"

"Who? There's no—"

"Come on, whenever a gorgeous, single male with all the apparent qualifications to be fantastic marriage material does not so much as have a girlfriend"—Tenley wagged her finger at him—"I know his heart was broken."

Jonas cleared his throat, smoothing his hand over his chest. "You think I'm gorgeous?"

"What? No, I mean, yeah, sure, you're gorgeous. But focus, Cocoa Beach, focus. Answer the question."

"What was the question?"

She walked on through the low-tide water. "She must have really broken your heart. I'm sorry." Tenley waved off her question. "You don't have to tell me. It's really none of my business."

"Cindy," he said, coming alongside her. "Her name was Cindy. We dated for a year and a half, got engaged, and were about six months from the wedding when I woke up one day to find a note stuck under the truck's windshield wipers. 'Joe, I'm so sorry. Forgive me. But it's better this way.'" He paused, facing the sunset. "Took me a week to find out what happened. A week living with questions and hurt . . . Felt like a lifetime."

"Wow, Jonas, I'm sorry I asked. But for the record, she must have been cray-cray to walk out on you."

"I thought so at the time, but looking back, she did me a solid. We would've been miserable as a married couple." He reached for a broken shell and tossed it toward the waves. "You're right, I'm the marrying kind. When I met her, I was ready to settle down. She seemed to fit the bill . . ."

"Love, for all its pleasures, can sure be blinding."

"What about you? How'd you meet your fiancé?"

"Starbucks. He was there the night the police told me Dad died. It was a little after midnight, I was tired, trying to write . . . I just stared at them, unable to comprehend what they were saying."

"I'm sure you were in shock."

"Felt like a weird dream. But Holt was at the next table, working, listening. He stepped in to help. We'd become friends after arriving at the same Starbucks night after night to write. He took me back to the apartment. Slept on the couch. Called my friends, called Blanche. I just wept on Dad's bed."

The memory flooded over her, and for a moment, she was back in the Murray Hill apartment, rushing through the door after school, dropping her backpack to the floor and raiding the kitchen.

"*What's to eat, Dad? I got another A on my paper. Mrs. Merkle said you had to have helped me. It's too good for a fifteen-year-old. Can we order pizza for dinner?*"

"*You tell her you have the blood of Gordon Phipps Roth in your veins.*"

"I'm sorry, Tenley. I can't imagine." He peered down at her, compassion in his blue gaze.

"It's okay. I'm healing." She brushed her hand over his arm. "And you? You're healing, right?"

He nodded, peering toward the sunset. "Cindy didn't just leave me. She ran off with my business partner, Mason. Took my designs and all the money, set up shop in Colorado with someone Mason met in design school."

"When was this?"

"Two years ago."

"Did you hunt them down?"

He laughed. "I should've. I'm a self-taught designer and worked hard on those designs. But I was too brokenhearted, and to be honest, too humiliated to *hunt* them down. You know what? It bothers me more that Mason took my designs than my girl. Who does that? Get your own designs. Creative work is personal, hard fought, mined from the deepest places of imagination. Well, you know, you're a writer."

"You've really thought about this."

"Yeah, because I felt like he took more than one piece of me with him. A piece I can't get back. How would you feel if you worked super hard on a story and Holt just walked off with it?"

"Sick to my stomach. Like I wouldn't want to write again for a long time."

"Exactly."

"So if you're more concerned about the designs than your girl, why are you sitting on the sidelines of the dating game?"

"Because I don't trust myself. How could I have been so blind? What sort of character flaw do I have that allowed me to be duped by both of them? Even when I realized Mason was also gone, I never suspected he was with Cindy. Of course, by then I knew the plans were gone, and I was going through every backup I had to find the originals. He took those too."

"And you had no idea?"

"Nope. Apparently everyone around me had suspicions but not me. I was fat, dumb, and happy."

"Fat, dumb, and happy?" Tenley patted his lean middle. A move that felt more intimate than teasing. "Hardly, Cocoa Beach."

He grabbed her hand. "So, have you figured out why you're engaged but not wearing your ring?"

Tenley pulled free, the exchange between them feeding a hunger in her heart to feel special, to feel loved. "Hey, I'm asking the questions here."

"Now I'm asking. Did you fall in love with him because he was there for you when your dad died?"

"I'm sure his compassion caught my attention, but no, that's not why. It took six months before we started . . . dating. I moved to a new place and he . . . came with me." The confession felt as awkward as it sounded, and she churned with the idea Jonas might change his view of her if she confessed to living with her lover. Tenley glanced toward the picnic area. "You know, I should go. Check on Blanche."

"Are you the marrying kind, Tenley?" Behind him, lights from the hotels and shops raised a golden glow along the shoreline.

"Oooh, foul ball. You can't ask a question that's been asked." She turned for home.

"Oooh, sorry, but I call fair ball. You asked me *why* I wasn't married. I'm asking if you're the *marrying* kind."

"Same thing."

"Nope, it's a different thing."

She sighed. "I don't know if I'm the marrying kind." Tenley faced Jonas as inquisitive seagulls landed beside them. "And I'm not sure why I don't wear my ring."

Jonas brushed the ends of her flyaway hair from her eyes. "Does he tell you you're beautiful? Because you are."

"Jonas, don't." She moved out of his reach.

"Joe!" The boy twins raced his way. "One game of football before we go. Dad agreed to play. Tenley, you want to play?"

"I'm going to check on my mom, but thanks."

"I'll be right there," Jonas said, taking hold of Tenley's hand. "Does he?"

"Why do you want to know? What difference does it make? Go. Play ball." But this time she didn't pull away. Didn't step out of his touch.

"I'm sorry." Jonas released her. "I stepped out of line. I just . . . ah, never mind."

"You just what, Jonas?"

"Don't do what I did. Don't stick with someone who doesn't love you. Your dad wouldn't want it. I'm pretty sure Miss Blanche wouldn't either."

"But he does love me." Bravado. She said it with the hope of it being true. He'd proposed, but Tenley couldn't remember the last time he'd said he loved her. Most likely in a moment of passion.

"Good. I'm glad. Because you deserve to be loved."

"So do you."

He grinned. "And that is why I'm not married. I haven't found *her* yet."

Tenley watched him as he joined in the football game, head and shoulders above his brothers, playing the quarterback, one of the twins trying to bring him down as he passed the ball.

He was stunning to her, effortless in his movements, his thoughts, his honest confessions. No, Holt didn't tell her she was beautiful. Well, once in a while. But it was perfunctory. Said when expected. Like when they attended a wedding or cocktail party. Or an awards reception on a Manhattan rooftop.

Jonas told her she was beautiful with her unwashed hair and stained robe.

Tenley curled her toes into the sand and for one long, aching moment, she wished to be *her*. The one who captured Jonas Sullivan's heart.

TWENTY-FOUR

Elijah

He spied her sitting on a Central Park bench under the spring trees, a pink bloom on the limbs.

He sailed home with the Gottliebs tomorrow, and he could not do so without saying good-bye to Birdie. Though being alone with her presented certain challenges. Could he restrain himself from wanting to kiss her once more?

He had debated posting the letter until he could no longer bear his own cowardice. This one was short and to the point.

Are you free to meet in Central Park Saturday next?

She replied affirmatively the same afternoon, and now there she was, waiting for him. A few years ago this sort of one-on-one meeting would have been unheard of, but Eli took advantage of New York's growing metropolitan ways.

"Good afternoon." Eli removed his hat and sat next to her, shoving his unruly hair aside. He'd see the ship's barber on the journey home.

She peered at him, then at the cyclist riding through the park. "Isn't it a beautiful day? There's no place like Central Park in the spring. I don't care what anyone says." When she faced him, she smiled.

"What do you make of those new carriages? I find them rather clever." He motioned to the street just beyond the wrought-iron gate as one of the newfangled collapsible-top carriages paraded down Fifth Avenue.

"Did you bring me here to speak of carriages?"

"No, indeed not. Did you have trouble coming away?" He glanced around, looking for her maid. "I hear from the Gottliebs your mama is very ill."

"She makes herself ill. But she can't last. She's only trying to manipulate me into accepting Alfonse."

"He proposed, then?"

"I did not accept him."

"I see." Eli surveyed the park, his heart pounding. "Was he angry?" *Hold steady, chap. Remember your family. Your honor.*

"He believes he will persuade me."

"You and I bear the same burden as the unlikely heirs to our family fortunes and legacies, responsible to carry on the names, our older brothers falling to an untimely death." He sighed, glancing to where a spirited colt dashed with its rider through the park. "I saw it over and over in the war—a fallen, fresh-faced lad, no more than eighteen, taking with him the hopes and dreams of his ancestors."

"It's a wonder men even go to war."

Eli smoothed his hand over hers. "I say votes for women."

"Hear, hear." Birdie sat so resolved and regal on the iron bench. "Do you miss him?" she asked after a moment. "I think of William every day, often unwittingly. A moment will pass and I realize I wished him home, sharing in a birthday or some celebration. He had such a gusto about every small thing."

"Sometimes I fear Robert was just a figment of my imagination. He was in day school when I was a wee lad in nappies, then off to Harrow School at thirteen. By the time I joined him there, he was a leader, popular and athletic, adored by the young chaps, admired by the older." Eli laughed at the memory. "He pretended not to know me for the first month of my first term. He claimed I had to make my own way, become my own man."

"I regret not being able to say good-bye. I fear William died alone and cold, longing for his mama and papa. Did he make peace with his Savior before crossing to the other side?"

"I was playing cricket when I was called to the headmaster's office. A place no young boy wishes to go. Robert had been missing for a day and a night. The headmaster implored me to give up his whereabouts, but I had no knowledge. They found him that afternoon, his mount standing guard. They believe he suffered from a heart condition since birth . . ."

"We did not even know William was ill. Then a cable arrived saying he was dead—" Birdie's confession broke with emotion.

"I watched them carry him off, pretending he was someone else's brother. But I cried myself to sleep for a month. I begged Papa and Mama to bring me home, but they assured me the greatest way to honor Robert was to excel at Harrow. Rise up and take his place."

"Death required me to pay attention to my life, to what I believe. A woman never knows when her life will be required of her."

"All the more reason to heed men like Whitefield and Edwards, who believed scripture. I pray Robert was at peace with the Savior when he died."

"I feel as if my life is being required of me now," she said, her voice low, edged with sorrow. "With Mama insisting I marry Alfonse. Don't you feel some the same way, Eli?"

"I've been groomed for this since I was a child, Birdie. If not as the heir, as a young man in the British Empire, where country and duty trump any man's heart."

"When Papa allowed me to go to Wellesley, I foolishly believed my life was my own." She twisted her hands in her lap and he laid his arm along the top of the bench behind her back. "But alas, it's not meant to be."

"Expectations, traditions, and the hopes of our ancestors fall on us."

"It is a burden I cannot bear."

"Dear Birdie, everything will be all right," he said with no real authority. His admonition was merely a wish. He could not rescue her and to even suggest it would do far more harm than good. "Have faith."

She affixed a smile, turning to him. "Enough of me. Tell me, how are you and dear Rose?"

He brought his arm back, the intimate moment passing. "We sail tomorrow for England." He dug his hand into his pocket for a wrapped item. "I saw this in a shop and thought of you."

"Oh, Eli." She pulled back the thin colored paper, exposing a petite porcelain dove. "You shouldn't have. . . It's beautiful. Thank you." Her eyes glistened when she looked at him.

"See here, the wings are raised, ready for flight." Eli lightly tapped the tips. "Yet it is the creature's eyes that fascinate me. Doves have excellent vision, you know. They see well at night. They are not easily distracted by looking to the right or left." He motioned from his eyes to hers. "Keep your eyes ahead. On your desire to pen your stories. Keep looking at Christ. I am convinced more daily we cannot do anything without Him."

"I am growing more convinced myself."

"Let this dove be a reminder. See here . . ." He reached for her reticule. "It's small enough to fit inside. You can sneak it home without raising suspicions. Though you are under no obligation to keep it."

"I'll cherish it always." She clutched the bird to her breast. "Will I see you again, Eli?"

For all his talk of dove eyes, he could not hold a steady gaze upon her. It hurt—physically pained him—to think of leaving her. "If God wills."

"You've given me more reasons to pray."

"Good, good. That makes me jolly." He held her hands in his. "Tell me we'll always be friends."

"Of course. Always. But you do love Rose, don't you, Eli?"

A rush of tears flooded his eyes and he looked away. To be talking to Birdie of loving someone else. . .

"We have affection for each other. She's busy preparing for the wedding with her mama." Eli smiled softly. "We arrive in London at the start of the season. Rose will be the talk of the peers. My family and friends have been writing to her already, welcoming her. She is anticipating her first view of York and Hapsworth Manor."

"She'll do you proud, Eli. I know it. And won't you be glad to be home? You've been gone a long time."

"Forever it seems. I left for Her Majesty's fusiliers in '99 and did not return until the summer of '02. In November I boarded the *RMS Celtic* for New York and my future bride, arranged for me by my mother and aunt whilst I was away."

"It is the life we lead, is it not?"

"Bound by our class and rules, our traditions. Me by my peers." Eli took her hand. "But not you. You're determined to make your own way. I'm impressed and proud." He brought her hand to his lips, kissing the top of her glove. "I wish you well, Birdie. May you find love and the greatest of joys."

"Same to you, Eli." She cupped her hand about his face. "Same to you."

He stood, ripping his heart away from her tender tone and delicate touch. "Good-bye, Birdie."

"Good-bye, Eli."

He walked on without glancing back, swallowing the roar in his chest until he couldn't breathe.

BIRDIE

The lines had been drawn, the gauntlet thrown down between mother and daughter, and the battle of wills commenced.

Tension filled the Shehorn mansion, borne by every member of the household.

Mama refused to attend the final parties of the season. She took luncheon in her room and feigned sickness. Five times she called the doctor to the house, so sure she stood at death's door.

Birdie dined alone with Papa night after night. "You know she's pretending."

"Nevertheless, she's worked herself up into a real fright. The doctor believes she might have a stroke."

Finally, after two weeks, Birdie knocked on Mama's door. "You cannot freeze me out forever."

But Mama did not respond. She showed no sign of weakening.

Society women called on her, but she denied them. Flowers and calling cards filled the grand hall.

Then two days ago, she called for the reverend. "I need to make peace with my Lord."

Tonight Birdie readied for the season's final ball, hosted by the Winthrops. Wearing an emerald green gown that caught the gold flecks in her eyes, Birdie made her way to Mama's bedroom.

"Mama, may I come in?" She rapped softly. "Mama?"

Hearing a cough, she waited, expecting the door to ease open. When it didn't, Birdie knocked again.

"Mama?" She tried the knob, and when it gave way she peeked around the door's edge to see Mama lounging on her couch in a dressing gown, a compress over her eyes. Birdie knelt next to her, stroking Mama's hand. "We're going to the Winthrops'. Don't you want to come with us?"

"How can I? I'm unwell, and my only child wants to throw her life away."

"Mama, I don't want to throw my life away." Birdie pressed her cheek against Mama's arm. "I want to do something meaningful, something of my own choosing. And if I marry, I want it to be for love."

Mama removed her compress, her blue eyes full of venom. "You live as if fairy tales were true. Is this about your writing? Those stories you pen when you think no one is watching?"

Birdie averted her gaze, wiping the surprise from her expression.

"Yes, I know all about your attic. I pay the staff to be loyal to me, not to you." Mama returned the compress to her eyes. "Go, leave me be. I'm unwell."

"Papa would be so happy if you'd attend the ball tonight," Birdie said.

"Leave me be." But just as Birdie arrived at the door, Mama sat up. "If Alfonse proposes tonight, and you accept him, I'm sure my recovery would be most swift."

"Good night, Mama."

Everyone at the Winthrops' was gay and lighthearted, dancing until the wee hours as if it were the first of the season rather than the last. Champagne punch was served at dawn along with a sumptuous breakfast of eggs, cheese, and croissants, and every fruit imaginable.

Birdie danced until her feet blistered, mere adrenaline keeping her upright. She danced for Mama, for the future she battled to make her own, and for Eli, who would never be hers.

At last Papa whispered, "Shall we retire home?"

Gladly. She was ready for her bed. At the door, Alfonse waited for them.

"He's asked to speak to you at home," Papa said.

At home, Percival greeted them. "I take it the evening was a success."

"Tremendous. The Winthrops closed the season in style. Our last hurrah before the disciplines of Lent." Papa glanced at Alfonse, nodding toward the parlor as if Birdie could not see them. "Pardon me while I check on Mrs. Shehorn."

Birdie turned to Alfonse, removing her hat and gloves, handing them and her coat to the footman. "If you'll pardon me"—she started for the stairs—"I'm rather tired. I think I'll go on to my room."

"Wait." He gently held her arm. "Will you sit with me in the parlor?"

"Are you proposing again?"

"I'm not giving up." Alfonse bent toward her. "You will be my wife, Birdie Shehorn."

"I'm afraid that's impossible."

Ire flashed in his eyes but he quelled it quickly. "Am I so repugnant to you?"

"Not in the least. But I do not love you, nor do you love me."

The pink hue of the morning filled the foyer, draping over the mail table and a long, rather thick envelope. From where she stood, Birdie could read her name.

Picking it up, she read the return address of Scribner's Sons and caught her breath. Clutching it to herself, she backed toward the stairs.

"Good day to you, Alfonse."

"Birdie, can't you sit with me—"

"I'm terribly tired." And trembling with excitement. "Alfonse, why don't we just agree we will not marry? Be freed from our fathers' agreement."

"That's not how it works, Birdie."

But she was gone, bounding up the stairs. What could a thick envelope mean? Perhaps they returned her story with suggestions for improvement before publishing.

She was so sure *The Tree* would meet their standards. She'd felt so, so *holy* while writing it.

Bypassing her room, she bounded up to the attic, her fingers trembling as she lit the lamp on her desk.

If they had accepted her story, she'd shout to the rafters. Maybe even try a cartwheel under the eaves. If they had denied her, she'd, she'd . . . Surely they hadn't denied her.

Slicing the envelope open with a letter opener, she dropped down to the settee and read.

Dear Miss Shehorn,

We were delighted to receive your submission along with many excellent entries. While yours was one of the final candidates, *The Tree* has not been selected for our publication, though we were impressed and moved by the vividness of your piece.

Please find enclosed . . .

The envelope contained her story. Her rejected story. She had failed. Not even Scribner's Sons wanted her novice work for a child's publication.

And she'd almost accused Barclay of stealing her novel.

In the cold, gray light of the attic, she collapsed sideways on the settee. She'd weep if she had the energy.

Glancing at the letter again, she thought of Eli and a collection of unbidden tears dripped from the corners of her eyes, splashing on the settee's thick upholstery.

TWENTY-FIVE

JONAS

Sitting on his back porch, cold root beer in hand, trying to figure what he wanted for supper, he thought of *her*.

It'd been almost a week since the family dinner on the beach, and she peppered his waking thoughts. Which was *no es bueno*. Since she was engaged. Never mind she didn't act or look engaged. The mere fact of it made her off-limits.

You'd think he'd have learned his lesson after Cindy. Be more cautious and wary. But *nooo*, here he was again, falling in love, heart first.

Tenley had caught him by surprise. He wasn't purposefully pursuing her, only trying to be a good neighbor. His head told him to back completely away, to not even enter the friend zone. His heart, however, said *so what?* If all he had was until the end of July with her, then he would feel whatever his heart wanted and deal with the consequences later.

Hey, maybe the more time he spent with her, the more he'd *not* like her. That worked for some people. Married people. With that in mind, he pulled out his phone and started a text.

You free? *Bob Newhart* night? I'll bring the ice cream.

But instead of hitting Send, he deleted the message and tossed his phone onto the wrought-iron table by his chair. *No. Just don't. She's engaged! Ring or no ring.*

Brooding, he decided to call Rob. See if he wanted to grab a burger. Just as he reached for his phone, it pinged with a message. Tenley? Nope. It was Mom.

You busy? Need you to do me a favor.

TENLEY

She woke from a dream, her face pressed against the smooth surface of her writing desk, her laptop screen dark.

What time was it? She snatched up her phone. Five o'clock.

Well, another day of writing shot to smithereens. Worse, she'd dreamed of walking on the beach with Jonas, his arm around her as he whispered she was beautiful.

Tenley mashed her hand against the wad of hair on top of her head. She was a hot babe all right in her man robe and slippers. But she couldn't find the motivation to change.

She wanted to hide. Pretend life had no deadlines, no cancer, no slick roads of black ice. No absent fiancés. No sexy furniture makers.

Uncurling herself from the chair, she stood in the golden light flooding the library, her heart still beating with a longing for Jonas inspired by the dream.

"Get out." She conked the heel of her hand against the side of her head. "Get out, get out, get out."

She'd not seen him since the family picnic on the beach almost a week ago.

This morning, Tenley had taken Blanche to see her primary doc about her wrist. Dr. Rocourt was pleased with how well she was healing. All things considered.

Now it was Monday afternoon and she'd drifted off to sleep. What was it about doing nothing that made her want to do nothing?

She'd forgotten all about her Téa Jones story. Where was she going with that anyway? She surfed the Internet for articles on writing, on overcoming writer's block.

"Write, don't think," was her favorite. What a bunch of baloney.

She'd been trying that for months and still had blank pages for a manuscript.

Brené e-mailed with an idea. "Just give me a rough, rough draft. Don't worry about perfecting the story, we'll do that together. Just spit it out."

Barclay was doing everything possible to help her. If only Tenley had an ounce of spit.

Then she did something stupid. She searched her father's and great-great-grandfather's works. They were prolific, beloved authors. Dad's last release still averaged five-star reviews. One of Gordon Phipps Roth's books, *The Girl in the Carriage*, was featured in a *New York Times* article about the upcoming anniversary edition.

Then she got even more stupid. She peeked at her own reviews. The one-stars. There weren't many, but they were blazing.

"*. . . she's published only because she's Conrad Roth's daughter and a descendant of Gordon Phipps Roth. I could write this sh—*"
Yeah, yeah, whatever.

Next one.

"Clearly all it takes to get published is to slap together four hundred pages of drivel, drop your father's and great-great-grandfather's name, and voilà, you're on the New York Times.*"*

"I wanted to love this book. I did. But the writing was bombastic and juvenile. Don't bother. We won't see anything else from this one-hit wonder."

Bombastic? Ha! *Well, your review is bombastic.*

Tenley slammed the laptop closed, covering her face with her hands. "Dad," she growled, "what do I do? Help me!"

After a moment she sat up, glancing at the photo resting on the back corner of the desk of the marchioness and marquess. Captured in the noir of black and white, they spoke of a time gone by. Of a life Tenley could not touch or even imagine.

Studying the marchioness, Tenley sensed the woman had a secret voice, a yearning to say something. But what?

Tenley surveyed the library. The marchioness had been in this very room. Sat in the light falling through the windows. Pulled books from the quirky shelves.

She set the picture back on the desk. "Did you sit here? Write letters? Address your Christmas cards?" Maybe the answers were in the stuck drawer.

She gave it a quick yank. "Hi-yah!" But nothing doing.

Grabbing her empty Diet Coke cans and stained coffee mug, Tenley started downstairs. Blanche must be up because yummy fragrances wafted from the kitchen.

"What's cooking, Blanche?" She found her mom on the veranda, her narrow frame lost in a pair of baggy shorts and a Ron Jon T-shirt, grilling steaks and smoking a cigarette.

"Give me that—" Tenley snatched the cigarette, stamping it out. "You're a chemo patient. Smoking is forbidden. Where did you get this?"

"The Menthol Bunny." Blanche made a face, casting a long look at the dead cigarette. "She came by while you napped."

"I was writing."

"With your face on the desk?" Blanche ran her hand over Tenley's cheek. "You have desk marks."

"Where are the cigarettes, Blanche?" Tenley held up her hands. "I'll scour your room while you sleep."

Humming, ignoring Tenley, Blanche checked the steaks. "I woke up with a hankering for beef. I drove to Publix for some Delmonico's. Potatoes are baking in the oven, and asparagus is waiting to be steamed. But the best part is dessert. Ailis is sending over her cinnamon cake."

"Mrs. Sullivan?" Tenley dug her hands into the robe's pockets, trying to be casual about Jonas's mom.

"One and the same. How do you like your steak? I like mine medium." The meat sizzled as gas flames kicked up.

"I don't eat steak, and why are there three cuts of meat?"

"I thought we could watch some more *Bob Newhart* tonight." Blanche waved the spatula at Tenley. "You have anything to wear besides that robe?"

Tenley glanced at her attire. She was wearing her weariness. Her discouragement. Her one-star reviews. "What's wrong with it? I've showered. Washed the robe."

"Anyone home?" Jonas came around the side of the house, jumping up the veranda steps, a grocery bag in hand. "Mom sent me over with her cinnamon cake, Miss Blanche."

"She's a doll. Just put the cake inside on the counter. Say, Jonas, look here, I have an extra steak. How about you join us for dinner? We're going to watch more *Bob Newhart*."

Tenley whispered over her shoulder, "You're as transparent as glass."

"Dinner?" He gazed between Blanche and Tenley. "If you're sure you have enough."

"We have plenty. Even made an extra potato."

How convenient.

"I'd be hard pressed to turn down a grilled steak." Jonas set down the bag. "I need to shut my truck off. I can take over grilling if you want, Miss Blanche."

"That'd be lovely. I always thought men were the best grill masters."

When he was gone, Tenley blocked Blanche from escaping into the house. "What are you doing?"

"Fixing dinner." A rosy heat flushed her cheeks.

"You're meddling."

"Now why would I do that? You're engaged to that cowboy."

"Screenwriter."

"Right. Why can't I remember that? Listen, I happen to enjoy Jonas's company. When Ailis told me she was sending him over with the cake, I thought why not have him for dinner?" She cut the air with a swipe of the spatula. "You don't have to stay. Go back to sleep at your desk."

"Maybe I will." She raised her chin. Two could play this game. "There's a little dive restaurant on US 1 I've been dying to try. It looked good." She started inside. "You don't mind if I borrow the car, do you?"

This time Blanche blocked Tenley's way. "Okay, fine. Ailis and I set this up. But is it so wrong for me to want my daughter married to a good man before I leave this earth? A man who I know will take care of her, love her, and support her? Not run off to Paris with some floozy actress."

"Married?" Tenley laughed. "We're barely friends. I'm engaged." Tenley waved her bare ring finger, proving . . . nothing. "And he's not looking for a wife."

"Oh, he's looking. You bet your bottom dollar he's looking. Once he finds the right girl, he'll—"

"Which isn't me, Blanche. Even if there wasn't the cowboy—"

"Screenwriter."

"Grrr, now you have me doing it. Even if there wasn't Holt, I couldn't get involved with Jonas. My life and career are in New York."

"Listen to me." Blanche eased her hold, standing back, shaking her head. "Those things fade. Glory fades. The excitement of a new love, of success, fades. Then what do you have? People come and go. They forget about you faster than they befriended you. All that matters at the end of your life is whether you loved others, gave generously, and had a faith that will carry you through to the next life."

"And you think I can find all of that here, with Jonas."

"Did I hear my name?"

Tenley whirled about, embarrassment rising. "Nothing, Blanche was saying she wanted you to take over grilling."

Jonas exchanged Blanche's spatula for the grill fork with a glance at Tenley. "Did you fall asleep at your desk?"

With a snicker, Blanche disappeared inside.

Tenley pressed her hand to her face, seeing herself as he might see her. It was frightening. "Jonas, will you excuse me?"

She ran upstairs, bolted herself in the bathroom, and leaned into the mirror. Really? Besides the line on her face, she had a gob of sleep in her eyes.

Thanks for the heads-up on that one, Blanche.

Washing her face, she let her hair down—it was clean for once—and ran a brush through the knots.

Pulling her suitcase from under the bed—she'd not even unpacked—she picked out a pair of shorts and a top, along with her favorite leather flip-flops.

It was then she caught her reflection in the dresser mirror. The robe hung off her shoulders, too big for her frame. With a glance down at her feet, she wiggled her toes in the oversize slippers. These things were not hers. Not the robe, the slippers, or the legacy of her father or great-great-grandfather.

Tenley sat on the edge of the bed, her clothes crumpled in her hands. If she wasn't her father or great-great-grandfather, then she was free to be whoever she was destined to be. Right?

However, if she wasn't defined by the success of *Someone to Love,* then just who the heck was she?

Flopping backward onto the mattress, she sighed, smacked by a wave of confusion, feeling more lost than ever.

What was her purpose? Why travel this journey called life if nothing really mattered?

TWENTY-SIX

JONAS

"I can wash dishes." Jonas powered off the TV, the last *Newheart* of season two in the can. Blanche had fallen asleep on the couch right after dinner, sleeping through two hours of the show. She roused herself and moved off to her room.

"Night, kids."

Tenley gathered the dessert plates with a glance at Jonas. "There's nothing to clean up. One pot and a few plates. I'll stick them in the dishwasher. Thank your mom for the cake. It was delicious."

"It was her grandmother's recipe."

"That's a romantic notion, isn't it? Passing down family recipes, cooking the same food your grandmother or great-grandmother cooked." Tenley headed for the kitchen and Jonas followed.

He wasn't ready to leave yet. He liked her company. Shoot, he liked everything about her. Even that stupid robe and knot of hair on top of her head.

So when she came down wearing real clothes, her hair combed and her face bright with a touch of makeup, he sank a little bit deeper in love. Yeah, he said it. Love.

Right down to a fluttering heart and a cotton mouth.

"Did your dad cook any of your grandmother's recipes?"

"He didn't have any. He was the man whose wife had the recipes. Then she left and he was on his own. But he was a good cook."

"Any recipes from him you can pass down?" Jonas found the dish soap and filled the sink with warm, sudsy water. "Want to hand me the pot?"

"He mostly grilled meat and steamed vegetables, boiled spaghetti and heated up sauce." Tenley passed over the pot. "Hey, Jonas, how do you know what you're doing is right for your life?"

He laughed. "What makes you think I know?"

"You seem sure of yourself."

"I'm a good faker." He rinsed the pot and handed it to Tenley. "Why do you ask?"

She wiped the pot dry, setting it in the cupboard. "Just had a thought maybe I'm not doing the right thing with my life. I clearly have writer's block and I'm afraid I've stopped caring."

"Is that why you're not wearing the robe and slippers?"

She offered a twisted smile. "Maybe. I got a look at myself in the mirror and it hit me—*This is not who I am.*"

"If I had the key to discover the right life path, I'd be the one writing a book." He ran his hand around the back of his neck. "Speaking of . . . I wasn't going to tell you, but I started reading *Someone to Love.*"

"Oh my gosh." Tenley flashed her palm, then folded the dish towel over the oven handle. "Don't tell me what you think. I've had my fill of bad reviews."

"It's good, Tenley."

"For a romance."

"For anymance. You have a way with words. I was drawn right in."

She regarded him for a moment. "Thank you."

"I mean it. I see what the E's like about Ezra. He's a good character. So for your next book, I say go for it. Have fun."

She made a face. "Now why didn't I think of that?"

He laughed. "Did I state the obvious?"

"Trouble is, I'm not sure I ever had fun writing. It's always been work or therapy. My assignments for school. Master's thesis—which was a very boring tome no one will ever read. Then I wrote out of grief, trying to find my way after Dad died."

"So can't you write for fun this time?" He wanted to reach for her and tell her everything would be all right. But he held back, nervous to cross more emotional lines.

She squinted up at him. "Write for fun, huh? What do you think? Should I try it without the robe and slippers?"

"Why not? Live on the edge. Keep the desk, though. I'll pick it up when the fun is over."

"Oh hey, speaking of the desk. The middle drawer is stuck and it's bugging me. Why won't it open? Can you look at it?"

"Let's go."

Tenley led the way, her fragrance like the beach after the storm. A little bit salty, a little bit sweet.

In the library the low light cast a romantic glow from the wall sconces. She flipped on the Tiffany lamp and Jonas knelt to examine the drawer. "Doesn't look painted over."

"I know, I slid a piece of paper through. Of course now I can't get it out."

"Something could be wedging it shut." Jonas tugged on the pull and the drawer slid open without any resistance.

"What?" Tenley shoved him aside, dropping to one knee to study the drawer. "This is crazy. I'm telling you it was stuck. I sat on this chair, propped my feet on the legs, and pulled so hard the desk almost toppled over."

"Well, it's open now." Jonas shoved the drawer back and forth.

"Know what?" She snapped her fingers. "I bet I got it loose for you."

He laughed. "Yeah, that's it. Sure."

"You think I'm crazy."

"No."

"I'm telling you it was stuck."

"I believe you."

"Then stop smirking."

He stood, dusting invisible dirt from his jeans. "Looks like there's nothing much inside. Papers, a figurine, a book. You can check it out later." He reached around her to push the drawer closed.

"My hero. Thank you."

Tenley extended her hand for a congratulatory shake, but when he took hold of her, he couldn't let go. Pulling her to him, he shut off his internal critic and lived in the moment.

"Jonas"—she gripped his shirt in her hands—"I think we—"

He bent toward her, kissing her without a word. He just had to taste her, to see if his feelings had any bearing on reality. After a moment, he broke away, pressing his fist to his lips. "I'm sorry—"

She tasted like her fragrance, sweet and salty, warm with a vibrating passion.

"Jonas, don't talk. Please, don't talk." She roped her arms around his neck, rising on her toes to meet him, her lips finding his. Finding the pulse of his heart.

Hesitation stopped. Doubt fled. He sank into the sincerity of the moment, holding her, wanting her.

He was breathless when he lifted his head, tapping his forehead to hers.

"Kiss me again," she whispered.

He surrendered to the moment, to her demand, his lips trailing along her cheek and down the nape of her neck. He reached for her hands, slipping his thumb over her fingers, then—

He stepped back. "We can't do this."

But she gripped his T-shirt. "Why? Why not?" There was a wild desperation in her voice.

"Because you're engaged. Because you just told me you don't know what you're doing with your life."

"So I can't kiss you." She grinned, slinking toward him. "You're a good kisser, Jonas."

"Yeah, well," he said, stepping away, breathing deep. "You're not too bad yourself. But I'm not the kind of man who steals another guy's fiancée. I was *that* guy, and it stank." He backed toward the door. "I shouldn't have kissed you, Tenley. I'm sorry."

TENLEY

He left her trembling and breathless. Dropping down to the chair, she listened to the sound of Jonas leaving.

His kiss . . . The sensation lingered with her. She didn't want to let go. But he was right, she was in an unsure place. And she was engaged.

Holt. Tenley rested her head against the back of the chair, eyes closed. She'd have to tell him. She didn't want lies in their relationship.

Taking her phone from her pocket, she texted Jonas.

Sorry.

Then she texted Holt.

Hey babe, call me.

Jonas's reply came quickly.

No, my bad. I'm sorry. I crossed the line. It won't happen
again.

Tenley sighed. But she wanted it to happen again. That gorgeous, kind man kissed her and she was undone. Not just by passion but by Jonas Sullivan.

The way he laughed at *Newhart*, cared for his parents, and took over grilling for Blanche. How he volunteered to wash dishes. Or the fact he never said a bad word about Cindy and Mason.

She wanted to know *everything* about him.

"Now what?" She dreaded the idea of confessing to Holt, but she wouldn't be dishonest. She was already being disloyal. She gazed at her left hand. She should haul out her ring and slip it on.

Tenley's gaze drifted to the desk. At least the drawer was unstuck. One less thing to bug her. Angling forward, she tugged on the pull to inspect the contents.

The drawer did not budge.

"What?"

Tenley squared off with the desk and tried again. The drawer refused to move. Impossible! She jiggled it from side to side and it still remained shut.

Jonas opened it, closed it, but Tenley was powerless to do against it.

TWENTY-SEVEN

BIRDIE

Spring was everywhere. In the garden. In the park. Along the avenue. New York was glorious.

As Birdie walked home from an afternoon of tea with Mrs. Minturn and her daughters in Murray Hill, her heart was full.

The Minturn sisters were independent, eager to talk about the arts and life in New York outside the season.

The youngest, Mildred, educated like Birdie, suggested she search the papers for writing opportunities. Seemed she was always finding an ad or some such seeking a skilled author.

Why hadn't Birdie thought of it before? It wasn't time to quit. It was time to pick up her stride. Mrs. Minturn, like Mama, was conservative and old-fashioned, but even she agreed Birdie should pursue her writing.

"Some women have needlepoint. Birdie, you'll have your stories."

What an invigorating afternoon. Wasn't it just like her song?

Do not be dismayed, you don't have to worry or be afraid.

Everything eventually worked out. Even Mama seemed to have given up on her scheme. She said no more about Alfonse, and as the season ended, she miraculously recovered from her sickness, having worn out her friends with her sorrows.

Papa postponed their passage to Paris, and Birdie wondered if indeed she might be free.

Last evening the architect arrived with plans for the Berkshires house, which revived Mama considerably. Papa announced they'd travel over at Easter to explore the land.

With a skip, Birdie took the steps to the front door, drinking in the sunlight and soft breeze, inhaling the perfume of garden honeysuckle.

Inside the house, Percival greeted her in the grand hall. "I trust you had a lovely afternoon."

"Indeed I did, thank you." She handed him her hat and coat. "The Minturn women are gracious and lovely."

"I've always found them to be so."

"Is Mama about?"

"Somewhere," Percival said. "She had the footman off on some chore or other. You know how she is after the season, wanting to clean or rearrange."

"Then the coast is clear." Birdie started up the stairs. "Oh, Percival, can you arrange for the copies of the newspapers to be brought to my room at the end of each day?"

"Morning and evening editions?"

"Yes, please. They can be cleared away the next day."

"I'll begin the chore tonight."

She hurried up to the attic with a germ of an idea—a story of sisters. Dinner would not be for hours, and with Mama occupied, she had time to write.

Humming to herself, she bounded up toward the attic, stopping cold when she saw a small glow slinking down the stairs.

At the entrance, she peered up. "Hello?"

She ascended the narrow stairwell to find Mama in the attic, sitting at Birdie's writing desk, the spring light falling through the high dormer windows and bowing at her feet.

"This is a lovely hideaway you have here, Birdie."

Birdie paused on the top step. "It's not a hideaway." Birdie glanced toward the corner. The settee was gone. "I come here to read."

"And write?" Mama kicked a box out from under the desk. The box where Birdie had stored her letters and diaries.

"Those are personal, Mama."

Her mother opened the middle desk drawer, pulled it free from the desk, and turned it over. Birdie rushed to catch the pages she kept inside, but nothing fluttered to the ground.

"I never imagined you'd steal away to this dark, dreary attic— cold in the winter, hot in the summer—and write venomous things about your mama."

"I don't write venomous things about you." Birdie dropped beside the empty drawer, then raised the box's lid. Also empty. "Mama, where are my things? What did you do?" She reached for the two side drawers where she stored pens and pencils, extra writing pads. Letters from Eli. The drawers had been cleared. "My letters, my stories. Mama! What have you done?"

"I've decided to clean out this attic." The woman went to the door, her footsteps echoing over the wide plank floor. "Been meaning to for quite some time."

"Yet your things are still here." Birdie crossed to the opposite side, where Mama's chests of linens remained along with rows of dining chairs from a table she no longer used. "What exactly are you cleaning and clearing?"

"I warned you, Birdie. Yet you refused to yield. You've played your game, now I must play mine."

"So you invade my privacy?" Her limbs trembled, and she

feared fainting. She could not remember being more enraged. "Steal from me?"

"I believe this house belongs to Papa and me. It is ours to do with as we please."

"Yes, but my writing, my diaries, my letters are mine to do with as I please. You know Papa would not approve of this, Mama."

"I know Papa is expecting you to marry Alfonse Van Cliff."

"Is that..." She stepped toward Mama, a fire in her chest. "You're manipulating me into doing your will? Into marrying Alfonse? He does not want to marry me. He's not called in two weeks."

"He has not called because you refused him. Twice."

"He's a wise man. I'll refuse him again."

"You think I don't know about your affection for Lord Montague? Well, he's marrying another, Birdie."

"I am well aware."

Footsteps echoed on the stairs. Birdie turned to see a footman and one of the hall boys emerging.

"Please take this desk down to the charity cart," Mama said. "Burn all papers in the incinerator."

They hustled to do as she bid. "Yes, ma'am."

"Mama, what are you doing?" Birdie tried to intercept the footman. "No, please, leave the desk."

But Mama overruled her. "Take it."

The young men hoisted the desk toward the stairs. In a panic, Birdie lunged forward, falling on the desk, gripping the sides with her weak arms. "The desk is mine. Mr. Van Buren brought it for me."

"Mr. Van Buren? How did you—" Mama wrenched her from the desk. "Act like a lady. You shame yourself."

But she did not care about shaming herself. She wanted her desk. Her writings. "So you choose to crush me just to have your way? Is that it? You must be the victor at all costs?"

"I'm winning, just as I told you I would."

The boys wrestled with the desk, inching it down the stairs.

"Wait!" Birdie lurched for the stairs, but Mama caught her with an iron grip. "I warned you, Birdie." Her countenance darkened with the power of her voice. "I warned you I would not be defeated." Mama released her. "Put on your favorite gown. Alfonse is calling this evening." She paused on the top step, becoming a dark silhouette in the light of the second floor. "When he proposes this time, you will say yes."

TENLEY

Thursday evening Blanche announced, "I need chocolate."

"So get some." Tenley looked up from reading e-mail. She'd spent a good part of the afternoon on social media, stalking other authors, reading *their* reviews.

Blanche stood in the library doorway, a new colorful turban on her shaved head.

When Tenley couldn't take Blanche's uneven locks anymore, she had driven her mother to the nearest barbershop. Blanche wanted a crew cut but the barber gave her a nice even overall buzz.

Then they shopped for turbans at the Merritt Island Mall. Blanche had a head covering for every day.

Tenley researched the best diet for chemo patients and shopped at the local health food store, fixing her a power smoothie every morning and afternoon. A bit of color slowly returned to Blanche's cheeks.

However, at the moment, she looked pale as she patted her lean belly. "I don't feel well."

"Then you won't want chocolate. How about some soup?" Tenley scooted away from the desk, calling the day quits.

When she wasn't reading other people's reviews, she thought of Jonas. And his kiss. Over and over. Even woke up in the middle of the night reliving the touch of his lips on hers. His scent and taste lingered with her.

She showered every day trying to wash that man out of her system. Even called Holt first thing in the morning—he never answered—trying to tilt her world right again.

But nothing worked. She just might be falling for him. No, no, no . . .

"I want chocolate," Blanche said, arms crossed in a stubborn stance. "I don't have chemo this week and nothing says celebration like chocolate." After four weekly treatments, Blanche had moved to one every other.

"Fine. Go get chocolate. I left the car keys on the hook by the door."

An e-mail from her agent, Charlie, popped up on her phone. Subject line: *Trip to NY.*

"Will you go for me? Like I said, I'm not feeling too well."

"But you want to eat chocolate?" Tenley tapped the screen to open the message. Some of her best moments in life began with Charlie.

Tenley, I sold your book at auction.

Tenley, you're on the New York Times *bestseller list.*

Tenley, Gonda Films optioned your book.

Tenley, you're going on a national media tour.

"Yes. Please."

She glanced at Blanche. "Fine, I'll run to Walgreens. What kind of chocolate?"

"Hershey's. Oh, and we need toilet paper. You'd best go to Publix."

"For toilet paper and chocolate?"

"And meat. We need meat."

Tenley squinted at Blanche. "What's going on?"

"Nothing." Blanche huffed and leaned against the door frame, hands in her shorts pockets. "I'm just telling you things we need."

"Chocolate, toilet paper, and meat."

"You're out of Diet Coke too."

"Fine. I'll go to Publix." Back to the e-mail.

"Now? My sweet tooth is pestering me for that chocolate."

"There's some chocolate syrup in the fridge. Have a swig. That'll tide you over until I'm done." She clicked on Charlie's e-mail. "Write a list. I'll be right down."

From: Charlie@McGuireLit.com
Subject: Next week in NYC (!)

Tenley,

How's it going? How's your mother? I hate to add pressure to you but Wendall called. They're concerned at Barclay. Brené isn't sure you're writing. She said she asked for a rough draft but you've given her nothing. However, we can salvage this if you get to New York for a day. We'll meet with them, show them what you have, brainstorm, strategize.

In other news, I landed you a spot on *Good Morning America*. I have a friend over there who works in programming and I pitched him the idea of you coming on with *Someone to Love*, as a recent Phipps Roth winner and, of course, his great-great-granddaughter. They're doing June brides specials all month and *Someone to Love* fits the theme. What do you say? They want you Monday morning.

Let me know but I already told them you would, so . . . If I
have to, I'll fly down and take care of your mother.

Charlie

P.S. Send me what you have of your manuscript. I'd like to
be prepared.

Tenley dropped her head to the desk. *Help me, please, someone.*
This was getting ridiculous.

She hit Reply and shot Charlie a short note.

I'll be there. Blanche doesn't have chemo until Thursday. I'd
send you what I have but I'm still working on it.

Tenley

P.S. Thanks for everything.

Closing her laptop, she headed downstairs. "Still working on it"
was a stretch. But she had the weekend to knock out something. In
the kitchen, Tenley drew a deep breath, reaching for Blanche's list.
Yep, this weekend, she'd marathon write. Get that girl Téa to talk
to her.

She scanned the list and grabbed the keys from the hook.
"Seriously? *Meat?* What kind?"

"Beef, chicken, whatever."

"Okay, what are you doing? What's going on?"

"Chocolate, lots of chocolate." She shoved Tenley out the door
with more strength than a woman of her physical challenges should
possess.

So she drove to Publix with the top down, cruising under a blue sky, the late afternoon still robust with heat. Tenley mulled over a trip to New York, excitement building.

It would be good to see her apartment. Sleep in her bed. She'd text Holt, ask him to fly home for a few days.

Though she wrestled with a bit of dread over meeting with Barclay, it would be good to talk to them face-to-face. Clear things up. Brené never *asked* for an early rough draft. She told Tenley she could submit one. At deadline.

Tenley gripped the steering wheel, gliding under a green light. She couldn't fail. She would *not* fail.

Blanche could be on her own for a few days. A little over a week since her last chemo, she was over the reaction period. Nevertheless, Tenley would ask Mrs. Sullivan to keep an eye on her.

At Publix, she grabbed a cart, stopped to sample a dish a woman stirred together in the makeshift kitchen, tossed a bag of Goldfish in the cart—even though they weren't on the list—and took a leisurely stroll down aisle one.

In the dairy aisle, she picked up a carton of chocolate milk, the idea of New York settling deeper, an anticipation growing.

She loved the idea of being on *Good Morning America*. Loved seeing Charlie. Oh, and she'd see if Alicia was free for dinner.

As she rounded the spaghetti aisle, she collided with another shopper. Moving her cart from his, she peered into the handsome face of Jonas Sullivan.

"Jonas. Hello." Dang if her lips didn't buzz.

"Tenley." He carried a basket with cold-remedy items.

"Getting a cold?"

"No, this is for Mom. She sent me on an errand."

"Funny. Blanche sent me on an errand for chocolate."

They stared at each other for a moment. Then Tenley remembered how he broke away from her, apologizing for his kiss while she begged for more. Her buzzing lips faded with embarrassment. "Well, have a good night, Jonas."

He touched her shoulder. "We okay?"

"Yeah, we're okay."

He nodded. Once.

"Except . . ." She paused, propping her foot on the bottom rack of the cart. "The drawer you unstuck is stuck again. The moment you walked out of the library, it was as if you were never there."

"Come on, it slid right open for me."

"Well, I can't open it. What'd you do to it?"

He angled toward her. "I shut it."

"Well, come and open it again, and this time don't shut it." As the words left her lips, she knew she wasn't talking about an old desk drawer. She was talking about her heart.

"I'll stop by on my way home."

"G-good." Tenley shoved her cart down the candy aisle, filled it with chocolate, and rolled through the express lane, completely forgetting toilet paper, meat, and everything else on the list.

JONAS

When he got to Mom's with a bag of cold medicine, he discovered she was not down for the count at all like she said on the phone.

In fact, she'd just walked in from work with two buckets of chicken, completely uninhibited by a runny nose and raspy cough.

Jonas set his bags on the counter. "What's up, Mom?"

She fake coughed into her fist. "I'm feeling better. Thank you for going to the store." Mom took the remedies from the plastic bag and stuck them in the kitchen's medicine cupboard.

"You called me at work saying you were sick and that no one else could go to the store for you." Jonas fell against the counter. "What are you up to? And don't say nothing."

"Nothing." She tore open a bag of cough drops and popped one into her mouth.

"Interesting, Tenley was there buying chocolate for Blanche."

"She's such a good daughter. Blanche is lucky to have her."

"You two are up to something." Jonas wrapped his arm around Mom and kissed her forehead. "But stop. She's engaged. She lives in New York."

"Blanche says he never calls, never visits."

"He's in Paris."

"For how long?" Mom held his arm. "Jonas, I've been praying. I think she's the one."

"For Holt. And until she decides otherwise, she's off-limits."

Out the door and in his truck, Jonas headed for Grove Manor. He'd fix that stupid desk drawer and be on his way.

No lingering, no tempting kisses, no letting his heart love what he could not have.

TWENTY-EIGHT

Real estate magnate Geoffrey Shehorn announces the engagement of his daughter, Elizabeth Candler Shehorn, to Alfonse Rudolf Van Cliff III, heir to the Van Cliff banking and Wall Street fortune. An October wedding is being planned.

—New York Times

Lord Montague, son of the Marquess of Ainsworth, presented his fiancée, American heiress Miss Rose Gottlieb, and her parents at court. His Majesty and Her Majesty were most charmed by the American beauty. She is said to have luncheoned with Queen Alexandra.

—Evening Post

Elijah

He'd become accustomed to her walking on his arm, strolling in silence as they faced the London season. He introduced Miss Rose Gottlieb to his peers, and to the king and queen.

She hosted her first tea with Mama, who informed Eli, "She was a delight."

Success all around. Her father was right, Rose was up to the task.

They returned to Hapsworth for a quiet weekend. Monday Rose and her mother would sail to Paris for an appointment at Worth's.

On this glorious afternoon, Eli invited her out for a stroll through the gardens. She was quiet when they were alone. Almost shy. This afternoon, her aura was rather somber.

"Isn't it a lovely day?" He bent to see her expression through the high sunlight.

"Very."

"You seem quiet, love." His cane tapped the green manicured path as they walked. Should he reach for her? He sensed a barrier against any intimate move. "Let's sit for a moment." He motioned to the bench under the weeping willow.

Rose sat, her smile weak, a weariness in her expression. "I'm a bit tired. So many parties."

"Yes, you've endured back-to-back seasons. Perhaps when you sail to France you'll find some rest."

"You don't know my mother." She sat back, hands folded neatly in her lap, the gentle country breeze teasing the soft loose hair about her face. "We'll take Paris and Worth's like soldiers."

"I've no sisters, but I know my own mother did quite a bit of damage to the accounts on her Paris shopping sprees." A rabbit hopped across the grounds, pausing to sniff the air and then moving on. "I hope you've enjoyed your time here. The next time we see one another will be our wedding week."

"Can we go inside? I'm sorry, Elijah, I'm just so weary." Rose started for the manor.

"Rose, please tell me, are you all right? I sense more than weariness about you."

"Please, Elijah, do not badger me." She hurried on, almost running, a watery desperation in her warning.

Without another word, they arrived at Hapsworth, stepping into the cool hall. Eli passed his hat to the footman, catching Rose as she bounded up the staircase.

"Tell me what bothers you."

She stopped and slowly descended, her cheeks flushed, her skirt gathered in her hands, her countenance on the verge of tears. Where was his lively, energetic Rose who charmed New York and London societies?

"I-I'm not sure I can say."

"Have a care, Rose. We are to be married. You must have liberty to speak." He motioned toward the front parlor. "Shall we?"

She agreed to go with him, standing instead of sitting as he rang for tea. It was early, but he wanted the comfort and distraction of pouring, stirring, and drinking. A few cakes would ease the edge as well.

Once Manfred took his order and left, Eli walked to the window and peered out.

"Did I ever tell you this is my favorite room in all of Hapsworth?" he said.

"No, no, you didn't."

"When I was a boy this was our family Christmas room. We had a tree in the grand hall, but Mama set up a smaller one in here, and this is where St. Nick delivered our gifts. So many. All the way to here." He laughed, tapping the edge of his chin. "Of course, I was much smaller then, but it seemed like a mountain of presents. On Christmas Eve I would sneak down at night with blanket in tow to watch and wait, falling asleep within minutes."

"We too had a smaller room for the family Christmas." She laughed softly. "We're so different yet much the same."

He warmed with her smile. Had life carried its right course, Robert would be talking with her now—a far handsomer and more charming bloke—offering his good name and title to this American heiress.

"Something disturbs you and I must know what, Rose. I'm to be your husband." He sat beside her, aware of her nervous fidgets and averted gaze.

"I know, Eli. I know." She hung her head, all but weeping. "I adore you."

"Then whatever is the matter?"

She started to speak, then stood, walking toward the door. "Wait here." She disappeared, the door closing quietly behind her.

He paced in front of the fireplace, nodding to Manfred when he brought round the tea. He poured a cup, then a second later Franz Gottlieb appeared.

"Lord Montague, Elijah, I apologize for leaving you to ponder so long."

"What's going on, sir?" He set his tea on the service tray, a sourness rising in his middle. "Where's Rose?"

"Lying down. She's not well. In fact, she's been unwell for quite some time now."

"Unwell? How so?" He moved to the pull cord. "I'll send for Dr. Howler."

"Eli, no, it's not necessary. He won't have the right medicine."

Franz walked the room, admiring the paintings and the gold tray ceiling.

"What medicine does she require? Out with it, my good man. What has happened? I fear the worst."

"Rose is ill with anxiety. She . . ." He paused and set his pipe to his lips, but struck no match. Eli resisted the urge to charge him, demanding an answer. "I don't know how to say this."

"Plainly, sir."

"Rose does not wish to marry you, Lord Montague."

He stepped back, Franz's confession resonating. "I see. What has changed? She was most eager when I proposed and when we sailed over. She's been well received in London and at court."

"Do not blame yourself, son. Rose is a tenderhearted girl. Our stay here has brought things to light. She's come to realize she'll leave us forever. That she'll be thousands of miles away from her family and friends. This trip is not just another grand tour. Her mother has been coaching her on her responsibilities as the woman of the house, especially a titled woman, and she's prepared to do what is required. But to be frank, she's terrified of leaving home. We believed experiencing London and Hapsworth would ease her trepidation, but it seems only to have heightened."

"I'm so sorry." Eli lowered himself to the nearest chair. "Shall we delay the marriage? Give her time?"

He'd been suspicious of her apprehension but felt sure she'd take hope in her future once she saw Hapsworth and found success among his peers. Hadn't he treated her gently if not with affection?

"I was of the same mind until my wife informed me she's neither eating nor sleeping. But just now, Rose confessed she does not want to marry you or become a great marchioness." Franz tucked away his pipe, bearing the tone and expression of a concerned father. "I've never seen her like this, Elijah. My light, my heart, has become a fragile, sad young woman. I'm afraid for her."

"Then we must break the engagement. I wish her no harm or ill. I'm greatly troubled by her distress." Upon his confession, the chain around his own heart broke, and he drew a long, deep breath. A lightness buoyed in his being. "May I speak to her?"

While not in love with Rose, he'd carried a fondness for her and had recently begun to hold hope for their marriage.

Franz moved for the door. "I think it fair and wise. I'll go for her."

"I'll not hold you to our financial agreement, sir."

He paused at the door with a sentimental grin. "She will insist you keep the financial settlement. I believe it eases her shame over her change of heart."

"I cannot accept. The money belongs to Rose and whomever she finally chooses."

"Since Rose wishes to break off the engagement, I myself will insist on a percentage of our original settlement. I'd require the same of any man who broke our contract."

Business. Contract. Words meant for men at Square Mile or Wall Street, not terms for lovers and marriage.

"Marriage should be a covenant rather than a contract," Eli said. "I'll arrange for a return of your money and stocks."

Mr. Gottlieb nodded. "I am sorry, Lord Montague. I thought you and Rose made a lovely pair."

"It's not meant to be."

When Rose appeared a few moments later, red emotion rimmed her eyes.

"Father told you." She entered, her countenance already a bit brighter.

"Though I wish the words had come from you." Feeling exposed and humbled, he was relieved to know the truth.

"Forgive me, Elijah." She crossed over to him. "I thought I could marry you. I'd dreamed of it since our aunts made the introduction. But it was just a foolish, girlish dream of romance. Then we entered the season and you proposed . . . such a lovely proposal . . . and I was very happy. I'd landed such a fine, noble man. But then I began to realize—"

Tears drifted down her slender, creamy cheeks. This would never do.

"Rose, don't cry." He passed her his handkerchief. "Not on my account. We will always be good friends."

Having grown up with a brother and attended an all-boys boarding school, Elijah had little experience with feminine emotions. But they moved him and he longed to comfort her.

"I've dishonored you and my family," she said, sinking down to the couch.

Eli eased down next to her. "Rose, have no more care about it. I release you from your promise. Let there be no shame."

"How can you be so kind?" She dabbed her cheeks with the edge of his handkerchief, then passed it back to him. "I feel I must repay you, do something for you in kind. Father said you refuse to retain the dowry."

"You owe me nothing but truth and the love of a friend. Keep your dowry for the man you do choose to marry."

As he spoke, he knew he'd unwittingly failed his family. Without the Gottliebs' fortune, Hapsworth would flounder.

"I suppose we were doomed from the start. I've never done well away from home. Did Father tell you how he rescued me from a French finishing school? Once home, I wouldn't let him or Mother out of my sight for a month." She laughed softly, showing a glimpse of her true self. "I'm still that little girl, Eli, at eighteen. Some nights I ask Mother to read me a bedtime story. And Father holds my hand walking through the park."

"Then you must go home." He brought her hand to his lips. "We are the better for having you with us these past weeks. One day, when it is right, you'll fall in love and marry the right man."

She leaned to kiss his cheek. "I still wish desperately to repay your kindness."

"You repay me by living your life well and remembering me in your prayers."

"I will." She stood to go. "Good night, Eli."

"Good night, dear Rose."

TWENTY-NINE

TENLEY

He did it again. Opened the drawer with a simple tug on the pull.

"This is a joke. Someone is trying to convince me I'm crazy." Tenley bent to inspect the trick drawer, pushing Jonas out of the way. "Let me try."

With ease, the drawer opened and closed. Opened and closed.

"What's the problem, New York?"

"I'm telling you, it wouldn't open, Cocoa Beach." Shoving the casing in, then out, she was convinced. "Okay, it works." But she left it open. Just in case.

"What's inside that's so important?" Jonas asked, standing over her, near her, teasing her with his warmth and fragrance.

"Stand back, let the girl have a look." She gently pushed him aside. *Space, please, give my heart space.*

The drawer contained a couple of old-fashioned pens, a porcelain dove with lifted wings, a black leather Bible with gold engraving, and a tattered manila envelope.

Setting each item on the desk with Jonas at her side—a position she was growing to like—she took one step away from him.

"What's in the envelope?"

Tenley reached for the Bible, a name engraved in the bottom right corner. *Mrs. Percy.*

"The marchioness's Bible." Bending back the cover, she read the inscription. "To the Marchioness of Ainsworth with love from"—she glanced up at Jonas—"Gordon Phipps Roth."

"Your great-great-grandfather?"

She nodded. "My great-great-grandfather gave the marchioness a Bible? I wonder how he knew her."

"Maybe she was a fan. I'm sure people in elite groups wanted to meet him."

"Dad had a picture of him with the king of England. I suppose I have it now, in a box somewhere. But neither he nor Grandpa mentioned a family friendship with aristocrats."

"Wonder why he gave her a Bible?"

"Good question. Maybe he thought she needed it. One of his grandsons did grow up to be a preacher."

"What about you? Do you believe?" Jonas palmed the small Bible in his wide hand.

She shrugged. "Dad never forced it on me. We talked about it. We had faith in the house. But we weren't Sunday church people."

"You should give this a read, then. See for yourself if it's true. Start with the New Testament, Gospel of John." He set the Bible on the desk. "What's in the envelope?"

Tenley slipped the contents out onto the desk, about three hundred onionskin typewriter pages. "*An October Wedding*, by Gordon Phipps Roth." She dropped to the desk chair and removed the rubber band, flipping through the thin pages. "Oh my gosh, a lost manuscript."

"A lost manuscript? What do you mean? Why would it be in this desk?"

"I have no idea." Tenley cuddled the manuscript, running to

the second-floor banister. "Blanche, was my great-great-grandpa ever in this house?" Then to Jonas, "A lost manuscript . . . one that never got published."

"What's all the yelling?" Blanche peeked out of the bedroom wearing a summer dress, a bright orange turban on her head, a rosy tint on her cheeks.

"Gordon Phipps Roth. Was he ever in this house?"

"Not to my knowledge. Why?"

"Did the marchioness know him?"

"Tenley, I was nine when my parents bought the house. I just remember a sweet old lady with really white hair. Odd, though, she died right after we bought the house. Most of her things were gone already but some things were left in the library. My mother adored the marchioness and refused to get rid of what remained."

"Right, okay." She offered up the manuscript. "I found this in the desk. A Gordon Phipps Roth manuscript."

"What in the world?"

"And a Bible. Good ol' Great-Great-Grandpa gave it to the Marchioness of Ainsworth."

Blanche made a face. "Then I guess they knew one another, then."

"Dad never said anything to you?"

"Never. He was a man. Didn't pay close attention to the family tree."

Tenley dashed back into the library. "This is incredible."

"What are you going to do with it?"

"I don't know." Tenley flipped through the pages, the precious, precious pages, her heart racing, her thoughts tumbling. A found manuscript. "Read it. I'm going to read it."

"You should find the owner. Like the head of the Phipps Roth Foundation."

"I'm the owner. I found it. I'm his two-times-great granddaughter."

She briefly considered the foundation run by Elijah Phipps Roth, a very distant cousin. Like two or three times removed. She barely knew him.

"Jonas," Blanche called up the stairs, "care to stay for supper? I'm feeling good today and I want to grill out again and bake some cookies."

Tenley's eyes met his and she knew. Jonas knew. He couldn't stay.

"Thanks, Miss Blanche. I need to get going." He reached for the drawer. "Look, open, closed, open, closed."

"Leave it open, just in case." She walked him downstairs to the door. "I'm going to New York on Sunday for a few days."

"Good. Have fun."

"Can you keep an eye on Blanche? Maybe let your mom know."

"Consider it done." He started down the stairs.

"I'll be on *Good Morning America* Monday."

"Really? Exciting. For your book?"

"They're featuring bride stuff all month and my agent got me booked on."

"I hope it brings a lot more sales. Do I say good luck or break a leg?"

She made a face, still hugging the manuscript over her heart. "Gee, I don't know."

"Then I wish you success. Break a leg and good luck." With a nod he started down the stairs.

Tenley leaned over the rail. "Thanks, Jonas. For everything."

He paused at the front door, peering up at her. "You bet."

When he'd gone, Blanche addressed Tenley below the second-floor landing, dish towel in her hand. "You're not giving him a chance?"

"I knew you were up to something when you sent me to the store."

"He's in love with you."

"I'm going to read this manuscript now. Do you need me to help with dinner?"

"You can ignore me but you can't ignore the truth. Go, read your manuscript. I'll call you when it's ready."

For a moment, Grove Manor felt like home and Blanche a normal mother, like the mothers of Tenley's childhood friends.

"Just be sure he won't be the one that got away."

"He'll check on you while I'm gone."

"I'll be fine." Blanche gazed up at Tenley. "You'll come back, won't you?"

"Do you have more treatments?"

"Yes, but—"

"Then I'll be back."

Blanche smiled, revealing the chocolate bar in her hand. "Thank you, Tenley. More than you know."

BIRDIE

She settled in the parlor with Mama and Papa, a cool evening breeze filtering through the window, Alfonse's ring on her finger and Henry James's novel *The Wings of a Dove* open in her lap.

She read the opening line a dozen times, the diamond on her finger catching the firelight and casting a strange glow on the page. On her.

Mama had won. Birdie was trapped. Caged. Broken after the exchange in the attic and the destruction of her desk and personal papers, she lost her will to fight.

Why was she resisting anyway? She had no options besides marriage. No publishing career. No other suitors. No job or future to speak of other than her charity work. She had joined the suffragettes and planned to fight for the woman's vote.

So when Alfonse knelt in front of her again and slipped the ring on her finger *again*, Birdie said yes.

He turned amiable and sweet, even a bit romantic. Last evening, he brought her a diamond bracelet from the Van Cliff vault.

"It was my great-grandmother's. I thought you'd like it."

Unable to focus on her book and the inspired words of James—oh, that she could write with such eloquence—Birdie glanced up when Percival entered.

"Mr. Van Cliff has arrived, sir."

Mama glanced at Papa, then Birdie. "Were you expecting him? What a surprise."

Papa stood, adjusting his waistcoat. "Send him in, Percival."

Upon Papa's word, Alfonse barged into the room, his coat unbuttoned and flowing, his eyes glowing.

"I'm sorry to disturb, but I have no choice."

"What's this?" Papa motioned for him to sit down as he reached for the decanter of port. "You seem troubled."

"When were you going to tell me, Shehorn?" He paced to the quiet fireplace, running his hand over his hair. "I'm shocked you'd keep such a thing from me once Birdie agreed to marry me. You know secrets have a way of unearthing. As did this one."

"What are you talking about, Alfonse? Sit down, speak plainly." Papa handed him the port, which he drank in one gulp.

Birdie focused on the page of the Henry James book, a tension filling her. What troubled Alfonse?

Mama sat in a statuesque pose, needlepoint in hand.

"I'm not sure how to begin." Alfonse commanded their

attention, his typically gallant nature eclipsed by frustration and ire. "I have recently learned that Birdie is of, shall we say, questionable birth." He glanced at her, pressing his lips in a tight, pale line.

The light in the salon dimmed as Birdie gripped the arm of the divan, Alfonse's voice a hollow echo chasing his words. She could not draw a deep breath.

Did he know? How could he possibly . . .

Papa guffawed as he filled his glass from the decanter. Birdie brought her focus back to the room, a dewy perspiration springing over her neck.

"Who on earth have you been listening to, Alfonse? My enemies? The slanderous papers?"

"I was at the club when Mack Van Buren decided to make a spectacle of himself."

Perhaps Mama's quick gasp was lost on the men, but it burned in Birdie's ears.

"Van Buren? You can't trust half of what he claims on a good day. After what he did to your father, to me, you should have no regard for his claims."

Birdie gripped the side of the couch, clutching her book to her chest, whispering prayers.

Please, make him be quiet.

"My thoughts precisely, but when one speaks so boldly . . ." Alfonse paced around and around and Birdie wished he would just sit. "Is it true that he is Birdie's father? She is his offspring?"

"Upon my word!" Papa thundered across the salon, confronting Alfonse nose-to-nose. "In front of the women! You may be engaged to my daughter, but you are not free to come into my home and slander us."

Alfonse reared away from Papa's ominous countenance.

"Why do you think I've come? To learn the truth. At the very least you must know the stories he is telling. I heard Van Buren with my own ears explain in great detail a liaison he shared with . . ." He motioned to Mama, unable to finish.

"Oh my—" Mama mopped her brow, swooning over the arm of the chair.

Papa rushed to her. "My dear, are you all right?" He patted her hand, reaching for the pull. "See what you've done? Upset my wife."

Percival entered and Papa ordered a glass of water and a cool, damp cloth. "Mrs. Shehorn isn't feeling well."

"I apologize," Alfonse said, a stutter in his words. "I didn't mean to . . ."

Papa faced him, fists clenched. "I assume you challenged him, Alfonse. Defended your future mother-in-law."

"I-I wasn't sure what to do. I was merely eavesdropping from another table, but he seemed quite adamant, with specific details. He spoke of how Birdie and I would have intelligent, good-looking children because of his blood, not yours. That the joke was on you and Father, because your grandchildren will have Van Buren blood. He was quite drunk and full of himself. The porters escorted him to one of the dormers not long after. But Shehorn, I must know. Whose blood will my children have? Yours or Van Buren's? I can't imagine how Father will react if he hears of this."

"How can you even ask? I don't know if your question deserves . . . Mine! Of course." Papa raged at Alfonse, then turned to Mama. "Perk up, Iris. Will you sit there and let your name be denigrated? Defend yourself."

Birdie hid behind her book, peeking over the edge, memories surfacing, a patchwork of images and voices.

Mr. Van Buren calling when Papa was away. Low whispers coming from the other side of the locked parlor door. The gift of the desk.

"Defend myself? I'm aghast." Mama gathered her decorum and focused on her needlepoint pattern. "Such foolish, outlandish accusations are not worth my breath."

"It's the epitome of jealousy," Papa said, pacing before the fire, burning twice as hot. "Tell Alfonse, Iris. How Van Buren wanted your hand but you chose me."

The tension in the room pushed Birdie lower behind her book, but her ears were alive with curiosity.

"You were going to marry Van Buren? Does my father know?" Alfonse stood beside the couch, hands locked behind his back. "I'm not sure he could abide it. His disdain for the scoundrel runs deep."

"Alfonse." Mama sat up straight, smiling sweetly. "We were both young. I had no idea of his ways twenty-five years ago. But my mama wisely intervened and I married Geoffrey. As for Birdie—I blush upon speaking of such intimacies—but she is most assuredly a Shehorn."

"So Van Buren told fairy tales to an entire table of cards?" Alfonse said. "Why would he do such a thing? I realize he's a liar and a cheat, but a man is most honest when he's drunk."

"Drunk liars only tell bigger lies." Papa poured a finger of whiskey and tossed it back, making a face as it burned its way down.

"So you maintain he made it all up?" Alfonse's countenance remained intense if not belligerent.

"Is there another explanation?" Papa demanded.

"Then I must challenge him. Ask him why he'd say such things about my intended's family."

"I'll sue him." Papa stabbed the air with his finger.

"And drag Birdie and me into court?" Mama rose up, fierce and undaunted by the proceedings. "You'll do no such thing, Geoffrey."

"He's defiled our good name."

"Our good name is just that: a good name. With a stellar

reputation. We do not need to defend ourselves against the likes of Van Buren. It's his reputation at stake, not ours." Mama moved to touch Papa's arm. "This is about Birdie and her future, the one we've worked so hard to give her. Why give Mack Van Buren one ounce of our precious consideration?"

Alfonse shook his head as he sank to the seat next to Birdie. "Then my apologies. I fear I've ruined my own reputation with you. I should not have assumed the . . . Well, please forgive me." He glanced from Papa to Mama.

The Van Buren and Van Cliff feud was legendary in the city, beginning with the Tammany Hall political machine, when a young Van Buren worked for Boss Tweed. The feud deepened when Papa and Mr. Van Cliff started a real estate proposition that Van Buren thwarted with his city hall connections.

"All is forgiven." Papa set his glass aside and took his cigar from the gold and silver ashtray, slowly relighting it. "I hope this is not some scheme to relinquish your duty and walk out on my daughter?"

"Of course not." Alfonse looked over to Birdie, reaching up to lower her book. "What are you doing hiding? Did we scare our little bird?" His laugh irritated her.

She slapped the book closed, settling it on her lap. "You did not frighten me."

"Birdie," Papa said. "What do you have to say to this? Do you forgive Alfonse?"

If she said no, would she be free? Birdie peered at Mama, a masculine voice echoing through the heavy closed door, a faint, distant memory.

"A desk, my love . . . You said she enjoyed writing stories and reading . . ."

"Birdie, what do you say?" Papa insisted, glancing up as Percival returned with a glass of water and a bowl containing a folded white cloth.

"I-I . . ." She glanced at Mama, whose eyes glistened in the lamplight as she slowly shook her head. *Please, Birdie . . .*

This was her chance. If she confessed what she overheard as a child, Alfonse might break their engagement. She'd be free. Yet at what cost to Papa? To Mama?

Even a suspicion of an affair would humiliate them. And what proof did Birdie actually have? None.

Birdie's mind reeled with implications. Would she lose Papa's affections? What little he supplied was a delight. Would he send Mama away? Despite their differences, a home without Mama would be no home at all.

"Birdie?" Alfonse said. "Do you have something to say?"

She lifted her gaze to him, then to her father, caught in her dilemma. "No, Papa, I have nothing to say."

"Then let's settle down." Papa exhaled and ran his hand along his muttonchops. "Alfonse, would you like something to drink? Iris, please, take your water. There, the cloth is damp and cool. My, haven't we survived quite a jolt this evening?"

"Thank you, Geoffrey. I'll have a brandy. Please, forgive my rash, foolish assumptions." Alfonse took Birdie's hand in his. "Do I have your forgiveness?"

"There's nothing to forgive."

"Shall we have some ice cream and cake?" Mama rang again for Percival. "Alfonse, I must remark on your integrity. Thank you for bringing this to our attention."

"Van Buren just seemed so sure, speaking of so many details. He described this room to the letter."

"He's a lawyer, of course he'd have details." Mama's voice carried newfound verve. "He's met with Geoffrey here before." Mama returned to her needlepoint in full confidence. Yet Birdie did not miss the tremor in her hand. "And he brought Birdie a gift once. A desk. Geoffrey, you remember."

"Do I?"

Mama. Oh, Mama. What a tangled web did she weave?

"Yes, we both found it quite ugly. Now, we will forget this night ever happened, won't we, Geoff? Alfonse and Birdie?"

"Of course, I remember now. Whatever happened to that desk?" Papa struck a match, lighting his cigar. "I'll have a word with the head of the club. Van Buren is a member only for the good graces of men like me, Gottlieb, and Roosevelt."

"I rather think you should leave it alone," Mama said, checking the door as the butler entered. "Percival, let's have cake and ice cream." She wrinkled her nose at Papa. "Doesn't ice cream sound lovely? It should take our minds away from the evening's disturbance."

Just like that, all was set aside, and Birdie's final hope for freedom faded. She breathed deep, shoving aside a sense of panic, resisting the urge to shout her suspicions.

Mack Van Buren was here. With Mama in the locked parlor. I heard them talking.

The clock in the corner ticked away the seconds and her indecision waned. No, she'd keep quiet, refusing to give innuendo a voice.

On her next breath, her lungs filled with air.

Alfonse returned to his jovial self. "It's early yet, shall we have a hand of bridge? Birdie, I've never heard you play the piano. Music might be nice."

"What a splendid idea." Mama spoke as a woman revived, moving over to the piano. "We've all kinds of new sheet music. Have you heard 'Sweet Adeline'? I can't get enough of it. What's your pleasure, Alfonse?"

"'Sweet Adeline.' I'm quite fond of it. Birdie?"

"Yes, of course." Music provided a soothing escape from her cares.

As she sat at the piano, Mama squeezed her shoulders, bending toward her ear.

"I don't know what you know or how you know it, but you will never mention this again."

THIRTY

TENLEY

"Miss Roth." The doorman hurried toward her as she entered the lobby, a distinct frown on his face. "Y-you're home. Were you expected? I'm sorry, I just came on shift." He reached for his iPad, scanning for some sort of notification.

"I didn't call ahead. This is a quick trip, Saget. A meeting with my publisher." She released her roll-aboard to him and started for the elevator. "I'm going on *Good Morning America* too."

"Is that right? Good for you." He fidgeted as they waited for the elevator. "H-how's your mother?"

"Doing well. Thank you."

Blanche had insisted on driving her to the airport, scrutinizing her trip, and asking a dozen times when she'd return to Cocoa Beach.

"You have my itinerary. I printed it out, stuck it on the fridge. Geez, you left me for twenty years and didn't care—"

"I did care. Very much."

"I'm just saying you'll be fine. I'll be back on Tuesday."

"I'll miss you is all. I'm used to your small sounds in the house."

At the airport Blanche clung to her longer than necessary. If she meditated on it, Tenley could still feel her warm, thin arms about her back.

The elevator arrived at the twelfth floor with a ping, inspiring a welcome-home flutter in Tenley.

Man, she missed her place. Her bed. Her loft office. Her stuff. Her space. Her view of the city.

"Shall I open the door for you?" Saget held out his hand for the key but Tenley declined, taking hold of her suitcase.

"Thank you, Saget. I'll take it from here." She pressed a five into his hand.

"If you're sure." He liked to go the extra mile. For the extra tip. "I'd be happy to go in, turn on lights, make sure everything is safe."

Tenley laughed, inserting the key in the lock. "I pay exorbitant fees for this place to be safe. It better be."

Inside, she dropped her keys in the bowl by the door and spread her arms. "Oh, home. I've missed you."

For now, she had two hours before meeting Alicia and Drake at Battery Park for dinner. Plenty of time to fill her soaker tub with bubbles and sink beneath the surface.

This was where she belonged. Not in that rambling house on the coast with Blanche and that bothersome, good-looking, was-he-for-real Jonas Sullivan roaming the beach.

Just inside the door, her packages—the ones she had ordered while procrastinating—were stacked along the wall from smallest to largest. Oh man, she'd ordered a lot of stuff and had the credit card bill to prove it.

Leaving her roll-aboard at the edge of the kitchen, Tenley flipped on a few lights, inhaled the afternoon view of Fifty-Third Street toward the south, and set her laptop on the coffee table. The apartment echoed with a peaceful quiet.

Looking in her laptop case, she retrieved Gordon's manuscript.

She'd read the entire thing the night she found it, staying up until three in the morning.

His well-paced story about a young woman's life in Gilded Age New York was beautiful. Raw and real, full of angst and hope. It made her long for her great-great-grandfather's talent. Why, oh, why couldn't she write like him?

"Grandpa, I need your words in my bones."

It also made her grateful for Blanche, despite the woman's weaknesses and failures. The heroine, Bette, had a nasty piece of work for a mother.

She returned to the long wall of windows and gazed down on Fifth Avenue. In Gordon's story, this very street was lined with extravagant Gilded Age mansions with opulent ballrooms and gaudy parlors.

But that was the era of building up and tearing down. The rich were so rich they thought nothing of razing their homes and starting again. Especially if a nouveau riche came along and built a newer, grander dwelling.

"I can't imagine," Tenley whispered against the glass.

Gordon wrote of riches and luxuries, the social seasons of operas and parties, silk gowns, and coy glances cast from behind Venetian fans. Men in tuxedoes smoking cigars and drinking port. Walking home by the gaslights at dawn under a soft falling snow.

Today Fifth Avenue was noisy and crowded with shops and high-rises.

She sighed with a passing longing to hear the waves curling against the beach beyond Grove Manor.

While she was glad to be home, so many weeks in Florida had changed her.

Pulling her phone from her pocket, she took a selfie with the view of the city behind her and texted it to Blanche.

I'm here. See you Tuesday.

Then she sent the image to Holt.

Guess where I am? Miss you. Are you coming?

She hit Send before thinking, but as she tucked her phone away, she wondered. Did she really miss him?

Grabbing her bag, Tenley headed for the bedroom and clicked on the light, kicking off her flip-flops and tugging her top over her head. She'd ponder her relationship with Holt on the subway ride to meet Alicia and Drake.

She'd just wriggled from her jeans when a movement under the bedcovers startled her against the wall.

"Who's here?" She clasped her shirt to her chest, glancing about for a weapon, reaching for the old brush she left on the dresser. "Holt?" She fumbled for her phone while holding on to her clothes and the brush, just as Holt popped out from under the blue comforter.

"Holt!"

"Tenley!" His dark hair twisted every which way over his sleepy eyes.

"What are you doing here?" She dropped the brush and set her phone on the dresser, slipping back into her top and snapping on her jeans.

"W-what are you doing here?"

"W-what are you . . . I-I'm meeting with Barclay tomorrow. And Charlie got me a spot on *Good Morning America* for their June brides feature." She eased toward the bed. "I was going to text you. . . You're back from Paris?" Sitting on the edge, she combed her hand through his hair and leaned for a kiss. "Why didn't you call? You could've come down to Cocoa Beach."

"Tenley . . ." He clasped her arm, moving her hand from his hair and angling away from her kiss. "There's something you should—"

From the other side of the bed, a lump rolled over and sat up.

"Nicolette?" Tenley slipped off the bed, crashing onto the floor. "W-what's going on, Holt?"

But she knew. The picture was clear. Her questions were rhetorical.

"I didn't think you'd be here. What happened to Blanche's chemotherapy?" Holt stepped out of bed, reaching for the T-shirt on the nightstand.

"What happened to three months of writing in Paris? And this is my place. I didn't think *you'd* be here."

Nicolette moved toward the door, her thin negligee exposing too much as it swayed about her lean frame. "I'll leave you two to talk."

"What the heck, Holt?" Tenley paced to the window, drawing open the shade. She needed light. The sun. The drift of cotton-white clouds. "You're unbelievable. I kissed Jonas and felt guilty for days." Reality settled over her, cold and deep. An involuntary shiver ran down her back. "I tried to call you to talk about it but apparently you were doing more than kissing with Nicolette."

"We're in love. We didn't mean for it to happen, but it did."

"Of course, all that drinking and nightlife in Paris. It's the perfect setting to not have an affair. You should've come to Florida with me."

"I didn't want to go to Florida. I've written more in Paris the last month than six months here."

"You make it sound like it's my fault."

"I'm just saying . . ."

"Saying what?"

"I think you gave me writer's block."

"What? It's not contagious, Holt." He was an idiot. "So you decided to cheat on me?" Tenley gazed down at traffic, the cold turning to a freeze, the shiver shaking down her legs. Oh, to be anywhere but here. "When were you going to tell me?"

"Certainly not now, like this."

"We didn't mean to, Tenley." Nicolette leaned against the door frame, drinking a bottle of water, sounding like a character from one of her movies. "Too much wine, I guess."

"Too much wine? Too much wine!" On instinct, she ran at Holt, ramming his chest, shoving him down on the bed.

"Tenley, hey—"

She pummeled his arm with her fist. "I trusted you."

As she whirled toward Nicolette, trembling, an image flashed across her mind and she saw herself through *their* eyes—weak and expendable. A bottle of wine and she didn't exist.

Dropping to the floor, back against the bed, Tenley sank beneath a surge of fear. Of course he didn't want her. She was nothing. An ugly duckling next to the beautiful swan.

Then Jonas's blue gaze flicked across her senses, and the tenor of his voice resonated in her.

Don't worry. Don't be afraid.

"Get out." She jumped up with purpose and pointed to the door. "Now. Both of you. Get your things and *get* out!"

"Come on, Tenley, don't be—"

"I said get out!" She leaned her nose to Holt's. "The engagement is off."

He laughed, glancing toward Nicolette. "She thinks we were getting married."

"I said get out!"

"Tenley, don't be angry," Nicolette crooned, easing across the room, fluffing her hair. "These things happen. I know. Been there."

"You realize he's only sleeping with you because you're famous. So he can get his script made into a movie."

"I know—"

"What? Don't listen to her. Babe . . . Nic . . . that's not true."

Tenley shoved past Nicolette for the door. "I'm going for a walk around the block. When I get back, don't be here. Leave your keys with Saget." And one more for good measure. "Now get out!"

Holt puffed out his narrow chest. "Hey, some of the things in here are mine. I bought the couch and the TV."

"Yeah, well, you cheated. And you lived here rent-free. They're mine now." Remembering her ring, she went to the dresser and pulled out the blue Tiffany box. She shoved it at Holt's chest. "Here, hope you can get your money back. I'll be back in five minutes. Don't linger."

Stepping into the hall, her bravado and adrenaline fading, she collapsed to the floor, quivering and weeping.

Cradling her head in her hands, she cried, warm tears trimming her cheeks. Tears for endings. Tears for the lies. Tears for the bank of empty days ahead. Tears for being such a fool.

When she sat up, she wiped her face on the edge of her T-shirt, then closed her eyes and rested against the wall.

"God, is this one of those moments where You get my attention? 'Cause if it is, then—"

She startled when her phone rang and tugged it from her pocket.

A fresh wash of tears rose when she saw Jonas's name. Clearing her voice, she answered, "Hey. Is Blanche okay?"

"Yeah, she's fine. But . . . are you? I'm on my way to see a customer, and man, I couldn't stop thinking about you. And not because of, you know, the . . . thing."

"I'm . . . I'm . . . good." Her chin trembled as she tried to respond with courage.

"You don't sound good."

She was unable to hold her tears. "Holt . . . with Nicolette. I found them together."

Jonas whistled low. "Ah, Tenley . . . man. I've been there. It stinks. I'm sorry, so sorry. I wish I were there with you."

"I'm sitting in the hall outside my apartment." Tenley dropped her forehead to her raised knees, a mixture of sadness and fear in her reluctant confession. "Know what's worse? I'm more embarrassed than hurt. I'm not sure I ever loved Holt. But who says yes to someone they don't love?"

"Bighearted people who believe, who want to give love a chance." His comforting deep voice coated her wound.

"Or just a warm body, a voice, to keep the loneliness at bay."

"You'll never be alone, Tenley. You have Blanche, your friends. Erin and Elaine would adopt you as their sister if they could."

"Only because I wrote one great book with one great hero."

"Ride the cynical train as far as you want, but they loved your book and now they love you. They couldn't believe how down-to-earth you were. You'll write another great book, and even if you don't, you don't have to worry or be afraid."

"You said it again."

"It's kind of a common phrase, Tenley."

"Did I tell you about the song?"

"What song?"

"Just a melody . . . with those words. When I was a kid I'd hear it at night when I was afraid, or when Dad was traveling and I was with the nanny. When I missed my mom. After Grandpa died. Even more recently, when I realized I was blocked."

"Sounds like a God song to me."

She sniffed and wiped her face. "God has songs?"

"He sings them over us. There's a verse . . ."

"Would He sing, 'Do not be dismayed, you don't have to worry or be afraid'?"

"Sounds a whole lot like something He'd sing."

"But why to me? I never talk to Him or worship Him."

"Maybe because He loves you. Maybe because someone was praying for you—"

"Dad and Grandpa."

"God's mercy cannot be quantified or understood. Just receive it."

"Just like that? Seems too simple."

He laughed low. "The best things in life are simple and free."

She exhaled, her tears drying, Jonas's calm manner filling her emptiness. "I'd better go. They'll be coming out soon. I only gave them five minutes."

"They're still there?"

She grinned, leaning forward. "You should've seen me. Told them to get out!"

"Now you're talking. Good going."

"When they leave, I'm going to fill the bath with hot water and bubbles then sink in over my head."

"Just don't drown, okay?"

"Thanks, Jonas. For everything." Seemed like she'd been saying that to him a lot lately.

"I'm praying for you, Ten."

When she hung up, she tucked her phone away and closed her eyes. Propping her hands on her knees, palms up, she tried to do what Jonas suggested.

Accept God's love.

"I'm yours, Lord. Even if I don't understand."

The simple comment changed something she could not see. She felt lighter, relieved. And oddly enough, not afraid.

THIRTY-ONE

BIRDIE

When the clock in the hall chimed eleven, Alfonse said he must go.

"Escort me to the door, Birdie." He reached for her hand and she could not refuse.

Percival helped him on with his coat, handed him his hat, and bid him good evening.

"Thank you for playing the piano tonight and singing. You're quite skilled."

"I'd forgotten how much I love to play."

"Do you sincerely forgive me, Birdie? For my accusation?"

She regarded him for a moment, the evening events a blur, her thoughts confused, her heart in turmoil. What could she say but, "Think nothing of it."

She had no more fight. She'd accepted him and whether she liked it or not, he was her world. The least she could do was protect her family.

Bringing her to him, he brushed his hand along her cheek. "We will be good together." His lips found hers for a cordial, warm kiss.

But there was more of a flame in the wall sconce than between them.

When he broke away, smiling, she let her heart speak. "Do you think we'll fall in love one day?"

He glanced down at his hat. "Isn't that always the intent?"

When he'd gone, Birdie wandered slowly up the stairs, the events of the evening still churning through her. Alfonse's abrupt disruption, the accusation, followed by a brief debate, all ending with cake and ice cream, and singing by the piano.

There was no real honesty in her family.

Bypassing her room, she headed up to the attic, where Mama had launched the beginning of the end. Tiptoeing up the steps, she found her nook empty, devoid of the desk and chair, her boxes, her stories, diaries, and letters.

Mama had wiped out her daughter's world so she could be triumphant.

"I thought I'd find you here," Mama said, rising into the room.

"It feels so sad and empty."

"I saved the desk from the charity cart. It's in the gardener's shed along with the chair."

Birdie batted away a wash of tears. "Thank you, Mama."

"I'll have them brought back up, though I don't know what you see in those odd pieces. Alfonse can buy you something much more grand and elegant."

"Because they are mine. Where I work, where I write."

Mama moved to the dormer window and stared toward the weak glow of the streetlights.

"What do you know?" Mama asked. "About Mack Van Buren and me?"

"What makes you think I know anything?"

"I saw it in your expressions. Believe it or not, I know you well, Birdie."

"Then why do you constantly try to change me?"

"*Change* is not the right term. I'd prefer the word *mold*. For your own good. Like my mother molded me." Mama leaned against the wall, arms folded. "So tell me what you know."

"I'm not sure I know anything."

"Birdie—"

"What Alfonse said. He is my father. That's right, isn't it?"

"Oh . . . oh . . ." Mama's knees buckled and she slipped down the attic wall, her plump form fainting to the floor, her fair complexion ghostly in the light. "H-how did you know?"

Birdie eased her down, crouching next to her. "Shall I call Papa or Percival?"

"No, no." Mama waved her off, propping one hand on the floor, breathing deeply, hanging her head. "So, have I finally come to my own comeuppance."

"Your expression that night told me the truth. To be honest, I was never completely sure of what I knew." She aided her mother into an upright position, then sat next to her.

"I wanted to marry him. Before I met your father. But he had no means or fortune. He was just a simple lawyer fresh from Yale. His parents were immigrants, laborers. My mother and father, along with everyone in our social circle, deemed him unworthy of me. An upstart only looking for a moneyed connection. He was well beneath us."

"Did you love him, Mama?"

"More than anything. Then I was introduced to your papa and I knew, Birdie. I knew my folly with Mack would only lead to trouble."

"Yet you bedded him well after you were married."

Mama shoved a loose lock of hair from her forehead, composing herself, her hands fisted in her lap. "An act I regret every day of my life."

"Is that why you treat me as if I must be controlled and steered only in your direction?"

Mama stared toward the attic's shadows. "There were times, I confess, you served only to remind me of my mistake. And the guilt was unbearable. My parents were right. Mack was trouble."

Birdie raised her face to the window as a light rain battered the pane. "Tell me, is he William's father as well?"

"No, no, Birdie, no. It was only . . . only the one time. A weak, lonely time in my life when your papa was away on business, increasing our fortune. But I make no excuse. I will never forgive myself." She raised her gaze to Birdie. "When I see you, I realize even good can come from our wicked choices. I regret telling Mack I was with child. You do realize if this comes to light, you are ruined. We are all ruined."

"He never demanded to see me? Or for you to tell Papa?"

"No. It was the one decent thing he did, God help us."

"If Papa was away, how did you convince him I was his child?"

"He's not one to calculate a woman's time. Besides, the timing needed no twisting. He arrived home shortly after."

"What a risk you took, Mama. You could've cost Papa everything. We could've been on the streets, you and I, a harlot and her daughter."

"But it didn't happen and here we are, safe, a solid family unit. You chose wisely tonight, Birdie. I'm proud of you. You could've broken Papa's heart."

"*Me?*" She held Mama's eyes. "If I chose wisely, then why am I the one paying? Why must I marry for position and society instead of love? You of all people must understand."

"Listen to me, Birdie." Mama composed herself, regaining her command. "Love is a fickle friend. You chose to love Alfonse and—"

"He kissed me tonight with all the passion of tepid tea."

Mama chortled. "He's being polite and gentlemanly."

"I do not find any of this funny." Birdie paced the length of the attic, walking through the cool shadows to where her things used to be.

"I suppose not. Are we clear?"

Birdie turned back toward Mama. "I'm not sure how clear we can be. You've lied to Papa and me for twenty-two years."

"What do you want me to do, tell him?" Finding her strength, Mama pushed up from the floor. "It would destroy him, me, you and our household."

"I want out of the agreement with Alfonse."

"And what reason would we give?"

"I don't know. That's for you to determine." Birdie loved her perch on the moral high horse.

Mama shook her head and started for the stairs, the composure of her old self returning. "If you want out of the agreement, you will have to tell Papa yourself."

"Is that what you want me to do? Tell him what I now know to be true?" How quickly she slid from her high perch.

"Yes, if you dare." Mama wagged her finger at Birdie as she descended. "But I know you, and you haven't the heart to break his. You haven't the heart."

TENLEY

The team around the table was all smiles, Starbucks coffees in hand, a plate of pastries in the center.

"You were fabulous on *GMA*." Kristen, VP of marketing, handed her a cold Diet Coke.

"Maybe we can make this an annual thing." Tenley twisted the cap from the tall bottle.

On her left sat Brené. Next to her was Paul, VP of sales. On his left, Wendall, executive publisher.

"Tenley," Wendall began. "We understand you had to leave your mother, so we appreciate you meeting with us today."

"My grandmother had breast cancer and it was hellish." Kristen shook her head, reaching to pass the pastry dish. "I don't envy you, Tenley."

"She's doing well despite the chemo. She broke her wrist in the midst of it, but even that's healing well."

The light conversation and morning success on *GMA* did not fool her. This was the calm before the storm. And Charlie was late.

"I thought you'd be tan," Brené said, laughing at her confession.

"Can't write on the beach."

The conference door opened and Charlie slipped in with an apologetic wave, taking a chair at the end of the table. Tenley smiled, relieved to have someone in her corner.

"So, Tenley," Wendall began again, slow and low. "How can we help you? We want you to be ready to go for a spring release, so the July deadline is imperative."

A slow thump of anxiety beat against her heart.

"Tenley, we're behind you, but be honest." Paul rested his arms on the table, linking his hands together. "Are you on track? I've convinced booksellers they have another hit on their hands."

"No one can guarantee a hit, Paul. You know that." Charlie made a face, defending her.

"No, but we have Conrad Roth's daughter." Wendall spoke directly to her. "That's more than half the battle. We can get her ready if the book lacks. Tenley?"

All eyes were on her, waiting, watching, blinking.

Wendall kept going. "Tell us now if you're still stuck. Because we need to take you off the schedule and get someone else on it. Rena Roberts has turned in her next book and is ready to go. We pushed her out until summer."

Rena Roberts. What was she, Super Girl Writer Chick? She'd released four books in two years.

"Come on, Wendall, that's a bit manipulative, don't you think?" Wise Charlie to the rescue again.

"Just saying. We're a business as much as a harbor for creative talent and good literature. If Tenley isn't ready to publish again . . . I've seen it. New authors burn out. Can't find the creative spark as quickly as others. Tenley's been through a lot in the past two years. It's understandable if she can't—"

"I'm good." She glanced around the table, raising her chin, pushing her shoulders back. "Yup. On track for July 31." She heard the lie hit the room. Too late to snatch it back. A dew of perspiration collected on her neck.

"I knew the beach would conquer your writer's block." Brené softly hit the table with her fist, smiling. "Don't worry about polishing it, Tenley. I'll take a rough draft and a sloppy ending."

"Great, but I think I'm in good shape." So that's how it was going to be. She spoke and lies exited her mouth.

"I'm so pleased. You never said how far you'd gotten in your e-mails." Brené tossed the conversation to Kristen, who talked of promos, links to *Someone to Love*, how to take advantage of the film release in eighteen months, and capitalizing on the sizeable e-mail list they'd built for Tenley.

For sure, another book tour. Paul, Kristen, and Charlie agreed to take the lead on working with the media, building up anticipation.

Meanwhile, Tenley tried not to run from the room in a panic. She had nothing and it was already June. Two months wasn't enough time to pen her next great novel. It took three to write *Someone to Love*, and she was fueled by intense grief and loss.

Just tell them. You've got nothing. No fuel. No inspiration. Unless fear of failure was a fuel, but it felt more like an emotional sieve.

The words lodged in her throat, refusing her voice.

"Tenley, so, what's the book about?" Brené adjusted her hip, New York–editor glasses. "I'm dying to know. If you create a hero as strong as Ezra, we definitely have a winner on our hands."

"Right, well..." *Think, think, think.* She sat forward, taking a long drink of her Diet Coke. "Well, I'm calling it *An October Wedding*."

What are you saying? Stop! You can't steal your great-great-grandfather's story.

"I like it already. New York is gorgeous in the fall," Brené said. "Can you give us the gist of the story?"

They were smiling. All of them. *Go to the Téa Jones story. Go to the Téa story.* But all she had there was a girl who didn't want to go on freaking date.

"Yeah, sure, so no one's ever heard of a book by that title? Hmm, okay. I just thought it sounded familiar."

"I'm sure there's one somewhere out there," Wendall said. "But titles aren't copyrighted. I like *An October Wedding* too."

"Well, it's set in the Gilded Age—"

"Tenley," Brené said, flashing a pleased smile. "It's like you read my mind. I've been dying for a Gilded Age story."

"The Gilded Age is hot now too," Kristen said. "A spring release would catch the wave."

"Are you doing a Consuelo Vanderbilt story or a Caroline Astor? Maybe a Minturn and Stokes kind of story?" Brené glanced around the table. "What do you men think?"

"I'm good." Wendall leveled his gaze on Tenley. "Anxious to hear more."

He knew she was lying, didn't he? Yes, he knew!

"Um, well, it's about a socialite, an heiress, you see, who is forced to marry a man she doesn't love."

"Ah, a Consuelo Vanderbilt story." Brené nodded her approval. "Does it have a happily ever after?"

"Yes . . . of course." Tenley leaned forward, propping her elbows on the glossy table. "Have you ever heard of the Marchioness of Ainsworth?"

Brené made a face. "No. Should I?"

"Not really. Just wondered . . ."

Brené shrugged and glanced at Wendall. "I'll check but it doesn't ring a bell. Is that who you're writing about?"

"Sort of but not really. I came across her name while research-ing. I thought I'd ask."

Wendall jotted a note and Tenley summed up the novel with a glance at Charlie for help. "And they lived happily ever after."

Charlie chuckled. "A Disney movie in the making. Know what, Brené, why don't we let Tenley finish her process, then you can add your thoughts on the edit?"

"Of course, of course." Brené reached out, squeezing Tenley's arm. "I'm so excited. I can't wait to read it."

Oh, what have I done?

"Brené, you don't think Tenley's voice is too young and hip to write about the Gilded Age?" Paul had remained silent until now.

Brené adjusted her glasses with a glance at Tenley. "Do you think you can handle this?"

"Absolutely." Because Grandpa Phipps Roth had done the heavy lifting, crafting the story and actually writing a masterpiece. Was she really going to steal—no, borrow—this story? Was she *that* desperate? "All women face the similar problems. Whether now or the Gilded Age. They want to be safe, free, and loved. They want to provide for their children. In the Gilded Age, women wanted to climb the social ladder. In the modern age, we want to climb the corporate ladder."

The summation pleased her. It was the first original idea she'd come up with since she sat down.

The meeting adjourned with small talk and pictures of Wendall's new grandbaby. Then Charlie offered to buy Tenley lunch, and they headed out.

Waiting for the elevator, he stood alongside her, eyes ahead.

"Do you really have a story about a Gilded Age girl?"

"Yes." Well, she did. Technically.

"So you *have* been writing?" His posture eased and relaxed.

"Sorta."

The elevator arrived and he entered behind her, waiting for the doors to close before he spoke. "Tenley, your career isn't the only one on the line. So is mine."

"You don't think I know that, Charlie?"

"Just making it clear. It's not fair, but it's true. Now where do you want to go to lunch?"

THIRTY-TWO

JONAS

Wednesday afternoon, the Sullivan cul-de-sac was a car-to-car parking lot. Jonas convinced Dad last-minute to forgo paying him back and throw the E's a graduation party.

They'd worked hard through college, graduated with honors, and deserved to be celebrated.

From his perch atop the deck with Rob, Marvin, and a couple of buddies from work, Jonas surveyed the festivities—his brothers hauling out the kayaks, the E's in a circle of their friends. Looked like Elaine had invited her friend Zac again. His eyes told him something brewed between them.

He'd wander down in a bit, chat with Zac, make sure he had the fear of Big Brother.

Coolers of drinks lined the patio and the upper deck. Smoke swirled from Dad's grill, scenting the air with juicy aromas.

With Julius, Cameron, Caleb, and Josh, he'd set up fifty feet of the heavy-duty plastic tables Mom borrowed from the church.

Now, with a cold drink in hand, he scanned over the roof of the house and down the street for signs of Blanche's Mercedes. Mom had invited Blanche and Tenley before Tenley left for New York but claimed she never heard back.

He tried not to read too much into his Sunday-afternoon conversation with Tenley, but if that wasn't divine timing—for him to call just when she sat outside her apartment, weeping—he didn't know what was.

Which led to thoughts of Tenley being free. She was no longer engaged. His heart kicked and screamed at him to go after her, but his head warned him not to go full throttle.

She needed time to heal. Finish her book. Figure out life.

Then there were the obvious obstacles. She lived in New York. He lived in Cocoa Beach. She was upper class. He was working class. Fine to flirt and steal a kiss, but were they a good match?

At the grill, Dad wiped sweat from his brow, balancing the last plate of meat Mom handed him.

"Rob, Marvin"—Jonas patted his buddies on the back—"I'm going down to help Dad."

As he crossed the lawn, greeting guests—"Hey, Mrs. Wallace"—he saw *her*. Talking with the E's, setting up new lawn chairs, the store tags still swinging from the metal legs. Tenley.

Behind her, Blanche talked to Mom and Connie Wooley.

When she looked up, he waved. Smiling, she started to cross over to him but the E's distracted her with their arriving college friends. Several of the women carried copies of Tenley's book, holding them out for her to sign.

"Hey, Jonas."

Tom Herman, a friend of a friend and noted contractor, a legend in the restoration business, walked his way.

"Tom." The two shook hands. "Good to see you. What brings you here, man?"

"I stopped by your house but you weren't home. Then I

remembered your parents lived nearby." He grinned, glancing about, taking an icy soda can shoved at him by Aunt Carol. "What's going on here?"

"My twin sisters' graduation party." He motioned to the cluster of women by the patio.

"Then I won't stay long." He popped the top and took a long drink. "Don't want to intrude."

"Intrude? Look around, man. All are welcome. It's a Sullivan rule and tradition." Jonas gave him the lowdown on the drinks and snack line, and the spectacular kayak race that would commence within the hour. "So why'd you stop by the house?"

"You interested in a job?" Tom let the question sink in. "Not that I want to steal you from Tug, but a friend of mine is opening a restaurant on the river. Seafood, burgers, tacos. He wants custom tables and chairs. I told him I knew a designer."

"*Designer* is a bit of a stretch, but yeah. I'd love to hear more." He'd resigned himself to another year at Crammer Custom Cabinets. The doors just weren't opening for design work. The grand he gave Dad wasn't going to buy his freedom anyway. He'd start over in the fall, reset his goals, save money, and design at night.

"I've got a shed full of reclaimed wood. Thought you could use it. Free just to get it off my hands. He needs twenty tables by September. Can you do it?"

"I'm your man." Without a doubt. "I appreciate this, Tom. You don't know how much."

"Send over a quote and I'll have him sign off." Tom flipped Jonas his card. "Don't go cheap. Include your salary. I know you'll be fair, and he can afford it."

"I'll get it to you in a few days." He felt suddenly lucky. Blessed.

"I heard what Mason did. Between you and me, I never trusted that guy."

Jonas arched his brow, making a face. "Now you tell me."

For the next few minutes, he soared a little, like an unseen weight had been clipped from his ankle. Tom wondered if the Seminoles could make another championship run this football season, and Jonas didn't see any reason why not.

When Tom said good-bye, Jonas turned at a touch on his arm.

"Hey, can I talk to you?" Tenley. This day was getting better and better.

"Absolutely." He pointed to the front of the house. "Let's get away from the noise."

He led her to the quiet through the sea of cars. Now that he had her alone, he didn't want to share her. Dropping the tailgate of his truck, they sat, legs swinging.

"I saw you on *Good Morning America*," he said. "You're a natural."

"Natural what?" She laughed, shoving her hair from her eyes. "Freak?"

"Come on now. You were relaxed and funny. The hosts loved you. Kept talking to you and ignoring the other two authors. Looking good without the robe and slippers too."

She laughed. "I think I might have hung up the robe for a while."

"Too bad, you're kind of cute in that thing."

"More like hiding in it."

She seemed lighter, brighter than before New York. As if she had stepped out from behind a dark cloud. "So, how are you doing? Have you talked to Holt?"

"He called once. We said good-bye." She absently rubbed her hand over her ring finger.

"As president of the local cheating-fiancés club, let me welcome you to our first meeting." He offered her his hand. "Jonas Sullivan, recovering fiancé. Two years."

"Tenley Roth, four days." When she slipped her hand into his, his weak resolve not to pursue her disintegrated.

"I know you're hurting and probably disappointed, but it gets easier, Tenley." Screams and splashes echoed between the Sullivans' house and the neighbor's. With one glance Jonas saw the kayak races had begun.

"Have you had a lot of breakups? I've only had one other boy-friend." She laughed softly, leaning close. "David Best. Tenth grade. Dumped me for a girl who was *easier*." She shook her head. "Man, if history doesn't repeat itself."

"Jenny Blanton. Senior year. Thought I was in love. She was the one."

"You were ready for marriage at eighteen? Not me. I had a bunch of living to do first."

"You're the one who said I was the marrying kind."

"Yeah. . ." She grinned. "I knew you were the marrying kind."

"My grandparents met and fell in love at fourteen. Married at nineteen and fell more in love every year. I adored Grandma. Idolized Grandpa. I wanted to follow their path, but Jenny had other ideas. Does that make me sound weak?"

"No, it makes you sound sweet. In every good way. What happened?"

"We went off to college. I was busy with baseball and she was busy with the Sigma Chis. You're right, history does repeat itself."

"Then came Holt for me and Cindy for you. Know what I think, Jonas?" She leaned forward, her hair falling over her shoulders, her toned arms exposed. "God must have someone better for us. We should be thankful we're no longer chained to idiots."

Jonas slipped his arm around her, pulling her to him as the breeze teased a strand of her hair over his lips.

He searched her face before kissing her, his lips touching hers in a sweet explosion of emotion. She fell against him, ratcheting up the intensity, filling him with heat.

Entwining his fingers though her hair, he kissed her again and again, not wanting to let go, yet letting go all at once.

He was in love.

"Hey, Joe!" Caleb's voice powered toward them. "We're racing and you're the ref."

Breaking the kiss, he breathed in and tapped his forehead to hers. "I'm going to kill my brother."

Tenley's sweet exhale warmed his neck. "You leave me weak, Cocoa Beach."

"I'm not playing, New York." He sobered, brushing his hands along the sides of her face. "But are we ready for this? You just broke up with Holt."

"More than Holt, Jonas. I'm leaving at the end of July." She peered into his eyes. "My life is in New York." She slid away from him, away from the pull of passion. "What's going to happen when I go home at the end of July?"

"I don't know . . . I don't know . . ."

BIRDIE

OCTOBER 8, 1903

The colors of fall painted Fifth Avenue with glorious golden reds and rustic oranges under a cloudless blue.

The air was crisp with the changing season, echoing with the *clip-clop* of horse hooves and the gleeful shouts of children.

A car motored past. A man on a bicycle raced alongside them.

A child shouted from the street corner, "Extra, extra, heiress marries today at St. Thomas!"

But to Birdie, sitting veiled in Papa's brougham, the world faded to gray. All around her life went on, gay and free, completely unaware she was about to walk the aisle to a prison, sentenced by the vows she'd make.

She'd wept uncontrollably while Fatine dressed her and styled her hair.

"You must stop crying, miss. See how swollen your face is? What will your groom say?"

Making Birdie lie down, Fatine pressed a cold cloth over her eyes, soothing her with sweet but empty promises.

"Everything will be all right. You'll see. What a fine day ahead. You're a beautiful bride, Miss Birdie."

Mama paced outside her room, knocking so frequently it was impossible to rest. "What is going on in there? Birdie, let me in. This is mere nonsense."

Gone was the equanimity between them. Mama took control of matters and fully convinced Papa that Mack Van Buren's story reflected his deplorable moral character, his lack of all social decency, and he should be booted from Papa's club.

A month later his membership was "mysteriously" revoked.

As the carriage moved through the city toward Broadway, crowds gathered on the street corners, cheering for what they could not see or understand.

"Are you happy?" Papa said.

"If you want me to be, Papa, then I am happy."

The carriage pulled along the church steps. Cheers arose as Birdie emerged, the wind pressing her veil against her cheek.

She wore a gown of nearly fifty yards of silk and lace swag, eight thousand pearls, and a diamond tiara. About her neck she wore a Van Cliff diamond choker. From her ears dangled matching earrings.

Head bowed, she walked toward the nave steps with Papa, fearing another rush of tears.

Newspapermen and photographers scurried after her.

"Miss Shehorn, over here. Smile for the *Herald*."

"Can you give us a quote for the *Times*, Miss Shehorn?"

But Papa's men shoved them aside, making way for her to enter the nave. As she approached, trumpeters blasted the good news—the bride is ready!—and the doors swung open.

Her waiting bridesmaids gathered round and Fatine fussed, fanning out her train and adjusting her veil.

"There now. So beautiful."

Beyond the sanctuary doors, organ music played. The melody stirred her to such an extreme she felt helpless to maintain control.

Lord, I'm afraid. Full of dismay!

Where was her song when she needed it most?

How she envied Rose Gottlieb, who had found the courage to follow her heart. When the news came of Eli and Rose's broken engagement, Mama panicked. She extended their trip in Paris, not letting Birdie out of her sight, checking her letters and eavesdropping on conversations.

When they arrived home, she assigned a maid or footman to follow Birdie's every move. She could barely use the water closet without someone peeking in.

She booked her days with parties, teas, and shopping until her life and her very thoughts were not her own.

But Mama had no need to fear. Eli did not contact her.

In July, Gordon Phipps Roth's new book released to great acclaim. Papa purchased a copy for her when they attended a lecture at the university where Phipps spoke about the life of a novelist.

She'd planned to read his book, but a late trip to Worth's and wedding plans consumed her summer.

During the afternoon of Phipps Roth's lecture on the life of a novelist, Birdie burned with each word.

She understood his struggles, his insecurities, the thrill of a completed manuscript, the fear of rejection.

She heard herself in his words. Yes, though he was far beyond her as a novelist, she ached to chase his path. At one point, she wanted to stand in her chair and shout, "Move over, Mr. Roth, I want to be a novelist too."

Resolved to return to her craft after her honeymoon, she sent her desk and chair to the home Alfonse purchased for them on Park Avenue.

But he returned them with a crisp note.

"No need. I've already purchased furniture for the home."

"Smile, dear girl, it's your wedding day." Papa set his top hat on his head and tightened Birdie's hand about his arm. He looked splendid in his tuxedo, his dark hair creamed back, splices of gray showing, his smile full and genuine. "Your nerves are getting the best of you."

The organ music changed and the doors opened. The guests rose as Papa led Birdie down the aisle.

With each footstep, a clacking rhythm sang through her, *I can't, I can't.*

She willed herself to stay upright. Leaned heavily on Papa. The congregation brimmed with hats and heads. Perspiration trickled down her back. Her heart raced. The slow stride down the narrow center aisle seemed to take an eternity.

From the corner of her eye, she caught a smiling face. The freed Rose Gottlieb. Their eyes met, and Rose nodded her encouragement.

Up front, Alfonse and his groomsmen watched and waited, their hair gleaming in the light, white spats covering their dark shoes.

At last they arrived at the altar, and Alfonse nodded toward her with a somber expression.

A quartet began to play and Miss Geraldine Farrar rose to sing "Oh Promise Me," her operatic soprano filling the church with power, pressing against Birdie until she was numb.

Fighting back tears, she peered at Alfonse and wondered that he looked no happier than she.

Geraldine concluded her song, her voice resounding off the marble, stone, and glass sanctuary even as she took her seat.

The reverend began. "Dearly beloved, we are gathered here in the sight of God and man to join this man and woman in holy matrimony. It is a solemn occasion, one to not enter into lightly. For it is written, 'He made them male and female. What God has joined together let no one put asunder.' Let us pray."

This was her moment. Her final plea. *Lord, if there be a way . . .*

". . . Lord, as these two pledge their lives one to another . . ."

If her pledge was filled with uncertainty and regret, would she not be committing a sin before God? Was He not to be obeyed above all others? Even Mama and Papa?

Birdie peeked through her veil at Alfonse's bowed head. Then at Papa. What would she say? How would she begin?

Upon his amen, the reverend turned to Alfonse. "It is my duty to ask you, Alfonse, if you are prepared to take your vows of marriage this day?"

Birdie's thoughts thundered. *Now or never. Now or never.*

Alfonse rubbed the back of his neck, glancing over his shoulder, toward the apse.

"Alfonse?" the reverend said. "Do you understand the question?"

"Yes, sir." Then came a movement from the apse side door, and a smile split his august face.

"Sir, I am not prepared to take the vows of marriage today." He moved aside. "But this fine chap will take my place."

Elijah Percy, Lord Montague, dressed in tails and tie, stepped around the flickering candles toward the reverend and the altar, taking Alfonse's place. Birdie gripped Papa's arm, swaying in weakness.

"I am prepared to take the marriage vows this day." Elijah held a steady gaze on her. "If Miss Shehorn will consent."

A photographer and his assistant ran in front of her, pausing long enough to snap a photo. Papa's arm muscle tightened under Birdie's hand.

"Birdie?" Eli said, hat in hand, a pleading in his eyes.

"Someone explain this to me?" The reverend eyed Papa. "This is highly unorthodox."

Alfonse moved in close to Birdie. "I know you don't want to marry me. The closer we came to this day, the more I realized I couldn't ask you to go against your heart. Then Rose Gottlieb came to me with an idea . . ."

"Why didn't you speak to me?"

He leaned toward her ear. "This was the only way. Like in war. The element of surprise."

Red-faced and bothered, the reverend demanded Alfonse's attention. "Explain yourself."

"Pardon me, but I believe this is between the bride and me." Eli shoved the men aside as he knelt before Birdie. "Elizabeth Candler Shehorn, I love you. With all my heart. If you feel the same, please, do me the honor of becoming my wife."

"Pardon me." Papa released Birdie to confront Eli, tapping him in the chest. "You will not see a penny of my money."

"Have I asked you for money, sir? Keep your accounts. I want your daughter's hand."

"Eli, yes, of course I'll marry you. Yes, oh yes." Her tears flowed—this time with relief, joy, and happiness.

Around the church, guests murmured and hummed, speculating in hoarse whispers.

"I mean what I say. No dowry—"

"Papa," Birdie said, "must you be so hard and bitter? He loves me and I love him."

Eli's blue eyes gazed with confidence at Papa. "Sir, if you think your greatest fortune is the size of your bank account, you've miscalculated. This beauty here before you is your greatest asset, and I'll devote my life to see her happy."

"Eli, are you sure?" Birdie whispered.

"My love, need you ask?"

Papa cleared his throat. "Birdie, is this what you want?"

"With everything in me, Papa."

He stepped away, nodding to the reverend. "Miss Shehorn will be marrying Lord Montague this afternoon."

"Psst, Geoffrey." Mama, her voice a tone above a growl, teetered on the verge of making a scene in front of her friends. "Might I speak with you?"

Birdie giggled, leaning into Eli as he took her hand and led her up the altar steps, following the reverend.

"Shall we begin?" The reverend cleared his throat, giving them a stern gaze. "Again. Are you prepared to take your marriage vows—"

"Yes, sir. Yes, indeed I am."

The Great Wedding Caper! Van Cliff Steps Aside for Lord Montague! Guests Aghast.

—New York Herald

Miss Birdie Shehorn Ditches Fiancé for British Aristocrat.

—New York Times

Do You Take This Man, No This Man? Shehorn Wedding Switcharoo.

—New York World

Bride Ditched by Groom, Her Mother Revived with Smelling Salts

—Evening Post

THIRTY-THREE

TENLEY

The house was quiet. Asleep. Ten o'clock and Tenley had work to do.

Upstairs in the library, she sat at the desk with her laptop open, staring at the blank page. Next to her computer? Gordon's manuscript.

If she just typed a few pages, got the juices going, she could take off with her own story. Lots of writers did free writing to get going. She'd just be free writing with someone else's words—her great-great-grandfather's words. She was sure he wouldn't mind.

Of course she'd not done a lick of research on the Gilded Age, but she knew a good bit from living on Fifth Avenue. She could research as she wrote. Or just lift a few sections from Gordon's book. He definitely had the Gilded Age feel.

She glanced at the door to make sure she was alone, nervous Blanche might wake up and surprise her. *What are you doing?*

Yes, what was she doing? Stealing?

Tenley shoved away from the desk and walked over to the bookshelf, staring at her setup.

It didn't help that she had stalked Rena Roberts for a couple of days, watching her interaction with fans on social media, feeling like a big hairy heel for her lack of engagement.

Rena was all smiles with a picture of her latest manuscript on the computer with the words *The End*.

Charlie texted to see how she was doing, adding a note that his youngest was getting braces.

If he had to choose between Tenley and Barclay, she knew his choice. Shoot, she'd make the same one.

This morning she had posted a picture of the beach on her Facebook page with a corny, "I am here. Where are you?"

The likes and comments piled up, most of her fans begging for her new book.

"All right, Ten, you're stalling. Look, copy Gordon's book until you take off on your own and then go back and edit. Make it all yours."

Back at the desk, she eased the middle drawer all but closed—she didn't trust it—set the dove figurine in the corner on top of the Bible, and arranged the picture of the marquess and marchioness on the other side.

So she began. *Chapter One*. For the legacy of her father, her great-great-grandfather, for Charlie, for Brené and Barclay Publishing. For herself.

If she survived this, she'd hang up her computer and seek another career. She saw a sign in a local McDonald's—*Accepting Applications*.

BIRDIE

Light broke through the slit between the draperies and Birdie, cradled in her husband's arms, traced her finger along his jaw, then over his soft, full lips, his breathing sweet and even.

"I love you, Eli Percy," she whispered.

He grinned, rolling over to kiss her, nestling down next to her, his body melded with hers. "I can't believe you're mine."

"Nor I you."

Yesterday was a blur—the ceremony and reception, their honeymoon ride to the Waldorf-Astoria.

Images of Mama's furious face surfaced. Of Papa hosting the reception with his chin held high. Of his tender kiss, his eyes glistening, as he bid her good-bye. Of the well wishes and exclamations of their friends.

"A wedding we'll never forget."

The Van Cliffs left the church in a quiet rage, demanding Alfonse explain himself.

Birdie overheard one guest say, "I came to see a wedding. So I stayed."

But she kept her gaze on Eli. She wanted to remember him above all else.

When the porter let them into their room and at last they were alone, Eli kissed her.

"I prayed for this," she whispered into his chest as he held her in the morning light.

"For me to make love to you?"

She blushed with a soft giggle. "To be rescued. Walking down the aisle, I begged the Lord to deliver me."

Hadn't He been singing to her all along?

Do not be dismayed. Do not worry or be afraid.

"Do you fear waking one day only to find it all was a dream?" he asked.

"That would be a living nightmare." She rose up on her elbow, not ashamed when the sheet fell away.

He'd been so patient and kind, tender on their wedding night. Mama had prepared her for everything but being with a man.

Anxious and shy, Eli ordered dinner for the room. Dining on roasted duck and vegetables, hot buttered bread and chocolate cake, they talked nonstop as Eli detailed every juicy tidbit of his trip to her altar.

"It was Rose, Birdie. She felt so grateful to be released from our agreement, she pledged to repay me. She suspected all along we had affection for one another. She approached Alfonse. When and where is still a mystery, but they devised a plan. When Alfonse wrote to me, I wondered if I'd not stepped into another world where dreams come true."

"But what about your family? What about saving Hapsworth?"

"I will find a way, love. I will."

His family was not happy over losing the Gottlieb fortune but agreed, in light of recent changes, Eli must follow his heart.

Oh, there was so much to talk about, and they had their entire lives to say everything on their hearts, but at last it was time to sleep.

Eli took her hand, walking her to their bedroom, kissing her, removing the pins from her hair, running his hands through her long tresses.

"My heart is bursting." *His kisses slipped along her cheek and down her neck.*

With a sigh, she clung to him, passions she'd never felt with Alfonse rising. Eli was not a cup of tepid tea.

"We sail home in three days," *he said, working the buttons of her leaving dress.* "I suggest we not leave this room until they come for our bags."

She raised up on her toes to kiss him, a sensual grin on her lips. "I'm all yours, Lord Montague." With a shiver, her dress fell at her feet. "But before we go, I must say good-bye to Mama."

Eli raised his head and gently brushed her hair from her eyes. "Let's not speak of your mama at this moment." With that he scooped her into his arms, carrying her away.

Birdie laughed. She was a free bird.

Did she feel the same in the power of daylight? More than ever. There was so much to explore about this man, from the joys of their wedding bed to her new home in Hapsworth to her role as a countess.

"I love you, Eli, so very much. Kiss me, darling, please kiss me."

He gathered her in his arms, bringing his lips to hers, his palm skimming the bare curve of her hip. She gave herself to him and to the joys of being a woman, and to the sheer happiness of being his wife.

TENLEY

"You're quiet."

"Thinking." Tenley slowed the Mercedes at the red light, the silhouette of Cape Canaveral Hospital behind them, doused in noonday sun. "But hey, this is a banner day. You got your cast off and have just one more chemo treatment to go!" She mashed the horn and rolled down the windows, leaning out. "Blanche Albright is almost done with cancer!"

"What are you? A boor? Roll up the windows, it's blazes outside."

Blanche was right about the heat. July temperatures had settled over Cocoa Beach with intensity.

"How do you feel? You're done."

"I feel like I've been run over." Blanche wore a bold blue turban on her head, the dark circles under her blue eyes telling of her ordeal. Her cheeks were gaunt and her skin pale.

"You'll heal."

"Pray to God the cancer doesn't return."

"It won't. It won't." Ever since the afternoon in New York when she invited God in, Tenley noticed a change. She talked to Him more. Loved Blanche a little bit more easily. Hoped more in Him, less in herself.

"How's the book?"

"Coming along."

Actually, it was done. She'd typed every blasted word of Gordon's. Once she started she couldn't stop. The story was beautiful and perfect. She changed nothing.

She'd stuffed the manuscript into the middle desk drawer and worked to make the story "her own." But it wasn't her own. It was his with updated language and more textured kissing scenes.

The light turned green and Tenley turned for home.

Four weeks of messing with the book and she had to be done. Turn it in. But did it sound like her voice? Would they recognize Gordon's?

The questions fed the tension in her gut. But if she backed off this book, her career was over. She'd have failed Charlie, Brené, and everyone who believed in her. Even Dad and Great-Great-Grandpa Gordon.

Either this was her book or not. If not, she'd wasted the last month. If it was, she needed to send it.

"Hey, Blanche, want to celebrate getting your cast off? Go

out to eat or just drive up the coast to Daytona? Or go south to Miami?"

But Blanche rested against the car door, her mouth slightly open as she slept.

Tears watered Tenley's eyes. "You sleep, Blanche. You sleep."

Reaching for the radio, Tenley finished the ride home with oldies from Ocean FM, musing over the last month.

Jonas came over on the weekends to watch *Newhart* or play three-handed euchre with Blanche or walk on the beach with Tenley, talking. They ate pizza, buckets of chicken, sandwiches, or Mrs. Sullivan's leftovers, Tenley's favorite.

He was working on furniture designs for a new restaurant, and every time he talked about it his countenance changed. He was born to do this.

There were no more kisses after the graduation party, and they settled into the routine of friends.

"I'm going back to New York, Jonas. I can't leave part of my heart here."

"Funny, 'cause you're taking part of my heart there."

But she ached to taste him some nights. Their good-byes at the door often stretched from a minute to two, to five, then ten, neither one of them wanting to say good-bye. If only someone would say, "Kiss me!" But neither one braved the barrier.

Just thinking of it now stirred her emotions. But she was cautious. She was wary. Both of them were keen with the reality Tenley was going home at the end of the month. Back to her life on Fifth Avenue.

Turning into Grove Manor, Tenley helped Blanche inside, tucked her into bed, and drew the shades to cut the afternoon light.

"I'll be back to check on you."

Meandering out the back door and toward the beach, she glanced back at the house. She hadn't wanted to come, and now she knew she didn't want to leave.

This place had changed her. Blanche had changed her. But Jonas, oh, Jonas. She would never be the same.

"You let me sleep." Blanche shuffled across the library without her blue turban. She carried a wooden tray of cut apples and oranges, a bowl of cherries, and a side of cheese and crackers.

"You usually do after chemo." For the last hour, Tenley had pored over an e-mail to Brené, ready to send the story.

Blanche dropped into the chair next to the desk, thin wisps of hair bouncing with dust beams in the three o'clock light, reached for an orange slice, and leaned to see the computer screen.

"So, you're all finished?"

"I think so." Tenley winced, pressing her fist to her lips. "I'm nervous."

"Said no author ever."

Tenley laughed with an exhale, running her hands through her hair. "I just don't want to disappoint them."

Lie. They'd love this story. No questions. It's a wonder Gordon never turned it in. *Why didn't he?* She might never know, and for now, she was grateful.

You did me a solid, Great-Great-Grandpa.

"Didn't you say your editor was fine with a rough draft? Doubt is just another color of fear, Tenley." Blanche layered a piece of cheese over a cracker. "So the book is good?"

"I think so. Different from *Someone to Love*."

"Cheese and crackers, so good." Blanche dusted cracker bits

from her top to the floor. "Are you ready to hit Send? Gotta tell you, I'm impressed you wrote a book so quickly."

"Yeah, it was a lot of . . ." Copying. "Late nights."

Tenley blew out a long breath. Here's where the whole plan blew up. From here on out, the book would become a living lie. One she'd have to tell for the rest of her life.

"How'd you come up with the characters? They were so real."

"How much research did you do? It's like you lived in the Gilded Age."

Shaking out her arms and legs, tipping her head from side to side, she stretched like an athlete about to run a race. Anticipation buzzed her nerves. One last time . . .

Are you sure?

Once she hit Send, the saga began. No turning back.

"Hit Send." Blanche shoved an apple slice with a cut of cheese into her mouth. "Am I usually this hungry after chemo?"

"No."

"I suppose there's always a chance they won't like it, Tenley." Blanche's cloaked confession eased the tip of Tenley's trepidation. Great, if they didn't like it, she had an out. She'd not publish the book but she met her deadline, fulfilling her part of the deal.

Blanche reached for another cracker, peeking over Tenley's shoulder. "Good to go?"

"Yeah, just thinking about—"

"Stop thinking. Just do it." Blanche reached around, tapped Tenley's mouse, and launched the e-mail through cyber space.

"Blanche!" Tenley panicked and fumbled with the mouse, trying to undo the e-mail. "I wasn't ready."

Her mother sat back in her chair. "You're welcome."

"I'm not thanking you! You had no right, Blanche." *Where was the undo option?* "That was mine to send. You think because I gave up Paris to help you that you can walk into my life and do what you want? Well, you can't." She rose from her chair, circling the library, aiming her self-loathing at her mother.

"Tenley, I'm—I'm sorry." She held an orange slice between her fingers. "I only meant to help."

"You want to help? Leave me alone." Tenley slammed her laptop shut and dropped to the chair, burying her face in her hands.

"Tenley?"

"What?"

"I think you were right. I shouldn't have eaten so much."

She glanced up as Blanche disappeared from the library, the sound effects of cancer and chemo spilling down the stairs.

THIRTY-FOUR

From: Queen.Brene@BarclayPublishing.com
Subject: Wow!

Tenley,

My family is livid with me. I spent all weekend reading your manuscript. I'm blown away. Blown. Away! It's like you found a piece of yourself you didn't know existed. It's your wit and voice, but I see shades of a deeper, more profound writer.

The ending had me in tears!

Now I see why you struggled . . . You were searching for that deeper place.

This book is going to be a huge hit, Ten. I can feel it. My fingers are buzzing as I type.

How did you land 1903 so perfectly? I tell you, I saw shades of your grandfather in your words. Did I ever tell you I wrote my senior paper on him?

Your talent knows no bounds, girl. I sent it on to Wendall and Paul. I think we're going to fast-track this.

As for edits, I've a few suggestions. Nothing major. I'll have notes to you by the end of the month.

Wow, Tenley. You should be proud. This has been a hard season for you, and we've added pressure, but you pushed through like a pro. I have a million questions about how you came up with this story. Message me when you're in town. We'll have lunch at Delmonico's. You know all the old Barclay deals were made there.

Love,

Brené

BIRDIE

OCTOBER 1907

After four years of marriage, she knew her husband's expressions. Tonight, in the dining room candlelight, he appeared handsome and calm, praising their fine meal but unable to mask the concern in his eyes.

"You heard from Len today?" Birdie asked. She'd seen the letter from his London solicitor on his desk.

"Yes." A simple answer as he took another bite of beef.

"Well? Are you going to keep me in suspense?"

His father had died in the winter and Eli inherited his title. He was now the Marquess of Ainsworth, lord and master of Hapsworth and the surrounding tenant farmers and village. He'd inherited great lands and a great debt.

"He reported on the death duties." Eli sat back, raising his wineglass. "W-what is new in your world, darling? How was the tea for the school? Did you raise sufficient funds?"

"We did very well, but you're not shutting me out of the business of Hapsworth. What did Len say?"

"You know what he said. The death duties are steep. On top of debts already incurred. It will take all of our wits and wherewithal to save us."

Eli used all of his wit and resources to save Hapsworth the last four years, but the death taxes would be more than he could manage.

His mama had moved to the London house after his father's funeral and never returned. In her grief she could not face Hapsworth and the memories.

"I've lost my eldest son and my husband while living at that place. I cannot bear it. Make it your own, Eli. It belongs to you and Birdie now."

Papa remained adamant about withholding a proper dowry but sent a generous financial gift every Christmas. The money was welcomed and helped sustain them but was no match for the rising debt.

"Let me write to Papa, Eli. Tell him of our predicament and—"

"And assure him his resistance to a marriage settlement was well founded? It would only prop up his opinion of my family's foolishness." Eli dropped his silverware against his plate. "Isn't it bad enough that I cannot protect you from what's to come?"

Birdie cast him a stern look. "I've told you, I do not need protecting. We are in this together. You've done more than most to save your inheritance, my love. Mark my words."

He'd ventured forward with a man bringing electricity to Yorkshire only to have the company fail within the year. They'd lost a small fortune.

His efforts to recuperate the loss through investments also yielded nothing. Trading was a long game, and they had neither the time nor the proper skill to play it.

"Thank you, darling, but I get no credit for trying."

"Then what shall we do?"

"I've no idea. I feel even my prayers fall short of the mark." He took up his utensils and sliced another bite of Mrs. Bourne's delicious roast. "How much did you bring in for the school? I need some cheery news."

"Enough for new chairs in every classroom."

"Splendid. The children will feel like kings."

"I'm sure they will." She tried to keep a straight face, but she had much more pressing good news. "I hope our son or daughter will attend the school and sit in the relatively new chairs."

Eli froze in midmotion, his gaze fixed on her. "Darling, what did you say?"

Birdie went about eating, having fun with his astonishment. "You heard me. I don't believe I whisper at this table."

"You said *our* son or daughter. Going to school. Are you with child?" His fork clattered against his plate as he left his chair and dropped to one knee beside her, kissing her hand. "Are you well? How do you fare?"

"Very well, so far." She beamed, feeling the warm blush of happiness. Four years in the waiting, their season had come at last.

"When? When will this blessed event be?"

"The doctor believes April."

"You've brought me good news indeed, love." He pulled her from her chair, wrapping her in his arms. "What are taxes and debt when we've a son—"

"Or daughter."

"—on the way. Yes, a son or daughter." He laughed and swung her around. "He'll be the ninth Marquess of Ainsworth. If we have a daughter, I'll go to the House of Lords and demand the laws be changed. She'll be the first woman peer to inherit the Ainsworth title."

Oh, the joy in his face was worth the painful years of waiting.

"You've made me very happy, Birdie." He kissed her long, lovingly, and deep.

"As you have and always will make me."

She loved him more than the day they married. More than when he brought her to Hapsworth. More than when he stayed by her side when she fell ill. More than when he wept openly over their first baby, a son, peaceful and stillborn.

"I promise you we will have a good life for our child if we have to sell Hapsworth to do it, Birdie."

"Begging your pardon, m'lord." Manfred entered. "You've a visitor. A Mr. Gordon Phipps Roth."

Birdie gripped her husband. "Gordon Phipps Roth? The American author?"

"I believe so, your ladyship. He's in the library."

"Did he give the reason for his visit?" Eli cast Birdie a curious expression. "Did you hear of him visiting York?"

"Not at all. I hardly know the man. And you know how I feel about him." She smoothed her hair in place, tugging on the edges of her gloves, straightening her strand of pearls. "Manfred, please send tea and sandwiches. We wouldn't want to appear inhospitable."

"I've alerted Mrs. Bourne."

When the butler had gone, Eli squared his bow tie and offered Birdie his arm. "I must admit my curiosity has the better of me."

"As does mine." She hesitated a step, holding Eli in check. "What could he possibly be doing here? You don't think he's come to confess, do you? Mercy, I can't imagine. Darling, if I in anyway appear rude or disrespectful—"

"Confess? It would mean his career. And you could never be rude. Or disrespectful." His voice mellowed with compassion and a soft twinkle lit his eyes.

But Birdie's throat had gone dry. She could be rude to Gordon Phipps Roth. She could! "I fear I might say what I've bottled up the last four years." Beneath her gloves, her fingers chilled with nerves. "And yet I wonder what in the world brought him to Yorkshire?"

"Shall we let him say his piece? I'm sure he'll explain. Then you can have your honest say. Now that you bring it up, I'm a bit miffed at him myself. Tell you what, if either one of us appears inhospitable, we shall clear our throats and say, let's see, ah, how about, 'Isn't it a lovely evening for guests?'"

Birdie made a face, laughing softly. "Yes, isn't it a lovely evening for guests."

Phipps Roth waited by the fireplace wearing a traveling suit, his hair the color of the night, curling and disheveled over his high forehead, the man beneath weary. Yet his eyes were bright, his step lively as he greeted Eli and Birdie with a slight bow.

"Sorry to barge in. I forget you eat so late here."

"No, no need to apologize. Please, be seated." Eli motioned to the couch by the fire. "We've tea and sandwiches on the way."

"How generous, but I didn't mean to be a bother."

Birdie took her usual seat by the fire, reaching for the book she'd been reading. A prop to keep her hands occupied.

"Mr. Phipps Roth, please, Birdie and I are curious as to the reason for your visit." Eli stood beside her. "What on earth are you doing in northern England? Are you lecturing?"

The author cleared his throat, his brightness fading as he took his seat.

The library was Birdie's favorite room in all of Hapsworth. She spent many a pleasant winter evening reading by the fire. She'd started writing again.

Mama even shipped over her desk when the scuttlebutt of the

wedding died down. It now sat in the far corner by the bay windows overlooking the grounds, a new typewriter at the ready.

"Nothing as grand as lecturing. I was in London on business. As you know, Barclay recently opened a London office." He reached inside his jacket pocket, retrieving a long envelope. "It was then I concluded this was the best time to give Miss Shehorn, rather, Lady Ainsworth, or is it Marchioness Ainsworth?" He passed the envelope to Birdie. "I apologize, I'm not quite sure how to address you."

"Birdie will be fine." She eyed the envelope, then Eli. "What is this, Mr. Roth?"

"Open it. You will see, Birdie. And please, call me Gordon."

Eli retrieved the letter opener from his desk, handing it to Birdie. "Go ahead . . ."

She started to slice open the flap, but sighed, setting the letter and the opener in her lap. "I'm sorry, but I feel I must speak up. Mr. Roth, it seems—"

"Please, call me Gordon."

"—something peculiar happened with your book, *The Girl in the Carriage.*"

"Birdie, open the envelope, then we can talk," he said.

But her adrenaline flowed. Her pulse thumped in her ears. She had courage. Or at least some profound bravado.

"You are a renowned and fine author, yet I could not help but notice how similar your book was to mine. The same one I submitted to Barclay. Do you recall that day outside Daniel Barclay's office? We spoke, briefly."

"I remember. Open the envelope, Birdie."

"I'd gone to see Barclay about my own manuscript. One I submitted to him and never saw again. And your title was *my* title. Or close enough to it." Her confession would not be tamed.

Beside her, Eli cleared his throat. "Isn't it a lovely evening for guests?"

She peered up at him. *No . . .* "It took me two years to finally read *your* book and I was dumbstruck to see my story between the binding." She peered up at Eli. "Wasn't I, darling?"

"Yes, you were." He reached down for the letter opener. "Let's see what Gordon brought round to us, shall we?"

She sighed. Yes, of course. With one quick flick, she opened the letter, her jaw set. How could he steal another author's work? No matter how unknown she might be. It was an outrage. Now that she had a chance to speak her mind, she was going to do so.

"It's a check," she said. "A very generous check." She passed the bank note to her husband, then addressed Gordon. "I don't understand."

"That is your share of the royalties from *The Girl in the Carriage*. I wish it could be more, but I spent a good portion upon my marriage in '05. I've also recently become a father, you see . . ." He gazed toward the fire, his hands clasped on his lap. "I feel rather humiliated by it all."

Birdie rose to her feet. "So *The Girl in the Carriage is* my story? Daniel Barclay claimed my manuscript was returned to me. But I never found it."

"He gave it to me the day you and I met in his office, though upon my honor I didn't know it was your manuscript." Gordon sounded contrite, his frame shrinking into the large red couch. "Though I am without excuse. I clearly knew the work was not my own. Barclay convinced me he'd hired someone to . . ." Gordon shoved his hand through his wild hair, a bead of perspiration on his brow. "To solve my problem. He assured me it was all completely aboveboard."

"But you're the great Gordon Phipps Roth. What problem could you possibly encounter?"

"I came upon a severe case of writer's block. My intended at the time had rejected me after years of pursuing her, and I fell into despair. Try as I might, I could not produce one coherent word. Barclay was desperate for another book, and when I went to his office to tell him he'd have nothing new from me, he handed me your manuscript. 'Do something with this,' he said. I read the most wonderful, fresh chapters. The story engaged me. I was envious of the writer's skill, really. Barclay suggested I rewrite the story, make it my own. Being the weak man that I am, I agreed. I'm ashamed now, but I was desperate enough to listen to him. My pride, my foolishness, my desire for fame and fortune . . . I've borne my guilt these past years and will continue to do so, but I must do something to make it right. The book has been a phenomenal success. More than any of us imagined. So, I come to you and your husband with some penance. Truth is, I loved the book so much I changed very little." He raised his gaze to Birdie's. "As I'm sure you are aware. Anyway, this money is small pickings compared to what you have in your accounts, but I hope it may bless you and ease some of my pain."

Numbed by his confession, Birdie searched for a proper reply, her ire fading. "I-I don't know what to . . . Barclay truly stole my manuscript?"

"We suspected it all along," Eli said.

"He saw something in your writing similar to my own and he was desperate to get a book out of me. He admitted his deed earlier this year. Confessed he thought an heiress didn't need her book published. She already had more than most. He believed your endeavor to write was merely a passing fancy. But I, the great Gordon Phipps Roth, was the next great American author." Gordon crunched his hands together. "The book has changed my career. I was acclaimed before, but now newspapermen and scholars alike regale me as quite possibly one of the enduring literary voices of our time. The sales have brought great reward."

"Because of my book?" Birdie's trembling legs could hold her no longer and she sank slowly to the nearest chair.

"Because of your book. Well, *our* book. I did a good bit of editing." He forced a laugh. "You are quite a talent, Birdie. I sensed it that day in the foyer. Any young woman who'd wait to speak to the great Daniel Barclay unintimidated . . . I do hope you're writing even now." He glanced at Eli. "Are you encouraging her?"

"Most assuredly. Just recently she's returned to her writing." Eli nodded toward her. "Birdie, darling, what do you make of this?"

She glanced between Eli and Gordon. "I hardly believe it . . . Why did you come now to tell us? Why not just keep the secret?"

Manfred entered with tea and sandwiches. Gordon moved to fill his plate and pour a spot of tea. "I turned in my latest book six months ago. I was quite proud of it. It's been several years since I've written a full-length novel. I've been traveling, guest lecturing. By the way, our story is beloved in France and Germany." He carried his sandwiches and tea to the fire. "At one time I feared I'd never write again. I owe a great deal to you and to my wife and son. Anyway, Barclay rejected the book." He took a bite of his sandwich. "Said it didn't have the voice of *The Girl in the Carriage*. That's when he revealed your name and his dastardly scheme. I believe he considers himself safe now that you're away, a grand marchioness in England, a peer and member of an established aristocratic family."

"You're a trusting soul," Eli said, pouring himself and Birdie a cup of tea. "What's to keep us from taking this news public?"

"Nothing at all. In truth, I've considered taking it public myself."

"You can't be serious," Birdie said. "You'll discredit yourself and disappoint readers everywhere."

"Were it not for my wife and child, I'd write the story myself and send it to the papers. But I must consider them." He sipped his tea, staring toward the fire. "But confession would ease my guilt and shame. And there is the fact that I live on the royalties your magical voice brought me, Birdie." He finished another sandwich, shaking his head. "Barclay hides it, but he's ready to do away with me. All of my prior works combined could not match the success of *The Girl in the Carriage*. I've concluded it's best to exit the publishing world on a success rather than a failure. We writers are too prone to despondency, are we not? But no, you, you seem quite happy."

Eli pressed his hand to her shoulder. "She told me tonight she is with child."

"Congratulations!" He jumped up to shake Eli's hand and to kiss Birdie's. "How thrilling. Our son is our greatest joy."

"But we have other woes." Birdie peered at Eli. "Death taxes and—"

"We're fine, Birdie."

Gordon's expression relayed surprise. "Then my payment came at an opportune time?"

"We're grateful." Eli sipped his tea. "What will you do now that your book has been rejected?"

"Find work. Come clean to my wife about the full extent of my troubles with Barclay." Gordon replenished his own tea. "I can seek a teaching position. Perhaps pursue another publisher, but that option comes with implied risks." He leveled his gaze at Eli and Birdie. "I fear I've lost my gift. My biggest success was not my own."

The room fell silent save for the ticking of the clock and the crackling of the fire.

"You should trust your wife, Gordon. She will help bear your burden." Birdie slipped her hand through Eli's. "And might I offer a solution that would help us all?"

TENLEY

The night before Blanche's final chemo treatment, she invited Jonas to dinner, insisting on making her *famous* lasagna. Tenley hovered around the kitchen's heady aromas, anticipating the evening and Jonas's arrival.

At the stove Blanche stirred the browning meat, the July heat pushing against the windows. A dark blue train of storm clouds rolled over the ocean.

Tenley loved the summer rains, the clap of thunder over the ocean, the tumult of waves crashing upon the shore, then at last, the heavy rhythm of rain against the tin roof.

It was then she knew. Someone more powerful than she commanded the storms, the sun, the stars . . . and He watched over her. The notion filled her with peace despite her own uncertainty and guilt. Yes, guilt.

As for Blanche, Tenley made peace with her over E-mail Gate. It wasn't her fault Tenley ripped off Gordon's story.

Twice she almost e-mailed Brené the truth. Twice an e-mail from her editor dropped into her in-box with another round of praise and palpable excitement.

Sinking deeper and deeper, Tenley knew what she had to do. Commit. Grandpa Gordon's story was now hers.

"I'm going to miss you when you go," Blanche said from the quiet, her attention fixed on browning the hamburger and onions. "I can't tell you how much I appreciate you coming."

"This won't be the end, Blanche. You'll visit me in New York. I'll visit you here."

She glanced up. "Will you? Really? When? Let's decide now."

Tenley snatched a piece of meat from the skillet. "I don't know. When I can."

"Thanksgiving?"

She shrugged. "We'll see. Maybe." Depended on how much of Jonas she could scrub from her heart by then. "Or you could come to New York."

Blanche nodded, wiping her eyes. "Yes, New York. It's lovely in fall. We could go to the Macy's parade."

Tenley smiled. "We could. Dad took me every year until college."

"Well, now it's your mother's turn."

Tears surprised Tenley. "Yeah, maybe. Sure."

Working together, they assembled the lasagna, layering noodles, meat, and cheese. Tenley slathered a loaf of bread with garlic butter to be heated when the lasagna was done.

"We're set. Brownies and ice cream for dessert," Blanche said. "Now come with me."

Curious, Tenley followed her mother to her room, where three dresses, all with a distinct vintage style, lay across the bed.

"Let's dress up. Which one do you want to wear?" Blanche held up a blue number with a button-up bodice and a flared skirt. "I think I'd like this one."

Tenley picked up the first dress, the red one with the Peter Pan collar. "This is pretty."

"One of my favorites." Blanche draped her dress over her arm. "I was wearing this when I met your dad. At a newspaper cock-tail party. I couldn't believe I was talking to Gordon Phipps Roth's great-grandson." She ran her hand over what remained of her hair. "He was charming, handsome, spontaneous. Then we got married, and he became responsible."

"Thank goodness for me."

"Yes, well, so, the blue dress for me and the red for you? I'll put Dean Martin and Frank Sinatra on the radio and we can iron these. Won't take long. Then let's set the dining room table with china and candles."

"Iron? Of what ancient ritual do you speak?" Tenley dropped the dress back to the bed. "If it's wrinkled I don't wear it."

Blanche sighed. "Why does this not surprise me? How can I forget you're the girl who wore a man's checked robe half the summer? Come on, I'll show you the ironing board. I'll shower while you iron, then I'll do my dress."

Tenley hesitated. "I don't know how."

Blanche paused at the bedroom door. "What?"

"How to iron . . . didn't have anyone to teach me."

She motioned for Tenley to grab the dress and follow. "Well, now you do."

They gathered in the laundry room off the kitchen, the lasagna smells setting Tenley's stomach to rumbling.

Blanche opened a small door on the back wall, and a short ironing board fell forward. "I learned to iron right here in this room. My grandmother taught me."

"How old were you?"

"Ten, eleven. Not long after we moved here."

"What was she like?"

"You remind me of her. Pretty, witty, sort of droll about life." Blanche plugged in the iron. "Devoted to family."

"I don't think I'm droll. Or devoted to family."

"You don't give yourself credit. If you're not devoted, what are you doing here? And you wrote Ezra like your dad. By your own confession. Yes, you're devoted. And droll. However, Granny, she smoked like a chimney. The smell of menthol reminds me of her to this day. Now, come on over here. Take your dress and fit the neck on the narrow end of the board. Good, now slide it down and straighten it out." Blanche pulled around a step stool and sat down.

"Are you getting tired? We don't have to—"

"We do. I'm fine. Just need to sit. Cancer isn't going to steal my last few days with my girl. This dress is cotton, so you need fairly high heat. The more delicate the fabric, the lower the heat. Some garments you even iron on the reverse side. Others, with a cloth in between."

"You need a university degree to do this." Tenley reached for the iron, winced when it shot out a puff of steam.

"You have a university degree. Next, test the iron's heat. Wet your finger and tap it against the bottom, see if it's hot."

"I don't have a degree in ironing. And you want me to what? Touch the iron? You're kidding, right? I'll burn myself."

"Wet your finger . . . go on . . . it won't hurt."

Skeptical and scowling, Tenley wet her finger good and slapped it against the iron, wincing.

"Hear that sizzle? Now you're ready to go." Blanche pointed to the worn spray bottle on the shelf. "Spritz a little water on the dress . . . good . . . hold the edge of the sleeve . . . You don't want to iron in the wrinkles, Tenley. Sort of defeats the purpose. Good, good, look at you. Like a pro. See, even an NYU graduate can iron an old cotton dress."

"What about this here?" Tenley pointed to the seam under the sleeve.

"That's the dart. Just shapes the bodice. Iron it but keep the seam flat."

In the warm laundry room, with a storm rolling in over the Atlantic, Blanche taught Tenley to press the wrinkles from a vintage red dress, the way her grandmother had taught her, and probably her mother before that and her mother. . .

THIRTY-FIVE

JONAS

The front door was unlocked. When no one answered, Jonas let himself in.

"Tenley? Miss Blanche?"

Making his way through the living room toward the kitchen, he found Tenley leaning against the porch rail facing the rain.

"Tenley?" he said, joining her. "I love storms over the beach." He peered down at her to see her blue eyes rimmed in red. "Hey, hey, why the tears?" With a sniffle, she fell against him. Jonas hesitated a second, then wrapped her in his arms.

"Blanche taught me to iron in the same room her grandmother taught her." Water dripped from the edge of the veranda roof, splashing against the board steps. "It's the first thing she taught me. Our first passed-down mother-daughter tradition."

"Didn't she teach you to dress yourself, tie your shoes, eat?"

She straightened, laughing softly. "I learned those by osmosis."

He chuckled softly and leaned against the porch post, his arms cold and empty without her. "Y-you still heading to New York soon?"

"Yeah."

He pulled her to him and trailed his fingers down her cheek, to her neck. "When you do, take this with you."

He touched his lips to hers, their connection starting slow, almost unsure. Then Tenley shifted into the moment, wrapping her arms around him, her body against his.

"I don't want to break your heart," she whispered when he raised his head, his heart pulsing with passion.

"Then don't." He kissed her again, letting his heart go when she cupped her hand behind his head, the palm of her other hand pressed against his thudding heart.

He fell back against the porch post, taking her with him. His body kicked into overdrive and if he didn't stop now . . .

"Tenley, hold up." He gently moved away from her, putting distance between them.

Overhead, the clouds rumbled and the rain thickened.

"We're coming up on the point of no return real fast." In truth, he'd arrived at it the moment he set eyes on her tonight.

He'd been fine the last month, hanging out with her on the weekends, watching *Newhart*, entertaining Blanche, but tonight when he saw her eyes rimmed with tears, he split his chest open and handed her his heart.

Kissing only confirmed their chemistry. They were good together.

She collapsed against the opposite post, stretching her hand to the rain. "I blame you."

"I blame you." He grinned, pacing the length of the wraparound. He was a goner. Good-bye and see ya.

"You're a good kisser." She pressed her lips together. "Too good."

He stared at her for a second, then laughed, holding up his hands, warning her to stay back. "Don't. My resistance against you is futile."

"I really don't want to break your heart." She sat on the steps, her toes curled over the edge, catching the drops from the porch overhang. "Or mine."

Jonas dropped down next to her. "If we're afraid of our hearts breaking, then maybe there's something real happening between us."

She brushed her hand over his hair and rested her head on his shoulder. "But I'm New York and you're Cocoa Beach."

"I know, but there has to be a solu—"

"Hey out there on the veranda." Blanche appeared at the door in her blue flared dress, a string of pearls at her neck and a white turban on her head. "You ready for dinner? Tenley, you're not changed. Put on the red dress."

"Right. After all that ironing, I should show it off." Her gaze met his. "I think we should just leave it."

"Where? Floating with no answer?" Around them the fat raindrops soaked the air, the ground, and him. "I think I love you."

She whispered against his skin. "That's the opposite of leaving it."

Standing, she went inside and he tried not to watch her long legs disappear through the kitchen, his hopes sinking with each echoing step.

"She'll come around," Blanche said.

"I don't think so." He smiled up at the woman who was clearly trying to matchmake with Mom. "But thank you for trying."

"I'm not done yet. Come on inside. What do you want to drink?"

He poured an iced tea, then helped Blanche carry out the lasagna, drawing up short to see the table covered with a linen cloth, white china, and glinting candlelight.

Tenley appeared in the door barefoot, wearing a red dress, a deep crease in the middle of the skirt where the iron must have gotten away, her sleek hair drifting over her shoulders. He couldn't breathe.

Sinatra's smooth voice crooned, "Fly me to the moon . . ."

And for the moment, that's exactly where Jonas was heading. To the moon. With Tenley as his rocket.

THIRTY-SIX

TENLEY

Friday afternoon, Tenley carried a load of laundry into the living room to fold while watching a rerun of *Blue Bloods*.

Blanche had decided to nap before Jonas came over to finish season eight of *Newhart*. Apparently the final show was spectacular, a television classic.

Separating her clothes from Blanche's, Tenley pushed aside the reality that a week from Sunday she headed home.

In many ways, Tenley ached to return to her life in New York. Monday the thirty-first she had lunch scheduled with Brené at Delmonico's.

Jer Gonda wrote to say he'd be in the city at the end of the month and wanted to set up a meeting. The screenwriter for *Someone to Love* was on her second pass and the team loved it.

And Alicia invited her to Addison May's birthday party.

But in so many other ways, she'd become suddenly attached to Cocoa Beach. The man, not the land.

Jonas came by every evening, even if just for an hour, sitting on the couch watching *Newhart*, talking, and just *being*.

Blanche insisted he come to dinner as often as possible, even if she wasn't always strong enough to cook. She really stretched Tenley's cooking skills, forcing her to learn the number of *at least two* other pizza-delivery places when everyone tired of Domino's.

Jonas in his quiet strength was so romantic, his hand barely touching hers as they sat together on the couch. Much to her disappointment, he never kissed her like he had that night on the veranda. He kissed her good night politely at the door.

Yet . . . two nights ago they found themselves alone on the couch, in the dark, the *Newhart* DVD fading to black.

He pulled her to him and they sank into the sofa cushions, into the wonder of each other.

He stopped just shy of letting his hands wander to intimate places, pushing to his feet with a heavy exhale.

"Good night, Tenley."

"Jonas," she whispered, "you can stay."

"Ha-ha, no, no. I can't. I've been pulling a Tim Tebow my whole life, waiting for the right girl and for marriage. Yeah, I know, no one does that these days. Besides, you're leaving in a week."

"Waiting?"

He flipped on the end-table lamp and found his keys, on the floor under the coffee table. "Yeah, read the Book. You'll get a sense of why."

"The book?"

"The little black one on the edge of your desk . . . the Holy Book."

"Ah." She rose up to meet his gaze. "But don't you want—"

"More than I want to breathe. More than I want to wake up in the morning." He pressed her hand to his heart. "I'm an inferno. But I have to do this right. I want to do it right. I have to honor my own vows to the Lord." He peered away from her, a soft blush on his cheeks. "It's hard to explain, but—"

"Read the Book." How could she be disappointed? He was willing to sacrifice his desires for One greater.

She'd never met a man like him. Not even Dad.

"Good night." When he leaned to kiss her on the forehead, she fell in love. Right then and there.

The clothes were folded and put away when Jonas walked in. He kissed her as she ordered the pizza, then asked about her day.

"I have a surprise. I brought my computer to show you my new designs." He'd been working on the tables and chairs for the new restaurant. Tenley didn't know anything about making furniture, but she wanted to see Jonas's work.

She joined him on the sofa, resting her head on his shoulder.

"This is going to be the bar." He manipulated a 3-D program to give her all angles of the design. "It'll have a driftwood look on top and reclaimed wood on the bottom."

"It's beautiful."

"Here's the table design. I had one like this before Mason took off with my stuff."

"Jonas?" She sat up. "Why did he steal your designs? Why not create his own?"

"Because he was lazy. I learned a lot from him, but I had more of an eye for it. A lot of his designs just didn't work." Jonas planted an affectionate kiss on her cheek. "I've had to kind of work through all of that again, designing these pieces, not reliving what they did. I mean, who steals someone else's stuff? Their best friend's to boot?"

A cold dread dropped through her. "Maybe he was desperate. Or scared. Had other things on the line besides himself." She twisted her hands together, an ember of regret flaring.

She'd kept to her commitment. Gordon's manuscript *was* hers. She'd stuffed the truth in order to sleep at night, but once in a while, guilt found room to bloom.

"I get being pressured. I watched you struggle with your

deadline, but you did it, Tenley. You put your mind and heart to it, sat at that desk, and got the job done. There's no excuse ever for stealing another man's work. Or woman's. Especially creative work. I sat up nights dreaming of designs. Mason stole a piece of me"—he slapped his chest—"when he took those designs."

He rested his head on the back of the couch with a soft laugh.

"Listen to me getting all worked up."

"Yeah, how about that . . ." Her laugh sounded nervous. Didn't it? "So, it still bothers you?"

"Sometimes. I've prayed, forgiven, even sent Mason pieces of designs I knew he was missing, but it just gets me how a man can want something so bad he'd steal. Or kill. Okay, look, here's the chairs."

But Tenley couldn't see for looking. She'd stolen for her own advantage. From a dead person. A relative. Certainly it was not the same.

She exhaled, shoving her hair from her face, pushing down the dark flash of panic. She had time to confess. At lunch with Brené. Yes, she'd own up during lunch.

A knock echoed from the front door. The pizza. "Jonas, can you get that while I find my wallet—"

"Don't worry, Ten, I got it." He pulled a folded bill from his pocket as he reached for the door.

Sure enough, the pizza had arrived, along with four guests—Wendall Barclay, Charlie McGuire, Brené Queen, and Elijah Phipps Roth. And they were not smiling.

"Hey, what are you doing here?" Panic gripped her as she shot Charlie a visual check. *Why didn't you call?*

He gave her an *I-tried* face as she patted her pockets for her phone. She'd left it upstairs.

"Tenley," Wendall said, somber and deep. "We need to talk."

BIRDIE

CHRISTMAS 1910

In the library, a fire blazed in the grate as she worked, a soft snow falling beyond the windows, the day's gray light fading toward evening.

"Well, darling, how's the life of a published author?" Elijah bent over her shoulder, kissing her neck, teasing and tickling her. He skimmed the lines of her typewritten page. "The End? At last. In time for the holiday."

"Holiday? I'm only concerned about the deadline. I must have this posted to Gordon by the morning or he'll not have proper time to edit and add what he wills before Barclay's deadline." She rolled the final page out and set it on top of the others, careful of the porcelain dove Eli had given to her. She'd set it on the desk as a reminder of his encouragement and love. "And I'm not a published author. Gordon Phipps Roth is."

This was her third book for, rather *with,* Gordon. She'd found she could write a story in a year, an exceptional pace according to Barclay. Though they had no knowledge of Birdie's agreement with Gordon.

Barclay published their first effort together, *Moonlight on the Hudson,* in '09. Their second, *The House in Murray Hill,* just this past fall.

This finished work, *Winter in New York,* would see the bookstores around Thanksgiving of 1911. Birdie had layered many of the scenes with the magic of Hapsworth, peering out her window as the winter snow drifted slowly toward the ground.

"He's the face, the fame. You're the brains. The talent." Eli poured a glass of port and stood by the fire. "Do I sound ungrateful? I don't mean it if I do."

"You're just defending your wife."

"I do wish you'd let me buy you a proper desk." He crossed the room to where Birdie sat by the floor-to-ceiling windows. "Look, it's battered and worn, the wood so dull."

"But I love this desk. It's battered and worn because I work here." She stretched her arm over the surface. "I've sort of an affection for it. This desk and I are old friends, partners. I sit here when I pray, when God inspires my stories."

"You mean Gordon's stories."

"Don't be a cynic. His latest book paid the wage bill and purchased us a new carriage. The one you love so well."

"Well, I do owe him for that, but still, I prefer to think of the books as *your* stories." He moved to the sofa and sat. "What do you hear from home? I saw a letter . . ."

"Mama and Papa are doing well. They want to come in July again."

Leaving the desk, Birdie stretched and rubbed the knot from the base of her neck. It was good to be done. Her back needed a rest.

"I love that you defend me, darling." She curled up next to Eli on the couch. "That you want to buy me a proper desk, but I have all I need right here in this room. If the rest of Hapsworth were to crumble, I'd be happy with you here, my desk and typewriter, the view of the grounds and a fire in the hearth. I love what I am doing. It gets me out of bed in the morning. It gives me purpose and joy. People say such kind, even profound, things about our stories. You've seen the letters Gordon forwards. We're touching hurting and lonely people as well as providing entertainment and advancing the written word."

"Doesn't it bother you, love, that it's his name on the jacket and not yours? That he gets the newsprint articles and invitations to lectures?"

"No, why would I want to be a lecturer? And I am in the newspaper plenty with the name Ainsworth. But one day I'll write my own book with my name on it. Gordon has suggested it himself."

"Do promise me you will."

"I promise." She caressed his chest and let him cradle her there. After seven years of marriage, she wasn't sure if her heart could beat without his.

"I wish I could give you what you really want." His blue eyes searched hers. "A babe for our nursery."

"It's not you who fails. It is I. But the doctor believes in time we will have a child. I am not sad, Eli. I do not feel I'm missing out. As long as I have you . . ." She could bear the loss of her son and daughter.

She'd given birth to a daughter in the spring of '08. Lady Amy Elizabeth Shehorn Percy.

But the Lord had only gifted her with a few days. The nanny found her unresponsive in her crib, the most peaceful expression on her face.

Birdie had not conceived since.

"I see how the other women look at you," Eli said. "I can only imagine their whispers. 'Why doesn't she have children?' 'What does she do with her time?'"

"Who cares what they think?" She kissed him playfully, teasing, "We do what we must to conceive. And as often as we can."

He laughed and kissed her forehead. "How did I win such favor with God Almighty to have you as my wife? Now, as for Gordon and your writing, I am all for it. Just don't let him take advantage, love. I'm glad we insisted Len draw up a formal agreement."

"I feel we are the ones who take advantage. Did you see the latest check?"

"I did, and I must say again I'm grateful." Eli stood, moving to the fire. "Though my pride is wounded to depend on my wife's earnings."

"Your latest ventures have proven worthy. We are meeting our obligations, keeping Hapsworth going, paying the death duties." She was honored to put her talent toward saving the ancient estate. "Now, what did you buy me for Christmas?"

"Must we do this every year? I shall not tell you. You're worse than a child."

"But I simply cannot wait two more weeks—"

Manfred entered from the far door, a small package in hand. "This just arrived for you, your ladyship."

"Thank you . . . Eli, is this your doing?" Birdie peeled away the plain brown packaging.

"Not I, love."

Inside she found a beautiful leather-bound Bible along with a note. "It's from Gordon."

Dearest Birdie,

I've been reading this book of late and find its poetry and truth comforting. When I spied this copy at a local bookshop, you immediately came to mind. I pray it blesses you as the perfect Christmas gift.

In these pages we find the story of a Savior who gave His life for all. Mine and yours. He commanded us to love like He loved.

Such words move me, and when I think of the gift you've given to me and my family, I want to weep for joy. I can never repay you. The royalties are only a fraction of my debt.

Yet I will endeavor to love you as Christ loved me. As you

have loved me. Unselfishly. I vow that one day we will take your book, not mine, to Barclay for publication.

My best to you and Eli in this joyous season.

Merry Christmas,

GPR

THIRTY-SEVEN

TENLEY

The group gathered around the dining room table and Brené led off.

"Can you explain this?" She pulled out a rubber-banded manuscript. "A Gordon Phipps Roth novel? Where did you get this, and why in blazes did you pass it off as your own?" She swore without a filter.

Tenley grabbed the back of the nearest chair to hold steady. "W-what are you talking about? A Gordon Phipps Roth novel?" Fear swelled in her heart and she could taste its bitter dregs.

Movement just beyond the dining room raised her attention. Jonas, his expression somber, his eyes full of questions.

"Did you steal *Someone to Love* too?" Wendall demanded. "Did your dad write it?"

"What? No. No! How can you say that?" She looked at Brené. "You wanted another great book and I gave you one." She worked on her weak defense by sounding indignant and unjustly accused. "W-who said it was a GPR book? Huh? I am his great-great-granddaughter, you know."

Brené turned to Elijah. "Go ahead, tell her. Man, Tenley, I am so disappointed. So very disappointed."

Her legs jellied and she had to cling to the chair to keep from fainting, to keep from looking back at Jonas. His dark expression sank through her and she shook with repressed tears.

Dear distant cousin Elijah produced a leather journal from a messenger bag.

"Brené and I have lunch now and then. Last week she was bragging to me about your new novel. Because you are a foundation award winner, naturally I was curious and asked for a sneak peek." Elijah opened the journal, setting aside loose, folded pages. "I'm going to read, if you don't mind."

He was patronizing her.

"'July 1947. I've come to the end of myself. My health is failing. I've a doctor appointment this afternoon, but regardless of his medical pronouncements I shall press on, working to see this latest book to the publisher. We are titling it *An October Wedding.*'" Elijah closed the journal and passed Tenley a set of yellow-edged folded pages. "Read these."

Gripped with her anxiety, she could barely move. Keeping her gaze averted, she reached for the pages. *An October Wedding.* Her strength buckled and she fell against the wall.

"Let me help you, Tenley." Wendall took the pages and read the opening paragraph of her—rather, Gordon Phipps Roth's—novel. "You stole his work." Matter-of-fact. No room for debate.

Sliding down the wall, she sat on the hardwood, her skin hot, her emotions too thin for tears.

"I-I found the manuscript in the desk upstairs. I searched online, asked you guys if you'd heard of *An October Wedding.* No one had. So yeah, I took my grandfather's story. I wanted to make it my own, but it was so good . . ." She buried her face in her hands.

"I typed in every word. I only changed things that didn't work for today's reader."

The silence in the room was stifling. It was broken only by the soft *click* of the front door opening. Jonas was leaving. She didn't have to see him go to know. She felt his presence slip away.

"Well, what are we going to do?" Brené said with a heavy sigh. "I knew your book sounded like Phipps Roth. I convinced myself it was because his blood flowed through your veins. I never imagined you'd steal someone's work. I just had marketing and promotions increase their budgets. Sales is ready to sell thousands of units into retail outlets. We've gone to auction on foreign rights."

"Don't kill me here," Charlie said. "But why not go with it? Phipps Roth is dead—"

"Because she didn't write it." Wendall gaped at him. "If I ever find out you were in on this—"

"He wasn't," Tenley said. "I promise. This was my doing."

Elijah folded the pages, returning them to the journal. "The family has looked for the rest of this book over the years, wanting the foundation to publish it, but never located it."

"Begging your pardon, Elijah, but family did find it," Charlie said. "Family is trying to publish it."

She could kiss him for trying so hard.

"Under her own name." Elijah was incredulous. "We're not going to let her steal GPR's work."

"We're publishing the book for the Phipps Roth 125th anniversary," Wendall said with a direct, stern glance at Tenley. "However, we will not be publishing your next novel."

ELIJAH

NOVEMBER 11, 1918

He folded the cable, flooded with relief. The war was over. The killing. The destruction. So many young Englishmen lost. So many good sons never to return home.

His knee had kept him from serving but not from remembering. What those boys faced . . . he knew all too well.

He had passed this war with the old guard, recounting their Boer stories, pretending they still mattered. But they were the past, worthless to their boys in arms. All they could do was pray. And, well, wasn't that the most ardent warfare of all?

Across the library, Birdie sat at her desk, hammering the keys of her typewriter. He'd come to love that sound. The *click-click* of his darling writing stories that changed their world.

Eli tucked the cable into his vest and crossed over to her, reading as she finished the sentence she was writing. She kept the porcelain dove sitting atop the Bible Gordon had given her on the desk's corner.

She glanced up at him. "Now what has you looking jolly?"

"You, of course." He picked up the last page she typed. "*The Berkshires*. Scandal and intrigue among the rich and famous. Did Gordon receive Barclay's approval for the title?"

"Just. That was his cable Manfred brought round this morning."

Eli returned the page to the pile. "Yet he's still not told them about you." Six novels Birdie had written for him, but his pledge to aid her publishing aspirations remained void.

"Don't make waves. I don't care. Need I remind you of our accounts?"

"Still, you work like no other woman of your station."

"They have children and their gossip. What do I need with it? Oh, did I tell you Consuela Churchill, Lady Marlborough, went on and on about the latest Phipps Roth book?" Birdie's sweet chortle brightened his spirit. "She *adored* it."

"In front of you? How did you keep from bursting out?"

"And endanger the secret? No. Besides, I rather like being the only one who knows. I still felt quite proud to hear her praise."

Eli's heart filled with pride. It was her writing and his management of the funds that saved Hapsworth and restored a part of their wealth.

He had intended to marry Rose Gottlieb for her wealth and pray he fell in love. Instead, he married for love and God brought him the wealth he needed to save the family estate.

Birdie stacked the pages, preparing to send them to Gordon. "Do you think Mama and Mack Van Buren will recognize themselves on the pages?"

"Surely you fictionalized their story," Eli said.

"Of course. I would never expose Mama, but Elise and Marcus's story is very similar." Drawing from real life created the best stories. "Papa still doesn't know the truth and I pray he never will."

Birdie's parents sailed over every other year for a month in the summer. July. When Birdie was not writing.

Iris Shehorn had softened toward her daughter, especially after baby Amy died, and the two managed a cordial relationship.

His own mother came for weeks at a time throughout the year, finding she actually missed her memories. She and Iris had become friends and July was a happy month at the manor.

He was a blessed man. Indeed.

"Darling, what is it?" Birdie turned, kissing him, examining his expression.

He retrieved the cable from his coat pocket. "It's over. The war."

"Eli. . ." She reached for the message, reading aloud. "Thank God, oh, thank God. Why are you just now telling me? This is wonderful news. Our boys will be coming home."

"It's the best news." He folded the cable back in his pocket. "But not all of our boys will be coming home. Only those who remain." He turned for his chair. He'd become something of an old man lately, nearing forty, preferring slippers and a good book by the fire to a London party or a house full of dinner guests. "Too many are buried on the battlefields of France. England may never recover, Birdie." He sat, releasing a heavy sigh. "Let this be the war that ends all wars. Having lost two babies, I cannot imagine how the parents of killed soldiers endure. Their futures gone with a single shot."

"So we will continue our prayers. And we will recover, love. We are England." She came to him, perching on the arm of his chair. He settled his hand on the familiar curve of her hip.

"*We* are England?" He smiled up at her. "My American darling . . . How did I deserve you?"

"I'm the lucky one." She stood, pacing away. "Eli, I thought I was expecting again."

He leaned forward, an anxious feeling in his chest. "Why do I sense a contradiction coming along?"

"There is no contradiction," she said with a slow smile. "I'm just past my third month."

"What?" Dare he believe it? "And you're just now telling *me*?" He charged from his chair, taking her in his arms. "Are you sure? We're going to have a baby?"

"Dr. Morris believes we are past danger. So yes, Eli, we are at last going to have another baby."

Tears welled in his eyes and he did not blink them away. "You . . . you continually make my world right."

"Because I am the most loved woman I know. And you know there is no force more powerful."

He kissed her with the same passion he'd felt upon their very first stolen kiss. The war was over, he was to be a father, and he shared Hapsworth with the love of his life.

TENLEY

When her judge and jury left, Tenley locked the door, frozen and numb, turned off the TV, and climbed the stairs.

At the library door she gazed toward the desk, where the worn Bible and porcelain dove remained. But nothing else. Elijah had asked for the original manuscript, which she handed over.

Elijah, along with Wendall and Brené, even Charlie, gave her a stony silence between awkward conversation and tense glances.

Easing across the library, Tenley brushed her hand over the desk, letting her tears fall freely. "I know you know the whole story, but whatever it is, the words are hidden in your scuffed surface. And tonight wasn't your fault. I knew better."

A slick of guilt covered her and she sank to the chair, the tears breaking, loneliness and fear wrapping their arms around her.

Stupid, stupid . . . She felt the magnitude of her decision when Jonas left, the *click* of the door a resounding gavel. His disgust was written all over his face.

When she'd wrung out her tears, she clicked off the Tiffany lamp and shuffled to her bedroom, exhausted.

Slipping off her shorts and top, she reached into the bedroom closet for the robe and slippers.

Draping herself in the red-plaid garment, she crawled into bed, tried to sleep. But in the dark, one thing became exceedingly clear.

She was a liar and a cheat. And she was in love with Jonas Sullivan.

Hearing Wendall *fire* her tonight hurt. But not nearly as much as realizing she'd done exactly what Jonas's best friends had done to him. The fact that GPR was dead sixty years didn't matter.

There was nothing left to do but go home and find a new life.

JONAS

Wednesday morning Jonas powered on the overhead fans, their motors blending with the song on the radio. With passion and poetry Jeremy Riddle sang about a holy God.

After popping open the mini-fridge for a water, Jonas stood in the giant doorway of his shop, facing the river. For the hundredth time today he thought of Tenley.

Three months ago, his life changed in a matter of seconds. He'd met a beautiful, funny, intriguing woman who scaled his romantic fears.

Then five days ago, in a matter of seconds, she changed everything. The way he saw her, the way he felt about her, the way he thought about her. And he hated himself for it.

She'd *lied*. Submitted another person's book as her own. Just to save her own neck.

While it wasn't fair to compare what she did to his situation, it brought up everything he loathed about Cindy and Mason.

Which made him all the more angry, because he'd convinced

himself he was farther down the recovery road. He thought he was ready for a relationship and the accompanying entanglements.

He swigged his water, returning to his workbench, where the first three tables for the restaurant were in process.

He knew Tenley was flawed, had her junk to deal with, but listening to the dining room confrontation over the manuscript shot him right back to where he was two years ago.

He'd left without a word and had not called her since.

However, her mother called the next day wanting to know what happened.

"Tenley's back to the red-plaid robe."

"You'll have to talk to her, Miss Blanche."

"But will you talk to her? She's muttering something about giving up writing. Fool girl."

"She might be right."

"What in the world is going on? Someone tell me."

"Talk to your daughter."

Another gulp of his drink and he lowered his safety goggles and reached for his sander. He had promised the restaurant owner he'd deliver the first three tables next week so they could start staging the dining room layout.

"Jonas?"

He whirled around to see Tenley at the shop entrance, her hair loose over her shoulders. She wore shorts and a pink tank top that matched the hue on her cheeks and flip-flops. No robe and slippers.

He powered off the sander. "Miss Blanche said you were back to the robe." He raised his goggles.

"Yeah, for a few days." She dug her hands into her hip pockets. "I just came to say good-bye. I'm leaving in the morning. Blanche is doing well, though I told her to call your mom if she needs anything.

I think she's going to look into one of those agencies to come help out a few days a week."

She spoke without confidence, her voice weak, her eyes full of watery sorrow.

"We'll keep an eye on her."

She nodded, gazing down. "I appreciate that."

"What are you going to do now that . . ."

She brushed her fingers under her eyes, biting her lip, sniffing back tears. Jonas crossed his arms, restraining the urge, the ache, to hold her. "I might go to LA for a few days, hang with my people, you know, the rest of the posers, fakers, and fibbers."

"Tenley—"

"After that, who knows?" She brushed at the tear dripping from her chin. "Beauty school. I always thought cutting hair would be interesting."

"I never took you for a quitter."

"I bet you never took me for a plagiarizer and a liar either, but voilà. Here I am."

He swallowed, pondering his next question. "Why'd you do it?"

"I don't know. Why does anyone do anything stupid? I was desperate. How could I fail after such success? I needed a book and I found one in a desk. A miracle, right? If I were smart I'd blame you for opening the drawer."

"You going to be all right?"

"Yeah, sure, why not?" She walked toward the workbench. "Are these the tables for the restaurant? They're really cool. I love the curved legs."

"I'm sorry I just left that night."

She peered at him, steady and clear. "You don't owe me an apology."

"It was too close, Tenley, to my own past."

"You see me differently now, don't you?"

"I don't want to, but yeah. I do." He removed the goggles from around his neck, tossing them to the workbench. "I tell myself you're not Cindy, nor Mason, but . . ." He shook his head. "It is the same, isn't it?"

Tears glistened in her eyes again. "Best thing that ever happened to me and I blew it."

"Hey, we didn't think we'd last anyway. You're New York and I'm Cocoa Beach."

She jabbed the air with her finger. "Right, exactly."

"You asked the other day where we were going to leave things. How about just leave them here?"

She nodded, working her way to the door. "So long, Cocoa Beach."

"Yeah, see you, New York."

THIRTY-EIGHT

TENLEY

She showered and packed and lay down on the bed, but sleep was nowhere near. Getting up, she shuffled into the library, clicked on the desk lamp, and sat at the desk.

A question started bugging her a few days ago. Just how did a Gordon Phipps Roth manuscript get stuck in the desk in the first place?

If the inscribed Bible was any indication, he was friends with the Marchioness and Marquess of Ainsworth.

She'd Googled them only to find a short Wikipedia entry. The nobles moved to Cocoa Beach from England in the late thirties, building Grove Manor on land owned by her father, Gilded Age millionaire Geoffrey Shehorn.

In their bio, there was no mention of Gordon Phipps Roth.

Tenley trailed her fingers over the desk, picking up the dove and the Bible. She'd promised Jonas she would read this book. She walked it back to the bedroom and tucked it by her phone.

She'd do it. Find out what love really looked like.

Back in the library to turn off the light, Tenley exhaled.

"Good-bye, library. I liked being here." She ran her hand along the dusty shelves, noting again the odd arrangement of the shelves.

She walked the length toward the back window, studying the section that stood an inch thicker than the rest of the shelves. Weird.

Maybe it'd fallen lose from the wall mount. Tenley leaned against the shelves, pushing, and startled when the shelf actually moved, swinging toward her.

"What in the world?" The library was full of mysteries. Leaning around the narrow opening, she peeked into a secret room. "Oh wow . . ."

Shoving the section open, Tenley stepped into a small space from another time.

It was boxy and cozy, containing an old easy chair, a side table and lamp, a bookcase, and an antique projector with film threaded through.

Turning on the lamp, she examined the single bookcase and the row of matching leather-bound books. A box sat by the chair, but the prepared projector had her curious.

She found the on switch, and the machine sputtered to life, moving the film from reel to reel.

The shadows cast by scratched celluloid appeared on the facing wall before a black-and-white scene of the beach filled the space, the sun dripping diamonds over the water.

Backing up to the chair, Tenley sank into the scene, gasping when the images of the marquess and marchioness behind the frame on the desk came to life on the wall.

The marchioness filled the frame, sitting in the library, at *the* desk, hovering over pages, turning them, making marks with a pencil.

"Look here, darling," an accented male voice instructed her. "Birdie."

She raised her gaze, smiling, her expression bright with a touch of lipstick, her hair neat and in place. She wore a patterned dress with a Cinderella neckline and pearls.

"Enough now, Eli love. I've work to do."

Tenley's chest thumped at the sound of her voice. Sweet but strong. American blended with British.

"I see you've finished your next great book." Eli tipped the camera over her shoulder.

The first line came into clear focus. Tenley angled forward. She knew that line. She'd read it a half dozen times wondering if she should change it or leave it.

She wished to escape. So much so her legs twitched of their own volition. Each time, Mama glared at her in warning.

"Eli, please." Birdie pressed her palm against the lens. "You know better."

"These are just our private movies."

"Still, I beg you. We cannot risk our secret."

"Secret, still." He peered round the camera. "When he comes to visit this summer, I'm going to have it out with him. How long must my wife be his ghost?"

"Please, you will do no such thing." Birdie turned to the camera, raising her hand to block the lens. "You know he's unwell."

"Well, when he's well again."

"Haven't you argued enough with him about it over the years? Yet here I am doing what I love and earning a handsome lot."

"Because I want your name on a book jacket. I'm very proud of you."

"Fine. But for now, go on. You're disrupting my work."

"All right, for you, love, I'll turn off the camera. I suppose these things do have a way of falling into the wrong hands."

"Precisely."

"Oh my gosh . . ." Tenley whirled, regarding the shelves and the box at her feet. "She was his ghost!"

Reaching up, she stopped the projector and angled the lamp to see the bookcase, examining the book spines. Gordon Phipps Roth. Every single one. Tenley retrieved *The Girl in the Carriage* and gently looked inside.

A first edition, 1903. Signed.

To Birdie. Yours, GPR

She pulled out *Moonlight on the Hudson*.

Another first edition, 1909. Signed.

Birdie, my dear friend and colleague. Your talents astound me. GPR

One book after another was signed personally to Birdie. Not Elizabeth or Lady Ainsworth.

Birdie.

She popped the lid from the box. Manuscripts. On top sat *The Girl in the Carriage* bound with a rubber band.

Beneath it, *Moonlight on the Hudson*. Then *The House in Murray Hill*, *Winter in New York*, and *The Berkshires*. Farther down, *Love on the Thames* and *West, Go West*.

Birdie *was* her grandfather's ghost. No, no, no, how could he . . .

Stacking the manuscripts at her feet, Tenley discovered a collection of letters. She pulled the first one from the yellowed envelope.

February 1943

Dear Birdie,

We've done it again, though I daresay, you've done it again. *West, Go West* is such a splendid tale and tribute to your dear brother. What a team we make. I owe you a debt I cannot repay. My love to you and Eli. I pray you are finding peace in these war days and solace over losing your dear son William. He was too young, much too young. A handsome, intelligent man who this world should not have to be without. You're in my prayers. Let's dedicate *West, Go West* to him and to your brother for whom he was named. To William the flyer and William the adventurer.

Yours, GPR

Oh my gosh . . . This was unbelievable. Tenley ran to the banister.

"Blanche, wake up. Did you know about this secret room? Blanche!"

Back in the library, Tenley restarted the projector, aching for more of Birdie's world, for more secrets to be revealed.

Eli was talking. "I'll go, love, but first, sing your song. The one from your childhood. It has comforted me more times than you know. Especially during the war and after losing William. Your voice is so lovely."

"It's not my song, it's the Lord's. He just allows me to sing it."

"Right you are, darling. So go on. My guess is He loves to hear you sing it as much as any human."

Birdie sighed and faced the lens. "If you will then leave me alone and go film your precious egrets, I will sing." Light fell on Birdie from an unseen window, her soft skin lightly lined with time. But she was beautiful, so composed and regal. Bet she'd never sloughed around for weeks in a man's robe without showering or combing her hair.

Her image against the wall, Birdie was as real to Tenley as if she stood before her in the flesh. She closed her eyes and sang, her voice sinking Tenley to her knees.

"Do not be dismayed, you don't have to worry or be afraid."

Chills crisscrossed Tenley's scalp and ran down her back and legs as her tears streamed, listening to this woman from the past sing her song. "How is this possible?"

"There. Is that good?" Birdie blew a kiss at her husband.

"One more time, darling. Nice and loud this time."

Birdie made a humorous face, then raised her song again, louder and clearer, the lyrics melting every regret, every fear, every bit of shame Tenley possessed.

"Do not be dismayed, you don't have to worry or be afraid."

The image faded to black.

"Rewind, rewind." Fingers trembling, Tenley fumbled with the mechanism. "Come on, come on . . . Help! How do you rewind this thing?"

She hammered the old metal side, willing the reel-to-reel to play again. Instead, it showed static scenes of the beach. A very different one from what lay beyond the yard now.

Finally finding a release, she threaded the thin film backward, seeing through the projector's light just when Birdie sang her song.

". . . it's the Lord's song . . . Do not be dismayed . . ."

Tenley raised her voice in weak, weeping harmony. "You don't have to worry or be afraid."

THIRTY-NINE

BIRDIE

MAY 1939

"This is splendid." Gordon along with his wife, Sweeney, toured Grove Manor with his hands locked behind his back. "I can still smell the lumber and the paint."

"We've only lived here a month," Eli said. "You're our first guest."

The maid, Mrs. Simmons, served tea on the veranda using Mama's things. She'd passed away the summer of '35 and left Birdie her jewels and china. Papa, bless his heart, died a year later from missing her. However misguided Mama's young heart might have been, she and Papa loved each other. In the end, isn't that all that mattered?

Birdie sipped politely, ignoring a touch of rude anxiety. Gordon had come to discuss their next project.

Perhaps, at last, her solo project?

"How does young Master William fare?" Gordon asked, reaching for a biscuit. He'd grown gray over the years, though success kept him youthful, confident. "Our Stephen has just become a father."

"I don't know what to do with myself," Sweeney said. "Empty house. Gordon traveling. The children in Boston."

"She visits them often," Gordon said, patting his wife's hand.

"William is well. Entering the RAF. He wants to be a flyer." Eli loved boasting of his intelligent pilot son. "He talks of nothing but aeroplanes."

The conversation focused on family and how Eli and Birdie finally decided to leave England for the warmth of Florida.

"We were both ready for change," Birdie said. "When my father died, he left us this land and a good deal of money, so—"

"—we turned Hapsworth over to my nephew, Earl of Montague, and built a beach cottage." Eli leaned toward Gordon. "When does Birdie get her own book?"

The author sputtered, spewing a bit of his creamy tea.

"Rather direct, Ainsworth."

Eli hammered his hand on the table. "We've been waiting and asking for years. Again and again you promise to bring her to Barclay, yet you do not."

"How can I? Her writing is my writing. We are the same. They will see the façade right away."

"Then claim you want to write with her. On a joint project."

"Impossible. I've no time. I'm lecturing and traveling. Again, our writing will be the same as my own solo works. I intended every bit to escort Birdie into her own career, but I fear we've built a ship we can no longer steer toward our own desires."

"Gordon," Sweeney said. "Have a care. Birdie's worked hard for you all these years."

"Of her own choice." He leaned toward Birdie. "Do you wish to lay down your pen?"

"No, but I wish not to be Gordon Phipps Roth for once."

"I'm afraid you will always be me. And the financial rewards are generous."

"We don't need the money," Eli spat, sitting back with his tea. "She inherited the Shehorn fortune. We need her to have her name on her books."

"Tell me how to go about informing Barclay." Gordon's expression drew taut. "We will all go down. Lose our livelihood. You may have the Shehorn wealth, but I do not."

"But one day I will have my own book, right? We will find a way?" Birdie said with a glance at Eli, then Sweeney. "I do not wish to retire."

What would she do with herself? Her son, her friends were in England. It was in writing that she felt the most free. The most herself.

"Yes, Birdie, we will figure a way to put your name on your own book."

"Then I'm satisfied." She squeezed her husband's hand. "Now, what thoughts do you have for the next book? I've been thinking about an English country woman who moves to America."

TENLEY

She bolted upright, hitting her head on the edge of a table, squinting through the darkness.

What time was it? She'd fallen asleep in the secret room, watching the movie of the Ainsworths over and over, reading their letters, flipping through the raw manuscripts.

GPR had a ghostwriter. But why?

Scrambling off the floor, Tenley burst from the secret room into the library full of morning light.

"No, no, no . . ." She bent over the top rail. "Blanche! What time is it? I'm going to miss my flight." The clock in her room said seven a.m. Dang it! Grabbing her suitcase, she started tossing her toiletries inside. No time to use them. And her dirty laundry . . . she had meant to do a last load.

"Blanche? Did you hear the taxi honk?" She couldn't hear a thing in that tiny room. She'd go to the airport and beg for mercy. Then sit there until she could catch another flight.

Phone? In her pocket. Wallet? In her purse. Rolling her suitcase into the hall, Tenley returned to the library to pack up her laptop. From the secret room, she gathered the correspondence between Birdie and Gordon, stuffing the letters in her laptop case.

"Blanche?" Tenley paused with a last look toward the library, then ran over to hug the desk. "Thanks for being my people. Don't let Jonas sell you to someone else. I'm going to ask Blanche if I can have you."

She shoved the bookcase-door closed with a mental note to come back this fall and investigate more.

Downstairs, she settled her things by the front door. "Blanche? You won't believe what I found. Hey, are you up for driving me to the airport?"

She breezed into the kitchen for a banana and glass of juice.

"Blanche, yo! You up? Did you know there was a hidden room in the library? Wild. The projector was in there loaded with film of the marchioness." Tenley paused by her mom's closed door, jamming the first bite of banana in her mouth. "Blanche?"

She knocked, then eased open the door, crossing over to the bed. "Mom?"

Eyes closed, hands folded on her middle in peaceful repose, a slight smile on her lips, Blanche neither moved nor breathed.

Tenley shook her gently. "Hey . . . Blanche? Mom?"

But she was gone. Sweetly gone. "Oh, Blanche, no." Drawing her hand over her mother's forehead, Tenley crawled in next to her, cradling her cold body, tugging the covers up to her chin, and wept softly against her arm.

TENLEY

The sunset over the Sullivans' cut of the Banana River flamed with red, gold, and pink. More glorious than Tenley had ever seen. The breeze mixed with dew and heat pushed against her, tangling her hair and forcing her to *feel*. Something. Anything.

Blanche's death came as the proverbial last straw. Tenley had wept for most of the morning, her heart excising every pain, every disappointment, the loss of Dad, the loss of Mom, the loss of her career and future. The loss of love.

Would she ever find her way?

She called Jonas. Together they found Blanche's will, which her lawyer, Mr. Brannon, executed to the last detail. Right down to a commemorative box of ashes for Tenley. Which now sat at her feet.

The rest of her mother's physical remains were to be interred at the Woodlawn Cemetery Mausoleum next to Dad—which he'd purchased for her two years after their divorce.

Together in death if not in life. *Dad, you're a saint, and I miss you.*

"Beautiful sunset." Jonas pulled a weather-worn lawn chair alongside her.

"You think it's Blanche telling me she's okay?"

"Or God telling you everything's going to be okay."

"Not to worry or be afraid? For God so loved the world . . ." Tenley repeated the verse that stuck out to her last night while reading Birdie's Bible.

She was starting to understand. Starting to see.

"Thank you for all of your help this week. I know you have a lot of work to do."

"You're welcome." He looked ahead, over the water, his dark hair curling in the breeze, his jaw dusted with a day's growth. He was beautiful. Truly beautiful.

Blanche's funeral commenced on the beach this morning with the Sullivans and a small gathering of her friends. Aunt Reese and her husband, Uncle Phil, flew in from Colorado. They were inside with Mr. and Mrs. Sullivan, perusing the cornucopia of casserole dishes the church ladies provided.

"Reese and Phil invited me to Colorado for the holidays," Tenley said. "But I don't really know them. They're strangers."

"You should go. Family . . . family is important." Jonas stretched out his long, tanned legs and watched the sunset. "They won't be strangers for long."

"I feel sad I can't have any more Christmases with Blanche."

"At least you had a solid three months with her."

"Saying yes to her invitation was the only thing I've done right lately."

"Then treasure the memories," Jonas said. "Have you decided what you're going to do with the car and the house?"

"And everything in between?" As Blanche's sole heir, Tenley inherited all her mother's worldly possessions. The boxes of photographs. The vintage dresses. The hats from her British period. "I don't know yet." She cut a glance his way. "Jonas, did you know there's a secret room in the library?"

"First I've heard of it, but I don't really know the house that well." He waited, listening.

"I found a bunch of manuscripts and correspondence. And an old reel-to-reel film. I think Birdie, the marchioness, was Gordon Phipps Roth's ghostwriter. Is that crazy?" He was the first one to hear her suspicion. It felt good to say it out loud.

He exhaled, making a face. "That would be hard to prove."

"Yeah, and after what I did, who would believe me?" She sighed. "I miss Blanche."

She felt the brush of his fingers against hers linking them together. They sat there until long after the colors faded and the night blanketed them.

BIRDIE

JUNE 1947

She turned to the last page of *An October Wedding*, the book of her heart. Her fictionalized love affair with Eli. But it would change. Gordon would make his additions, turning it into their trademark story.

It'd been more difficult than she imagined to pen her own story, remembering her battle with Mama, whom she'd give about anything to see one more time.

How blessed she'd been to be spared a loveless marriage with Alfonse, and Eli with Rose.

She was forever in debt to those two.

In the writing and the journey into her past, she remembered her brother, missing him and how he brightened every room and every dreary day.

But it was her grief over losing her son that had fueled her passion to write about her youth, about an age and time gone by, about her passion for Eli and the exciting journey she called her life—beginning the day Alfonse dumped her at the altar into Eli's waiting arms.

"Hello, my love."

She glanced up to see Eli entering the library with his confounded new gadget, a movie camera, edging it over her shoulder.

"I see you've finished your next great book."

"Eli, please." Birdie pressed her palm against the lens. "You know better."

"These are just our private movies."

"Still, I beg you. We cannot risk our secret."

"Secret, still." He peered round the camera. "When he comes to visit this summer, I'm going to have it out with him. How long must my wife be his ghost?"

"Please, you will do no such thing." Birdie turned to the camera, raising her hand to block the lens. "You know he's unwell."

"Well, when he's well again."

"Haven't you argued enough with him about it over the years? Yet here I am doing what I love and earning a handsome lot."

"Because I want your name on a book jacket. I'm very proud of you."

"Fine. But for now, go on. You're disrupting my work."

"All right, for you, love, I'll turn off the camera. I suppose these things do have a way of falling into the wrong hands."

"Precisely."

He lowered the camera and knelt next to her desk, which had become her dear companion. "Are you happy, Birdie? That we left England for Florida? That you wrote for Gordon?"

She kissed him softly, an intimacy she'd never tire of sharing. "I've zero regrets."

"Nor I." Eli glanced at the manuscript. "Wouldn't it be nice if this one had your name on it, though?"

"I've already sent the first chapter to him. I think Gordon's health concerns Barclay, but they've set a release date for next year. Now go. Though this book doesn't have my name on the cover, our story will be on the pages, forever immortalized in print."

"That does delight me." He raised the camera. "I'll go, love. But first, sing your song. The one from your childhood. It has comforted me more times than you know. Especially during the war and after losing William. Your voice is so lovely."

"It's not my song, it's the Lord's. He just allows me to sing it."

"Right you are, darling. So go on. My guess is He loves to hear you sing it as much as any human."

Birdie sighed and faced the lens. "If you will then leave me alone and go film your precious egrets, I will sing."

Birdie closed her eyes and lifted her voice for the camera. "Do not be dismayed, you don't have to worry or be afraid."

Birdie fit the manuscript into the envelope, a late-afternoon rain dancing against the library window.

Stretching, she slipped the typewriter cover over the machine. Picking up the mimeographed copy of *An October Wedding,* she wrapped it with a rubber band and walked to the room behind the library shelves.

"Oh Eli . . ." She shoved aside the projector, much too large for this small room, but he insisted on keeping it in here. And when they had a whole grand house to spread out in.

Opening the box, she set the manuscript inside. Number sixteen. She sat in the chair, facing the wall.

She read in here at night, surrounded by her books. They were hers. Her babies. Every last one written with love. The world may not know her, but God knew. He saw. And one day, she was sure, one day He would reward.

Wasn't laying down one's life for a friend the ultimate act of love? Wasn't that the sacrifice Christ made for her? Her sacrifice cost her nothing but fame. Her book earnings paid very well, though Eli suspected Gordon doctored the ledger now and again.

Below her, the house phone jangled in the phone room, vibrating up through the floor.

The maid's footsteps hammered across the hardwood and were followed by her quick, low, "Grove Manor, how may I help you?"

Birdie stepped out of the room, swinging the bookshelf into place. When she looked up, Delphi darkened the library door. "Mrs. Ainsworth, the call is for you."

"Who is it?"

"Mrs. Roth."

She hurried down to the phone, a panic spreading through her. "Sweeney, is everything all right?"

"It's Gordon, Birdie. He's gone. My beloved husband is gone."

FORTY

TENLEY

She waited outside Elijah Phipps's midtown office, the sign on the door reading *Gordon Phipps Roth Foundation*.

After the funeral, she had spent another week in Cocoa Beach going through Blanche's things, organizing pictures, and sitting by the ocean remembering her. Remembering Dad. And contemplating her life.

She dug through the library's secret room and found even more fascinating information on the Ainsworths, including ledgers of income Birdie had earned for each book.

At night Tenley crawled into her bed wrapped in the red robe, more from sentiment than fear now, and read notes from Blanche's friends and ex-husbands.

She read *An October Wedding* on her laptop again. Then before turning out the light, she opened Birdie's Bible, which was beginning to feel more and more like her own, and read the Gospels.

Finally, she was finding her way.

Now in New York, Elijah's door swung open and she stood, reaching for the backpack at her feet.

"Tenley, come on in." He stepped aside for her to enter his lavish office, his demeanor detached.

"Thank you for seeing me, Elijah." She hesitated, then dropped her backpack into the chair facing the desk. "I am really sorry about everything—"

"At least we found the lost manuscript. You're lucky we didn't discover your indiscretion after it was published."

"Dodged one there." She mimed flicking sweat from her brow.

"Guess you've figured out you shouldn't steal someone else's manuscript."

"Gotcha." Two thumbs up. "As if I haven't heard or thought of that already."

Elijah sat behind his desk, rocking back, tapping his fingers together. "What can I do for you?"

"I found something that might interest you." She pulled the film canister from the backpack along with one of the manuscripts, the original copy of *The Girl in the Carriage*. "Before my grandparents owned the house in Cocoa Beach, it belonged to an English couple. The wife was the American daughter of a Gilded Age millionaire."

"I assume this is going somewhere."

"Don't you think it's weird that our great-great-grandfather's manuscript was found in an old, nondescript desk in Cocoa Beach? In a house he never owned?"

"Not at all. He could've visited. Many celebrities and aristocrats were fans of Phipps Roth. In fact, I'm named after his good friend Elijah Percy, the Marquess of Ainsworth."

Tenley grinned. The story was coming full circle. "Remember that as I go on. So, why was Gordon's manuscript in the desk?"

"Just go ahead and tell me, Tenley." Elijah motioned to the film canister and the manuscript. "You obviously have something to say."

"Our grandfather was a fraud. I don't know when it started,

but I think it was with his breakout book." She tapped *The Girl in the Carriage*. "Birdie Shehorn Percy, the American heiress who became the Marchioness of Ainsworth, was married to the man you're named for, Elijah Percy, Lord Ainsworth. She, dear cousin, was Gordon's ghostwriter."

Elijah laughed. "Is this how you make yourself feel better? By lying about Gordon?"

"Not at all. But it's true and this is how I fix what *he* did."

Tenley retrieved Birdie's letters and the copy of the manuscript of *An October Wedding*. "Did you read *An October Wedding*?"

"Not yet, but I—"

"The origins of the story are in their correspondence. On the film, Birdie and her husband Eli discuss how she was writing for Gordon."

"You've got to be kidding."

She handed him copies of the letters. "Those are duplicates. I have the originals. I also have copies of her financial ledgers." She reached again into her bag. "I had the film converted to digital. It's on this DVD." She dropped the disk onto his desk. "Elijah, Gordon never wrote one book on his own after *Living with the Hamiltons*. *The Girl in the Carriage* is a collaboration of some kind with the marchioness."

"You can't be serious. That book changed his career." Elijah shuffled through the letters, sighing louder and louder, his face flushed and taut. "Tenley, we've built a whole foundation on his work and reputation." He stood, shoving his chair into the mahogany credenza. "You want to dismantle it?"

"No, I want it to fulfill our grandfather's promise to his ghostwriter. Put her name on a book."

He scoffed, pacing to the window and peering out over the city. "Which will effectively dismantle his name and reputation."

"Then let's find a way to keep his legacy while doing what he never did. Give Birdie her own book. Publish *An October Wedding* with her name, not Gordon's. We owe her this, Elijah, as his descendants."

"I can't do that. I have a responsibility to the board. We don't know she really wrote for him."

"Read the letters. Watch the DVD."

"And Barclay has the book. You think they are going to put an unknown's name on it? They're planning a fancy gilded edition."

"I don't care. *An October Wedding* is her personal love story. She wrote sixteen books for Gordon. We can find a way to do right by her. Elijah, if you don't help me, I'll go to the press with this."

"How do you propose we go about it? March into Barclay's with an 'Oh, by the way'?"

"Yes. A thousand bucks says Wendall already knows."

Elijah made a face. "Nah, he couldn't. How could he? If this is true, Gordon clearly kept it a secret."

"I bet old Daniel Barclay knew. Even if the family didn't, we have all the proof we need to show Gordon Phipps Roth was a fraud."

"Whoa, there's no *we*. Just *you*. I'm not going to be a part of his undoing. This foundation does a lot of good, Tenley. Programs for literacy. Grants for libraries. For young novelists starting out. Awards. As you well know."

She slipped the film tin into the backpack. "Here's the deal. I'm going to get Birdie Shehorn Percy Ainsworth's name on a book. Even if I have to expose our great-great-grandfather to do it." She started for the door.

"Why . . . why are you doing this?"

"Don't you see, Eli? He took her work just like I took his. Only I didn't know. Not that ignorance is an excuse. But for, I don't know, forty years, Gordon knew Birdie wrote for him and *never* said a word. He made his living off of her. Fine, it appears she was complicit. She made a living too. But he died owing her something. Her name on a book. *An October Wedding* is the fulfillment of that promise."

With a sigh, Elijah sank to his desk chair. "We always thought he never finished it."

"Because the manuscript was with Birdie, in Florida, all along. Now do you see my point? Elijah, let's finish what Gordon did not."

When Tenley came up with this plan, the notion burned in her gut for days. A small fire at first, then an inferno. It was her first matter of serious prayer. The more she prayed, the brighter the idea flamed.

Justice. It simply felt like justice. And for some reason, God had assigned her the task of executing it.

"So what's your plan?" Elijah said.

"Take all of this to Barclay. Ask them to publish it with her name."

"That's publishing suicide. She's basically a debut author with no face, no website, no Facebook or Instagram account. She can't do interviews or blog tours."

"But I can."

"Can we put Gordon's name on it too?"

"Yes, that would be lovely." She sank to her chair with a wash of tears. "Thank you, Elijah."

"I suppose this assuages some of your guilt?"

"I'm not doing this for myself." She inhaled a pure, deep breath. "After what I did, no publisher will want me. I don't think for a moment Wendall has kept his mouth shut. I'm applying to beauty school. I'm doing this for her. Because she deserves it. And from whatever corner she's watching from heaven, I bet she's cheering.

For me, it feels . . . great. Like I'm finishing something that's been waiting for a very long time."

JONAS

The August morning promised to be hot. But the collective breeze off the river and the Atlantic gave him hope.

Standing on his patio, watching the sunrise, he found his thoughts drifting to Tenley. He missed her. She'd texted of her success with Elijah Phipps and the foundation.

They'd not talked much since, but the way she had stepped out to right a wrong challenged him.

He'd played it safe with his heart far too long. He called Mason last night to see how things were going. Genuinely smiled when the man said his shop was booming and Cindy was pregnant.

Did the man apologize? Nope. But Jonas forgave, and when he did, confidence surged. Clearly his designs were working. He had talent and the confidence to venture out on his own.

Tenley asked him to check on Grove Manor. Seeing the desk in the library, he wondered about restoring it. But something about its appearance, the worn places from an old typewriter and from where arms rested, told him the desk was in its perfect condition.

Tenley had returned his thousand dollars, so technically the desk wasn't his. It was hers. And exactly where it belonged.

For one wild moment, he considered driving it to New York, then decided not to go there. Emotionally or literally.

But today? He had a long Saturday ahead, crafting tables and chairs.

He was about to go inside when Dad came through the house, shoving through the sliding doors, waving a check.

"Second installment."

"Dad, come on, I told you not to worry about paying me back." Jonas squeezed past him for the kitchen, dumping the last of his coffee in the sink.

"Your mother and I insist. Her boss gave her a bonus and we paid off a few more bills. We're catching up."

"God has taken care of me. The restaurant job came at the right time."

"Please, son . . ." Dad set the check on the counter with a quick pat, and Jonas saw the need in his eyes to pay back what he owed. To have the dignity and respect of not being beholden.

"Then thanks."

"Heard from Tenley lately?"

"Did Mom put you up to asking?"

"No. Okay, maybe. We both like her. She fits into the family."

"Not going to happen. We're from two different worlds."

"Ever stop to think her world needs yours and vice versa?"

"My world doesn't need hers." Jonas washed out his mug and put it in the drainer. "She doesn't need mine."

"Okay, let's get to the real issue. Hearts. Her heart needs yours. You need hers."

Jonas headed for the workshop, Dad following, crossing to his door. "I'm not sure I trust her. She stole another author's work. Tried to present it as her own."

"But she took responsibility. She's paid for her sin. Don't you think she deserves some compassion? A second chance? If you're to be like Christ, and He can forgive you . . ."

"I forgive her. I just don't know if I want to trust her with my heart."

"Well, you can't make that decision from all the way back here. Got to get up close."

Jonas laughed, sliding open the shop door, clicking on the lights and overhead fans. "I can see fine from here."

"What if you had nothing but your career? Estranged from Mom. I was dead. You were an only child. What if you had great success on a furniture design and then . . . *nothing*."

"I wouldn't steal another designer's work if that's what you're asking. Even if I didn't know whose it was."

Dad walked over to the workbench, admiring the second set of tables Jonas was finishing. "Just wondering if you're splitting hairs to push her away 'cause you're scared."

"I'm not scared." Jonas slipped on his goggles and gloves. "Just cautious."

"Cautious and scared often look a lot alike." Dad slapped him gently in the gut. "Remember when the sheriff came and put us out of the house?"

Jonas collected his tools and geared up for the work. "Kind of hard to forget."

"I was scared."

Jonas peeked over at his dad. "I don't remember feeling you were."

"Couldn't sleep. Couldn't eat. What had I done to my family? The boy twins were babies, the E's young enough to be innocent but old enough to notice things."

"We survived, Dad. And we're the closer for it."

"Your mom kept telling me to reach out for help, but I couldn't bring myself to do it. What kind of man can't support his family?"

"Dad, a lot of men find themselves out of a job or caught in debt."

"But I was a hard worker. How did I get there? One evening to get out of the cars, we took a walk downtown, remember?"

"The E's cried for ice cream all the way home."

"It broke me. I couldn't buy my kids an ice-cream cone because I was too prideful to ask for help. I asked the next day. Turns out there was a family looking for a renter. Another man in the church knew of a job. We spent a week in the cars when we could've had a nice home and a job because I was looking at the world through my pride. Don't miss out on this girl because you're looking through your pride, or hurt, or past experience, I don't know what, but you do. Figure it out."

"Look, even if I did figure it out and go after her, she doesn't want me, Dad. So we're even."

"My eyes tell me she loves you."

"Well, Mom's been saying for years you need new glasses."

With a chuckle, Dad headed for the door. "I've got to get to work, but Joe, no man ever hit one out of the park by keeping his bat on his shoulder."

Dad and his fatherly baseball metaphors. Jonas brooded as he started to work.

Now Tenley was on his mind. On his heart. He couldn't concentrate, so he yanked off his gloves and sent her a text.

How are you?

He waited. When she didn't text back, he poured a second cup of coffee and went back to work. He was just about to fire up the jigsaw when his phone pinged.

Okay. How are you?
Good. Building tables.

Yay!

How's New York?

It doesn't have a beach.

That's OK, we don't have Broadway.

Elijah and I met with Barclay. They didn't know Birdie wrote Gordon's books. They were shocked. I'm working on getting An October Wedding published with her name on it. We think it will be a Gordon Phipps Roth novel by Birdie Ainsworth.

Wow. I'm proud. Not your name?

Nope! ;)

He missed her. So much his heart ached.

Been reading Birdie's Bible. Starting to understand some stuff. Ha! #thickheadsoftens

His pulse raced, connecting his head and his heart. A small idea developed. He typed his next message, hesitated, then pressed Send.

What's your address again? Need it for my contacts.

1214 5th Avenue, Apt 11, Manhattan 10029

Thanks.

Closing up the workshop, he decided Dad was right. If he wanted to make a decision about Tenley, he had to get up close.

FORTY-ONE

TENLEY

She paced the length of her empty apartment, phone to her ear, listening to Charlie. A skilled, sharp agent, he took forever to get to the point. She wanted to end his sentences for him.

". . . so I had lunch with an editor over at . . ."

Tenley sat in the rickety lawn chair she had found by a Dumpster. After disinfecting it with a Clorox shower, she deemed the apartment worthy.

Otherwise, the place was empty. She'd arranged for Saget to take away everything but Dad's chair, Grandpa's old dresser, and her clothes.

The rest she sent away with her past. With Holt. With writer's block. With her failures. She was starting over. She had a new faith and fresh hope. Time to rebuild from there.

She'd repaid her advance to Barclay and restored some of her relationship with them.

They refused her plans for *An October Wedding*, but with Elijah on her side, Wendall returned the book to her, forgoing the option to publish.

"We want to protect Phipps Roth's and Barclay's reputations."

So she asked Charlie to shop Birdie's manuscript.

Royalties from *Someone to Love* sales along with Dad's earnings would keep her until she figured out what to do with her life.

But she'd been dreaming of writing again. Stories popped into her head all day. Her writer's block was broken.

Of course, she was no longer in command of her life. There was a new leader aboard. Jesus.

For fun, yeah, she signed up for beauty school. Maybe, just maybe, she'd find a glorious story in the process of making women beautiful.

"Charlie?" she said.

"—and I told him . . . What?"

"Did you sell the book or not?"

"I sold the book. To Daisy Jackson Publishing."

She put her forehead to her hand. Done. Justice. "Thank you."

Charlie rattled off details. "They're a small press but they loved the book. The team is young and hip, savvy on social media. They made a good offer. But Tenley, they don't want to touch Gordon Phipps Roth's name, so I sold them on you. They are big fans. The release date is early next year. *An October Wedding* by Birdie Ainsworth. Presented by Tenley Roth.

The moment was worthy of tears.

"They want a meeting. We can set one up later in the week."

"This means the world to me. Really, Charlie."

"Here's what I'm thinking . . ."

A knock hit the door. Still listening, Tenley rose to answer. Saget stood in the hall with a couple of men carrying a piece of furniture under a moving blanket.

"Charlie, hold on. Saget, we're taking furniture out, not bringing it in."

"The man said it was a delivery for you." The doorman shoved past her. "Where do you want it?"

"What is it?"

Saget removed the moving blanket. "A desk."

The men set the piece in the middle of the living room right where the sunlight spilled through the window. Her desk! Birdie's desk. With all of its glorious nicks and worn edges.

"Jonas!" She ran to the door. "Where is he?"

"Who?" Saget and his men stood around the desk. "Look, is this where you want it? These guys get paid by the second."

"Yeah, it's fine. Where is the man who sent up the desk?"

"In the lobby."

She mashed the elevator button a hundred times. "Come on, come on." Then pulled the twenty she was going to use for lunch from her pocket and smashed it into Saget's hand. "The tip."

She was just about to dash for the stairs when the elevator arrived. The doors opened to reveal Jonas standing alone in the car.

Tenley flew into his arms, wrapping herself around him as he caught her, gripping her tight.

"You're here."

"If you don't mind, we'll wait for the next elevator," Saget said, reaching in and pushing the close-door button.

"I'm here. I never should've let you go." He fell against the elevator wall as she kissed him over and over.

"I love you, Jonas. I do, I just do."

"Oh, I love you too, babe. I don't care about the manuscript. I just want you."

His lips covered hers and her heart stilled. Quieter than it had ever been. He turned her against the wall as they rode down to the lobby with his hands on her waist, his kiss going beyond her lips to the core of her being.

She drank him in, each movement slaking the thirst she never knew existed. Every other love, every other kiss had been a prelude to this one.

In Jonas's arms, she was no longer lost. But found.

"You're going to marry me one day, right? Really soon," she said.

"Oh, absolutely. You'd better believe it."

BIRDIE

APRIL 1968

She faced the shoreline, the wind and the waves, missing England. Missing Eli, gone five years on this very day. She reflected on her life.

Behind her, Grove Manor cast a long shadow over the beach. Lately, she'd begun to feel the hollow echo of the place, rattling around alone, hosting afternoon tea, trying her hand at knitting, sewing, and even painting.

Once in a while she thought of writing again, but when Gordon died, her creative river suddenly stopped.

She felt full, satisfied with her body of work. Starting over under her own name seemed more daunting than hiding her secret.

Besides, she feared her own publication might somehow expose Gordon. Or worse, bring accusations of plagiarism down on her. She shivered, the echo of that long-ago day in Barclay's office still with her.

She lived well with her inheritance and book earnings. The wind whistling over the beach put her in mind of her song. How it comforted her. Even now.

Do not be dismayed, you don't have to worry or be afraid.

How true those words had been of her life. Turning back for the house, the evening sunset lighting her path, she climbed the stairs for the library. Her old typewriter perched on its well-worn grooves, waiting for her to type again. But her story had been told.

"Birdie, are you here?" The front screen door slammed, and her friend and Realtor Marian Grace arrived with the family interested in buying the house.

"On my way."

Birdie reached for the typewriter cover and settled it over the machine, pausing for a silent moment. Right here at this desk, the girl in the carriage had lived a most wondrous life.

Good night, old friend. Good night.

EPILOGUE

The brim of her wide beach hat shaded the pad of paper resting on her beach towel. Lying on her belly with Jonas's leg intertwined with hers, Tenley dreamed up a new story.

"Know what I love about today?" Jonas said, sleepy and low, in a way that made her tingle.

"That it's Saturday?"

"Nope. That I'm married to you."

She leaned over to kiss him, his eyes closed and his tanned skin glistening. "You're married to me every day."

Eight months ago . . . Was it eight or nine? She always lost track with Jonas. One happy day blended with the next.

Anyway, they tied the knot on the beach behind Grove Manor, sixish months after Jonas formally proposed in New York.

Tenley gave up New York and the idea of beauty school and moved to Cocoa Beach, where Jonas and the Sullivans taught her how to live in a family, large and messy with an array of personalities, and how to love well.

One of the E's asked her on their wedding day, "Is Jonas your Ezra?"

With tears Tenley nodded. "Very much so."

Birdie Percy, Marchioness of Ainsworth, became a published

author last year, 113 years after *The Girl in the Carriage* was published with Gordon Phipps Roth's name.

Charlie, the slick agent he was, got the rest of the story from Wendall. Turned out he'd inherited his great-great-grandfather's diary, and the account of *The Girl in the Carriage* was detailed there. Daniel Barclay wasn't any more proud of himself than Phipps Roth for publishing a stolen manuscript. He just never did anything about it.

The release of *An October Wedding* started slow, but as Tenley hit the promotional trail, the book picked up momentum and hit the bestseller lists.

She sat on talk show sets and regaled the audiences with tales of Lady Ainsworth, an American Gilded Age heiress.

She'd found her holy grail—to do something so worthwhile for another. Even posthumously.

Biographies were being written about the Shehorns and Percys. Next week Tenley would fly to New York to be a part of a documentary. Movie talk arose from Hollywood.

"Hey." She tapped her sleeping husband on the shoulder. "Did you mark on your calendar the premiere of *Someone to Love*?"

"December 7. Got it. Three months to figure out how to get out of wearing a tux."

"Give it up. You're wearing one."

He rolled over, pressing his hand along her back, then recoiled, laughing. "You're sweaty."

"You don't say?"

Jonas's business took off after the owner of the restaurant showed off his designs to his friends. He'd built pieces for restaurants and hotels in the Bahamas, Miami, and Dallas, with new clients calling every day.

And, surprise, she was a churchgoer. Grandpa would be proud.

Little by little, Sunday morning was becoming her favorite time of the week. A time to just be and to absorb the worship, the prayers, and the insights of the Word.

God was cool.

"Hey." Jonas sat up, taking her hat from her head, setting it on his own. "Want to go inside? Work on that baby we've been talking about?"

Tenley grinned, gathered her notebook and towel, and slipped her hand into Jonas's as they walked up the path to Grove Manor.

She never imagined how her life would change when she said yes to Blanche, choosing Cocoa Beach over Paris. A decision that in the moment made no sense.

How a dull old desk with a stuck drawer would open doors she never imagined.

This was a season of triumph. Not as an acclaimed, bestselling, award-winning author but as a wife, a lover, a daughter, and a friend to Birdie Percy.

Birdie and her desk . . . Well, she finally had her book. And Tenley finally had her home. And this was just the beginning.

ACKNOWLEDGMENTS

Let's see . . . where to begin. A book is mostly written in solitude but rarely in a vacuum. So many people come alongside an author during the writing process. It's hard to remember everyone.

There are the usual suspects . . . Susan May Warren, the bees-knees of writing partners. She's a brilliant author, teacher, coach, and friend. Her help in the crafting of the story was invaluable.

Beth Vogt, another stellar author and friend, my FaceTime partner. She helped with the nitty-gritty of this book when I wasn't sure quite what to do.

My editor, Karli Jackson. What is not to adore about you? You're smart, beautiful, and have one of the easiest and best laughs around. Thank you for your insight and work on this book.

My second editor, the fabulous Erin Healy. Thank you for your help and labor on my behalf. We both put in hours over the holiday and that's never easy. You wisdom is evident in these pages.

Daisy Hutton, Kristen Golden, Paul Fisher, and the entire HarperCollins Christian Publishing team. It's an honor times a hundred to be working with you all to bring my stories to the world.

My thanks and appreciation to the HCCP sales team, the boots on the ground force as well as Jason Short and the rocking digital team.

Most of my research was done online and reading books. So thank you Caroline Astor and Consuelo Vanderbilt, once the Duchess of Marlborough, for your stories. Writing about the Gilded Age came with more bumps than I anticipated. It's hard to make such wealth and extravagance, even the mind-set of the Gilded Age society, relatable on the page. I did my best.

My friend and fab author, Leigh Duncan, for sharing stories of growing up in Cocoa Beach in the '50s and '60s.

As always, much appreciation to my dear husband of twenty-five years for enduring the writer's life. I was thinking the other day, "When did we ever talk about me leaping into writing?" In fact, we never did. I quit my day job on our first anniversary and started casually writing during the day. I finished a book, an epic WW2 novel in two years. Too long! Then I went to a writer's conference and the ball started rolling. I don't ever remember him saying, "Why are you doing this?" He just embraced it. Supported me and never, ever challenged the God-designed destiny on my heart. Hero? You bet. Love you, babe!

To all of you, who give your time and precious dollars to buy a book. Thank you. You are the reason I do this.

Above all, I have to acknowledge Jesus. I wouldn't be here without Him. The Prince of Peace is the Prince of my heart. Thank You for everything!

DISCUSSION QUESTIONS

1. Tenley has reached rapid success. Now she's afraid she's a fraud. Fear has paralyzed her. Have you let a fear hinder you? Or someone you know? How can you conquer it? Remember, fear is not your leader!

2. Birdie is trapped in high society. She has more than most can dream of but her personal freedom. Can you think of a time society, or fear of what others thought, kept you from pursuing your own dream?

3. How do we respect the conventions of society, honor our families, yet pursue the things God has put on our hearts? Share times God has opened doors for you.

4. Elijah is another one trapped in societal convention. Would you marry for money? Would you marry for position? Our ancestors did it quite often.

5. Tenley is estranged from her mother for good reason. But there's a longing to be with her. Do you have a relationship that's strained? How can you begin to mend it? Forgiveness doesn't mean the other person was right.

6. Birdie also struggles with her mother. How can we love our parents yet not be crushed. How can we love our children yet not dominate them?

7. Jonas is a great guy! I loved writing him. How can we model his generous heart in our every day lives?

8. Tenley wears the robe, literally, of her anticipated failure. While you may not get up every day and put on an old robe, are you seeing yourself dressed as a failure? How can you be transformed by renewing your mind. Romans 12:1–2?

9. Walking down the aisle, Birdie knew her life was no longer hers. Yet, God had a surprise planned. Share times God broke into your life and things changed!

10. Tenley justifies her actions with the book she finds in the desk. Did you relate to her or were you disgusted? Be honest, under pressure, how many of us would've done the same thing? Or in fact have done something similar. (P.S. I have indeed written all of my books!)

11. It's the massive failure with the book that causes Tenley to woman-up. It's the best thing that could've happened to her. How has failure or disappointment worked for good in your life?

12. Birdie is quite humble in her journey. Would you do what she did for Gordon Phipps Roth?